Whispering Sands

Whispering Sands

STORIES OF GOLD FEVER AND THE WESTERN DESERT
by ERLE STANLEY GARDNER

Edited by Charles G. Waugh
and Martin H. Greenberg

William Morrow and Company, Inc.
New York   1981

The stories in this collection were first published in *Argosy* magazine
on the following dates:

Sand Blast   July 21, 1934
Law of the Rope   March 11, 1933
Gold Blindness   March 8, 1930
Written in Sand   October 25, 1930
Blood-Red Gold   September 30, 1930
Carved in Sand   June 17, 1933
Fall Guy   March 22, 1930
Priestess of the Sun   December 6, 1930
Golden Bullets   June 7, 1930

Library of Congress Cataloging in Publication Data

Gardner, Erle Stanley, 1889–1970.
    Whispering sands.

    CONTENTS: Sand blast.—Law of the rope.—Gold blind-
ness.—[etc.]
    1. Adventure stories, American.   2. Gold mines and
mining—Southwest, New—Fiction.   I. Waugh, Charles.
II. Greenberg, Martin Harry.   III. Title.
PS3513.A6322W5   1981   813'.52   80-29460
ISBN 0-688-00474-1

Printed in the United States of America

First Edition

1   2   3   4   5   6   7   8   9   10

BOOK DESIGN BY BERNARD SCHLEIFER

Foreword

The Whispering Sands stories are a series of twenty-one tales that Erle Stanley Gardner wrote for *Argosy* magazine between 1930 and 1934. Each of the stories is (what was then) a contemporary western set somewhere in the deserts of the United States or Mexico. Each is told in the first person, each concerns crime and gold, most are also romances, and all but the first two feature Bob Zane as the protagonist.

Mr. Gardner was a natural-born storyteller, and these works are, like most of his writings, immensely entertaining. Indeed, unwary readers will probably take only one sitting to speed through the entire book. But Gardner also always provided a great deal of unusual information.[1] In this series you will learn many things about the desert —such as the tactics of night fighting, the value of canned tomatoes, and two ways of concealing a campfire. And maybe most important are the inspirational values implicit in the stories. Upbeat and optimistic, these works are peopled with active heroes rather than the passive and ineffectual victims so favored by the literary mainstream. Gardner touts the virtues of self-reliance, faith,

[1] In fact, an Arizona district attorney once was able to convict a murderer by using information gleaned from *The Case of the Curious Bride*, a Perry Mason mystery.

and fair dealing; he makes us believe that we can achieve
great things by trying; and he makes us want to try.

"Gold Blindness" was the first Whispering Sands story
published. Set in the Funeral mountain range east of
Death Valley, it is a tragic love story that features a fascinating portrait of the moon ceremonies of a dying Indian
tribe and an unforgettable description of Auno, a young
Indian maiden educated at Berkeley.

"Fall Guy" was the second story to appear. Its protagonist is Sid, who seems to be an older, less well educated version of Bob Zane. Along with his young friend
Phil Ryan, Sid is a mine guard assigned the task of getting
something on the slippery outlaw Pedro Gallivan. Their
job is complicated by an involved romantic situation in
which Phil loves a sort of desert welfare worker, Dixie
Carson, who loves a weak-willed eastern gentleman, Walt
Hedley, who loves a no-good society woman, Miss Westing, who loves the reprehensible Gallivan. Interestingly,
two of this story's peripheral incidents, a discussion of
Colorado Basin wheel ruts sticking up into the air and
the teaching of self-reliance in the desert, were later to
turn up as central themes in two other series' stories—
"Written in Sand" and "Sand Blast."

Bob Zane, who is the narrator of all the remaining
stories, never gives his age and rarely reveals anything
about his physical features or his background. Nevertheless, it is possible to form an impression of the man from
his behavior, his reported conversations with others, his
observations about life, and his descriptions of the typical
desert dweller.

Zane is a prospector evidently in the prime of life,
probably in his forties or early fifties. Unlike Sid, Zane
doesn't reminisce about his experiences with the Earps
and Clantons or complain about getting old, or say there
are some things he can no longer do. On the other hand,

while he still confesses to looking at young women, he doesn't seem troubled by the passions or impetuosity of youth; his present role seems rather to be matchmaker for others, with, at best, a kiss of gratitude as reward. For example, in the whodunit "Carved in Sand," Zane's impulsive young friend, Pete Ayers, gets himself deeply in trouble with the law by attempting to help Margaret Blake, a young woman whose father has been accused of murder. To save the couple and give their affection a chance to grow into love, Zane employs superior desert knowledge and tracking ability to put his finger on the actual culprit.

Physically, Zane probably resembles those other individuals he describes as having been shaped by the desert. So he has gray eyes, firm lips, and a face that is bronzed and deeply lined by the burning sun. His voice has a "dry husking whisper in it that's like the sound of a lizard's feet scratching along the surface of a sun-baked rock." His clothes have been soaked in desert sunshine and dust until they are a nondescript gray. His whipcord lean frame possesses great endurance and his slow, deliberate way of moving belies lightning-fast reflexes.

Zane has been prospecting for a long time and has spent many years roaming around the western deserts. But he continues this life-style out of enjoyment rather than need. To him adventure is in finding gold, not in having it, and he has quickly blown all but the last of the several fortunes he has made. However, by the time of "Golden Bullets," which seems to be the chronological end to the series, he has finally tired of the desert and is leading a life of luxury in Los Angeles. Still, he finds he periodically longs for his old home and will occasionally visit the desert for excitement. In this story, for example, he returns for a brief stay and ends up deep in the rugged Sierra Madres of Mexico where gold is so plentiful that it is actually used to make bullets. There he undergoes torture as he tries to save a young woman prospector from a band of fierce Yaqui Indians.

On rare occasions, perhaps when he is bored or needs a grubstake, Zane will interrupt his prospecting to take a job as deputy or special investigator. "Law of the Rope" finds him serving as an agent for the board of directors of The Bleaching Skull Mining Company. Here he tries to discover who is behind the string of murders and robberies that plague their Greasewood Mine. After his job is done, however, he appears to return quickly to his search for gold.

He is intelligent and has apparently received some education, for he speaks well and is sometimes capable of poetic expressions such as "The town of Mojave squats in the sunlight like a gigantic spider . . ." or "The desert waited with white-hot arms, and swallowed those who entered into a silence that was like that of the grave."

Zane is observant. As he says: "Little things count for a good deal in the desert. The man who lives in the desert must observe everything, no matter how small, otherwise he won't live long."

He is also extremely curious. If he must investigate to make sense of what he sees, he does so. This trait has involved him in a number of adventures such as his Colorado Basin experience called "Written in the Sand." Here his attempts to discover why an embittered young woman would steal into the desert to eavesdrop entangle him with a ruthless gang of double-crossing robbers.

One of Zane's most admirable qualities is a strong sense of justice, and he is particularly sensitive when a woman is involved. In "Priestess of the Sun" he briefly encounters a young city woman wearing snakeskin shoes. Later he stumbles across those shoes at what appears to be an ambush site in the Mojave Desert. Deeply outraged, he starts a rumor of finding her skeleton and plants a map to set himself up as bait. Still, the chances he takes are calculated ones, based on his belief that he knows the desert well enough to outmaneuver his foes in it, and usually his assumption is accurate. But in "Blood-Red Gold" he meets his most formidable opponent, someone who, for the first time, seriously challenges Zane's superior grasp of desert warfare. Harry Ortley is a brilliant thinking machine whose mind works with ball-bearing efficiency. Unfortunately, he is also psychopathic, unscrupulous, selfish, and merciless. In his haste to bring Ortley to justice, Zane seriously underestimates the man and is lucky to survive.

To Zane, the desert is a woman. She is ever restless and ever changing: her dunes alternate with broken rocks and mountains, her chilly nights with burning days, and her absolute silence with whirling sandstorms. Yet she is always the same: awesome miles of barren waste operating under immutable laws. She is the cruelest country in the world, yet she is the kindest. Her rabbits are the swiftest; her rattlesnakes are the deadliest; her coyotes the most cunning. Even her plants have to be coated with a natural varnish and studded with thorns. The desert is the world's greatest natural obstacle, and Zane feels that life can progress only by overcoming obstacles. In civilization, people do not have to be tested. There are fancy veneers and distractions which allow them to hide from others, even from themselves. But they cannot hide from the desert. Its vastness and nothingness force them to look inward, and those who cannot accept their findings panic and flee to their doom. Those willing to learn, who are clear of mind, keen of eye, and swift of hand, may live long; those who are not will die. For only by knowing and embracing the desert can one survive in this never-ending contest which results in self-respect and tranquility.

Zane loves this fascinating lady. And perhaps the reason he seems not to have married is because he cannot find another as exciting and satisfying. The desert satisfies his desires for adventure and a simple, self-reliant life, and it is these desires rather than the weaknesses of the greedy such as gambling or drinking which keep him prospecting. Indeed, when he has the chance, he is likely to try to salvage city slickers by forcing them to undergo the desert's rite of passage. For example, in "Sand Blast" he goes back east and rescues George Ringley, an old partner's dissolute son, from gangsters. Then, to try to straighten the young man out, Zane drags George back to the western deserts and maneuvers him into a position where he must demonstrate his character by defending a young woman from a gang of claim jumpers.

The desert plays a leading role in each of the Whispering Sand stories and, to those who know the desert well, her whispers are her most enchanting feature. Late at night, in the silence, the sand often brushes against the sage or the cactus and sometimes rubs against itself or the soft sandstone to make a soothing, crooning whisper much like that of a mother reassuring her child. Sometimes just before sleep or while awakening, one seems to hear the whispering form into words and sentences. Many people, including Zane, believe that these are desert messages which lodge in the unconscious and provide them with warnings, guidance, and love—messages that result in special intuitions.

One cannot help but think that such whispers inspired Erle Stanley Gardner himself, for he camped out much of his life and did a lot of his writing while traveling in various western deserts. Mr. Gardner is, of course, best known for his work in the mystery field; indeed, sales of his books that feature investigators such as Perry Mason, Doug Selby, and Lam and Cool exceed 300 million copies. But Gardner thought of himself not only as a lawyer and a writer but also as a westerner, and during his career he was to produce over seventy western novelettes and short stories.

In fact, Gardner bears a striking resemblance to his most notable western protagonist, Bob Zane. At the time the stories were written, both were middle-aged; both were of average height, intelligent, and curious; both were experienced in the ways of the desert, had a strong sense of justice, and were convinced of the values of desert living. Gardner spoke contemptuously of New Yorkers and seemed to enjoy destroying their city by flooding, as in "New Worlds," or by bombing the bejazzers out of it, as in "As Far as the Poles." Zane is disgusted with urbanites and continually refers to them as "city" folk. Gardner kept taking visiting New York editors on camping trips into the desert to see what they were made of, and Zane lures people out into the desert to try to develop their characters.

But Gardner found writing westerns frustrating, because he felt that editors had false ideas about what the West was really like and did not appreciate, and sometimes interfered with, his intent to portray it accurately. He was also a hardheaded businessman who realized that the real money lay in novels and not shorter works. So when his Perry Mason novels caught on, Gardner shifted his attention more and more to detective novels, until finally by 1935 the desert's beautiful whispers were rarely heard again in his works.

CHARLES G. WAUGH and
MARTIN H. GREENBERG

Contents

Sand Blast

I COOL RECEPTION

THE HOUSE WAS a magnificent palace. It sat back from the streets, surrounded by fresh green grass which was kept moist by fountains of spray that spouted up from a buried water system.

There were great shade trees around the house, furnishing rich patches of green color against the stucco of the walls, forming deep pools of inviting shade beneath them.

I felt out of place as I looked around at the shade and the grass. Grass is something we don't have in the desert. It seems an awful waste of water somehow to have all this water cascading over a lawn just because it looks pretty.

I was halfway up the stairs and wondering whether a butler would hold out a silver platter for me to put a card on, when the door flung open and Pete Ringley himself stood in the doorway.

He was heavier than when I'd seen him last, and the fat was a moist, well-nourished, puffy fat that made his face look round and plump, like the breast of a picked goose.

"Bob Zane!" he shouted, and then came galloping across the porch to slam me between the shoulders with

17

a hand that had lost nothing of its strength. "The same
as you were seven years ago!" he said. "You haven't
changed a particle. You haven't aged a day. You look
hard and fit, as though you could start out for Death
Valley with nothing but a burro, a canteen of water, a
sack of beans and a roll of blankets."

I looked at him in surprise. "Of course I could," I said.
"What else would I want?"

He laughed and whacked me between the shoulders
again. "Come on in," he said. "I was looking out of the
window when the taxicab drove up. I saw you get out,
and couldn't believe my eyes for a minute. Lord! but it's
good to see you again."

I followed him into the house and didn't say much.

"Well," he said, as he paused in the doorway of the
living room, "what do you think about it?"

"It doesn't look much like the old cabin down in the
cottonwoods," I told him.

He laughed at that, but there was something wistful
in his laugh.

A door opened and a woman entered the room. She
was young, stylish, tailored, manicured, hairdressed, mas-
saged, powdered, perfumed and lipsticked, and her finger-
nails had been painted.

"Dearest," said Pete Ringley, "I want you to meet the
best friend I have in the world—Bob Zane. Bob, this is
Evelyn—the wife."

I started to shake hands, then remembered something
I'd read somewhere about a man not shaking hands until
a woman offered him hers.

She didn't offer me hers.

Pete Ringley kept on talking. "Bob Zane," he said,
"was my partner out there in the desert when we struck
it rich. Lord! what a battle we had with those claim

jumpers. Bob is the fellow that saved my life. I've told you about it, dearest."

"Lots of times," she said in a voice that was without interest.

Pete Ringley laughed again. "We sold out our claim that spring," he said. "Two hundred thousand dollars cash was what we got."

He looked over at me, and there was the glitter of a fighter in his eyes. "I always wanted to come back to civilization," he said, "and let my money make money for me. I had my boy, George, you know. I thought he needed a father's care. I came on East, and my money made lots of money for me. And then I met Evelyn and married her."

Evelyn Ringley looked me over coolly.

"What did you do with your money, Mr. Zane?" she asked tonelessly.

Pete Ringley laughed booming merriment and answered the question for me.

"Blew it in!" he said. "Went down to Los Angeles and blew it all in, and then went back to the desert to look for more."

She looked at me as though I had been a specimen of something that was under glass.

"And I never was so tired of money in my life," I told Pete. "I can remember how fed up I was when I got down to the last twenty-five thousand dollars. I went through that in a week and it was the longest week I ever put in."

"Why didn't you save it?" Evelyn Ringley asked.

"I don't want money, ma'am," I told her. "I want the desert. I want the making of money. I want the thrill of fighting; the adventure of searching; the big spaces of the outdoors."

"I'm quite sure," she said icily, "that you're entirely welcome to them. Are you going to be long, Pete?"

Pete looked a little flabbergasted.

She turned and left the room. Pete put a hand on my shoulder.

"No, ma'am," I called as she went through the door, "he won't be long."

"Don't mind her," Pete said. "She is a city girl. All of her interests are in the city. She doesn't understand anything else."

She was ten years younger than Pete, maybe fifteen— it's hard to tell. There wasn't a wrinkle or a line on her face. It was all smooth, as though it had been molded and then plastered over with some kind of a pink plaster so it wouldn't crack or weather.

"Where's your bag?" said Pete Ringley. "You've got to stay here for a week anyway. You can't go back . . ."

"In about an hour, Pete," I told him. "This isn't my country."

There was genuine disappointment on his face.

"Oh, listen," he said, "I haven't seen you since we signed the deed to the mine. We've got to have a little celebration, just for old times' sake."

I grinned at him and shook my head. "Where can we talk?" I asked.

He led the way to a room on the second floor.

"This is my den," he said. "No one ever disturbs me here."

It was a comfortable room. There were a few relics of the old days scattered around—a pair of *alforjas*, with some of the hide pretty badly worn, where the pack ropes had rubbed. There was a battered Stetson, with a sweat-grimed band, a hat that had absorbed so much sunlight and desert dust it had turned gray like the desert. There were an old *riata*, a gold pan and a shovel that was covered with gilt paint and tied with a ribbon.

I looked at the shovel.

"That was the shovel," he said, "that we turned over the first gold of our bonanza with."

"Why the gilt paint," I asked, "and the ribbon?"

"That was Evelyn's idea," he said. "She thought it should be decorated somehow. She said that it had brought her gold, so we should put gold paint on it."

I didn't say anything. Pete looked uncomfortable.

"Of course," he said, "it sort of takes away the charm of the thing, but Evelyn wanted to have her way about it, and she's a city girl. She knows what's proper in such matters."

"Yes," I said, "she's a city girl."

I looked at the woodwork of the den. It was a peculiar light color. It looked comfortable and weatherbeaten.

"Like it?" he asked.

I nodded.

I went over and felt of it. It looked like the old driftwood that would be found around the washes in the desert where cloudbursts had carried it along for a mile or two, and then the sand had blown across it.

"What kind of wood is it?" I asked.

"It's the way it's treated, Bob," he told me. "It's given a sand blast."

"A what?"

"A sand blast. They blow sand against the wood through a nozzle. The sand is sent out under pressure. It cuts the wood, and then they wax the surface. It gives it that weatherbeaten appearance."

I nodded and kept my hand on the wood. It seemed to give me something to tie to, something that I could understand.

"I came to see you about the old Chuckwalla claims," I said.

He frowned and shook his head. "I don't remember any Chuckwalla claims," he said.

"You remember the time that the burro stepped on the canteen, and—"

"Why," he said, "that stuff wasn't any good!"

"It is now," I told him.

He looked at me curiously.

"There's been a big change in the desert," I told him. "The price of gold is going up. What's more, it's easier to get transportation now than it was. Those Chuckwalla claims were low-grade, but they were uniform in gold content. There's all kind of rock in there. With the increased price in gold and the chance to get at them, it's one of the biggest propositions we've ever tackled."

"Why," he said, "I'd clean forgotten about those! As I remember it, I threw the samples away."

"No," I told him, "we didn't throw them away; Sally Ehlers got them."

His face lit up. "That's right," he said. "Sally was there. That was the time we found the kid out in the desert. Her dad had been killed. She'd taken the wrong road and run out of gas. What was she—around thirteen or fourteen, wasn't she? Just a kid."

"She isn't a kid any more," I told him. "She's grown up. She's a young woman. She put herself through business college, got a job as a stenographer in a law office, and then went out to Blythe and became a notary public. She does stenographic work and notary public stuff. She's got the desert in her blood; she can't keep away from it."

He looked moodily meditative.

"Gosh," he said, "it makes me feel old to think that that kid has grown up. Remember what an impulsive little kid she was?"

I nodded.

"She remembers where the claims were," I said.

"Well," he told me, "what about it?"

"I think we'd better go out and relocate them," I said. He shook his head.

"I'm finished with the desert, Bob," he said. "It's cruel."

I looked him over.

"It's not cruel," I said. "It's kind."

His laugh was scornful and bitter.

"Kind!" he exclaimed. "My God, Bob! Have you forgotten the burning heat of those suns? The shimmering sand that burns up through your boots until the soles of your feet blister? Have you forgotten those days when you can cook an egg simply by putting it out in the sun and leaving it for five minutes? The days when the air is just like the breath out of a furnace, when the moisture dries right out of your blood and your muscles shrivel? Have you forgotten those awful desert winds? The bitter cold of the winter nights? The everlasting sand? The rattlesnakes? The Gila monsters The tarantulas? The centipedes? The scorpions? My God! It's so cruel that even the bushes have to grow thorns in order to protect themselves, and nature coats their leaves with some kind of a resinous substance. If it wasn't for that the water would evaporate right out of them!"

I shook my head at him and smiled.

"No," I said, "I haven't forgotten those things. I just came from the desert, Pete. But that's why the desert is so kind. It's cruel to those that don't understand it; to the person who can understand her moods she's a kind and loving mother. There's nothing that develops character like cruelty, and the development of character is all life is for."

He shuddered.

"Lord!" he said. "I hate to think of it. Honestly, Bob, I was more than a year getting enough moisture in my muscles so that I could look good in a dinner coat. I was all stringy and shriveled like a mummy. No, Bob, I'm done with the desert. If you can make anything out of those claims, go ahead and do it. I've built up quite a fortune making investments, and right now I'm in the middle of a business deal that is going to more than double my fortune."

"I'd like to have you go back with me," I told him. "Perhaps when you got back to the desert you'd feel a little bit differently toward it. You used to get along pretty well in the desert."

He shuddered and shook his head.

"I couldn't stand it, Bob," he said.

There were lurching steps outside the door. The knob rattled.

Pete Ringley frowned.

"No one disturbs me in here," he said.

The words had just left his lips when the door opened and a young man entered the room.

He was big and tall. He hadn't filled out yet, but he was enough like his father so I knew him at a glance. This was the "kid" that Pete had always talked about around the campfires; the kid that Pete had determined to send through college; the kid who was going to have the advantages of all the education that his father had missed.

I looked at him. He was drunk.

He wasn't offensively drunk; it was just the type of drunk that comes from taking two or three drinks on top of a hangover. The eyes were moist and watery; the skin was a rich pinkish red, as though he had been putting hot and cold towels on his face after he shaved, trying to get his nerves steady. His hair was glossy and black, and it swept back in waves that were as glossy as the wing of a blackbird. The waves were too regular, too artificial. It looked as though some one had put them in with a hot iron.

Pete frowned.

"I'm busy, George," he said.

George grinned easily.

"That's what Evelyn said," he told him. "But she said that she didn't think it was anything important—nothing that you cared about particularly."

Pete flushed.

"George," he said, "shake hands with Bob Zane. Bob Zane was my old desert partner."

George Ringley gave me a hand that was cool and just a little flabby.

"How're yuh?"

I squeezed the hand a bit, just to see if there would be any resistance. It was like squeezing a dead trout.

George pulled his hand away and looked at it.

"Big he-man stuff—outdoor man—wide open spaces and all that, eh?" he asked.

Pete Ringley scowled at him, and there was a look of hopeless resignation on his face.

"What is it, George?" he asked.

"Got to see you, guv'nor, before I go out. Got to see you within the next hour. It's important as hell."

Pete stared steadily at him.

"I presume," he said, "that you're in some kind of a jam over money matters, and that you think it's important as the devil I should come to your rescue. Is that it?"

George smiled at me.

"The guv'nor," he said, "is a great student of character. He should have been a detective."

He grinned at his father.

"I'm sorry," he said, "but you know how those things

are, Dad. You were young once yourself."

"I'll see you sometime this afternoon," Pete Ringley said.

"It's got to be within an hour, guv'nor," George told him; then, as he saw only ominous silence stamped upon his father's face, he smiled affably at me. "Be seeing more of you, Zane," he said.

When the door had closed I looked at Pete Ringley. Pete's face was apologetic.

"Don't misjudge him, Bob," he pleaded. "He's an awfully good boy, an awfully good boy. But, you know, his mother died when he was five. I was out in the desert prospecting around, scraping up a little money here and there to send back to keep him in school. Then we struck it rich and I put him through college. He had the best that money could buy. Perhaps I indulged him a little too much. I was trying to make up to him for the years that he hadn't had enough."

"What college did he go to?" I asked.

"Harvard," he said. "Why?"

I tapped the woodwork.

"Why didn't you send him to your old college?" I asked.

"My college?" asked Pete. "Why, Bob, you know I never had any college."

I tapped the woodwork again.

"The same college," I said, "that took this cheap wood and made something distinctive out of it—the college of drifting sand."

He looked at me for a moment before he got the idea, then he laughed nervously, and his eyes didn't meet mine.

"He's a good kid," he said, and jabbed his finger against a push button.

"We're going to have a highball, Bob," he said. "I've got some genuine uncut whiskey."

II THE SNATCH

I had told Evelyn Ringley that I wouldn't detain her husband long, and I kept my promise to her. Exactly fifty-seven minutes from the time Pete had met me on the porch, he was saying good-by to me. There were tears in his eyes and he was sorry to see me go, but he hadn't urged me forcibly to stay. It was plain that his wife thought I wouldn't mix in well with some of the guests who were coming in during the latter part of the afternoon to play bridge.

Poor Pete was in something of a daze. It seemed strange to him that his old partner would come on to see him and leave within less than an hour. Yet he realized as well as I did, perhaps better, that there was nothing else I could do.

I wouldn't let him send the liveried chauffeur and the family sedan down to the depot. I insisted that he call a cab.

The cab started away with a lurch, and had gone about a hundred yards when a light gray roadster came tearing down the driveway from the big house.

George Ringley was at the wheel. The car gathered speed and swept past us at better than fifty miles an hour.

George saw me and slammed on the brakes. The big car swayed slightly. The tires screeched a protest. George gave the wheel a deft twist, sending the roadster up close to the cab.

"Didn't know you were going so soon!" he shouted.

I nodded.

"Get out," he said, "and I'll take you wherever you want to go and get you there in half the time."

I grinned and shook my head at him.

"No," I said, "thanks all the same. I prefer the cab. I'm nervous about automobiles."

His smile was humorous and patronizing. He looked on me as some wild outlander. He was still drunk—not dead drunk, but just pleasantly oiled. His face wore a grin of complacent self-satisfaction, and I gathered that the interview with his father, which had taken place a few moments before I left, had been entirely satisfactory to the young man.

"Okay," he called. "Good luck."

His foot pressed down on the throttle. The car shot ahead like a frightened jackrabbit and left the taxicab rattling and swaying, as though it had been standing still.

The cabdriver shook his head dubiously.

There was a traffic signal at the corner, where a through boulevard crossed the one we were on. George Ringley went through the red light just as it was changing. An officer blew vigorous blasts on his whistle. Ringley didn't pay any attention to it at all.

A black Cadillac sedan came up from behind, traveling fast. I looked at it casually, wondering if every automobile in the city traveled at such a terrific rate of speed. There were four men in the sedan. As it swept past, I saw that the rear license plate was loose, dangling and flapping in the breeze which sucked up from behind the car.

Just before it got to the corner, the metal license plate came loose and dropped to the curb, where it skidded along for some ten or fifteen feet.

The traffic officer blew his whistle and held up his hand.

The big Cadillac didn't stop at once. It looked as though the driver was going to make a run for it. The officer was mad by this time. He reached for his hip. The Cadillac stopped. The officer pointed to the license and said something. The signal was against us and we had stopped. I saw the driver jump from the car, run to the license, saw him exchange a few words with the cop, then pull out his card case and show something to the officer.

"His driving license," said the cabdriver in response to my question.

The traffic light changed. We went on across the intersection and passed the black Cadillac, but within a block it passed us, and by that time it must have been going sixty miles an hour.

I saw something as the car passed me the second time which I hadn't noticed the first time. There was a peculiar hole in the front fender of the car. It was the kind of a hole which would have been made by a steel-jacketed bullet.

I wondered about that hole. It looked as though some one had shot at a tire, and the bullet had glanced, then torn its way up through the fender. The license plate was bolted on now. They'd done a hurried job. I wondered why they were in such a hurry.

The boulevard they were following ran along for a couple of miles through a sparsely settled district given over largely to golf and country clubs. Then the road swung into a densely populated district once more. It was the best shortcut to the depot. Pete Ringley had built his house out in the exclusive section, where he had plenty of elbow room and was within easy walking distance of the country clubs. People in that section paid more attention to clubs than to offices.

The cabdriver jammed the brakes on hard.

"Look over there," he said.

I looked.

The roadster George Ringley had been driving was in the ditch. The fender on one side was badly crumpled. The car rested on its side. One of the front wheels was still turning, barely moving, but turning, nevertheless.

"Stop the car!" I shouted to the cabdriver.

He had it stopped by the time I had wrenched the door open. I got out and looked around the wreck. There was no trace of George Ringley. He had vanished, apparently, into thin air. I looked the seat over. There was no sign of blood. The windshield was cracked. The car had evidently skidded into the ditch. I looked the fenders over once more. They were crumpled, and on one of them was a smear of black, as though it had collided with some object that had been painted black and had scraped off part of the enamel.

"What do you suppose happened?" asked the cabdriver at my elbow.

"Too much speed," I told him. "He skidded into the ditch. Some car came along and he picked up a ride in it. Let's go."

The driver looked the roadster over and nodded.

"I'll say one thing," he said, "he didn't lose any time."

"Oh, he may have been five minutes ahead of us," I told him. "Let's get to the depot."

The cabdriver shrugged his shoulders. After all, it was no affair of his. I reentered the cab and we drove to the depot without incident. I paid off the cab, entered a telephone booth and called Pete Ringley. I had some little difficulty getting Pete on the telephone. There was a butler or valet, or something, who wanted to know all about me. Finally I heard Pete's voice.

"Pete," I said, "George passed me in a roadster. I was in the taxicab. We got a mile or so down the boulevard and saw George's roadster in the ditch. George wasn't anywhere around. Have you heard anything from him?"

He hemmed and hawed and hesitated.

"Come on," I said, "out with it."

He lowered his voice. "Yes," he said, "I've heard, Bob, but I can't tell you over the telephone."

"Sure you can," I told him. "What is it? Is the boy hurt?"

"Not hurt, Bob," he said, "he's been snatched."

"Been what?" I asked.

"Snatched," he said; "kidnaped. It's a new racket that's sweeping the country. I suppose I should have anticipated something like this. I'm supposed to be a very wealthy man. George is an only child. They telephoned just a minute ago and told me to get fifty thousand dollars in hundred-dollar bills if I ever wanted to see my boy again. I wasn't certain that it was on the square, but if you saw the car I guess it is."

"You're notifying the police?" I asked.

"Good Lord, no!" he said. "That's one thing I don't dare to do! They told me that if I notified the police or said anything about it, the boy would be killed instantly."

"Suppose they meant it?" I asked.

"Of course they meant it," he said.

"What are you going to do?"

"Get the money, of course. I can get more fifty-thou-sand-dollar-cash stakes, but I can't get another boy. Money doesn't mean a single damn thing at a time like this. It's a question of getting my boy back."

"Can I help you?" I asked.

"No," he said. "Don't say anything about it. I can get the money without attracting any attention. I've got four or five times that much on deposit in banks here in the city. Naturally, I'm worried, but worrying isn't going to help any, and if they knew I told a soul it might be bad for George. That's why I'm telling you, Bob, because I know I can trust you, and I want you to keep the information under your hat."

"I'll keep in touch with you," I said, "and see how you come out."

"You won't need to," he told me. "As soon as George is returned the newspapers will have the story and then the police will start trying to trace the kidnapers. It'll be in big headlines all over the country then. In fact, I'd rather you didn't call up, Bob, because I want to keep the line clear for communication with the men who have George. They're going to tell me where to take the money."

"How soon will you have it?" I asked.

"The money?"

"Yes."

"I can get it within a couple of hours," he said.

"Okay," I told him. "I wish there was something I could do."

"So do I," he said, "but there's nothing any one can do. It's simply a question of raising ransom and raising it fast. And I'm not going to make the mistake of taking a single soul into my confidence. The authorities always bungle cases like this."

I expressed my sympathy once more and hung up the telephone. My train was due to leave in half an hour, but I didn't bother about it. I got my bag from a checking stand, went to the lavatories, took out my big six-gun, with the shiny leather holster, black and polished from much exposure to sun and wind, and strapped it around my waist underneath my coat. I knew there was some sort of a law against it, but I didn't care particularly. I had a hunch and I was going to play it.

I got a taxi and made time back to the intersection, where the cop was still on duty. I got out and walked toward the cop.

He saw me coming and surveyed me frowningly.

"You've got some information that I want," I told him, pulling a ten-dollar bill from my pocket.

He looked at me and at the ten-dollar bill, and his expression was uncordial.

"It's okay," I told him, "not only something that you

can give out, but something that you should give out in connection with your duty."

"What is it?" he asked.

"I was driving a car," I said, "when a Cadillac sedan bumped me. At the time I didn't think it had done any damage. I thought my rear bumper had taken care of it. But when I got home I found that the gasoline tank had been punctured. Now that sedan dropped its license plate when it got to the corner, and you took a look at the operator's license of the fellow that was driving it. Do you remember the name?"

"So that's how that license plate got loose," he said.

"Yes," I said. "He sideswiped me as he went past."

"Why didn't you say something about it?"

"I didn't think any damage was done."

He pulled out his notebook and thumbed the pages.

"I think," he said, "the name was Watson. Yes, here it is—Carol P. Watson. And the address is seven four nine three Ridgeway Drive."

I passed him the ten-dollar bill.

"That's all right," he said. "Just a matter of accommodation. I'm glad to do it for you."

I didn't say anything, but kept the ten-dollar bill poked at him, and he took it without making any further protestations. I climbed into my cab.

"Seven four nine three Ridgeway Drive," I said, "and drive like the devil."

It wasn't a long run out there—not over fifteen blocks from the place where George Ringley's car had been forced into the ditch. There was a black Cadillac sedan parked in front of the place, and I saw there was a bullet hole in the fender.

"This the place?" asked the driver.

"Just keep on going," I said, "until you come to the corner. Stop there for a little while and wait."

I figured that, knowing the cop had the address which was on the driver's license, the men probably wouldn't keep George Ringley there. It was too dangerous. There was always the chance that Pete might notify the police after all, and the traffic officer might have been observant. On the other hand, they'd made all of their plans to use the place as headquarters, and it would take them a little while to get some other place ready.

I waited in the cab for fifteen minutes. Then a man came out of the place on Ridgeway Drive, opened the door of the sedan, got in behind the wheel and started the motor.

A minute later two men came out of the door, waited for a moment and took the arms of a third man. They kept the third man between them. They walked down the driveway and bundled the man into the sedan. The car purred into motion.

I had a glimpse of the man who sat between the two in the rear seat as the sedan went by. The man was George Ringley.

"Follow that Cadillac sedan," I told the cabdriver. "If you get a chance run alongside of it. I want to talk with some men in there."

He looked at me curiously, but snapped the car into motion. We ran four blocks before we got a chance to run alongside. The Cadillac was moving slowly, keeping within the traffic regulations. Evidently the men didn't want to chance being arrested for some minor traffic violation. They'd had a taste of that and didn't like it.

The taxicab rattled alongside.

"Get over to the curb," I said. "I want to talk with you."

The Cadillac speeded up.

As it shot into fast motion, I squinted down the sights of my big six-shooter and pulled the trigger.

The right rear tire went out with a bang. The big car rose and then settled. It skidded around and suddenly came to a stop. The driver opened up on me with a big automatic. One of the men in the back stuck a gun out through the rear of the car.

The automatics were pumping like firecrackers. My big range gun thundered. The driver of the car jerked, twisted and slumped down over the steering wheel. A bullet from the gun in the hands of the man in the rear struck the frame of the door within an inch of my head. I thumbed the hammer of my big .45, and he caught the slug right in the chest.

The taxi driver had jumped to the ground and was sprinting like a deer. The man who sat on the other side of the seat, with a gun on George Ringley, suddenly started to fumble with the catch on the door. George sat motionless. His face was white. The man reached the sidewalk, ran two steps, turned and fired. My bullet caught him in the side of the shoulder, spun him half around. He dropped to the sidewalk, got up to his knees, swayed for a moment, then dropped forward on his face.

George Ringley recognized me. His eyes were as big as teacups. He floundered out of the car.

"Can you drive this cab?" I asked him.

He nodded.

"Get started," I said, "and make it snappy."

Windows were up in some of the houses. Some one was screaming for the police. A big fellow, with a bald head and a close-cropped white mustache, appeared in a window with a short-barreled, nickel-plated revolver in his hand. He held it out at arm's length and emptied the gun. One of the bullets struck the sidewalk in front of the cab; none of them came nearer than ten feet.

"Get started," I told George Ringley. "You haven't got all day, you know."

The cab shot into motion and swayed over as it took the corner. I leaned forward where I could watch George Ringley drive.

"A top-heavy old bus," he said.

"Take it easy," I told him, "after you get away from here. We want to escape attention."

"How did you know?" he asked.

"Never mind that now," I said, "just keep moving, and watch what you're doing."

"Don't worry," he said, "I can pilot this crate. It's top-heavy, but I can make it all right."

"Don't go home," I said.

"No?" he asked.

"No," I said, "there are some other members of the gang between us and the house. Go up to the Union Depot."

"Why the Union Depot?" he asked.

"Don't argue," I said. "Get started."

He swung the car toward the Union Depot. I looked at my watch. It was too late to catch my train.

We came to a boulevard stop.

"Better leave the cab here," I said. "They'll be tracing it directly."

He stopped the car.

"But listen," he said, "I want to know what it's all about. Why shouldn't I telephone—"

"You're going to do exactly as I tell you," I said.

"But I want to telephone father."

"You poor simp!" I said. "Don't you suppose I telephoned your father?"

His face showed relief.

"When?" he asked.

"Just before I went out and picked you up," I told him. "Now come on and get busy."

"What do you want me to do?"

"Help in trapping the kidnapers."

"I'll sure as hell do that," he said. "The devils crowded me off the road, then sideswiped me as I went into the ditch. It's a wonder I wasn't hurt. They wanted fifty thousand dollars from the guv'nor. Think of it! Fifty thousand dollars!"

I signaled a passing cab which was running along the boulevard.

"Union Depot," I told him.

I picked up my bag at the Union Depot, chartered another car which took us to the airport.

Half an hour later we were seated in a cabin plane, with the motors warming up.

"I don't understand," George Ringley said. "Father couldn't have known just what you were going to do."

"Shut up," I told him. "Don't ask so many questions. This is all a scheme to bring the kidnapers to justice."

"It looked to me as though they got plenty of justice," he said. "My God! You never missed a shot! They fired half a dozen shots to your three, but every one of your three counted."

"Never mind that," I said. "Quit talking about it."

The pilot gunned the motors. We ran down a cement runway. The plane tilted as it took off, swayed slightly in a gust of wind, then zoomed upward in a sharp banking turn.

"Where are we headed?" George Ringley shouted.

"Straight west," I said. "Your father wants you to do a job for him while you're hiding."

"Hiding?"

"Yes," I said, "so they can trap the kidnapers."

George Ringley shrugged his shoulders.

"I guess it's okay," he said in a voice that showed tired resignation, for all of its attempt to make itself audible above the roar of the motors.

He sat back in the comfortable cushioned chair, looking down at the city and the farms of the countryside as it unwound below us like some huge panorama which was being run by clockwork. His eyes closed, and he started to nod his head.

He'd been pretty drunk and the booze was wearing off.

The nose of the plane was pointed toward the desert.

III   A LONG-EARED CADDY

Few people know very much about the country between Palo Verde and Ogilby.

There's supposed to be a road that runs through there. The maps vary. Some of them show the road as being impassable; some of them show it as an abandoned road; some of them show it as a road that traffic can get through on.

Over to the west is another road which runs between Niland and Ripley. In between is a big triangle of waste desert, with the Chocolate Mountains rearing their deeply washed sides in a shimmering atmosphere of intense heat.

Up toward the apex of the triangle, where the two so-called roads run together, is the city of Blythe, a few miles west of the Colorado River, and on the main highway which runs from Mecca to Phoenix.

Sally Ehlers met us at Blythe. She looked George Ringley over.

"I can see a resemblance to your father," she said. "I knew him back ages ago when I was a little girl."

George Ringley surveyed her with eyes that were keenly appreciative.

"Not so awfully long ago," he said.

She nodded.

"So long ago I hate to think of it," she said. "So you've come out to represent your father in re-locating the Chuckwalla claims, have you?"

George Ringley looked over at her and grinned.

"I guess that's what I came out here for," he said. "Bob Zane wouldn't tell me. He only told me that he was acting under secret instructions from my father, and that what we were going to do was to be shrouded in the utmost secrecy."

Sally Ehlers met my eyes.

"It's a good thing you figured on keeping it secret, Uncle Bob," she told me. "Big Bill Ordway knows what's happening."

"How do you mean?" I asked.

"He happened to remember about that big low-grade proposition that you and Pete Ringley brought in seven years ago. You remember, at the time you didn't know just how much it was going to run. Then, when you found out that it would cost at least a dollar and a half a ton more to work than you could get out of it, you told it around as a joke—the big bonanza that fizzled out."

"And Ordway remembered it?" I asked.

"Yes," she said, "Ordway figures that you'll be starting out to re-locate it. He hasn't said anything, but I know what's on his mind. He's hanging around town, but he's got an outfit all ready to start. He's got an automobile all packed and provisioned, and then he's got a string of burros so he can start on a minute's notice."

"But why do we have to keep it a secret from Father —what we're doing, I mean?" George asked.

Sally Ehlers looked at me.

"You do whatever Bob Zane tells you," she said, "and you'll come out all right."

"Has Bill Ordway got any men with him?" I asked.

"I think so," she said, "but I don't know who they are.
But there are five saddle burros in the string, and three
pack burros. All of them are fast walkers. He's been
holding them here in town ever since you left for the
East."

"Has he been trying to pump you at all, Sally?" I
asked.

She nodded her head. "He's been asking lots of questions. They seemed like aimless questions," she said, "but
I knew he was fishing around for something."

"You think he remembers the whole thing then?"

"I'm sure he does."

I looked about me at the blue vault of the cloudless
sky, at the shimmering heat waves which radiated from
the horizon. The Palo Verde Valley was a veritable oasis,
with irrigation water transferring the desert soil into green
fields of alfalfa, with huge shade trees breaking the direct
rays of the fierce sun and casting welcome pools of deep
shadow. But out beyond stretched the desert, a vast
shimmering waste of sand, broken here and there by
clumps of greasewood or sage. Out toward the Chocolate
Mountains there was no travel. The desert waited with
white-hot arms, and swallowed those who entered into
a silence that was like that of the grave.

Occasionally, figures returned from the desert. Sometimes they did not return. When they did not return, the
shifting sands of the cruel desert covered that which had
happened. Occasionally, some prospector would blunder
upon a pile of bleached bones. Sometimes trail-wise eyes
would decipher that which had happened; sometimes
there would be a scribbled note left by the hapless victim
of the desert. More often there was nothing.

George Ringley's tone was casually optimistic.

"Oh, well," he said, "we've got nothing to worry about.
We can go out there and make the location and get back
inside of a day or two, can't we, Zane?"

I shook my head.

Sally Ehlers smiled. Her eyes were black as chunks of wet obsidian and as expressionless as those of an Indian, but now there was a tolerant smile in them which even George Ringley could decipher.

"Oh, I know I'm green to the country," he said, "but, after all, the desert isn't like it used to be. I've read books about it. You can drive an automobile almost anywhere now."

"Not where we're going," I told him.

"No?" he asked.

"No," I said. "We're going to go by the most direct method. We're going to go right to the claims we're going to locate. Then I'm going to come on back and record the location notices. You and Sally are going to stay on the ground and hold the claim against all comers.

"You want *me* to go?" asked Sally.

I nodded.

"Particularly," I told her.

Her eyes had a frowningly thoughtful expression.

"Just why?" she asked.

"Because," I said, "you're a notary public."

She remained thoughtfully observant.

"Just the three of us?" she asked.

"Just the three of us," I told her.

"When do we start?"

"Sometime within a day or two," I told her. "I want George to get toughened up so he can stand the desert."

"Oh, don't mind me," he said. "I play a pretty good game of golf now and can toddle around for thirty-six holes when I have to. I can tire the caddies out, if it comes to that."

"The desert," I told him, "isn't like a golf course."

He looked out at it and made a grimace.

"I'll say it isn't," he said. "What does a man do for a bath out there?"

"You've got a perpetual shower bath," I told him.

He looked at me uncomprehendingly.

"The perspiration," I said, "streams out of your skin and is evaporated by the sun."

He rubbed his hand over his moist forehead.

"It comes out faster with me," he said.

"After you've been here awhile," I told him, "you dry out and get so you don't sweat all the time. You get accustomed to the desert."

"Like a mummy?" he asked.

"Like a mummy," I told him.

"I don't think," he said, "I'm going to like the desert."

"You never can tell," I told him, "until you get out in it. Then you either love it or you hate it. And if you hate it, your hatred is bred of fear, nine times out of ten."

His eyes met mine with a calm, steady glitter.

"I'm not going to be afraid of it," he said.

"You're going to like it, then," I told him.

"Well," he said, "no matter whether I like it or whether I don't, you don't need to wait around to get me toughened up. If we want to start, let's go."

"You stick around here and talk to Sally Ehlers," I told him, "and I'll browse around a bit and see what I can find out."

I left them, with George Ringley bending over her with just a slight stamp of patronizing tolerance in his manner. Sally's eyes were enigmatical, but she was tense as a poised cat getting ready to pounce.

My prowling around consisted of rounding up the string of burros I had left in a river-bottom pasture and getting a bunch of provisions and canteens together. I did it unostentatiously. The stuff was packed in an automobile, taken down to the river bottom and dumped out. I put on the packs down there.

About dusk I hunted up Sally Ehlers.

"Where's the golfer?" I asked.

"Over at the hotel," she said.

I found him in his room. He had changed to the clothes I'd picked up for him to wear—a pair of overalls, boots, a light-blue shirt and a straw hat.

"Looks like the devil!" he said.

"Never mind what it looks like," I told him. "We're leaving about ten o'clock to-night. You'd better get some sleep. I'm going to give you a caddy you won't tire out on this trip."

He grinned at me.

"Has the caddy got long ears?" he asked.

I liked his grin. Now that some of the booze was sweating out of his system, he reminded me more and more of his dad when I'd first known him.

"The caddy," I told him, "has long ears."

IV INTO THE DESERT

The desert has as many moods as a woman and the desert at night is as different from the desert at day as is winter from summer.

The night was moonlit. Our burros filed out in a long shuffling file, the sound of their feet in the sand and the creak of the saddle leather being the only noises which marred the tranquillity of the calm desert night.

The moon was almost full. It rode in the heavens like a vast ball of silver, and the white sand of the desert caught the moonlight and flung it back until the whole surface of the desert seemed to be bathed in some mystic shimmering pool of white light through which we plunged in shuffling Indian file, casting grotesque shadows which were like splotches of ink on the glistening sand.

George Ringley had enough of his father in him so that the desert thrilled him with its vast mystery. But he had been bred in the ways of the city, and the tranquil silence, which seemed to blot out noise as a blotting paper absorbs ink, made him nervous. He started to whistle in a low key.

"Silence!" I called to him.

We shuffled on in absolute silence.

The calm tranquillity of interstellar space stretched unbroken down from the high places and rested like a mantle upon the surface of the desert.

We shuffled along until the moon set, which was about an hour or an hour and a half before daylight.

As the moon dropped down behind the western horizon, I called a halt. We huddled together, a little compact group of figures.

"Can we make a fire?" George Ringley asked, and shivered slightly with nervousness, fatigue and the chill which comes before morning.

"No," I told him; "it isn't safe. We'd make too easy a target against the light of a campfire. We'll wait until to-morrow and see if we're followed. You'll be warm enough in a couple of hours."

The burros took the opportunity to rest, standing dejectedly, their ears flopping forward, pulled by their own weight. The three of us sat in a little huddle. The moon dropped down below the rim of the western desert and swift darkness marched silently across the cold surface of the desert. The stars blazed with steady brilliance.

"It's lonesome," said George Ringley suddenly.

I said nothing. Sally Ehlers laughed lightly.

"You'll get used to it after a while," she said. "But there's always the mystery."

The stars seemed gradually to draw farther back into the heavens, until they became mere needle points of light. One of those swift desert breezes sprung up which come from nowhere and blow the sand in scurrying clouds, sending it hissing against the cacti, rattling through the greasewood, and at times, when the wind becomes stronger, making that most peculiar and subtle sound of all—the whispering, slithering noises of sand scurrying over sand.

George Ringley spoke, and now the spell of the desert had impressed itself upon him sufficiently so that his voice was a whisper.

"It seems as though the sand is talking," he said.

"Yes," I told him. "Those are the sand whispers. You hear them in the desert when you're camped out on the sand. The desert seems to talk."

We sat and listened to it in silence. The whole desert seemed to be stirring. The little sand wraiths swirled and streamed about us in the darkness, each giving its little mysterious hissing whisper, until it seemed that the desert had a thousand tongues whispering warnings to us.

Then the east turned to gold. The gold showed a splash of vivid crimson where a few little clouds nestled over the eastern mountains. The stars were absorbed in a steely blue as the light grew stronger, and abruptly the sun plunged over the rim of the mountains and sent long, level rays flooding the desert.

George Ringley's laugh was nervous.

"Say," he said, "there was something spooky about those sand whispers, wasn't there? It almost got my goat for a minute."

The wind had died away as the rays of sunlight searched out the glistening sand of the desert. The mystery of the desert dawn, the peculiar thrill of the desert whispers, were but memories. The glaring light of common day transformed the desert into a vast waste of sand, cacti, greasewood and sage.

"The desert is a law unto itself," said Sally Ehlers, glancing at me to see if I intended to make any statement.

I swung into my saddle without a word.

"We're going on?" asked George Ringley, and I thought there was a trace of weariness in his voice.

"Going on," I said, "during the cool of the morning."

"How about coffee?" he asked.

"After it gets too hot to travel," I told him.

We shuffled along for an hour. The sun started burning the desert with a fiery heat. The horizons began to dance and shimmer. Mirages chased their way about the distances, giving the effect of shimmering pools of water in which were reflected the heat-tortured outlines of the mountains.

About eight o'clock I called a halt. It was hot by that time, a dry heat which seemed to drain the very life from one's body. Little gnats buzzed about in front of the eyes or stung through the skin.

George Ringley's eyes were a trifle bloodshot. His lips were commencing to crack. His laugh was nervous.

"I'm not so certain that I can keep this up day after day," he said, and looked quickly at Sally Ehlers.

"You should," I told him, "be able to do as much as a girl, shouldn't you?"

I tried to make the question without scorn, merely as a matter of casual inquiry.

He flushed and stiffened.

"I was only kidding," he said. "I'll do as much as any of you."

We unpacked the burros. I built a little fire, made coffee, and we had some eggs and bacon. Then we had a can of that desert luxury, pure watery tomato juice drained from a can of tomatoes. After that, we ate the tomatoes on bread. I kept looking at the back trail. Sally Ehlers watched me anxiously. George Ringley ate in silence, his eyes on his food. Occasionally he made irritable swipes with his hand at the little gnats which got in front of his eyes and buzzed about steadily or crawled in his ears.

"It doesn't do any good to fight them," Sally Ehlers said. "It just makes you nervous."

"How do you stand them?" asked George Ringley, and this time there was no discounting the irritation in his voice.

"You simply learn to be patient," she said. "It's one of the lessons that the desert teaches you."

"Oh, damn the desert!" he exclaimed irritably.

I shifted my eyes to his. His locked with mine for a moment, then dropped.

"We can get some sleep here in the shade," I told them. "You two sleep and I'll keep watch."

"What are we keeping watch for?" George Ringley asked.

"To see if any one is riding on our trail."

The two of them lay down in the shade of a patch of greasewood. The shade was scanty. The gnats were troublesome. Sally Ehlers put a handkerchief over her face and slept. George Ringley twisted and turned, moaned in fitful sleep. Occasionally he would give a convulsive start and sit up to stare groggily at me from bloodshot eyes.

About noon I saw a little cloud of dust on our back trail. Half an hour later I could make out moving dots, and then the dust settled and ceased. The moving dots became invisible as they blended with the shade of tall greasewood bushes.

I waited until I was certain they were not coming on, and then crawled into a clump of brush. Sally Ehlers heard me and sat up.

"See anything?" she asked.

"Yes," I said. "Eight burros. They've stopped a couple of miles back there. They spotted us, probably through binoculars. They'll wait until we move on. There's nothing more to be done."

"I'll watch," she said.

"You don't need to," I told her. "They're simply going to keep us in sight."

I put a bandanna over my face, drove a little stick into the ground to hold the cloth away from my nostrils and dropped off at once into dreamless sleep.

The sun was low in the west when I awoke. Sally Ehlers had a little fire going and was teaching George Ringley some of the first rudiments of desert cooking. Ringley's lips had commenced to crack; his face was an angry red; the eyes were bloodshot. His manner was the grim, dogged determination of a runner who finds himself commencing to weary in a race, but who is determined to hang on.

After our simple meal of plain desert fare, I sent George out to pick up some of the burros that were browsing about. Sally Ehlers moved over toward me and said in a low voice, "Just what are you planning to do, Bob?"

"What do you mean, Sally?" I asked.

"You're not going to go out and locate that mine with Bill Ordway's gang on your trail, are you? You know what would happen. We'd never get back to record the claim, in the first place, and in the second place, you could never hold possession against Ordway's gang."

"Perhaps I could," I said.

"And perhaps you couldn't," she told me. "I never did understand why you came out here with just the three of us. Why didn't you get two or three men that you could depend on?"

"Because," I said, "I'm taking George Ringley to finishing school."

"Finishing school?" she asked.

"Did you ever see wood that had been treated by a sand blast?" I asked her.

"What's that got to do with it?" she wanted to know.

"A lot," I said. "All of the roughness is stripped away. All of the glitter and veneer is gone. That which is left is just the true substantial wood, honest and rugged."

"Well?" she asked.

"That," I told her, "is what's going to happen to George. He's had too much civilization, too much moisture —not enough hardships. He needs a dose of the desert, needs to have the sand drift against his character, cut away all of this loose, flabby flesh and strip him down to his naked soul."

"You certainly don't intend to locate this mine with Big Bill Ordway and his gang on your trail, do you?" she asked.

I grinned at her, went to my saddle bag, took out a canvas sack and pulled out some ore.

She looked at it and gasped.

"Free milling ore!" she said. "Where did it come from? Have you struck a bonanza, Bob?"

"No," I told her, "that high-grade ore came from a mine in Nevada. They struck a pocket in there that was so rich it had more gold than rock."

She looked at the specimens with appreciative eyes.

"Aren't those pretty?" she asked.

I nodded.

"Here's what's going to happen," I told her. "I'm going to go to a place about two or three miles from the Chuckwalla claims. I'm going to stake it out. It'll look like a regular claim. I'll pretend that I don't know Bill Ordway's on my trail. Then I'll leave you and the kid in possession of the claim, and I'll start back to record the location notice. But I'll start in the moonlight, so that I'll run right into Big Bill Ordway's gang. You know what'll happen. They'll hold me up, take the notice from me, tear it up, probably take my burro, leave me afoot and tell me to keep moving."

"They'll take your guns away from you," she said.

"Sure," I told her, "but I'll cache some guns along the road. I've got some extra ones in the packs. Then Ordway will move on down and dispossess you two. It'll be up to you to see that the kid doesn't actually do any shooting. You can explain to him at the last that you're overpowered by superior numbers and that you've got to get out."

"Then what'll happen?" she said.

"Then," I said, "Bill Ordway will put some of his gang in to keep possession of the claim, and he'll take the rest of them and make a run for the county seat, to record his location. After he's done that we'll move on to the Chuckwalla claims and locate them at our leisure. In fact, I'll make our fake location a few miles south of the Chuckwalla claims, so that when we start back they'll be right in our road. After Ordway turns me loose in the desert I'll mosey on up to the Chuckwalla claims and locate them. I'll pick up the guns on the way up there, so that I'll be armed and ready to stand my ground in case anything should go wrong. But it won't."

She nodded slowly.

"You think that's going to make a man out of George?" she asked.

"It's all going to help," I told her. "We're all going to get out in the desert and get right down to brass tacks. It's a cinch Ordway will take some of our provisions and water. He'll leave us stripped down just as close as he dares to."

"You don't think he'll shoot?" she asked.

"Not if he gets possession of the claims without shooting," I told her. "Ordway is smooth. He knows that if it comes to a lawsuit, his men can testify to one thing and we can testify to another; that if he's got possession, that's all that counts. If there's any shooting, of course, Ordway will shoot back. That's where you've got to come in. You've got to see that there isn't any shooting."

She nodded, and about that time George Ringley came back leading a sleepy-eyed burro, with a couple more following along behind.

We put the stuff on the burros and started out.

Ringley didn't look quite so well. His face was slightly swollen from the sunburn. His eyes were red-rimmed and bloodshot. His lips were badly cracked. There wasn't any grin on his face any more, but there was a dogged determination in his eyes.

We shuffled along through the late afternoon, through the twilight, and then through the calm moonlit night. The burros plodded patiently and steadily. There wasn't any trace of Big Bill Ordway's gang, but I knew that they were on my trail. I knew that they respected my knowledge of the desert and would do everything they could to keep us from finding out that we were being followed. The farther we got into the desert the more they'd drop behind, figuring that they could always follow our tracks.

Our burros walked along at a good pace, steady and monotonous, but a pace that put the miles behind. I saw George Ringley sway several times in the saddle, and knew that he was dropping off to sleep. I could also tell from the way he sat his saddle that he was getting pretty sore. But he hadn't complained.

Around midnight we dropped down into a little cañon, and I built a fire and brewed a cup of strong tea apiece, which was better than drinking the lukewarm water from the canteens, which had sloshed around until it commenced to taste strongly of the metal.

Ringley dropped to sleep by the campfire, and I could see that Sally Ehlers was getting pretty near the point of exhaustion.

"Another five miles," I told them, "and we'll camp and get a little sleep while it's cool."

The burros pushed on for that last five miles. I got the packs off, hobbled a couple of the burros, let the others run loose and pillowed my head on a saddle.

"You're not keeping a lookout?" asked Sally Ehlers.

I shook my head.

"No," I said, "we don't need to. Just drop off to sleep and get a good sleep. We may have a hard day to-morrow."

George Ringley was too tired to argue; too tired even to get into his blankets or undress. He simply flopped on the sand, pillowed his head on his saddle and dropped off to sleep. Sally Ehlers covered him with a blanket, because the desert would get cold just before dawn. I kicked off my boots, rolled myself in a blanket and was almost instantly asleep.

That night the desert talked again, but George Ringley didn't hear it. The little sand swirls scurried around over the country, rustling against the sage and greasewood, whispering strange secrets of the desert. But George Ringley slept on. And yet I knew that he was hearing the noises of the desert, despite the fact that he was sleeping. One may shut his ears to the sound of the desert, but the desert stamps itself upon one's soul just the same. George Ringley might not have consciously heard the noises of the drifting sand, but those sand whispers were doing things to his soul, nevertheless.

A professor of psychology camped with me for a while. He was out on the desert getting rid of a spot on his left lung. He told me that the subconscious mind was always receptive; that man's environment stamped itself indelibly upon his character, because of the innumerable little things that were soaked up by the subconscious mind, without the consciousness being aware of it.

I didn't get it in just the terms that he expressed it, but I got the idea all right, and I knew that it was the truth. I'd seen men in the desert before. The drifting sand blasts through the veneer of their character, just the same as the sand blast ripped the surface off of the wood in that house of Pete Ringley. Sometimes, when the sand got done, there was honest, sound wood down underneath, and sometimes it was just a rotten heart that had been covered with a veneer of highly polished wood. I've seen both kinds in the desert, but I've never seen a man in the desert who didn't get stripped of his veneer and get right down to the stuff that was underneath.

George Ringley slept until about an hour after sunup. Then the gnats and flies got to bothering him and the heat of the desert started doing its stuff.

He sat up and rubbed his eyes.

I had breakfast almost ready, gave him some coffee and flapjacks. Sally Ehlers looked as fresh as she had the day we started.

"What's the program?" asked Ringley.

"Feel that you can ride a little today?" I asked.

When I mentioned riding, I noticed his face twist in an involuntary grimace, but he nodded his head.

"Sure I can ride," he said.

"We'll work on for an hour or two," I said. "When it commences to get hot we'll stop again. We're going to try short trips from now on. The burros will stand up better, and it will be a lot easier on you."

"Never mind me," he said.

Sally Ehlers flashed me a glance.

I didn't say anything.

We finished breakfast, got the burros up and got another nine miles behind us. Then we slept until late afternoon, had another meal, got the burros up, and about seven thirty came down a long slope and looked over toward the Chocolate Mountains.

Sally Ehlers rode up beside me.

"Aren't those the Chuckwalla claims?" she asked, nodding her head to the left.

"Those are the ones," I told her. "You ride on with George for a piece. I'll catch up with you later."

She nodded and said something to George. They went on.

It was a full moon, and the sun had set just a few minutes ago in the west. The big moon was climbing over the eastern horizon, not red like some huge pumpkin, as it is in the impure air of the cities, but showing a pure delicate silver from the minute it climbed into view.

I made certain that Bill Ordway wasn't crowding us too closely, and then I took a shovel from the pack and buried a rifle, a pair of six-shooters and plenty of shells. I smoothed the ground over and made certain that a tracker wouldn't spot the place, particularly in the moonlight. Then I threw the pack rope back into place, got on my burro and urged him to speed. I caught up with the others within about a mile and a half. After we'd gone another half mile I said, "This is the place, Sally, over here to the right."

"You mean this is our camp?" asked George Ringley.

"This is close enough to it," I said.

He heaved a big sigh of relief, got from the saddle, tried to walk and fell flat. His legs were too stiff to function. After a minute or two he got up and grinned.

"I hope we stay here for a day or two," he said.

I took some provisions and a little extra water, backtracked for a ways, and buried the stuff. Then I swung back so I could watch our back trail. Not that I expected to gain anything by it, but I knew that Bill Ordway would be suspicious if I made things too easy for him.

Bill was playing his hand pretty close to his chest. I knew that he was following along the trail. I knew that he knew we'd camped. The moonlight was almost as bright as day, but I did not see any trace of him or his men.

The next morning I took some location notices and started locating claims. George Ringley watched me with big eyes. Sally Ehlers seemed nervous and tense.

"Now," I told them, "I'm going to leave you here with these claims. You can prowl around and do a little prospecting. It would probably be a good thing if you did. I'm going to go on back and record the claims. I'll make a quick trip, then I'll pick up some more provisions and come back to you just as soon as I can. I shouldn't be gone over four or five days. I'll take a fast-traveling burro and one of the packs, and I'll shuffle right along."

George Ringley looked around at the hot surface of the desert.

"Shucks!" he said. "There isn't a human being within a million miles of us. We could leave the government mint exposed right here, and there wouldn't be any trouble."

Sally Ehlers didn't say anything.

"Well," I told him, "it will give you a good rest anyway."

I put some provisions on the pack, not too many. I took a rifle and strapped a six-shooter around my waist.

I nodded to Sally Ehlers and shook hands with George Ringley.

I had the samples of high-grade ore in my saddle bags, and took care to see that the flap of one saddle bag was open so that a corner of the canvas sack was visible.

V THE HOLD-UP

My burros shuffled off at a rapid pace. Behind me, the serrated line of the Chocolate Mountains was sharply outlined against the deep blue-black of the desert sky. The air was so clear that it was possible to see every detail for long distances until the heat waves started distorting the scenery.

From time to time I turned in my saddle and looked back at the claim we had staked out. I could see two figures standing there watching me. From time to time they would wave. At length, the heat waves started making them do all sorts of weird dances, and then I dropped down into a depression and rode along a sandy wash, the claim shut from my sight.

I was following the trail we had made in going to the place we had located. Had I been trying to avoid Bill Ordway, I naturally would never have taken the same trail, but would either have kept on going until I hit Niland or Ogilby, and then gone by railroad to the county seat, or I would have swung back in a big circle. As it was, however, I played right into their hands, but kept a sharp watch to see if they were hidden along the trail. At that, they made a good job of it. I had no warning of the ambush until the hot rays of the sun glinted on the blue-steel barrel of a rifle within less than twenty yards.

"Stick 'em up!" said a man's voice.

I hesitated just a moment, not long enough to actually collect lead, but long enough not to make my obedience seem suspicious.

A voice from behind me shouted: "Get them up quick, Bob, or you'll get perforated!"

I turned.

Another man was hidden behind a rocky outcropping some fifteen yards to the rear. They had me between a cross-fire. I elevated my hands. A third man came out from the sandy wash. He was Bill Ordway, a big, ungainly figure, with a paunchy stomach, cheeks that were flabby and a mouth and eyes that were hard as steel.

"Get off the burro, Bob," he said, "and unbuckle your six-gun as you get off. Don't make any sudden motions. You're between two fires."

I slid to the ground and unbuckled my six-gun.

"March over against that rock," Ordway said, gesturing with the barrel of a six-shooter.

I backed over against the rock.

"Search his burro, boys," said Bill Ordway. "You'll find a description of the claim in the saddle bags probably."

"Perhaps he's got it on him," one of the men said, walking up with a rifle in the crook of his elbow.

"We'll make sure of that, too," Ordway said. "Don't worry."

One of the men went through the saddle bags. I heard him exclaim when he found the gold.

The three men clustered together for a moment, their eyes bulging as they saw the gold. Then they uncovered the notice I had ready for recording. They were excited, but not so excited that they overlooked their hand. They kept me covered. After a while, Bill Ordway came over to me.

"Looks pretty good, Bob," he said. "Too bad you didn't locate it first."

"How do you mean?" I asked.

"That's our claim," he said. "Didn't you see our location notice?"

I twisted my lips into a sneer.

"A fat chance that it's your claim," I said.

"Sure it is," he said. "We located it yesterday. We were starting back to record it when we saw you go on past. Then we watched you go in and jump our claim. We were coming down to do something about it when you rode right into our arms. We had our location notices there, all duly in order."

"Not when I located it," I said.

"Oh yes we did," he said. "You can't pull that stuff on us, Bob Zane, no matter how smart a guy you think you are, nor how much experience you've had in the desert."

I shrugged my shoulders.

"Oh, what the hell's the use?" I said. "You're going to steal the claim—go ahead and do it and cut out all the conversation!"

Big Bill Ordway said nothing. His face was cold and determined. His hands patted my pockets. Searched for a shoulder holster under my armpit.

"Okay, boys," he said, "he's clean."

He made further search, looking for any additional location notices. When he had satisfied himself that I had none he nodded toward the desert.

"All right, Bob," he said. "You've got the reputation of being a good man in the desert. Take a canteen of water and a couple of cans of beans and start."

"How about my burro?" I asked.

"You never had any burro," he told me.

"I can't get very far on water and a couple of cans of beans," I said.

"You can get as far as you're going," he told me, "and don't think we don't know it. You'll probably beat us into Blythe, but it won't do you any good. There are too many witnesses against you. Do you understand?"

"Understand what?" I asked.

"Understand that you tried to jump our claim," he said. "You couldn't make it stick. We were on the ground and in possession. You did the best you could, but we were there first. Do you get that straight?"

I shrugged my shoulders.

"All right," he said, "get started."

I made a gesture of resignation, started walking along through the hot, blinding sand of the desert, my head forward dejectedly, the two cans of beans they had given me thrust in a bit of sacking and thrown over my shoulder, the water canteen pounding on my hip as I walked. The others got on burros and rode away. I watched them until they were out of sight, then I started shuffling along once more. After a while I took care to leave my tracks where it wouldn't be too easy to follow them, picking out the rocky stretches and working along those, until I found an outcropping, up which I climbed until I struck a ridge. I worked along the ridge and headed over toward the Chuckwalla claim.

I was just digging up the rifle and revolvers that I'd cached, when I heard the sound of distant shooting.

The hot, dry air of the desert absorbed the sound, until the roar of the guns sounded like the dull pop of distant firecrackers.

I sat and listened to the firing for some little time. I couldn't figure it out. Sally Ehlers had specifically understood that she was to keep George Ringley from doing any shooting. I figured that Big Bill Ordway wouldn't shoot unless he had to. He was perfectly willing to commit murder, but he didn't want to do it.

I put up monuments and made a location on the Chuckwalla claims, then I got the stuff ready to take into the recorder's office, and sat and waited.

The firing was still going on.

I couldn't figure that out. The shadows were commencing to stretch across the desert. It was nearly time for me to take some definite action, and Big Bill Ordway and his gang were still popping rifles over the rocky ridge which prevented me from seeing what was going on.

The more I thought of it, the less I liked it. Finally I went around and took down all of my location notices and leveled the location monuments. Then I shouldered my rifle, saw that the two six-guns were working freely in their holsters and started trudging back toward the place where I'd left Sally Ehlers and George Ringley.

I didn't go by the same route that I had come, but worked around the ridge toward the west, so that I would be coming up on the attackers with the sun at my back.

The firing continued. The sun was just touching the rim of the western hills when I got to a point where I could see what was going on.

Sally Ehlers and George Ringley had built themselves a rock barricade, a first class little fortress. They'd built it in such a way that they commanded the surrounding country. Big Bill Ordway and his gang were strung around in a big circle. They had the place virtually surrounded. There was a big peak off to the rear, but it was pretty much out of rifle range, and they hadn't tried as yet to get up on there and drop shells down into the fort, but I could see them crawling around in gullies and washes, looking like black beetles dragging themselves across the white sand. Occasionally they'd fire a few shells, apparently in order to keep the defenders from getting into a position where they could deliver an accurate fire.

The pair in the fort were holding their fire, sending, however, an occasional well-placed bullet. From where I was, I could see the dust rise up near one of the crawling figures.

I carried a small pocket telescope with me, one that had a small field but a great deal of power. I used it occasionally to trace formations with. Bill Ordway had evidently figured a telescope wouldn't do very much harm. He hadn't bothered to take it. I got it out, and in the dying light focused it on the field of battle.

What I saw didn't give me any additional information. I could see that Sally Ehlers was taking care of the east end of the fort, George Ringley of the west end. As I looked through the telescope, I could see an occasional flick of dust where a bullet struck, or see powder fly from one of the rocks in the fort.

Looking over Big Bill Ordway's gang, I figured he must have six or seven in all, which was more than I'd figured him for. Some of the gang must have kept out of sight when he picked me up.

I could see that Bill Ordway was getting his men placed in strategic positions. Under cover of darkness, they could work in to the fort, but there'd only be about half an hour of darkness after the sun went down, and before the moon came up. They'd have to work quickly.

On the other hand, it was certain that Ringley and Sally Ehlers weren't getting anywhere. They were simply holding themselves in a state of siege. But, of course, Bill Ordway didn't know how long they could hold out.

While I was watching the battle, I saw a figure wave his hand two or three times, then two other figures started over toward him. I shifted the little telescope and saw that the man who had given the signal was Big Bill Ordway. The pair came over to him, and they had a short conference. Then the two started walking back toward the north, slipping from cover to cover at first, until they were pretty much out of range of the pair in the fort, and then coming out into the open, walking rapidly.

I couldn't figure that for a minute, and then all at once, the explanation struck me.

Ordway was afraid that I was going to get back to Blythe, pick up some men who would stand back of me, and come back into the desert. If they hadn't jumped the claims by the time I returned, the men would find themselves out of luck. Therefore, Ordway had sent these two men to follow on my trail and ambush me at the first opportunity.

I sensed then that Sally Ehlers had decided that she was going to make enough racket with the firearms to bring me to the ground, knowing that when I heard the shooting, I would realize that she had, for some reason, violated the instructions I had given her.

I couldn't figure just what the reason for that violation was, but I had enough confidence in her and her judgment to know that she was doing what was right.

Having brought me to the scene of the conflict, she was continuing to shoot from time to time in order to keep the others at their distance, and to let me see exactly what the situation was. Obviously, therefore, she expected me to do just what Bill Ordway expected me to do—go as rapidly as possible to some of the towns in the Palo Verde Valley, notify the authorities and bring them back with me.

But could they hold out until that time?

I doubted it.

The moon would be rising some forty-five minutes later every night. After two nights, the interval of darkness would be amply sufficient to enable Bill Ordway to get his gang together and to rush the defenders. I couldn't possibly make it to Blythe and back in time to keep that from happening.

I decided, therefore, that before I took any definite steps, I'd find out something about what was going on, so I started looking around, using the telescope and shifting my position from time to time. Before it got dark, I had discovered several things. One of them was that the men had dumped all of their provisions by their burros, and that their burros were located in a little wash down by the foot of a butte. There was no one guarding their base of supplies.

I started working against approaching darkness, moving around toward the place where they maintained their base of supplies. The gang were fully occupied with the business in hand. I got to within about a hundred and twenty-five yards of the place without being detected. I nestled behind a rock, got my rifle pressed against my cheek. It was pretty hard to see with the leaf sights, but I put up the peep sight and got a good bead on the pile of canteens.

The canteens jumped and jiggled as the bullets crashed into them. Six shots and the water supply of Bill Ordway's gang was pretty much ruined.

The peculiar thing was that no one paid any attention to what was happening. Rifles were banging all around in a brisk fusillade, and apparently every one of the gang took it for granted that the shots were being fired by some other member of the gang.

I reloaded the rifle, slipped back from behind my rock, worked down a slope and started circling so that I could get into a position where I could help Sally Ehlers and George Ringley if it became necessary.

Darkness settled rapidly, and I knew that Ordway would try a rush if he could do it before the moon came up.

I managed to get a good place of concealment down behind a little bunch of rocks. And I flattened out so that I was as close to the ground as possible.

VI NIGHT TACTICS

It gets dark rapidly in the desert. The stars began to appear. The western heavens showed a glow of light, but darkness was settling on the desert like a thick blanket.

I lay looking up at the bright patch of sky, and suddenly saw something move. A moment later I saw the form of a man crouched low, moving along the little ridge which communicated with the slope on which the defenders had made their fort.

Back of the first figure came another and then another.

I nestled my gun against my shoulder, didn't try to use the sights, but shot entirely by the feel of the weapon.

I pulled the trigger. The big gun jarred into recoil, and, spitting orange flame, shot lead into the night.

That first shot came as a surprise. I flung two more at the attackers before they suddenly realized that they had been outflanked. I doubt, at the time, if they thought I had doubled back to assist the defenders, but they figured that Sally Ehlers or George Ringley had left the little fortress, under cover of darkness, and had moved out to intercept them.

There was a sudden fusillade of shots, little pinpricking bursts of flame which showed red and angry in the darkness. Bullets whizzed overhead, spatted against the rocks or zoomed off into space with long whining screams.

I heard the sound of footsteps pounding along the ground as the men charged.

I didn't lose my head as a novice at night fighting might have done, and return the fire. Nor did I arise to meet the charge. I simply pressed myself flat against the desert and lay there.

The men had been almost a hundred and fifty yards off when I fired my shots. Charging a hundred and fifty yards through darkness isn't a thing that's easily done, particularly when one is not certain that one's enemy will remain in any certain place.

Before the men had come fifty yards I heard the jarring impact of one of them falling to the earth as he stubbed his toe on a rock. Another crashed into a patch

of cacti, and as the needles pierced his legs he let out a
yell of pain. The others were swinging to one side, their
charge stopped of sheer inertia before they had reached
the place where I lay concealed. I heard them muttering
cautious comments, then huddling together for a conference. It was possible for me to hear every word they said.

I recognized Bill Ordway's voice.

"It's the girl," he said. "She's got more sense than the
fellow. She's detoured out to the side to ambush us. She's
sneaked back to the fort now."

A man's voice said, "Don't be too sure she's gone back
to the fort. She may be sticking around here somewhere.
Whoever she is, she shoots like the devil. She got Bert in
the leg and one of those bullets went through my Stetson."

"Well, come on," said Bill Ordway. "If she's out of the
fort there's only one left. We can rush it before the moon
comes up."

"I've lost my bearings now," one of the men said.

"You can see the outline of that peak against the sky.
It's up the slope just to the right of that."

"Damn it!" said a man's voice. "I wish they'd do a little
shooting so we could tell just where they are. We've
moved over here to the side and I don't know just where
the place is now. We don't want to go floundering around
there in the dark."

The little knot of men gave a murmur of assent.

"This is no time to go blundering around if we don't
know where we're going, and what we're going after, Bill,"
a man's voice said. "We'd better go do something about
Bert's leg. The bullet went through the upper part of it."

"Oh, the hell with Bert," Ordway said. "Are you fellows going to stand around here and talk until the moon
comes up, or are you going to follow me?"

He pushed on ahead.

I waited until he was almost lost in the darkness, and

then, when I could see just a vague indistinct blotch of shadow, I fired again, shooting by the feel of the weapon, and shooting low.

I heard a man yell, then once more the darkness was ripped by stabbing flashes of flame.

Two or three of the men came charging toward me. I heard Ordway shouting at them to let me go and to rush the claim. His orders, however, were not obeyed. The men didn't relish the idea of having an enemy in the rear.

The two defenders in the fort held their fire. I figured they probably either sensed some friction in the attackers or else they realized that their strongest defense lay in keeping the location of their fortress sufficiently indefinite to prevent the attackers from making a direct charge.

I heard men crawling about me through the darkness, and sat tight. They worked on past me. One of them came so close that I could hear his labored breathing. They drew together some twenty yards on the other side of me, and I heard them whisper, but I wasn't able to distinguish the words, but I could hear the hissing sibilance of the whispers.

I sat tight and didn't move.

There was a glow of rosy light in the east. I heard Bill Ordway cursing his men for fools. Then the rim of the moon appeared over the eastern mountains. The first rays of the silvery moonlight gave some degree of weird visibility to the desert.

My own position was just a little dangerous. The enemy were all about me and the moon was coming up. However, I clung to my little depression in the sand with the rocks that I had flung about me, casting enough shadow so that I blended with the other shadows which were cast by the rays of the rising moon.

After a moment the men walked over to join Ordway, and as they walked they went within some ten feet of me, but they didn't see me. Nor, on the other hand, did I open up on them. I figured that I was hopelessly outnumbered if they actually got me cornered, and that my best defense was to sit tight until they had found the punctured canteens.

The moon slid slowly and majestically into the heavens, illuminating the desert with its silvery rays. The attackers decided that there was nothing more they could do that night, and I heard Ordway instruct a couple of men to keep working up toward the fort, until they got as close as they dared, firing from time to time in order to keep the defenders from getting any sleep. Then Ordway and the balance of the crew went over toward the place where they had left their burros and supplies, in order to cook a meal.

I waited for four or five minutes and then heard a sudden hubbub from the place, and knew that the men had found what had happened to their water.

After that I heard a shrill whistle, then the sound of steps crunching the sand, and Bill Ordway's hail.

It was answered by one of the men who had been detailed to work up on the fortress.

Bill Ordway called him over and said: "Somebody's shot hell out of our canteens. The water's all leaked out, there isn't enough there to last us for more than half a day, not after the sun gets up."

There was a moment of silence. Then one of the men said, "Well, that settles it. We've got to head back toward drinking water."

Bill Ordway muttered a curse.

"Here's where I fool you," he said. "There's plenty of drinking water in that fortress. I'm going to keep you fellows right here. If you want to get any water you've got to rush the fort."

There was a moment of silence while the men digested

that remark. Then one of the men started a low-voiced protest, but Bill Ordway turned on his heel and walked away. He crunched the sand with his feet, within less than five yards of the place where I lay concealed. After that there was an interval of silence and then the men turned and went back toward camp, muttering their protests. The fortress was left unmolested.

I saw the glow of a campfire. From where I was I could hear the rumble of voices. Voices that were raised in an argument, but evidently Bill Ordway had his way. The campfire continued to burn, and the men didn't start back toward Blythe. If they had been faced with the necessity of making a forced march in the desert without water, they would, of course, have started while the moon was in the heavens, and while the desert was cool.

I moved on up closer to the fort, working my way to within about seventy-five or eighty yards, until the defenders saw me and a couple of bullets came pretty close to me. Naturally, they thought that I was one of the enemy, and I didn't tell them anything to the contrary. I had a plan that I wanted to work out.

I burrowed my way down into a depression in the sand, and sat perfectly tight. After a while I heard the thud of running feet.

The charge toward the fort had commenced.

Rifles blazed. Two of the men dropped to the ground, the balance spread out and took to cover. There followed a period of isolated sniping, the men working around, trying to sneak on the fort under cover of the shadows cast by the moon.

But the moon was higher in the heavens now, and it was illuminating the desert with a species of silvery light that made objects almost as visible as under the noonday sun. The pair in the fort kept up a steady fire, and after a while the attackers were beaten off.

Once more they held a council of war. This time I wasn't close enough to hear anything that was said, but I could hear the distant murmur of voices sounding like the indistinct roar of a waterfall, and once or twice I heard Big Bill Ordway's voice as it boomed forth above the whining arguments of the men.

Two of the men had been wounded. I gathered that their wounds were serious. There was hardly enough water in the whole outfit to last them for a forced march to Blythe. In the end, apparently two of the men were dispatched for water and help. By this time, Ordway's gang had been so seriously weakened that an attack was out of the question, but Ordway detailed one of the two remaining men to keep up a desultory fire on the fortress in order to keep the defenders from getting any sleep.

I sensed the strategy when the two men left, and the man who was chosen to keep firing on the fort took up a position within some fifty yards of where I lay concealed. I was, in fact, almost between the two fires.

I listened to the roar of the guns and the whining bullets as they passed overhead, and some ten or fifteen yards to my right. Then gradually I dropped off to sleep, knowing that we held all the trump cards in the game; but I didn't want to play those cards. I wanted George Ringley to play them.

I dozed off and on during the night. Big Bill Ordway relieved the man who was doing the sniping shortly after midnight.

VII THE HERO

Along toward morning the night wind came up, and the desert commenced to whisper. I lay and dozed, keeping an eye on the place where Big Bill Ordway had fired his last shot, keeping my rifle ready and sleeping with my senses alert.

It was around four thirty in the morning when I heard the noise of crunching sand. A noise that wasn't made by the night wind.

I cocked my rifle and nestled it up against my shoulder. The noise seemed to be coming from the direction of the fortress.

I sat silent and alert, my rifle ready.

A man came crawling along the desert, working his way by inches, stopping from time to time perfectly motionless and peering about him. He was dragging a rifle along the ground.

I couldn't be sure, but I thought it was George Ringley.

I let him pass.

The wind, which had been sending the sand in little drifting eddies, died away, and the desert became calm and still. The creeping man had passed beyond the scope of my vision. Once or twice I thought I could see him, but I wasn't certain. There were too many shadows in the desert as the moon slid down toward the west, and it was difficult to pick out which blotch of darkness was cast by the figure of the crawling man.

Suddenly I heard a roar of rage and then the thud of a blow. Two men rose up, apparently out of the face of the desert, and started a terrific hand-to-hand struggle. They were perhaps sixty-five yards away.

I jumped up and ran toward them, my rifle at the ready.

I could see another man running from the place where the outlaws had made their camp. A man who ran with heavy, awkward strides, a gun in his hand.

I circled the combatants and headed toward this man. He was intent upon the struggling figures, apparently, trying to distinguish which was which. As I got within a few feet of him he raised his gun.

I flung my weapon to my shoulder.

"Hold everything," I said in a low voice.

The man whirled toward me.

"Drop that gun," I said, "or you're a dead man."

He fired, and at the same time I squeezed the trigger of my rifle. His bullet whizzed past my cheek, my bullet gave that unmistakable *thunk* which is made by a bullet when it impacts living tissue.

I saw the man jerk around as though he had been pulled by some invisible string. He staggered for two or three steps and then pitched forward on his face.

I looked back.

The two men were struggling. Apparently, they had been entirely unaware of the shooting.

Abruptly one of the men staggered backward.

I saw the smaller man swing a clubbed rifle, heard the smashing impact, and then the big man went down. I dropped to the desert.

George Ringley ran past me, going toward the place where the men had established headquarters. He was gone for perhaps three quarters of an hour. It was commencing to get light in the east when he came back.

I chuckled when I saw what he had done. He had loaded up all of the provisions on the burros, and was bringing them back with him. He picketed them near the fortress.

The stars began to recede to mere needle points of light, and once more a mysterious wind started the desert talking.

I relaxed. There was no necessity for me to enter into the picture—not just then.

I kept close to the ground, working with the caution of a man stalking a deer, taking advantage of every bit of shadow I could find, and gradually moved off to the east. By the time the rising sun cast its first rays over the peaks to the east, I was more than a mile from the fort.

After that there was nothing to it.

The men who had been sent by Bill Ordway to follow my trail had apparently followed it back to the place where I had fired my shots into the canteens.

By that time they knew what had happened. They came up to the camp where they had left their stuff. In the light of the early morning they could see their burros tied up back of the little fortress. Bill Ordway was staggering about, apparently still punch-groggy. Two of the men lay motionless on the desert, black blotches which were already commencing to attract the circling buzzards.

The men held a brief conference, then turned and started trudging through the sand, walking with the quick, anxious steps of men who are running a race with desert death.

After a moment Bill Ordway started running after them.

I waited until the figures had vanished into the heat waves of a distorted horizon, which, even so early in the morning, was commencing to dance a weird devil's dance.

I started approaching the fort from the east. When I knew that they had seen me, I put my hat on my gun barrel and waved it. After they had recognized me, I walked on to the fort.

Sally Ehlers had a bloodstained handkerchief wrapped around her left arm. Her eyes were starry. George Ringley was grinning. His eyes were red-rimmed and blood-shot. There were powder stains on his face. His hair was tousled, there was dirt and grime all over him. His knuckles were bloody and there was a livid bruise on one cheek, but his grin had an expression of triumph.

"Where were you?" asked Sally Ehlers. "We kept

shooting so that you'd know something had gone wrong."

"I had quite a time getting here," I said. "What happened?"

Sally Ehlers, her eyes gleaming with excitement, reached down into the loose sand at the base of the little fortress, scraped away the sand, and pulled out a rock which gave a yellow glistening gleam in the intense sunlight.

"Look!" she said, and held it out to me.

Her hand was trembling so that she could hardly hold the rock.

"You see what happened," she said. "We started to locate this claim knowing that it was just a fake, and that you were using it as a blind to lure the claim jumpers—"

"I didn't know that at the time," said George Ringley.

"Of course you didn't," she told him, smiling. "That was a secret that Bob Zane and I had between us. But, of course, as soon as we found this rich gold, I had to tell him. Then, you see, we simply *had* to hold the claim."

I nodded slowly. "I see," I said.

I took the chunk of rock from her trembling hand. "More of it?" I asked.

"Lots of it," she said in a voice that quavered with excitement. "There's a ledge of it up there, and it is almost pure gold. It glitters in the sun."

I turned the rock over and over in my hands.

"What's the matter, Uncle Bob?" she asked. "You don't seem very excited about it."

I didn't know whether I should break the news to her or not, but while I was hesitating my face told the story.

"Good heavens!" she said. "Don't tell me it's—"

I nodded.

"Yes, Sally," I told her, "it's what they call 'fool's gold.' It's a crystal formation that frequently occurs in gold-bearing rock. There may be some mineral content in here, but it's a cinch it isn't any bonanza of pure gold."

She gave a little gasp of disappointment.

"Oh," she said, and sat down on one of the rocks as though her knees had become too weak to support her.

George Ringley wanted to fight about it.

"Look here," he said, "don't be too sure about that. Sally Ehlers said it was gold. We've put up a big battle for that gold, and personally I'm going to require something more than your say-so before I figure it's all a false alarm."

Sally put a swift hand on his arm.

"No, George," she said; "if Uncle Bob says it's fool's gold, that's what it is."

Her eyes lifted to mine. There was a funny expression in them.

"Then," she said, "we violated your instructions all for nothing. There's been a fight. Men have been killed. We risked your life and I risked George's life, all for a lot of fool's gold."

I shook my head, smiling down at her.

"No," I said, "you're only looking at the debit side of the ledger. There's a credit side."

"What?" she asked in a tone that was too innocent.

I nodded my head toward George Ringley.

"Do you realize the vein of gold that you've uncovered?" I asked her. "You've uncovered a fighting character that is going to go far in the world. This boy managed, with your assistance, to beat off Big Bill Ordway's whole gang. They were experienced desert fighters. They've been notorious claim jumpers for the past ten years, and you and George broke up the entire gang. You'll be given the thanks of every miner between here and Mojave. Moreover, you've accomplished something that a great deal of money had never been able to accomplish."

She looked from me to George Ringley.

"Sand blast?" she asked, and her smile was enigmatical.

I nodded.

"Exactly," I said.

"How about the Chuckwalla claims?"

"There's nothing to keep us from locating them," I said. "Ordway's gang is all busted up."

She nodded slowly. "Just as you say, Uncle Bob," she told me.

I held her eye.

"Sally Ehlers," I said, "have you lived in the desert all your life and been fooled by fool's gold?"

She smiled.

"George found it," she said.

The plane slanted down from the cloudless blue of the California sky, to drop to a three-point landing as gracefully as a seagull dropping to a sand bar.

Pete Ringley was the first one out of the plane. He ran across the cement and grabbed his boy by the arms. They looked in each other's eyes for a moment and then started pumping hands up and down. Sally Ehlers came over and Pete Ringley threw an arm around her. I walked up and caught the glint in Pete's eyes.

"You damned old pirate," he said. "I should have you arrested."

"Remember the woodwork in your study, Pete?" I asked.

He looked at me, wondering if perhaps I had gone entirely crazy.

I nodded toward the boy.

"Take another look at him, Pete," I said.

Sally Ehlers burst into rapid-fire conversation.

"You'd ought to be proud of your son, Uncle Pete,"

she said. "Do you know what he did single-handed and unaided? He busted up the Bill Ordway gang of claim jumpers. Here it is in the paper. Take a look for yourself."

She whipped a copy of the Los Angeles *Times* from under her arm, snapped the paper open, and let Pete Ringley look at the big headlines which streamed across the front of the page with a picture of George Ringley occupying a prominent position in top center of the page.

Pete's eyes lit with a sudden glow of pride. He grabbed the paper.

"Humph!" he said at last, when he had read the account. "And where was Bob Zane all that time?"

"I couldn't get there, Pete," I said. "I heard the firing, but there was nothing I could do. By the time I got started they had the place surrounded and I couldn't get through them."

Slowly the gleam of hostility faded from Pete Ringley's eyes.

"I think," he said, "I'm commencing to see."

"Aw, it was Sally that worked the whole thing for me," George said. "I'd never have had the courage to do it. She showed me how to build the fort and all of that stuff."

"Who showed you how to bust out of the fort and lick Bill Ordway in a hand-to-hand battle, kid?" I asked.

He shuffled his feet and hung his head in embarrassment.

Pete Ringley looked at me and sighed.

"Well, Bob," he said. "We're starting all over again."

"What do you mean?" I asked.

"That big business deal I had on," he said, "turned out to be a skin-game. I was the one who got skinned."

"You mean you've lost money, Dad?" asked George Ringley.

"Lost money?" he said. "I've lost everything. I been cleaned out, lock, stock and barrel. I had enough money in my pocket to buy an airplane ticket when I got Bob Zane's wire, and that's about all."

"Your wife?" I asked.

A look of pain clouded his eyes for a moment, then he shrugged his shoulders and made a spreading gesture with his hands.

"She was a city woman," he said, as though by way of extenuation.

Sally Ehlers gripped his arm.

"But," she said, "you've got the Chuckwalla claims. Bob Zane located them in your joint names."

Pete Ringley looked at me.

I managed to look glum.

"Yes, Pete," I said, "I located them, but they didn't look so good when I made a second survey of the property. I'm afraid that ore doesn't run uniform."

Sally Ehlers gave a gasp.

"Why, Uncle Bob," she said, "I thought the claims were going to be bonanzas."

"You never can tell about gold, Sally," I told her.

"Well," Pete said, "let's get started somewhere. We can't stick around here, and I don't like the noise of civilization. I want to get out in the desert where it's silent."

The two young folks walked on ahead. Pete Ringley fell into step beside me.

"Listen, you old sidewinder," he said, "what the hell's the idea about that second survey of the claims? We made a complete survey that first time."

I grinned at him.

"You know, Pete," I said, "I think when she comes to think it over, Sally Ehlers might feel a little embarrassed if the son of a millionaire should propose to her to-night. She'd probably turn him down just to make sure that she wasn't marrying for money. But if she thought that he was the son of a poor desert prospector . . ."

I broke off and shrugged my shoulders.

Pete looked over at me and a slow grin came over his face.

"And those claims are just as good as they ever were?" he asked.

I gripped his arm.

"A damn sight better," I told him.

He heaved a deep sigh.

"All right," he said, "let's get out of these damn dude duds and get out in the desert where we can hear the silence."

I nodded toward the couple on ahead.

"Why the devil do you suppose we filled the gas tank before we drove up to the airport?" I asked. "You bet your life we're headed for the desert."

Law of the Rope

I DESERT DEATH

LITTLE THINGS count for a good deal in the desert. The man who lives in the desert must observe everything, no matter how small, otherwise he won't live long.

The desert is the cruelest mother a man ever had, and therefore the kindest. Man develops through his sufferings. The pleasures which come in between are the mental bromides which enable us to carry on. Our only real progress is made through overcoming suffering or hardship.

If I hadn't lived so long in the desert I wouldn't have investigated the moving speck. We were approaching the end of the road, and my roan was tired. He was still full of spirit and stamina, but he was tired. The moving speck caught my eye and held my attention.

It wasn't a deer; it wasn't an antelope, and it wasn't a man. It looked something like a burro, and yet it seemed to be too high in the back for a burro.

I glimpsed it winding around the base of a butte, then it vanished.

I pulled the roan in and looked around me. Mile on mile of empty space, aching with silence, a weird horizon of sharply serrated mountains that thrust knife-like edges up into the blue vault, a horizon that danced in the sunlight as the heat waves distorted the distant mountains.

I dropped the lead rope from the packhorse, swung one knee over the horn of the saddle, and rolled a cigarette while I scanned the base of the desert butte. The roan had seen the speck too.

Perhaps he knew what it was. His ears were cocked forward and his nostrils slightly dilated as he looked at the place where the speck had disappeared.

I made fire to the cigarette, inhaled an appreciative lungful of smoke and touched the roan lightly with my spur. He knew at once what I wanted, and started a shuffling lope through the white sand.

Distances are deceptive in the dry air of the desert, and at the end of ten minutes we seemed to be no nearer the butte than when we had started. The roan continued his pace-devouring stride, although we were climbing a slope and the footing was soft. We angled around the slope of the butte and came at length to the place where I had seen the moving object.

I looked down in the sand, reading the trail, and knew at once what it was that had gone around the base of that butte.

It was a burro, and a burro that had a pack on his back.

A burro, with a pack, which is loose in the desert, means a desert wayfarer in trouble, and the code of the desert is that one must always aid the wayfarer who is in trouble.

The horse knew as well as I did what I wanted. I left everything to the horse.

He drifted around the shoulder of the butte, went down a pitch on the other side, and I saw the burro nibbling at a bit of sage in a cup-like depression between the buttes. I rode up to him and looked at the pack.

A desert man can tell much from the way a pack is thrown. Men who have worked as forest rangers usually have a certain system. Professional packers throw their ropes in another way; and men who have gone in much for hunting use a distinctive method of balancing the pack and throwing the hitch. There are all kinds, from diamond hitches down to squaw hitches, with various modifications in between.

I concluded this pack had been thrown by an old desert man who had been out from his base of supplies for about two days. There was water in the canteen, a light bed roll, and a pair of *alforjas* filled with a miscellaneous assortment. The tarp which was thrown over the top was grimed with desert dust and sooted with straggling ashes from countless camp fires. I tossed a rope over the burro's neck, made a half hitch around the horn of the saddle, and spoke to the roan.

We swung back around the shoulder of the mesa, down a long slope, around a short ridge of hills, through a little valley, and then I saw another speck. This speck was a black blotch which was lying motionless on a sandy slope between two clumps of stunted sage.

The sun was getting a bit toward the west now, and the shadows were lengthening. The shadow which was thrown by this object seemed as black as a pool of ink dropped on the white sand of the desert.

I knew what it was when I was more than a hundred and fifty yards away.

At first I thought perhaps the man might have collapsed with a sprained ankle or because of the heat. But as I rode up and took in the details of the grotesque pose, I knew that he was dead.

I dismounted when I was twenty or thirty yards away. The burro didn't make any objections, but the roan was side-stepping around a bit and snorting. I knew then that the death had been violent, and the roan was smelling blood.

I moved forward cautiously and, as I walked, I pulled

my six-gun from its holster and watched the surrounding country.

Ordinarily we don't wear six-guns in the desert. The man who has one is usually a tenderfoot or a crook. But this trip was different. I was going into a section which remained wild.

It needed but a glance to tell what had happened. The man had been shot from some distance with a high-powered rifle, used by an expert. There had been but the one shot, and it had gone full into the heart.

The man had never known what hit him.

He was about fifty-five or fifty-six years of age, and had a gray stubble along the angle of his bronzed jaw. He was attired in an old pair of faded overalls, a jumper and a shirt. The hat was an old Stetson which had been soaked in desert dust and sunshine until it showed only as a nondescript gray. Everything about the man indicated an old desert rat who knew the moods of the desert.

Tracks showed that there had been two burros, and I spotted the second burro not over two hundred yards away. This was a saddle burro, and there was a scabbard on the side of the saddle, with a rifle in the scabbard. I went up to this burro and looked the saddle over.

I would have said that the man had been shot from some sort of an ambush. Certainly he never knew that he was in any danger. The rifle was in the scabbard, the reins were caught on the horn of the saddle.

Evidently the man had been riding along when suddenly he received that shot, full through the heart.

I unsaddled both of the burros and turned them loose. I knew that they could shift for themselves in the desert. I couldn't be bothered carrying them along with me. I went back to the body and examined it once more. There was a six-gun thrust down the front of the man's belt, and apparently he had made no attempt to reach it. It was stuck snugly in its holster. The left hand held a small glass jar, hermetically sealed, with a screw top. In that jar was a piece of paper.

I took the jar from the dead man's hand. I could see that the paper had writing on it, but I couldn't see exactly what that writing consisted of. I slipped the jar into my saddle bag, took the tarp and covered the body with it.

Tracking back the burros and getting the direction in which the man had been traveling, then looking at the path the bullet had taken through his body, I was able to get a general idea of the direction from which the shot had come.

I mounted the roan and started shuffling along in that direction. Pretty quick I came to a place where a body had lain in the sand. It was possible to see prints made by the elbows and by the buttons on the coat, also little holes where the toes of the boots had rested.

There were half a dozen cigarette stubs scattered around in the rocks, the ends of several burnt matches, and a single empty rifle shell. That rifle shell was from a .303 rifle.

I prowled around and found where the man had walked into his place of concealment. He wore high heeled cowboy boots. Backtracking, I found where his horse had been stationed, and figured that the horse was a big, fast cattle horse that had been trained to stand when the reins were dropped over his head.

I didn't disturb the evidence any, but simply looked it over. Then I went back, picked up my packhorse, and started on.

Behind me stretched the flat desert, across which wound a road of sorts, a road that could have been traveled by automobile.

Ahead of me loomed mountains and the road which wound up the Box Cañon, a grade that was far too steep for any automobile to negotiate. In fact, it could hardly

be dignified by being called a road at all. It was merely
a wide back trail.

II   DESERT MYSTERY

From here on, I left civilization behind. The hands of the
clock turned back through two or three decades. I had
heard of Greasewood before. In fact, I had been there
once or twice in the earlier days. In those days it had been
a prosperous mining community and the road had been
such that supplies could be freighted in by wagon.

Those were the days of the ten- and sixteen-horse
wagons that crawled up through the hot country; horses
harnessed in long strings, two abreast, and driven by the
"long-line skinner" who sat in a saddle on one of the
"wheelers" and controlled the team by jerks on a long
line. The leaders had bells attached to their collars so that
any one coming along the road from an opposite direction
could be apprised of the big freighter that was crawling
along the grade.

Then had come the change. The mines on the mesa
had closed down, and the town of Greasewood had become a ghost town with only a few desert rats making
headquarters in the deserted buildings.

The desert closed in and claimed the once prosperous
mining community for its own, engulfed it in vast silence.
Then the crash in the stock market started the depression,
and the depression had placed a premium upon gold.
Once more the yellow metal was king. Greasewood once
more became a city.

The outstanding event of the gold boom in Greasewood was the reopening of the Bleaching Skull Mine. A
New York concern sent out some laborers who went into
the old tunnels and started to burrow into the face of the

rock along the line of a drift which had been abandoned years before.

Within the first fifty feet they had struck the rich vein of ore which had faulted out back in 1906. Excitement raced across the desert, fanned to a white-hot, fever heat. Prospectors poured into the city of Greasewood by the score.

The mine was taking out ore that was literally studded with the yellow metal; ore that was known in mining parlance as "jewelry rock."

My roan plugged steadily up the long, deep grade as the purple shadows filled the valley. Higher and higher we wound up into the land of the distorted peaks. Gaudy-colored rock outcroppings caught the glint of the setting sun and transformed the country into a riot of color.

I turned off of the trail, angled down a slope, and found a little valley in which I could make camp. I wasn't anxious to camp too close to the trail which led out from Greasewood.

That night the desert talked.

A wind sprang up from nowhere and whisked around the weird peaks with whistling noises, swooped down upon the sandy slopes, picked up little particles of sand, and sent them scurrying along, rattling against sage and cacti, giving the effect of some weird, hissing whisper which filled the darkness.

People who have lived much in the desert are familiar with this desert talk which comes at night.

I lay and listened to the sand talk, watched the stars quietly wheeling across the heavens, and dropped off into dreamless sleep.

I was up with daylight, saddled, packed, and away. By seven o'clock I topped the pass and could look down upon the mesa where the town of Greasewood held forth.

Many of the old houses were so dilapidated as to be unfit for human habitation, and their places had been taken by tents which had been packed in on horseback and flung up here and there, little blobs of white which caught the rays of the morning sun.

The smoke from cooking fires rose straight up for the first hundred feet or so until it struck an area of lighter air and spread out in a blanket of haze which covered the valley.

As I rode closer I could hear the voices of men, the laughter of children, and the lower tones of women. The sides of the hills were scarred with mining dumps, long pack trains were commencing to shuffle out over the road, and men on horseback loped about, starting the business of the day.

I dropped down off of the last slope, and put my horses at a lope as I went along the side street, past the tents, where children came to stare at me curiously.

I rode directly to an unpainted, rather ramshackle building which had stood for more than a quarter of a century without attention. It had been fixed up by such patchwork as was necessary to make it habitable, and over the door was a board upon which had been lettered by an unskilled hand: "THE BLEACHING SKULL MINING COMPANY. GENERAL OFFICES."

A man came shuffling to the door when he heard the hoofs of my horses on the road, and stared at me with uncordial eyes.

"I'm Bob Zane," I told him, "and I want to see Frank Atwood."

The man looked at me for a moment, turned without a word, and vanished into the interior. I swung from the saddle and dropped the reins over my horse's head, tied the lead rope of the packhorse to a rail.

There were quick steps on the board floor, and a young, well-knit man in khaki and polished puttees came bursting out into the morning, his face wreathed in smiles, his hand extended.

"Welcome to Greasewood, Bob Zane!" he exclaimed, and pumped my hand up and down.

"You're Atwood?" I asked him.

He nodded. "Frank Atwood, manager of the mine here. They wrote me that you were coming."

"Where do I stay?" I asked him. "And where can we talk?"

"We can talk right here, and we'd better talk before you pick a place to stay. Let's come in here. I've got a private office where we can go over things."

He led the way into a private office, ensconced himself importantly at a desk, and indicated a chair.

I dropped into the chair, tilted back against the wall and rolled a smoke, and sized him up.

He wasn't a desert man. He was city bred, a college-trained mining engineer.

"Before we start talking," I told him, "I want to get in touch with the sheriff."

"What's the trouble?" he asked.

"Nothing in particular," I said, "except a dead man on the trail. Somebody had done him in from ambush with a .303 rifle. The fellow who did the job was a good shot."

Frank Atwood stared at me. "Another murder?" he said.

I shrugged my shoulders. "I don't know about the 'another' part of it," I told him, "but it sure is a murder."

"You don't know who the man was?" he asked.

"No. Some fellow who was traveling out of Grease-wood with a saddle burro and a single pack."

"I wonder who it could have been?"

I didn't make any suggestions, but contented myself with putting the finishing touches on my cigarette and striking a match to the end. Atwood got up and strode to the door. He jerked it open and said in a low voice: "Sproul, will you go and round up the sheriff for me? Get him here right away."

A voice grumbled an answer.

I filed away in my mind, for future reference, the fact that this man, Sproul, stayed pretty close to the door of Frank Atwood's private office when there was a conference going on.

Atwood came back and sat down.

"Where was the man shot?" he asked.

"Right through the heart," I said.

"You couldn't tell anything about the motive?"

"No."

"Do you know how long he'd been dead?"

"Sometime around about noon yesterday was when he got his. I came along about three or four o'clock."

"How near the main road?"

"About four hundred yards, but you couldn't see it from the road."

He looked at me and sighed, and then fidgeted uneasily in his chair.

"I understand that the directors sent you in," he said, "with unlimited authority to take such action as you see fit."

I puffed on the cigarette and said:

"The directors told me to coöperate with you."

"Oh, yes," he said, "of course. That's understood. But I mean that you are to have a free hand in regard to methods."

"Yes," I said.

"You're generally familiar with conditions here, I take it."

"I'm not so sure about that," I told him. "I haven't been here for years."

"We're contending with all sorts of lawlessness," he said. "We haven't got our transportation facilities opened up yet. We're getting out a lot of high-grade ore, and we have a payroll which we have to meet. All of that makes for trouble. We're being troubled with bandits and an element of lawlessness that the sheriff doesn't seem able to handle."

"Why can't he handle it?" I asked.

"He's a local man," said Atwood, "and he has local prejudices to figure on."

Steps sounded in the passage outside. Some one knocked on the door. Atwood opened it.

I gazed into a pair of steel-gray eyes which surveyed me from behind steel-rimmed spectacles, a face that had been bronzed by desert suns, and deeply lined. The hair was iron-gray and it peeped out from beneath the rim of a battered Stetson.

Atwood said: "Bob Zane, shake hands with Bill Hostler, the sheriff here."

I got up and shook hands.

The sheriff said: "You wanted me, Frank?"

"Zane does," said Atwood.

The sheriff looked at me, and I told him what I'd found.

"Is that all?" he asked, when I'd finished.

"That's all," I said, "except for one thing."

"What's that?" he asked.

"The man had a glass jar in his hand," I said, "and in that glass jar was a paper. The glass jar was sealed with a screw top that had been put down tight. I didn't open the jar, but I figured the paper might be important, so I brought it along."

"Where is it?" he asked.

I reached in my pocket and took out the round glass container, and set it on the table.

Hostler stared at it curiously. Frank Atwood picked up the glass and turned it around and around.

"Well?" he asked.

"Better open it, I guess," said the sheriff.

Atwood unscrewed the top and fished out the piece of paper.

It was a piece of brown paper such as had evidently been used at one time as a wrapping paper.

"Good Lord!" said Atwood. "It's a copy of the agreement that Doug Drake reached with us just before he left for the city!"

"What agreement's that, Frank?" asked the sheriff.

Atwood got up and crossed the room to a little safe. He got down in front of it and started spinning the combination.

I reached over and picked up the paper. It felt funny in my fingers. I twisted it a bit, and then tried to tear off a corner. The paper was tough and the corner didn't tear until after I had bent the paper so that wrinkles came in it between my thumb and finger. I looked at Bill Hostler, the sheriff, to see if he saw what had happened. He was staring at the paper too. Then he picked it up and tore a little piece from the other corner.

Atwood was back from the safe by that time, carrying a piece of paper, and he looked at us as we looked at each other, but none of us said anything.

Atwood put a piece of paper down on the desk, and I saw it was a carbon copy of the paper that had been in the glass jar.

"Doug Drake settled his difference with the Bleaching Skull Mining Company day before yesterday," he said. "He wasn't going to say anything about it until he had recorded the original. He was on his way down to get it recorded."

Sheriff Hostler looked over Atwood's shoulder and read the writing that was on the paper.

"How did it happen the agreement was drawn on this kind of paper?" he asked.

Atwood grinned.

"We made the settlement at his house," he said, "and I've had enough dealings with Doug Drake to know that when he was ready to sign was the time to get him to sign. I had an old piece of carbon paper in my pocket, and he scraped up some brown wrapping paper that had been around a purchase he had made in the city, and we executed the agreement, the original and one copy, right then."

Hostler said, slowly: "Well, that agreement seems to give the mining company the complete right to go into the property that's been in dispute."

"It does," said Atwood. "Drake got tired of fighting us."

"What do you do under those circumstances?" I asked. "Bring the body up for an inquest?"

Sheriff Hostler shook his head.

"I have a general understanding with the authorities on those things. We notify the people that are interested and overlook the red tape."

"Who's interested in this case?" I asked.

"A daughter," said Frank Atwood, "named Bessie Drake. I guess you'd better tell her, sheriff."

Bill Hostler looked over at me and said: "Was the man about fifty-six, with gray hair and light blue eyes, a fellow who weighed about a hundred and fifty, and was about five feet eight inches tall, wearing blue overalls and a patched jumper?"

I nodded and said: "One of the burros was grayish and it was an old 30-30 rifle that was in the saddle scabbard."

Sheriff Hostler reached for his hat.

"Well," he said, "I'd better go break the news to Bess."

When the sheriff had gone I asked Frank Atwood a question:

"This man Drake left here, you say?"

"Yes, he left here two or three days ago."

"And had the agreement with him?"

"Yes, he was taking the original out to have it recorded. I had the duplicate copy here in the safe."

"Who's this Theodore Sproul who is a witness?" I asked.

"That's Ted Sproul who's outside here. I'd better get him in."

He went to the door and called: "Oh, Ted."

A man came in who had black eyes that were virtually expressionless. His face showed no expression whatever. His mouth was wide and firm. He wore a shirt which was open at the neck, and a handkerchief which was knotted around his neck. He wore overalls, cowboy boots, a vest, and a cartridge belt with a six-gun dangling on his hip.

The black eyes regarded me in steady, questioning appraisal.

"Bob Zane, here," explained Atwood, "is a man who has been sent in by the directors to sort of assume charge of our campaign here against lawlessness. Sproul, Mr. Zane, is one of our guards here who has shown considerable aptitude for the work."

Sproul grinned and said: "Thanks."

"You'll work under Zane, Sproul," said Frank Atwood.

The black eyes came to my face again and the face twisted in a slow smile.

"That'll be a pleasure," he said. "I've heard of Bob Zane."

"How many other guards have you got?" I asked.

"Two," said Atwood. "There's Sam Easton and Phil Stope."

"What's been your main trouble?" I asked.

"Everything," he said. "We've lost payrolls and high-grade ore. We've been hampered at every turn by vicious lawlessness. For the most part, the inhabitants of the town seem to be fighting us. We're the big mining company here and every one hates us because we control most of the property."

"That makes it interesting," I said.

"Don't it?" said Ted Sproul, and grinned.

"But you must have some definite idea of who you're fighting," I said. "It isn't just a question of isolated lawlessness. There must be some head to it."

"There is," said Atwood slowly, "but we can't get a line on him."

Ted Sproul spoke in his slow desert drawl.

"He's right," he said, "we can't seem to get a thing. Stuff disappears, payrolls are held up and stacks of high-grade ore vanish. The man who does it has an uncanny knowledge of just what he's after. He's got some kind of a spy system, because he knows just what we're doing.

"For instance, when we get in a payroll, we start three separate pack trains over the grade, only one of them having the actual cash. This bandit never makes the mistake of getting the wrong pack train. He seems to know right where the money is, and he goes after it."

"The men are all masked, of course?" I said.

"Oh, yes, sure," said Sproul, "and they have a sweet habit of shooting from ambush. They kill first and rob afterwards."

"Suppose this man Drake met up with one of those bandits?" I asked.

"Of course he did," said Atwood. "You see, he was carrying the cash consideration for the agreement, amounting to over fifteen thousand dollars."

"How come?" I inquired.

"Well, it was this way," said Atwood. "As you will see by the agreement itself, there was a cash payment of fifteen thousand dollars which was paid. I made out a check to him, and he didn't want the check; he wanted cash.

We've got a little bank here in which we keep a certain amount of money—not too much, but enough to cover our emergency expenses. I got him to endorse the check, took it to the bank, got it cashed, and delivered the cash to him myself."

"So, evidently," I said, "somebody knew in advance that he had this fifteen thousand dollars, and arranged to take it by the most efficient method possible."

"That's it," said Atwood; "only the man didn't need to know very much in advance. Drake was using burros, and this man could have used a horse and gone on past him on the trail."

"That doesn't leave us much to work on," I said.

"Well," Atwood told me, "never mind that. That's a problem for the sheriff to handle. That's the reason we have our own mining guards. The sheriff has to look after the general crime that takes place in the county. We have our own guards to look after those crimes which affect our interests, and Lord knows there are plenty of them!"

"You don't figure that this crime affects the mining company then?" I said.

"Certainly not," said Atwood. "We paid the consideration for the agreement and got it executed. It's binding on Drake's heirs."

"Well," I said after a pause, "I presume that you've got something in particular lined up for me to do at the start."

"There's one thing," said Atwood, "that we'd like to have you ready for. And that's a payroll that's coming in some time to-morrow. We're bringing it in considerably in advance of the time that it's due, and we're sending it in as provisions. The money is in a shipment of flour, concealed in the flour sacks."

"This comes in to-morrow?" I asked.

"It starts up the grade some time to-night."

"Why the night business?" I asked.

"We figure that there's less chance of an ambush at night. They've got to come out with more of a direct attack. The horses can travel at night, and we're going to run the stuff right on through. It should be in here about half past two or three o'clock in the morning."

"Okay," I said. "I'll give that some attention. Is there anything else?"

"Nothing I can think of right now," he said.

I told them I'd see them later, and went out.

III NIGHT CONVOY

I found a place where I could stable my horses and see that they had some feed. Prices were like they were in the Klondike during the gold rush, but everybody seemed happy and prosperous. There was a general merchandise store which seemed to be doing quite a business, and I figured that would be a good place for me to get a line on the various people.

I loitered around looking the people over and picking up an earful here and there. Apparently no one knew who I was, or why I had come to town. I hung around for a couple of hours.

While I was standing there waiting, there was a swirl of motion, and I turned to find myself staring into a pair of very black and very burning eyes.

She was about five feet two inches tall, dressed in a khaki skirt and blouse, with a big Stetson that had seen service. Yet her complexion was smooth and well cared for. It wasn't the lily-white, peaches-and-cream complexion of the town girl, but was a clear olive tint that showed the contour of her face smoothly and without blemish.

"You're Bob Zane?" she asked.

I nodded.

"You don't know me," she said, "but I want to ask you a question or two."

I stood there feeling uncomfortable, but not being able to place just exactly where that feeling came from, or what caused it.

"You're the man who discovered the body of Douglas Drake?" she asked.

I nodded.

There was a slight hint of moisture in the eyes, but no quivering of the mouth.

"I'm his daughter," she said.

I wondered if perhaps there was going to be a scene of weeping, but after a moment I could see that there wasn't. She blinked back the moisture from her eyes.

"I'm sorry about him," I told her.

She nodded her head.

"I've heard," she said, "that he had a paper with him."

I nodded.

"A paper," she asked, "by which he conveyed everything to the mining company?"

I nodded again.

"Then," she said slowly, "I've got nothing."

"There was a cash payment, I believe," I said. "Do you know whether or not he had that with him?"

She said, "I don't know anything about it, but there must have been some motive for—for—for killing him."

"I'm sorry," I told her. "I wish there was something I could do. Perhaps if you have any suspicions you could tell me."

"No suspicions," she said.

I stood, looking down at her, wondering what I could say or what I could do. She was a typical desert girl, strong and self-reliant, vibrant with personality—a daughter of the sun and the sand. Yet her father lay out there in the glittering sunlight of the desert, covered over with a tarp, awaiting the arrival of the official burial party.

Abruptly she turned on her heel, flung a "thank you" over her shoulder, and walked away.

I walked out of the store, went over to the livery stable.

"Horses fed?" I asked the attendant.

He nodded.

"Okay," I told him, and flung a saddle on the big roan. The attendant watched me as I tightened up the cinch and adjusted the bridle.

"Going to take the pack?" he asked.

"No," I said.

He looked as though he wanted to ask some more questions, but I did not look as though I wanted to answer them, so after a while he went away. I went to the pack and got out my carbine, which I put in a saddle scabbard and tied to the saddle, so that it hung under my leg. Then I put some concentrated food in the saddle bags and climbed into the saddle.

"Where can I find the sheriff?" I asked of the man at the livery stable.

"I think he went up to the mine," he said.

I nodded and sent the roan up to the mine at a lope.

Frank Atwood came to the door to meet me.

"Where's the sheriff?" I asked.

"He went out to take a look at Doug Drake's body," he said. "He only left a little while ago."

"Where do I meet the payroll?" I asked him.

"Down at the foot of the grade," he said. "It's going to be in to-night—earlier than we expected. I was trying to get in touch with you. Did you get my message?"

"No," I said, "I didn't get any message. I just got to exploring around."

"Well," he said, "you'll have to start inside of a couple of hours. I'm going to have Ted Sproul go with you if you want."

"I don't want," I told him. "I'm going to play a lone hand."

He stared at me an instant.

"Any way you want it," said Frank Atwood, shrugging his shoulders; "but I would suggest that you take at least one man with you, maybe two."

"No," I said, "I'm playing a lone hand."

The smile left his face.

"All right," he said, "have it your own way," and then he added, "It's your own funeral."

The roan was big and strong and used to the desert. We made time up the trail. I overtook Sheriff Hostler within the first ten miles.

He looked at me with mild surprise. "Going out for something special?" he asked.

"Heard you were going out and thought I'd jog along for a ways."

He nodded.

We rode along in silence. Most of the way the trail was wide enough for the two of us to ride abreast. I waited for him to say something, but he kept quiet.

We'd reached the summit of the trail and were working down through the colored mountains on the other side when I said to him abruptly: "What are you waiting for, sheriff?"

He turned and looked at me with mild surprise. Then, as he let his eyes lock with mine, the surprise left them, and his face showed a great weariness.

"I'm waiting," he said, "for somebody to back my play."

"All right," I told him, "I'm going to back it."

He didn't say anything to that, and I didn't say anything more.

Fifteen or twenty minutes later I looked back and saw dust on the trail.

"Somebody coming," I told him. We waited to see who it was. After the horse got closer, I saw that it was a woman riding.

"Probably Doug Drake's daughter," I said.

The sheriff squinted his eyes, and I saw his mouth twitch at the corners, then settle into firm lines. After a moment he nodded.

"Yes," he said, "it's Bessie Drake."

She rode up to us and nodded her head as casually as though she had been strolling down Broadway and met a couple of acquaintances.

"I want to go," she said.

"It isn't going to be easy, Bess," the sheriff told her.

"You don't think I'm a fool, do you?" she asked.

That was all that was said. She swung her horse in alongside of ours, and we went trotting down the trail.

We got to the body along late in the afternoon. Bess knelt beside it and the sheriff and I walked away for five or ten minutes, then Bess came to us, and said: "All right."

The sheriff had a shovel on his saddle, and I helped him dig the grave. It was hot there in the desert, but the ground was dry and it didn't take us long.

The girl watched, dry-eyed, as we lowered the body into the grave. She was grim and silent.

After the grave had been filled in she asked me in a calm voice: "Can you show me where the man lay in ambush?"

I piloted her and the sheriff over to the place.

They looked the ground over. Neither one of them said anything. They just prowled around. After a while the sheriff said: "Well, I'm going to start back. Are you going with me, Bess?"

She thought for a minute and said: "No, I don't think I will."

The sheriff turned to me. "How about you, Zane?"

"No," I said, "I'm going to wait here for a little while."

I didn't want to tell either one of them that I was expecting the pack train to show up for the payroll.

The sheriff turned to the girl and said: "If you want to take your father's pack in, Bess, there'll be some packs over the trail. They're sending some stuff out from the mine, and taking some stuff in all the time, you know."

"Yes," she said, tonelessly, "I know."

The sheriff got on his horse and rode away. I climbed on the roan and went back to the end of the road and sat there watching the shadows get longer, smoking an occasional cigarette, and soaking in the silence of the desert.

After a while I heard the crunch of feet in the sand, and Bess came riding up behind me.

"I just wanted to say thank you," she said.

"You're welcome," I told her.

She turned, spurred her horse and started up the trail toward Greasewood.

It was about dusk when I heard the tinkle of bells, and a pack train came down from the mesa country. The man in charge came over to me.

"You're Bob Zane?" he asked.

I nodded.

He said: "We're from the mine. We came down to get a load of flour. Atwood said you'd know about it."

"I know about it," I told him.

He hesitated a moment, and then squatted down on the desert beside me and rolled a cigarette.

"All alone?" I asked him.

"I've got my son with me," he said. "He'll be over after a while."

We sat and smoked and then a young lad about nineteen or twenty, with an eager face and alert eyes, came over and joined us.

"The horses all hobbled, Harry?" asked the man.

The boy nodded his head. "All staked out, dad," he said.

We sat there and waited.

The sun set and shadows came along the desert. After a while we saw the headlights of automobiles coming along the road, jolting and swaying. It was getting dark by the time they pulled up. There was a truck loaded with flour, and a car filled with men. The men were armed.

The man who had charge of the pack train evidently knew the truck driver. They talked together in low tones for a while, and then the sacks of flour came out on the ground. The boy brought up the pack train and I helped them throw the sacks. The man on the truck gave some papers to the packer, and the packer signed a receipt. Then the cars turned and started grinding their way back over the long desert miles.

"All ready," said the packer to me.

IV ROPE LAW

We started up the winding trail. By that time it was pitch-dark, save for the grayish illumination which covered the surface of the desert from the steady stars.

After we'd gone a mile or so, I rode up to the head of the pack train and spoke to the packer.

"We're going to stop here for a minute," I said.

"What for?" he wanted to know.

"I want to know where the money is," I said.

"It's in the flour," he told me.

"I know that," I said, "but what sacks?"

"I'll show you," he said.

He showed me the packhorse that had the marked flour sack with the money in it.

"All right," I told him, "I'm taking this money out."

"No, you're not," he said.

"I'm sorry," I told him, "but this money is coming out," and I took out my knife and ripped open the pack and the flour.

He said: "My orders don't cover that at all. My orders were to bring the payroll in the flour sack."

"Your orders were to act under my directions, weren't they?" I asked him.

He hesitated for a moment, and then said: "Yes, I was told that you'd be in charge."

"All right," I told him, "I'm in charge," and took out the money.

It was in sacks in the flour, the sacks filled with bills of various denomination. The entire payroll was in currency.

I managed to get the payroll in my saddle bags.

"All right," I told him then, "go ahead with the pack just as though nothing had happened."

He shrugged his shoulders and spoke to his son.

The pack train got in motion.

I waited on the roan until I could hear the bells of the pack train getting mellow in the distance. Then I started poking along behind. I had a theory and I was going to test it.

I'd been moving up the trail slowly for about an hour when suddenly I saw the pinprick of a ruddy flame against the darkness of the mountains. Then I heard the crash of a shot which echoed from rock to rock. Then there were more flames and more reports. I heard the thud of galloping horses, a hoarse voice shouting a command, and then there was no more firing for a few minutes.

I stopped the roan, eased the carbine from the saddle scabbard, and waited, watching the trail ahead.

After a while I heard the sound of galloping hoofs, and got my roan crowded well over to the side of the the trail up in a little draw where the trail cut through a dry wash down the side of a mountain.

Two horses came thundering past. They were pack-horses and had been loaded with flour. The flour sacks had been cut open, and the flour had sprinkled over the sweating sides of the horses until they looked like ghosts.

I held the roan steady while the horses went by, and after a while two more horses came past, then a third and a fourth.

Ten or fifteen minutes passed, then I heard the sound of a trotting horse coming down the trail as though it held a rider.

I waited until a black blotch silhouetted against the stars, and saw where the rider was sitting. Then I nestled the stock of the carbine against my cheek.

"You can either stop there or stop a magazine full of lead," I said casually.

The voice that answered me sounded almost hysterical.

"Don't shoot! Don't shoot! It's Harry!" said the voice, and I recognized the young lad who had been helping his father with the pack train.

I rode out from the shadows and his horse snorted and stopped.

"What is it?" I asked.

"I'm tied," he said.

I slipped the carbine into the saddle scabbard, but eased the six-gun from my belt as I rode alongside of him, and reached out an exploring left hand. My right hand held the gun in readiness.

What he said was true. He was bound, his arms tied to his sides, his legs tied to the stirrups.

I got out my knife and cut him loose.

"What happened?" I asked.

"A stick-up," he said. "They shot first, and killed my father. They tied me on my horse and started cutting open the flour sacks. I managed to get my horse started down the trail. I thought maybe I could find you."

"That's all you know?" I asked him.

"That's all I know," he said.

I looked at the sky. The moon was just coming up.

"You haven't any weapons?" I asked him.

"No," he said, "they took those."

"Any idea who the men were?" I asked him.

"No," he said, "they wore cloth masks and didn't do much talking."

"All right," I told the boy, "we're going to start."

He fell in behind me without a word and we started the horses up the trail.

After a few minutes I came to the scene of the hold-up. There was no mistaking it because flour had been spilled all over the trail until it looked like snow. Harry's father lay sprawled in the trail, a hole in his forehead, his face and clothes all covered with flour. We moved the body and covered it. Harry was sobbing softly.

I picked up the trail of one of the men who had ridden in from a place up the slope, and found where he had been waiting. There wasn't enough moonlight to read track very well, but I could see that he had sat there for some little time. I back tracked around and finally saw something lying on the ground. I walked over to it. It was a Stetson—the same hat that Bess Drake had worn that afternoon.

I sat staring at the hat in the moonlight while the boy watched me.

After a few minutes I walked back to my horse, climbed in the saddle, put spurs to the roan, and we went up the trail. The boy came riding up the trail behind me.

Halfway down the trail on the other side, we slowed

abruptly. I didn't like the way the roan was keeping his ears forward.

"Can you hear anything?" I asked.

He listened and then shook his head.

I started the roan again, but kept my hand close to the six-gun.

We rounded a little shoulder, and on the trail ahead I could see something moving. I stopped the roan and took a good look. It was a lone horseman. As he swung broadside on, in a patch of moonlight, I recognized the horse. It was the one the sheriff was riding.

I put spurs to the roan and we came up on the gallop. Sheriff Hostler turned to stare at us as we came up.

"What's happened?" he asked. "You seem all lathered."

"Have you seen Bess Drake?" I asked the sheriff.

He shook his head, peered past me to the boy, and said: "Hello, Harry, what's the trouble?"

"There was a stick-up down the trail," I said. "They killed Harry's dad. Bess is missing."

The sheriff looked at me, and as the moonlight touched the side of his face I could see that his jaw was set, and his lips clamped in a thin line.

"Are you coming with me?" I asked him.

He stared steadily for a moment and then said: "Yes, Zane, I'm coming."

"All right," I told him, "let's go."

He swept his horse into a gallop and we went tearing down the trail, leaning over on the side as our horses careened around the curves.

We hit the flat, galloped through the dark, deserted streets of Greasewood and thundered up to the office of the mining company.

There were lights on.

I climbed from the saddle, untied my saddle bags, threw them over my shoulder, and walked into the office with my six-gun at my belt, the carbine in the crook of my arm.

Frank Atwood was fully dressed in his pegged riding breeches, his puttees all nicely shined and polished. His eyes were sparkling.

"You got in all right?" he asked me.

I flung the saddle bags on the desk.

"There's the payroll," I said.

He pawed at the sacks with feverish hands.

"Good work," he said. "Did you have any trouble?"

I stood the carbine in the corner.

"No trouble," I told him.

He looked up at me as I came toward him, caught something in the expression of my eyes, and fell back.

I slammed my right fist straight into his jaw and banged him back against the side of the building. He made a dive for the front of his shirt, and I crossed over a left that threw him off balance, twisted his hand away from the shirt, ripped open the shirt and pulled out a six-gun which I dropped on the floor.

He stared at me with panic-stricken eyes, and lips that were white.

"What I want first," I said, "is to know where the girl is."

"What are you talking about?" he said.

"You haven't got time," I told him, "to pull all that stuff. Tell me where the girl is!"

"I don't know what you're talking about," he said.

I looked over my shoulder at the sheriff. The sheriff was standing very grim and very white, but with eyes that were very steady.

"I guess we'd better get a rope," I said, "and clean this thing up real desert fashion. You can tie a hangman's knot, sheriff?"

Atwood stared at me and started to yammer.

"You're crazy!" he said. "You've gone stark, staring crazy! I don't know what you're talking about. What do you want?"

"Listen," I told him, "that paper was a forgery; the one that Doug Drake had. You wanted to get possession of his property and you wanted to get some money. So you made a check payable to him for what was supposed to be the purchase price of the property, forged his signature as an endorsement, and cashed the check yourself at the bank. You didn't have any difficulty doing that because it was a mining company check, and the endorsement was a good forgery anyway.

"You went into the city and had some expert forger forge the agreement selling out to the mining company. You sealed it in a bottle because you were afraid that if you left it loose on Drake's body it might blow away, or if they didn't discover the body right away, the decomposition might ruin the writing.

"You came back and waited for Drake to come out, or had one of your gang lying in ambush for him. When Drake showed up the man shot him and put the glass jar with the paper in it, in Drake's hand. Then you waited for the body to be discovered."

"You're crazy!" yelled Atwood. "You can't prove a word of what you say."

"No, I'm not crazy," I told him. "If you'd known the desert a little bit better you'd have known that you were betraying yourself. The paper showed on its face it was a forgery."

"How do you mean?" he demanded.

I told him: "Paper that's been in the desert gets so dry it hasn't any tensile strength at all. You should have been in the desert long enough to know that. You try to put stuff in a paper bag, and at the least jar the paper bag will rip open. You can take paper and tear it easily.

Paper that's been in a moist climate is hard to tear. When you sealed that forged agreement in the glass jar, you didn't do it in the desert at all, but you did it somewhere out on the coast. The jar was hermetically sealed, and when the paper was taken out, it still retained the moisture that had been in it when it was on the coast.

"Paper crinkles differently in the desert than it does on the coast. The sheriff noticed it, and I noticed it. As soon as I saw the way that paper lay on the table, I knew that there was too much moisture in it for it to have been written in the desert and sealed in a jar here. That paper was written somewhere out on the coast, and sealed in the jar.

"In short, Atwood, you're the one that's been the head of this gang of thugs that has been preying on the mine and the payroll shipments. Knowing exactly when they were coming, why you knew exactly how to play your hold-ups. But the game's up now!"

He pushed back from me, staring with a white face.

"Sheriff," he said, "the man's gone crazy! He's accusing me of crime."

Sheriff Hostler said, slowly: "He's right, Atwood. As soon as I felt of that paper, I knew it hadn't been signed here in the desert."

Atwood's eyes held a glint of desperation. Suddenly I saw that glint change into a stare of triumph.

I jumped to one side, and as I jumped, a gun crashed from the corridor of the office building, and a bullet thudded into the wall.

I whirled. There was another shot as I whirled.

Sheriff Hostler staggered and spun half around. Ted Sproul, his lips drawn back from his teeth, eyes glinting with the light of a killer, flung up his gun for a shot at me.

I fired from the hip, and at the shot he was blasted backwards as though he had been jerked by some invisible hand.

I sensed motion behind me and knew that Atwood had made a grab for the revolver I had taken from him.

I swung around and lashed out with the barrel of my six-gun. The blow caught him on the side of the head, just as he had the gun in his hand ready to fire.

He fired, but the bullet went wild.

Two more men came rushing into the corridor, shooting as they came, and I sent bullets down the corridor, firing rapidly.

Sheriff Hostler sat down on the table, blood pouring from a shoulder, but his eyes were steady and calm.

He said to me: "I'm afraid they got me hard. I've combed the hill country pretty thoroughly, and I'm satisfied that they bring their stuff here to the mine some place and store it right on the premises. If I pass out be sure and look around."

Atwood lay on the floor moaning. Ted Sproul was motionless on the floor of the corridor. The other men who had fired at us had stepped back out of sight.

I went over to the corner and picked up the rifle. Then I reached up to the gasoline lantern and turned it down. The flame flickered for a few minutes. Then darkness descended on the office.

"Can you make it out of here?" I asked the sheriff. "I'm afraid they may dynamite the place."

"I'm going to be all right," he said. "It was the shock. They got me in the shoulder, and the bone's pretty well splintered."

I supported him, and eased him down the passageway.

We had gone about half way when I heard the sound of whispered voices, and men came shuffling into the corridor.

"Stop where you are!" I said.

The motion stopped. Then a voice said: "What's the trouble?"

I said: "We've found the bandits who have been looting the mine. Who are you?"

A voice said: "It's all right. I'm Harry. I've got some of father's friends. There's a dead man out here, and another man got on a horse and galloped away as we came in. I think he was wounded."

Sheriff Hostler said: "It's all right, now, Zane. You can trust these men," and suddenly became a dead weight on me.

Back of us in the office somebody moaned, and I could hear the sound of a body crawling along the floor.

"Better get a light," I said, "and see what's happening in there."

Somebody brought up a light from one of the other rooms in the office. I could see a crowd of desert men, hardbitten miners who were the type who wouldn't stand for funny business.

Then as they raised the light so that they could see into the interior of the office, I saw something else.

Ted Sproul had managed to crawl into the office. He had a knife in his hand, and he had groped his way to Frank Atwood. I looked at what had happened, and my soul felt sick.

Sproul leered at us.

"All right," he said, "I'm ready to go now. Bring on the rope. He was the one that got me into it."

I heard the men make restless motions behind me, and knew that my time was short. I pushed my way toward him.

"Where's the girl, Sproul?" I asked.

His eyes were feverish, and his face was the color of desert sand. His voice was so weak I could hardly hear.

"The old mine had a drift over by the old shaft house," he said. "It's abandoned. We used that as a storeroom for the stuff we took. The girl ran on us to-night and tried to avenge her father. We had to take her along. She got one of the men in the leg—a pretty bad wound. We knew she was wise. Some of the men wanted to kill her. I didn't want to until after we'd seen Atwood. I thought it was time to clean out."

He swayed drunkenly, sitting there on the floor.

I heard shuffling steps behind me, as of men moving purposefully. I turned and saw a body of miners filing down the corridor. They had a rope, and in the end of the rope was a noose with a hangman's knot.

Ted Sproul looked past me and saw the men and the rope.

Law had come to Greasewood—the law of the rope!

I camped the next night in a little depression between the mountains, down in the desert country, pretty well down the trail. Bess Drake was with me.

We had ridden until late. The horses were picketed, the packs on the ground, the ashes of the little camp fire on which we had cooked our meal were blowing fitfully in the desert breeze.

"Why didn't you tell me," she asked, "that you knew who was the head of the gang?"

"Why didn't you tell me," I countered, "that you were going to try and ambush them when they held up the pack train?"

She said simply: "I wasn't sure that I could trust you then, Bob Zane."

I said nothing, and we sat for a while in silence, the little circle of golden coals paling and glowing, as the wind swept over it.

"And you knew it all?" she asked, "as soon as you took that paper from the jar?"

"I knew," I told her, "that the paper had never been sealed in that jar in the desert country. I knew that it had been put in the jar where the air was moist."

She waited for a few minutes without saying anything.

The wind freshened, and the first faint sounds of the sand whispers commenced to come to our ears.

"Bob Zane," she said, softly, "do you ever feel that the desert is alive? Do you ever feel that there's something about it that demands justice—something that betrays men who are dishonest?"

I didn't say anything, because I knew it was a question that didn't need an answer.

After a moment she went on:

"See what happened in this case. Atwood robbed the people who employed him. He murdered, and he forged a document which he thought would stand inspection anywhere, bolstered up by his perjured testimony, and that of Ted Sproul. The desert came along and stamped that document as a forgery, so that you and Sheriff Hostler would tell it the minute you saw it. It seems as though it wasn't just chance. It seems as though there must have been something bigger—something omnipotent that betrayed those men to their undoing."

I started to say something, but then the wind in the desert changed, and the sand started to stir restlessly, making little whispers.

I settled back, and reached for my blankets. I knew that there wasn't any use of making an answer—the desert was answering for me.

Gold Blindness

I DESERT WHISPERS

Oho! So you're interested in the little yellow pellet, eh? Look again! Virgin gold! It's a nugget, worn smooth by rubbing around the bottom of a stream. And here's another. Look! But don't look too long.

You'll become gold blind if you're not careful. Oh, yes, you can. Men get snow blind from the glitter of snow, and they get gold blind from the glitter of gold.

A story connected with it? Rather.

In Ensenada I first heard of the gold. Like all of those things, it came in whispers. The desert's full of whispers. The sand whispers to the cacti as the wind blows it against the green stalks, and sometimes you'll even hear the sand whispering to the sand.

Sure, it's the wind—if you want to figure it that way. I'm not a fool. The sand blows along the desert and gives off a peculiar sound. It's just the wind, and the sand. But sometimes when you're asleep in the desert you can hear the sand whispers, and you'll wake up. Then there's a minute, just before you get fully awake, that you can hear the sand talking.

But that's not the whisper I heard about the gold. That came from an old engineer, a mining man, a prospector, an adventurer.

He was dying at the time. We all thought it was TB. He kept wasting away, getting thinner and thinner, and he coughed most of the time.

You know how the beach stretches along the ocean there at Ensenada. There's the city, then there's the sand, and then there's the bay of Todos Santos. By day it's a deep blue, warm as milk. By night it reflects the stars. There's not much surf, just a lazy waving of the water that splashes in little sheets of hissing foam.

One night this mining man told me his story. He was pretty far gone, and he had to whisper it.

We sat out on the shore. The stars glittered and reflected from the water. There was a little wind, just enough to make the sand whisper. Tiny waves hissed up on the shore, as though they were whispering back to the sand. And the sand blew along on the warm breeze and whispered to the water, and the engineer whispered to me. Behind us, the lights of the town showed as pin points of brilliance against a jet background.

Of course, I didn't believe that fellow at first. It was like all those other whispered tales you hear in the desert. The country's full of them.

He told me of a small trading station up east of the Funeral Range, and of a trader who kept faith with the Indians.

"The Injuns never had a pawn room," he said. "They paid for everything they bought, provided they could not trade for it. An' they always paid a little back room, sort of private. . . ."

I waited for the engineer to go on, but he had a fit of coughing that almost laid him out. I wasn't much interested—not then.

Finally he managed to whisper again.

"I went one night an' peeked in through a little knot hole," he said, "an' saw the trader weighin' out gold dust.

He spoke Injun to the customer an' asked if he didn't have anything to trade. The Injun gave him a hard-luck story about how he'd lost all his stuff so the medicine man had let him take the gold. The trader nodded an' finished weighin' out the gold."

That sounded goofy enough, but I nodded real seriously. The man was dying, and there was no call for me to start an argument over something that was none of my business.

He had another spell of coughing. Then he went back to whispering, telling me about how he explored the country where the Indians lived, and finally found a cavern that was gold from grass roots to bed rock, and about how an Indian medicine man shot a little arrow into his shoulder and breathed a curse.

And he told about how he got a stake of gold and started out of the country, and about how he got sick and the gold got heavy, and about booming drums that followed him and sounded inside his ears, and about a snake that followed him wherever he went, and about how he woke up one morning and found the gold gone, and about being sick ever since and being afraid to go back.

I nodded as grave as a judge.

Then this engineer rolled back his shirt and showed me where the arrow struck.

He was all wasted away to skin and bones, but the scar was there, all right. And the funny thing was that he had started to get sick right around that scar. You could see where the flesh had turned a reddish purple and the muscles had shriveled.

That made me think.

Two days later the engineer died.

They buried him out in that big graveyard across the wash. You know the place. It looks bigger than the town. Maybe it is, Ensenada is an old town; lots of people have died there. And the Mexicans keep up graves. They respect the dead that way.

Somehow or other, I couldn't get him off my mind. Perhaps it was because I spent so much time sitting on the shore near the bay, and the waves whispered as they hissed up the beach, and the sand whispered back to the waves, reminding me of the dead engineer and the story he'd whispered.

Finally I knew I had to go after that whisper, so I packed up my things and started out in my little flivver.

II A TIGHT-MOUTHED TRADER

Maybe you know Death Valley. It's a desolate stretch. But the engineer had said east of Death Valley. So I went up the Funeral Mountains. I traveled by night so it'd be cooler, both on me and the car.

Rhyolite's right over the hump on the Funeral Mountains. You know, the Ghost City of Nevada. It was moonlight when I went through, a full moon. At the time I didn't appreciate the real significance of the full moon. That came afterward.

But the city stood there, desolate, silent, deserted. The white buildings, the banks, the depot, the big schoolhouse, all standing white in the moonlight, looking as though they were swathed in winding sheets.

I went on east and then turned to the south. I didn't know just where I was going, but I knew the general direction. For two weeks I scouted around the country, through the Pahrump Valley, through the Amargosa sinks.

Daytimes I'd laugh at myself for being a credulous fool. But nighttimes when the wind would blow and the sand would begin to whisper as it drifted along, I'd get to thinking I could hear the whispers of the dead engineer. And when I'd hear those whispers I'd begin to feel it was all right again.

Finally I came to a place where there was a belt of artesian water, and some mountains, and a bit of greenery, and there was a board shack that showed it was a small trading station.

I went in, just as I'd been doing at all the trading posts, and right away something seemed to tell me I was on the right track.

The man that came out to see what I wanted was a thin, dour fellow with little puckered lips and eyes that were not much bigger than peas.

I told him I wanted to look at some Indian blankets, so he showed me his stock.

Then I got to talking about business and told him I'd like to see the pawn room.

You know those pawn rooms. The Indians go broke and take their silver finery, maybe a turquoise belt or necklace, their spurs, their guns, anything they happen to have, and pledge it for grub.

Those pledges are always redeemed. The trader keeps a separate little room for 'em. Maybe it'll be months, maybe it'll be a year, but the Indian always comes back and pays up, gets his finery, and goes away. Maybe he'll have to hock it again within a week.

The trader shook his head.

"I've got no pawn room," he said.

Whereupon I knew I was at the right place.

"You wanted Indian blankets," the trader said, looking as though somebody'd slipped a lemon in under his tongue.

I grinned and stuck out my hand.

"Flint's my name," I told him, "Jim Flint, and I'm just roaming around, looking the country over. I was wondering what sort of blankets these redskins made. They seemed to be a pretty shiftless bunch around here."

He took my hand, but his clasp did not have any warmth in it. He just stuck his paw into mine and then let it drop as soon as I opened my fingers.

"Goin' to be here long?"

"Maybe a week or two."

He thought for a minute. "Well, Mr. Flint," he said, "the Indians ain't shiftless."

I yawned as though I wasn't much interested.

"If you want any grub I can sell it to you," he said, after a bit.

"Later on, not right now."

The trader nodded and went back into the tiny office where he'd been when I came in.

That left me nothing to do except go out. I'd liked to have talked awhile, but he wouldn't talk.

I strolled over to the edge of the ditch where the artesian water went down into the little alfalfa patch, and there I made camp.

The Indians came past and looked me over. I bought a little grub from the trader, but that was all that happened in a week.

Then I sneaked up one night and looked the place over, the trading post. I wanted to see that mysterious back room where the cash transactions took place.

I'd found out about the trader. He was McLaren, a hard-bitten old Scot who could keep his mouth shut in fourteen different languages. He was a naturalized citizen and was always discussing the sanctity of the Constitution. But that was all he'd talk about.

This night the moon was old, and I took advantage of the darkness before moon-up. I sneaked around the place, looking for the room. I found it, all right. It was a little back room, to one side of the office, adjoining the cubbyhole of a kitchen where McLaren lived and did his own cooking.

I could see from the partition studding and the nails
that there must be a room there. Also, I could see where
there had been a knot hole, but it was filled up with putty
now, and a sheet of something was nailed on the inside.
Tin, I guess. I poked the blade of my knife through, and
it felt like tin.

It was ticklish business. I started boring a small hole
right where two of the boards came together. I had to
work slow, so as not to make a noise, and I rubbed dirt
in it, so it wouldn't show from the outside where the
boards had been scraped.

I didn't finish that hole for two nights, what with having to work slow, and the moon coming up and all. At
last I got the job done. Then I started watching. Every
night after dark I'd go up and put my eye to the hole and
wait.

But I didn't notice anything out of the ordinary. Once
or twice I saw McLaren walking through the room. But
I never saw an Indian come in the place.

I found out McLaren had some booze hidden there,
though. Twice I saw him break out a bottle. I made up
my mind I'd ask him some day about how it happened
he believed in the Constitution so hard and yet kept a
stock of hooch in his place.

After a couple of days, when it got slap dark of the
moon, McLaren said he was going away to get some stock
for his store. I offered to run the place for him while he
was gone, but the old fellow shook his head and didn't
even thank me.

"It's dark of the moon," said he.

"What's that got to do with it?"

"The Indians won't trade during the dark of the moon.
It's some sort of a religious business with 'em."

I pretended to be awfully glad.

"Then I'll ride down on the truck with you and pick

up some little stuff I need. It'll be company for you, and
if you should have a breakdown you wouldn't have to
leave the truck and go for help."

He wasn't cordial, but the code of the desert's a
strange thing—something that a man don't dare run
against—and so he agreed.

I made up my mind I'd see what sort of money he
used in paying for his stuff. Not that I was going to take
any advantage. It was simply a business proposition. I
thought there might be gold in that Indian country. I did
not want any of McLaren's gold. I wanted to find some
of my own, but I didn't want to go on any wild-goose
chases.

He went to San Diego for his provisions. Why he went
there I don't know. Maybe because of wholesale prices.
He went to a bank first. I told him I wanted to cash a
check. He nodded and introduced me to his banker.

I've never seen a banker with such fishy eyes or such
a cordial handshake. That banker started shaking hands
with me while McLaren started for an inner office with
the cashier. He was still working my arm up and down
like a man jacking up a car when McLaren came out.

And then McLaren got cordial. He acted like he didn't
have a care in the world. He cracked Scotch jokes, and
he endorsed the check I wrote on a Los Angeles bank,
and he kidded the banker. He was like a two-year-old colt
just turned into pasture.

Quickly the cashier came out of the little inside room,
rubbing his hands.

"Your credit is one thousand four hundred and ninety
dollars, Mr. McLaren," he said in a low voice.

McLaren made some figures.

Now, why should a banker have to wait a while to tell
a man how much he had deposited? There was only one
answer. The cashier must have been weighing out gold
dust in that inner room.

I didn't say anything, McLaren didn't say anything. But McLaren gave a guarded glance at the banker, and the banker replied with a slight nod of his head.

I remembered how the banker had held me with his long handshake, keeping me from following McLaren into that inner room. And I remembered how the banker's cordiality had vanished into thin air when McLaren came out.

I got my check cashed, after which McLaren and I went out of the bank, went to a wholesale house where McLaren bought a bunch of stock. He paid for it with a check. I wanted to start back. McLaren wanted to go to Tia Juana. We went to Tia Juana.

McLaren was not the Scotchman of the joke magazines when it came to the booze. We swapped treats for a while, and then McLaren started to spend. Not that he was throwing any money away, but he was buying all the drinks.

I switched to beer. Even then I was feeling a little uncertain about the sidewalk when we got started back, and Mac insisted on stopping in one of the *cantinas* for a last shot of oil.

Then was when he did the funny thing.

He pulled out his purse, couldn't find any small change, turned the purse upside down, and some gold nuggets fell out.

There were only three of 'em, and they wouldn't have run over five dollars, but they were virgin gold.

He scooped 'em up quick and dropped 'em back in his purse.

After a bit he started to explain.

"Pocket pieces I've had ever since I used to be a prospector, years ago. I've carried 'em in that purse for years and years."

He leered at me like an owl leering at a titmouse.

I nodded and sipped my beer.

He gulped down his whisky, looked at me again, and took a deep breath.

"Flint, you been like a brother to me. I'm going to tell you the real truth."

That sounded better. I sat my beer glass down and tried to act only half interested.

"There was a prospector came into the place and wanted me to grubstake him. He showed me some gold and said he'd stumbled on a place where it was thick. I gave him a hundred dollars' worth of grub, and he left me the nuggets. I ain't never seen the prospector since."

I pretended my ears hadn't been expecting anything else. He was getting drunk, but he was an awful liar.

"Do you s'pose we could smuggle a bottle across?" he asked me, putting his head over toward me and peering with a strained expression in his eyes, like a drunken man will.

"We could smuggle two bottles, one apiece," I told him.

We did.

In a room in a San Diego hotel I poured whisky into him. He seemed to suspect I was getting him oiled, and he had the thought of the gold on his mind, all right.

When the second bottle was half empty he leaned forward, holding the edge of the table.

"Goin' tell you real truth about thash gold," he said.

I moved over closer.

"Jush like a brother to me, Jimmy, old boy," he went on, swayed, straightened, filled his glass and drained it at a gulp. "I came on old prosh-pector . . . awful shick . . . dying. I did besht I could, but prosh-pector died. I wash a thief. I went through hish roll an' found half pound gold dusht. Thish what's left."

And then he sagged over on the table and went to sleep.

I put him on the bed, went down, checked out of the hotel, and caught a night train out. At Las Vegas, Nevada, I outfitted. It was a funny outfit, but I was going on a funny errand.

III   WATCHED

I knew the country pretty well, and I went into the Indian country from the back way. It was hard going. I had a burro to ride and two to pack, but I took it easy. And I did not get clean into the Indian country. I stopped just below the summit of the range that ran into the desert.

There was timber here, water, and lots of game.

I shot a buck and built a fire. I used green wood, so the fire made lots of smoke. I cut up the venison and started to jerk most of it. A ham and some backstrap I hung up in canvas. I kept the fire going most of the time, and, as I said, it made lots of smoke.

I didn't see anybody at all.

Next morning I went out with my rifle as though I was hunting. But all I did was scout around the ridges above camp.

And I found what I was looking for. The trail of a moccasined foot. I backtracked it to the place where the Indian had squatted behind a clump of brush and watched my camp.

Then I walked all up and down that ridge so my tracks wouldn't show as having just trailed the Indian, and I put up a target and did a little shooting. Then I went back to camp and let the fire go out.

I stayed there four days without seeing a soul.

But, every morning, I'd take a short hunt and always I'd find moccasin tracks. Sometimes they'd watch me from one angle, sometimes from another. Sometimes there'd be two or three, sometimes one. But they always had me watched. Yet I never saw the faintest flicker of motion on those hillsides.

And the air's so dry up there, and it's so high, that the sun just floods light all over the country, all except in the shadows. The shadows are sharp, and contrast with the sunlight so it's hard to make the eye see into 'em. The Indians watched from the shadow. They must have followed the shadows around.

On the fifth day an Indian came up the cañon. He was carrying a gun and acted as though he was trailing something. When he looked up and saw my camp he acted surprised. Too surprised. In the first place, any Indian would have smelled the camp before he rounded the bend. In the second place, he wouldn't have acted that surprised over anything. But I pretended I didn't see anything wrong in the way he acted.

He came into camp and smoked a cigarette Indian-fashion.

That is, he squatted on the ground, and his first six puffs were ceremonial puffs. They always smoke that way. First they puff to the four directions. Then they puff up toward the sky and down toward the ground.

After a while he looked around at camp. "Killed deer," he said.

"Four days ago."

He nodded. "You stay four days one camp."

"I stay long time one camp."

"Hunt?"

"Little bit."

That was a pretty long conversation for an Indian to have with a stranger, so he went back to smoking.

Ten minutes passed. The Indian said nothing. I got confidential.

"I may be here six months."

"One place?"

"Naw. I get tired of being in one place. I'll move camp around a little bit."

He waited for me to go on.

"You see, the doctors tell me I gotta live the simple life out in the open for a long time."

He grunted at that. After a while, he said some more.

"You stay down trader's for a while?"

I nodded and let my face all break out in smiles.

"Did you see me down there? I don't remember you. Sure, I've got some things down there yet. But I went in to see the doctor in San Diego, and he said I'd have to get up higher in the mountains."

The Indian grunted again. Then he lit another cigarette, and went through the same rigmarole of smoking it.

Indians always do that, but you've got to watch sharp to catch 'em at it. They turn their heads casually, as though they were looking around at something, and you don't figure they're turning so as to blow the smoke at the four points of the compass, then up toward the heavens and down into the earth. They want the spirits propitiated before they smoke. It's like saying grace over a meal.

After a while my visitor went away without saying anything more.

I stayed in that same camp a week longer and shot another buck and jerked most of the meat. I didn't see another soul.

Then I moved down the cañon half a mile and made another camp. I stayed there five days, cut across a ridge and pitched a camp in a clump of timber. It was cold there in the mornings, and I stayed only three days. Then I worked toward the foothills.

Finally I began to see Indians. They didn't keep out

of sight so much. Now and then one would walk against the skyline and stand there as though he didn't know I was looking at him.

I never paid any attention.

When I shifted quarters the next time I moved within half a mile of an Indian camp. I didn't let on I knew it was there.

For a day or two I lay low, and then I went hunting. A couple of Indians stopped me and said there wasn't any good hunting around there, but I told them I wasn't in a hurry to get my game. After that they let me alone.

I'd been there for a week when I came on *her*.

It's not very often you see an Indian before that Indian spots you. But I did that with Auno. She was engaged in a ceremonial dance on a little flat of sandstone. It was just after sun-up and the air was still pretty crisp.

I saw her shadow first. Shadows are sharp in those mountains, and the sun was low enough to make hers long. The shadow moved and I thought I'd seen a deer. Then I moved over a bit and caught sight of the tawny skin weaving in a series of supple gyrations.

She was playing some sort of queer flute. I could hear the sounds of the music after I listened. I tried to work nearer, but she saw me.

I passed her going toward the camp. She wasn't even breathing hard, but she'd been staging a sun-up dance and must have run for three or four hundred yards as fast as a deer.

She looked at me with smoky eyes.

"You findum deer?" I asked.

"No findum," she said, then, after a moment: "and you don't need to talk that synthetic pidgin English to me. It happens that I was educated at Berkeley, and I majored in English."

I stood on one foot then the other, trying to think of the proper comeback for that one. There wasn't any.

Then she smiled. "What were *you* looking for?"

"Just walking."

"Why are you camped here?"

"For my health."

She let her eyes drift away for a flickering instant, then turned them back on me, as glittering as obsidian, as expressionless as ebony.

"If you would like to camp in the desert I know where there is gold."

I did some rapid thinking. I know Indian psychology.

"I am not interested in gold. I want health, and I must live in the mountains."

"A white man—not interested in gold!"

I shook my head doggedly.

"It is an evil. Money is only a way of storing food. But people go mad over it, and they ruin their health seeking it. I, too, had my money madness, and then I lost my health. Now I only want to live. One needs very little gold to live."

She smiled at me, and, as I was admiring the white luster of her perfect teeth, flashing against the tawny silk of her skin, she turned and slipped into the shadows.

Two days later I saw her again. After that she made it a point to keep in contact with me. I figured the tribe had delegated her to see what I was doing and keep track of me.

I was willing.

Gradually she began to talk more. And I think I convinced her that I wasn't looking for gold. Her name was Auno, and she was the only pretty girl in the tribe. It was just a handful of people anyway, not more than a dozen families.

After a while I got acquainted with them. Among

them were Hanebagat, the chief, and Bigluk, a young
fellow who was sweet on Auno. And then there was
Wailo, the medicine man.

I don't know how old Wailo was. Nobody did. He
had some blue tattooing in his face, but the features had
wrinkled so much that it showed only as a blotch. No
design to it any more.

Age had withered him until he was a dehydrated shell
of a man with wrinkled skin and shriveled arms and legs.
But he was as straight as a young pine, and he had eyes
that were like thunderclouds when the lightning first
starts to play around the dark places.

He said nothing, although his eyes were on me all
the time.

I'd been there three months before I learned about
the moon ceremony.

It was an ancient rite, handed down from the time
when the tribe was powerful.

It took me quite a while to get the straight of it. You
see, they weren't Piutes, and they weren't Navahos, and
they weren't Apaches. I'd have guessed they were an off-
shoot of one of the Pueblo tribes that had drifted through
the Navaho country, picked up some Piute and Apache
customs, and then settled somewhere around the Death
Valley.

Age, disease, changed conditions and white encroach-
ments had done the rest. They were the last remnant of
a dying people, and they knew it—all except Auno, the
girl.

She used to try and pep them up, tell them of the
future, predict that they would come back to their own.
But the others watched her with somber eyes and said
nothing.

It's hard to watch anybody die. Death seems to send
a shadow that hovers about the dying one for quite a

while before the soul slips its moorings. It's harder still, to watch a dying race. That shadow of death seems to be with the very infants. The children play, not like normal children, but like young corpses that are walking hand in hand with death.

But it was the moon ceremony I was thinking of.

The new moon was the time for the very young people to sit out, all by themselves, on the sacred mountain. When the moon went down it was time to go back to camp and bed.

Then, when the moon got into the first quarter, the lovers went forth into the moonlight, and returned when the moon had gone down.

The full moon was the warriors' moon. It was for the men in the prime of life.

After that the older people came in. They went forth to worship on the wane of the moon. The last quarter was reserved for the sages.

Those Indians ushered in each phase of the moon with a lot of powwow and old Wailo would beat a tom-tom and wail through some song. It differed for each phase of the moon.

Wailo's personal moon was the very last of the fourth quarter, the one that came up just before the sun. There wasn't anybody else as old as he was, so he went forth alone to worship.

By that time I was down living with the tribe, almost adopted—thanks to Auno. And I remember the first time I heard Wailo at his ceremony of moon worship.

It was a little before dawn, and it was cold; cold with the dry, chilly cold of the desert places, cold with the soul-shuddering mystery just before dawn.

The old moon was riding the heavens, looking like a bit of pitted gold, and it was cold, too. I awoke with a start to hear something going *boom-boom-boom*.

I lay in my blankets and shivered, first with the cold,

then with the awful note of that tom-tom and the song that was going with it.

It was a wailing chant, coming in from the distance, borne on the thin, cold air without an echo. It was the voice of an old man trying to sing—the song of the old moon, the song of coming death, the song of a dying race.

I tried to get back to sleep, but I couldn't.

With the red streaks of dawn in the sky Wailo came stealing back to camp. He was all decked out in paint and he moved as silently as a gray ghost.

Then the tribe got up. Little fires began to burn. There was the sound of moccasined feet on the hard ground. And it was time for me to get up.

All this time, I hadn't seen anything of the gold, or anything that looked like gold. But I did know that the tribe wasn't dependent upon trading, in the ordinary sense of the word.

The women wove blankets. There were some sheep, and there was a little cornfield. But the work was all done after the manner of those who are sure of their living, and work only to get what they need.

Besides, there were the coin buttons. That's the fashion of Indians in that country. They take dimes, quarters, sometimes even half dollars, solder a bar on the back and use the coins for buttons and for ornaments. When times get hard they clip the bar off and use their "buttons" for money.

The clothes of this tribe had silver buttons, and they never came off. Whenever any one needed anything at McLaren's trading post, they had a way of getting it. Old Wailo seemed to be the treasurer of the tribe.

So I figured they had a placer deposit somewhere around, and that Wailo had persuaded 'em that it was magic, and only the medicine man could take out the gold.

After that I commenced to watch Wailo.

I figured he must have a stock of the gold in the village somewhere. Maybe he knew I was watching him, but I don't think so. Anyhow, he didn't lead me to anything. I watched him, and that's all the good it did me.

But he never seemed to leave the village. He was always around, saying very little, his puckery lips sucked into his mouth, his thundercloud eyes darting around the camp, seeing everything.

During the dark of the moon the tribe dedicated the night to those who had already died. They sat up around big fires, talking in low tones of the dead, and there was a circle where the ghosts were supposed to sit and warm their hands. There were places for the big chiefs who had passed on.

The tribe slept most of the day, after those night communions with the dead.

IV   LOVERS' MOON

I got an idea during those long sessions around the spectral fires. When the new moon came I went to Hanebagat, the chief, and told him that I was the same as a member of the tribe now, and that I would go out on the ceremony of the first quarter of the moon. He agreed.

The word got spread around, and Bigluk made a protest to the chief. It was easy to see how his mind worked. There weren't more than five or six of them that came under the lovers' moon, and Bigluk was afraid I'd get too thick with Auno. He'd always preëmpted her for the moon ceremonies before.

But Auno whispered to Hanebagat, and the chief stood pat.

When the moon came to the first quarter, Wailo got

out the sacred drum, put on some ceremonial paint and chanted a song that was supposed to be the thrilling song of love. But he knew the race was dying, and sadness crept into his voice. The chant sounded more like a dirge, for all its swing and occasional burst of noise.

After the chant we went out onto the sacred mountain, walking hand in hand. On the mountain we separated, each going by himself.

That was the ceremony. The young men were supposed to meditate upon the hunt and upon warlike deeds. The girls were to think of the tanning of skins, the cooking of food, the rearing of a family when they should get married.

If one of the young men chanced upon one of the young women after they had separated, he could talk with her. If they stayed together until the moon set, then it was equivalent to a marriage ceremony.

Of course, all the young men in the tribe wanted to marry Auno. But Bigluk seemed to have the best chance. He was big and surly, and he sort of kept the others away. There wasn't one of them, though, that hadn't tried to find her on the mountain after they'd separated.

Custom decreed that the women should leave first. After a few minutes the young men walked apart.

There were only three young women. One was very fat. The other was homely. The third was Auno. There were only three men beside myself. One of them was rather ugly.

After the girls had gone, the men separated and I found myself out on the moonlit mountain. Below was the camp. One of the warriors started a chant that ran for a few bars, then wailed into silence. Here and there a shadow flitted.

Auno was an adept at keeping separate. They could find her, have a little chat, and she'd glide off like a shadow. But, for the most part, they couldn't find her.

I sat in the shadow of a clump of juniper and watched Bigluk. He tried to trail her for a while, but that was too slow. She could make tracks faster than he could find them in the moonlight. So he got in the shadow of a pine trunk and searched the mountain.

Finally he was off like a deer.

I watched him. He ran fast and well. He jumped into a brush clump, and there was a sound of struggle, the low laugh of a woman, the exclamation of a man's voice, and Bigluk came out, looking disgusted.

The fat girl was clinging to his arm, pouring words at him. Bigluk was shaking his head. He jerked his arm free and went down the mountainside, peering into brush clumps.

Far above him I heard a low laugh that sounded like the tinkle of a bell.

He turned and charged like a mad bull. But he might as well have been chasing a shadow. He became dignified then and walked about with slow steps, pacing in the moonlight, no doubt meditating upon his life. But I noticed that he had his eye peeled for every bit of motion.

When the moon went down we started for camp, coming in one at a time, in silence. Then we rolled into the blankets.

The next night it was the same, and the next.

I didn't move around much. I kept up there on the mountainside, mostly in the shadows. The fat girl found me once on the second night, but I left her. She'd have been willing to stay until the moon went down, which, as I said, would have been the same as marriage.

On the fourth night the moon was pretty strong. It was about the last of the ceremonial phase given over to the younger people. Bigluk had charged around as usual. Once he had caught Auno, and they had talked for fifteen or twenty minutes. I couldn't hear what they said, but he was doing most of the talking, and his voice was getting that note in it that comes to people when they're desperate over something.

Auno left him. That was the custom; either could leave the other and the other must not follow.

Bigluk walked into the shadows and stayed there.

I went out into the moonlight, walking, thinking. I knew it was no use to look for Auno. She could hide from the keen eyes of the Indians, and it would be too simple for her to elude me with my civilization-dulled senses. She could hide from me so easily it would make me seem absurd. I could no more hope to find her than I could to elude the fat girl.

The fat girl talked a little English, and she put herself in my way, so I'd have to either talk to her or be rude.

I paused for a few minutes, talked.

"You no go 'way," she said, and her eyes were bright.

I laughed.

"You too good-looking to waste yourself on white, Missa Flint. You get nice Indian."

She parted her lips and the moon gleamed on her teeth.

"I make you good squaw . . . *I show you plenty gold.*"

She lowered her voice for the last few words, glanced quickly around her.

I knew the danger. If other ears overheard, the fat one had pronounced her death sentence. But she had the keen sense of an Indian, and there wasn't much chance any one would have been in hearing.

I looked at her, hesitated.

She gently tilted one shoulder blade with a seductive motion.

I got a grip on myself.

"Gold no good," I said sternly. "Gold only good to buy food. Out here plenty food. One needs not much gold."

And I walked away.

It was a struggle, and I wasn't sure why I hadn't said "yes" to the girl. I could have married her, got her to show me where the gold was, and then sneaked back some night, got what I needed for a stake, and left.

Maybe they'd have trailed me, maybe not. A man can go far in a night when he has to, and a rifle in the mountains gives the one who is fleeing a lot of advantage over those who follow.

And I was pretty good at losing a trail myself. I was wearing moccasins, and there are a lot of little tricks of losing trail in that country—ledges of rock, boulder-strewn creek beds where cloud-bursts leave their trails, long drifts of ridge which are exposed to the winds which blow in the mornings, fallen logs—oh, there are lots of ways of making it difficult to follow tracks.

Of course, it was foolish, but I began to get inoculated with something of the philosophy of the tribe. Why work in the treadmill of civilization? Civilization taxes you almost a hundred per cent for the privilege of participating in it.

You have butchers to make your kills, machinery to carry you from place to place, do your work. And yet one really lives in caves. They're made out of concrete instead of cut into the side of a precipice, but they're caves just the same, steam-heated caves. Your liver gets sluggish, and you lose the capacity to enjoy life. Out here we were free. We weren't mere cogs in a machine.

As I walked and looked at the moon, I inhaled great lungfuls of air and wondered if there mightn't be something in the philosophy of Wailo, after all.

I rounded a bush and Auno got to her feet with a single bound, like a startled deer. Then she paused, poised on one lithe limb, half turned.

"Don't run, Auno," I said.

She settled back on her two feet, looked at me.

It was well done, but I knew that her ears had heard my steps long before I came to her. Perhaps they had heard the conversation between the fat girl and myself.

"I was thinking, and you startled me," she half whispered.

"Thinking of what, Auno?"

She raised her head, looking at me with half-closed eyes, then tilted her neck, after the manner of a listening deer.

"He comes. You will go with me and we will avoid him."

I listened, but could hear nothing save the faint rustle of the night wind on the moonlit slope of the mountain. But her delicate senses had apprised her of the coming of Bigluk.

"Very, very softly," she said, as she nestled her warm hand confidingly in mine and guided me along the moonlit game trails that networked the side of the slope.

We crossed the ridge and were in shadow. Then she paused, listened, and led me into the deeper darkness.

"Now we are safe."

Reluctantly, I let go her hand. Of a sudden I realized what this girl had come to mean to me.

"So you would not marry, get the gold and desert the tribe?" she cooed.

"You heard, then?"

"I heard."

I shifted my weight from one foot to the other, not knowing just what to say next.

"Why?" she asked.

"Because I do not care for gold—no, I'll be honest; that is not it."

She came closer to me. I could feel the warmth of her body, glowing through the soft tanned fawnskin of her clothes.

"You are not like other white men. You are more of a man, less of a hog?"

"It is because I love you!" I told her, and swept the girl into a tender embrace.

Quick as I was, she could have avoided me had she desired. Her splendid muscles functioned as easily and swiftly as those of a springing cougar. But she slipped into the curve of my arm and, after a moment, raised her red lips to mine.

For long minutes we stood, close to each other, I feeling the warm fragrance of her breath on my cheek.

The moon slid lower in the velvet sky.

"It is not the gold?"

"It is not the gold."

And, at that moment, gold seemed sordid to me. I resented the very use of the word.

She sank to the ground, pulled me down beside her, slipped her head upon my shoulder, laughed, sat snuggled close to me, patted my cheek and hair, kissed my eyes, looked up at the star-studded sky, and rippled into another laugh.

"Soon the moon sets, Jimmy."

"You will go back with me, Auno beloved?"

For a long minute she was silent, thinking.

I knew when a sudden thought came to her. I could feel her body stiffen in my embrace. The hands were at my shoulder where her head had been, pushing us apart.

"Perhaps it is because you knew I loved you, Jimmy. You still want the gold, but you would rather have the gold *and me*, than the gold and her."

I was on my feet, words poured from my lips.

I convinced her heart, but the thought remained in her mind.

"We will see," she said, and made a single writhing motion which gathered the cloak of darkness about her as a tangible thing. One moment she had been there. The next she was gone.

The moon set, and I returned alone to the camp.

V   ORDEAL BY GOLD

That was the last night of the lovers. Thereafter Auno avoided me. And Bigluk had muttered some comment to the elders of the tribe. I detected a feeling of hostility which had not before been apparent.

The full moon came and went.

One morning the air was calm, still, cold. I set out with my rifle, going more for the exercise than anything else, for there was plenty of meat in camp.

A bush ahead of me showed a ripple of motion. I flung up the gun, and Auno stepped out into the trail.

"Are your eyes still the eyes of a white man?" she asked, tauntingly. "Do you not know that a deer would not be on the windward side of the bush? Think you that a deer would shut off his vision on the same side that his nose was blind?"

I muttered something about having seen motion and acted automatically.

She laughed, beckoned for me to follow.

She picked her way down a game trail, came to a cañon, paused, looked about her, her eyes snapping, every muscle poised, tense.

Then she took my hand. Together we raced up a bed of smooth rock, worn down by the torrents of many cloud-bursts.

She paused where a branch cañon came into the main cleft in the hills, parted a bit of brush and disclosed a worn trail.

I followed her without a word.

The trail ended at a rock. Behind the rock was a place which yawned black and forbidding, the entrance to a cave.

She slipped into it, grasped a torch from a place in the wall, lit it, and advanced.

The smoking flames of the pitch torch gave weird shadows which danced about on the wall of the cave. A damp smell of musty ages was in the atmosphere. A bat flew past, almost knocking against my shoulder.

The girl stopped, held forward the torch.

I saw where some subterranean stream had cut a channel through the cave, leaving coarse bits of gravel, bigger rocks worn smooth. I saw where a dike of rock came across the course of that ancient stream, making a dam. And I saw something else, pebbles that were not pebbles, but glittered here and there as the light of the torch struck them.

Mostly they were black, but in places the black oxidation had been rubbed away and the gold showed through. I had seen black gold in places before.

"Behold," she said, "the treasure of the tribe. There is more here than many men could possibly carry away."

I knew she was right.

Auno moved the torch, and I saw a row of something white, something which sent a sudden chill through my bones. They were skeletons, three of them!

There they sat, grinning into the dark depths of the cavern, grouped in a row upon a little shelf in the rock.

"And these," she went on, "are the white men whose greed betrayed them. These are the skeletons of those who would have looted our treasure, stolen from us that which is ours."

"Murder?" I asked.

"Bah!" she spat, an expletive of disgust. "Murder, is

it? Didn't the white men crowd us out of our own country, banish us to the burning desert? And now that we
have a little of the precious metal in our possession, they
must come even here and grab that, too!"

I decided not to argue the point.

"Yes," she said, and her voice was low, almost crooning, "these men discovered our secret, tried to steal our
treasure. The braves trailed them, cut off their escape
and returned the bodies to the cave. They wanted the
treasure so much! Let them remain with it always.

"But they were foolish, Jimmy. They took the gold
and started over the mountains toward the road. But
had they been wise, they would have gone out into the
desert. There they would have had heat and thirst, but
the shifting sands would have drifted in over their tracks.

"Wailo guards the treasure. And in the mornings when
there is a very old moon and Wailo is on the mountainside, a man could enter here, wait until dawn came, and
then slip out. He would get far before he would be
missed."

I thought that over, the last sentence in particular.

"You are telling me how _I_ could steal the gold?"

She nodded.

"Why?"

"Because either you love me, or you love the gold.
I want to find out which. If it is the gold, take what you
can carry and go. If you love me—well, then when there
comes a new moon again, Jimmy, and we walk upon the
mountainside, perhaps—"

Her voice trailed into silence.

I grasped her in my arms. The torch fell sputtering
to the floor, flickered a minute, and went out. There in
the darkness of the cave we embraced and I whispered
that gold meant nothing to me.

Of a sudden, she broke away.

"Quick!" she breathed, and grasping the still smoking torch, led me farther back into the black recesses of the mountain.

There was the sound of feet upon the gravel floor of the cave. Some one stumbled, halted. A match blazed, a torch flared, and I could see Wailo, the magician, peering about the shadows.

His wrinkled skin seemed as coarse as an elephant's foot-pad. But his eyes glittered with an undying spirit that made the flames of the torch glitter in dancing reflections.

For several minutes he stood, listening, watching. Then he stooped, gathered some of the gold and retraced his steps. The torch was extinguished, and darkness fell upon the cave.

We sat, she in my arms, and waited until an hour had passed. Then we, too, sought the sunlight.

I thought much of that cave during the next two days. But mostly the thoughts came to me at night. I wondered if I had dropped so low as to be unworthy of Auno's confidence.

That fine, clean girl meant more to me than anything in the world. Beauty, charm, perfect health; and we could live the care-free life of Nature's children out in the desert, out where the tumbled mountains stretched their glistening sides down toward the Armagosa sink, down toward the bitter waters of the poison river, toward the shimmering heat of Death Valley.

Then I thought of the gold. Try as I would, I couldn't get the yellow metal out of my mind. I thought of what it would buy.

Then I realized what the Indian girl had done. She had put my soul to the test. If I had greed, she had shown me how to take all the gold I could carry and escape. If I had spoken the truth and cared naught for gold—then the next new moon would see us walking together down from the mountain.

The nights passed. I slept less. The thought of the gold tortured my mind.

Then came the old moon, the last night of the withered moon when there was a mere streak of crescent light riding in the heavens a half hour before dawn.

And then I heard the faint *boom-boom-boom* of Wailo's drum as the old man communed with himself. I thought of the shriveled arm, the wrinkled face, thought of how he had been with the tribe when he was a young man and walked on the mountainside in the light of the new moon.

And I remembered what Auno had said, that this was the safe time to steal the treasure. I tried not to think of the cursed stuff, but my thoughts turned to the gold.

A clammy sweat clothed my body. I raised myself on one elbow. The camp was silent.

Faintly, I could hear the chant of Wailo's song of extreme age, the chant that greets the grave. The drum gave forth hollow boomings, throbbing like a pulse of the night. It seemed to lift me up . . . to lead me . . .

Waiter, bring me another bottle; and bring a bottle for my friend here, too.

Take the price from this sack. See, it contains gold. There is lots of gold, pure virgin gold. My friend and I are celebrating—celebrating my return to civilization.

Written in Sand

THERE are nights when a camp fire seems to profane the desert, and this was one of them. The moon hung low and round in the heavens, and the Colorado Basin was bathed in warm, mellow light like the amber of old wine.

But I wanted fried potatoes for breakfast, and I'd put off cooking them until the night got cooler. Boil potatoes for half an hour, then let them stand overnight, cut them into slices and fry them with onions, add a little bacon and wash down with coffee. That's a breakfast that'll stay by you. That's why my camp fire was crackling away under the desert moon, and the water was bubbling and steaming over the potatoes.

Off to the west, a mile or so, was Signal Butte. To the east, the lights of Calexico and Mexicali twinkled like brazen jewels. To the north, the Superstition Mountains basked in the light of the mellow moon.

The flames of the camp fire died down to a bed of glowing coals. A light breeze came up from out of the night, and the desert commenced to whisper.

Desert whispers are funny things, and they vary just as the desert varies. Up around Death Valley the desert whispers will be hard and hissing, filled with an ominous

menace. Down here by the border, they'll be languid, romantic, dreamy.

But the Colorado Basin's a funny desert, anyway.
Down by the Superstition Mountains, where the whole
valley is under sea level, and the soil is composed mostly
of silt that's been washed down by the big river, the
whole desert's entirely different from what it is a hundred miles north. Deserts are like that. At times you'll
have high stretches covered with giant cacti and greasewood. Then you'll have barren places where even a stray
sage can't get nourishment. But always you will hear
whispers. They're the heritage of the desert.

Of course, those whispers, aren't really voices. I know
as well as you do that they're the noises made by the
sand scurrying along on the wings of the desert winds
and rustling against the cacti and the sage. And then,
when the wind gets stronger, you can hear the sound of
sand rustling against sand, the strangest whisper of all.

But here's something to think about: Those sand
whispers somehow or other color the whole desert country. Meet a man who's lived a long time in the desert,
and there'll be a husky hiss in his voice, a dry whispering
note that brands every word he utters. And the desert
teems with other whispers, whispers of lost mines, of
fabulous fortunes buried by the Spaniards when the
Indians turned hostile.

I was thinking about those whispers when the desert
began to whisper to me. The ashes glowed in the breath
of the wind. The sand scurried by and made little whispering noises, tantalizing sounds that were almost words. I
strained my ears to listen—and while I was listening I
heard the other sounds that weren't whispers.

There was the sound of feet in the dry wash, feet that
weren't accustomed to walking on sand. They shuffled,
stumbled, stamped a couple of times as the man lurched

forward, then shuffled again. They came nearer. A head
and shoulders showed in the moonlight as a man came
up out of the wash.

"Howdy," he said, while he was still thirty yards
off, and his voice was anxious.

"Howdy," I said.

He came toward me then, and the moonlight sent a
short black shadow splotching the white floor of the
desert until it looked like a moving blot of ink.

"You're Bob Zane?" he asked.

"Yes," I told him, and waited.

He sat down by the camp fire and held out his hands
to the coals as though it had been cold. But it was a warm
night.

"They told me I'd find you out near Signal Butte. I
had a hard time trying to locate you. Then I saw your
fire."

I waited until he looked up from the coals. Then I
said, "Yes."

He looked back into the fire right away.

"My name's Lucas," he said, "Pete Lucas. They tell
me you know the desert from A to Z."

"Nobody really knows the desert, Lucas," I said.

He shuffled his weight around as though the sand was
uncomfortable. He rubbed his hands, and then held them
toward the coals some more. What he wanted to say
didn't come easy. I didn't give him any encouragement.
Talk that's hard to say out on the desert ain't the sort of
talk that's easy to listen to.

The red embers caught the front of his face. The
moon silvered the silhouette. All in all, I got a good look
at him. He was about forty years old, and he had something to conceal.

His head moved in swift jerks on a nervous neck.
His mouth was weak and the chin was pointed. The nose

spread out into wide nostrils. The eyes were weak and watery. The big sombrero that he'd tilted back was obviously new.

"You could help me," he said.

I didn't say anything. Any man that had any proposition to make to me could make it unaided.

"I need somebody that knows the desert."

I kept silent.

He looked up at me, his watery eyes blinking in the red light of the glowing embers.

"If a gent had been out in the desert to some sort of a secret place, could you track him to that place? If you got started within, say, twelve hours?"

I shook my head.

"I might, and again I mightn't. Winds come up awful fast in the desert countries."

He sighed and let his eyes blink out over the desert.

"But suppose you got started a little sooner?"

"Well, how much sooner?"

"Three or four hours."

"That sounds more like it."

"What sort of a proposition could I make you—in money?"

"I don't know. What could you?"

"I could offer you a thousand dollars for the job. But you'd want to be awfully certain you could do it. If you fell down it would lose me a lot of money."

I ventured an innocent comment:

"We could track him some other time."

"No," he said, shaking his head, "he wouldn't make any more tracks."

I said nothing for a while, but listened to the sand whispers of the desert. The moon looked like a great pumpkin just over my head. The mountains were purple shadows against the golden glow of the night sky, and the sagebrush cast black shadows.

My visitor was looking at me now, staring straight and steady, but that was because I was looking out into the desert. As soon as I turned my eyes back to his face, he started looking at the coals again. The sand whispered little snatches of sound that were almost words but weren't.

"Maybe we'd be crowding too close on this fellow, and he'd get wise," I suggested.

"No. When we start there won't be nothing to be afraid of along that line. It'll be just a question of finding out where he went. There'll be two sets of tracks, one going out, one coming back."

I added to his words, sort of casual-like:

"And the man that made 'em will be dead?"

He jumped back from the fire and got to his feet.

"I didn't say that!"

"No; so you didn't! It must have been that the desert whispered it to me."

He stood, teetering back and forth on his feet.

"Pshaw!" he said after a bit, and turned and strode away into the desert just like he'd come, his feet shuffling, the black shadow bobbing along over the silvery sand.

I drained the water off of the potatoes and spread my blankets.

I thought there was something else that moved out there in the desert. Coyote, maybe, but I wasn't sure. Twice I got a glimpse of motion, and then there wasn't anything except the moonlight, the warm night, the sighing wind and the sand whispers.

I got under a light blanket, saw that my burro was all jake, and pillowed my head on the saddle.

I started drifting off to sleep the way a man does in the open desert. And the sand whispered a lullaby. My muscles relaxed, and isolated thoughts flitted through my brain. The sand whispers became words and strung out into a whole sentence.

There was something startling in that sentence, something I should know. It snapped me wide awake, it was so important. I felt the sense of the whisper slipping as I woke up, and I tried to hang on to what it was. But it was no use. I snapped wide awake to the moon that was shining down in my face, and the whispers were nothing but sand rustling against sand.

I didn't go back to sleep again right away. There was something I was trying to get, like reaching for a lost dream. Sometimes I almost knew what it was, but never well enough to get it fixed, just a hazy impression.

The wind went down as suddenly as it had come up. The moon shone steady and brilliant, and I went to sleep.

Daylight found me slicing the potatoes with onions. The bacon sizzled in the frying pan, and then I dumped in the onions and potatoes. When they were browned to a turn I washed them down with coffee.

But all the time, I was thinking of the man with the broad nose and the watery eyes, whose hands had seemed cold so he had to toast 'em over the embers of the desert fire. I remembered the flicker of motion I'd seen out in the moonlight. Somehow or other, the desert whispers seemed concerned with that flicker of motion.

The sun came up over the Chocolate Mountains, and the long shadows settled over the desert. Right away it commenced to get hot.

I got my camp stuff staked out in the shade of a mesquite clump and saddled my burro. Then I went out to where I'd seen that flicker of motion. The tracks in the desert told the story.

The man with the watery eyes, who had given the

name of Pete Lucas, had come floundering over the desert with shuffling feet. Some distance behind him had been a dainty-footed girl walking as lightly as a young doe. While Lucas had been talking with me, the girl had been lying down on the slope of a sand dune where she could watch him. I didn't think it was close enough to enable her to hear what had been said.

When Lucas left, she left, too, following him.

I backtracked the girl for a ways, trying to get a good imprint of her foot. It was dainty and small, but she handled her feet as though she knew what she was doing with 'em.

I got a track in a patch of silt soil that was a good one. It showed that the left heel had a little chip gouged out of it, probably by a rock. For the rest there wasn't anything except tracks of a woman's shoes.

I rode the burro into Mexicali. I like it south of the border, like to watch the types that come and go; besides, it's all a desert country and the desert has got into my blood. When you first see the desert and get out in it, you'll either like it or you'll hate it. Most of the time, if you hate it, it'll be because you're afraid of it. Then, after a while, when the desert gets into your blood, you'll find it motherly.

But it's a jealous mother, and it only takes care of its own. Those that know the desert and respect its power get along in it. Those that get flippant are likely to be found some place with circling buzzards, swollen tongue, and fingers that have had the flesh ribboned from the bone through delirious digging for water.

The desert's got me. I have to be out in it. It's in my blood. I don't stay long around the border ports. It's an interesting sight to see—once in a while. After that you want to forget it.

But I did want to see if I could find a girl with the heel of her left shoe chipped.

I found the guy with the watery eyes, and I kept him from seeing me. The gambling tables were just opening up, and the big horseshoe bar in the old Owl, that's now the A. B. W. Club, was swinging into action.

This chap, Lucas, was looking for somebody. After an hour or so he found him; I could tell by the expression in his eyes. The vague, watery look vanished, and the eyes snapped to hazel hardness. The flat nose expanded until the nostrils were two black, round holes, and Lucas wet his lips with his tongue.

I followed his eyes to the man he'd spotted. He was a big man, with a great dome of a forehead and eyes that were puckered in thought. He wasn't accustomed to the desert places, and the sun hadn't been kind to his skin. The eyes were red-rimmed from drink and sun, and he seemed a little bit shaky. He took a couple of cocktails, and then went to the gaming tables. He gambled until noon, and then he had some lunch. He played roulette and he was about a thousand dollars ahead. After lunch, he ran into a streak of bad luck. His pile melted, and as it melted he began to plunge, which is the wrong way to gamble. Any old gambler will tell you to crowd your luck when it's coming your way, but to hold 'em close to your chest when you're cold.

And Lucas kept watching the big chap with the dome forehead, keeping in the background, watching, watching, watching.

About three o'clock in the afternoon, when the big chap was down to his last stack, luck turned. He rode it hard. He bet the limit straight up and won time and again. The chips were scattered all out in a big pile. They changed croupiers half a dozen times. He just kept on winning and winning and winning.

Then when he must have had five thousand dollars in front of him, the chap with the watery eyes walked up and tapped him on the forehead.

The big man had just won a bet. His face was flushed with liquor and success. He turned impatient eyes as he scooped in the chips, and then froze into startled inactivity. His jaw sagged until I could see his pink gullet. The eyes bulged until the red rim seemed an inch wide.

"Pete Lucas!" he said, and his voice held nothing of welcome.

Lucas laughed, and the laugh was harsh.

"You're not having to go out in the desert to-night, eh, Sam Slade?"

"Out in the desert—how—what do you mean?"

"You know what I mean."

Slade scooped his chips toward the croupier.

"Quitting," he said.

"Afraid you might lose some of 'em back?" the croupier sneered.

Slade's eyes snapped cold and hard.

"You heard me," he said.

I didn't like the expression of his eyes. I've seen killers before, from outlaw horses to rattlesnakes. He had the look of a killer. The croupier saw it too, and he didn't say anything. He rang a bell, and the money came in.

Then, when he had the money all laid out, Slade did a funny thing. He divided it into two equal piles, and Pete Lucas took one of the piles. Somehow or other, though, it was just what I'd been expecting.

Then they walked into a restaurant, the San Diego Bar and Café.

That suited me. I wanted eats, and they make 'em good at the San Diego. Chinese cooks and waiters, anything you want: venison, quail, doves, lobster, oysters. I sat down where I could see them when they went out. No use to try and see 'em while they ate. The booths had curtains up the side, and were built for privacy.

I had some broiled baby lobster, some quail on toast and a bottle of Tipo wine that dated back ten years—

you can get it if you know the ropes.

Low voices came from the booth where the two men ate. Once I heard a sharp exclamation, and a chair scraped back. Then a voice talked low and fast, and I heard the chair being pulled back to the table. After that there was more talking.

Then the Chinese waiter disappeared, and a pair of jet-black eyes bored into mine over the top of a serving tray.

"Want some dessert?"

It was a girl. I'd place her at around twenty-three or -four. She knew her way about, and she'd lived. There was a snap to the jaw that was all business. Her eyes were like a couple of ripe olives. The complexion was clear and dark. The hair was a piled mass of midnight clouds that framed her face.

"Well?" she wanted to know.

I shook my head. "Nothing more."

She dropped the curtain and went toward the other booth. I looked at her as she bent over, picking dishes off the table. As she reached for a dish across the table, there was the flash of a silk-stockinged leg as she kicked it out behind her to keep her balance, and I caught a glimpse of the heel.

It had a chip gouged out.

There it was, a little drama of life taking place right before my eyes, and yet I couldn't get it pieced together.

I paid my check and sipped my wine until the glass was empty. Then I went out into the streets of the desert town. There was the usual crowd of tourists, and there was something else—low-hung black clouds, that scraped the tops of the mountains and sent black streamers trailing toward the ground.

Rain in the desert. It happens, but mighty infrequently.

The rain started within fifteen minutes, and the silt

soil turned to a slick mud on top of a hard foundation that was like grease smeared on cement. People tried to walk across the street and their feet flew out from under. Automobiles skidded and slid into a devil's dance that swept 'em against curbs with crushed wheels or crashed 'em into each other.

The rain came down in swift torrents for half an hour, and then there was a rift in the clouds, a patch of blue sky, and the sun was shining.

People who knew the desert stood on the sidewalks to see the cloud effects. The tourists lapped up the booze and plunged into the gambling games. The desert showed clear and sparkling, the clouds melted as by magic, and the sun's rays beat down.

Then, right in the middle of my speculation as to what I was going to do next, there was the scream of a woman. It was a knife-like scream, thin and drawn with terror; and then the sound of a shot crashed out.

A Chinaman shrilled a staccato sentence in Cantonese, and scuttled out of the San Diego bar like a frightened quail scurrying for cover. Another Chinese followed on his heels. A tipsy American bellowed for the police. A bartender in a white apron came out and looked up and down the street. A khaki-clad little brown man with a heavy revolver swinging from his hip sprinted for the door, slipped on the wet mud that had been tracked to the pavement, skidded into the arms of the bartender. The bartender took him in.

I managed to be well in the lead of the crowd of gawkers that pushed in.

The girl with the black eyes was on the floor. There was a little pearl-handled gun near her right hand. And there was a red streak along her forehead. The eyes were turned way up into her head, and were fluttering nervously.

She looked as though she'd been creased by a bullet,

and then slammed to the floor with a good punch. I made for the booth where Lucas and Slade had been eating. It was empty. There was a litter of dishes and some wine bottles, and a couple of glasses still half filled with whisky. The two men had gone.

The Chinese began to filter back from shelter. They were furtive-eyed, utterly dazed. They shook their heads with lots of "no savvy's" until an interpreter came up.

Then there was a lot of jabbering in Cantonese, and the interpreter told the story. It was painfully simple. The Chinese waiter had been approached by the girl, who asked him to take five dollars and let her wait on the tables for half an hour. He had done so. There had been a scream, a blow and a shot, and there was the girl. That was all he knew. He hadn't seen any one who had been eating. The girl was waiting on them.

That's the way with the Chinese. When they want to disguise the truth they always hang together and get a yarn that's got just enough of truth in it to make a good foundation for whatever falsehoods they want to add.

The Mexican police took charge, the girl was taken out on a stretcher and things went on the same as ever.

I poked around the gambling halls trying to find a trace of the two men. Nothing doing. I made inquiries about the girl. They'd taken her across the line over into El Centro. She was seriously hurt with a concussion and possible fracture. She was unconscious. The doctor's orders were against any visitors when she recovered consciousness.

The two men had disappeared as utterly as though they had been wiped out.

The desert settled back to its whispers, to the monotony of cloudless skies and sun-swept days. The last I heard of the girl she was conscious, expected to recover, but not saying anything as to how it all happened.

And there was another funny development. The night

of the shooting a Mexican had sold a team of horses and a light cart to two men. They had driven off. Three days later the team had been discovered northeast of Holt-ville. The horses had been running. There was blood on the dashboard.

Apparently the horses had been wandering on their own for nearly two days. They'd struck some alfalfa and were feeding when discovered. But they were encrusted with dried sweat and had been traveling without water.

Gold was reported in the Panamints; a new strike, placer. I always liked placer. It's a one-man proposition, no great outlay for mill and refinery, no blocking out of ore and looking for capital, no delving underground. And again, I always liked new strikes.

So I flung on the packs, saddled the riding burro and started the trek north. Sometimes I thought of the girl and the two men, and sometimes at night the desert would whisper strange sounds, sentences that seemed to indicate I was to have more of them, was to write a closing chapter to the incident. But I could never make anything more out of it than whispers.

If I was awake enough to listen, I was too awake to understand. If I could make sense out of the sand whis-pers, it was because my consciousness was dulled with sleep, and I wouldn't wake up until morning, trying to remember the sand whispers like I would a dream.

The placer proved to be a bunch of hooey, put across by some get-rich-quick mining company that was un-loading stock in Los Angeles; but I had to cover half of the Panamints and a shoulder of the Funeral Range be-fore I discovered it was a plant. By that time I was think-ing of the border again, and I turned the burros back there.

On the map, if it's large-scale enough, you'll find a little place that's listed as Andrade. It's on the Colorado, just west of Yuma, where the California boundary takes a jog down the river. And that twenty-odd-mile jog of boundary takes in some of the toughest border country in the States, bar none.

It's a saying in the customs at Tijuana that the farther east you go the tougher it gets. They have reference to Mexicali. Go to Mexicali and you'll hear the same thing. The farther east, the tougher the border. They have reference to this jog in the boundary.

Anyway, the place is listed on the map as Andrade. Go there and you'll find it's Cantu on one side of the line, and Los Algodones on the other. You won't find anything that looks like Andrade.

And there's lots of action at Los Algodones. They say there's never been a border crew there for six months that didn't have white hair. The theory is that six months on that post will give any of 'em white hair.

Anyhow, I went to Los Algodones, across the drifting sand hills that never stay put, but march like great white ghosts across the face of the desert. My burros were staked and watered, and I had an evening on my hands. I tried roulette and won, and got tired of it.

The evening begins at Los Algodones at around three o'clock in the afternoon. It's over by six. Ask any of the wise ones why they don't keep that section of the border open until nine o'clock, the way they do at Tijuana and Mexicali, and see what he says. If he's a wise one he'll say it with a smile. If he uses words, it's an odds-on shot he won't be one of the wise ones—or else he'll be figuring on leaving the border.

I went into the Log Cabin and rubbered around for a while, and then I went to one of the places where the girls hustle drinks for a commission. It's all done right out in front. A square of dance floor, a greasy-skinned orchestra, a long bar, girls who can flick eyes over a face and classify the character at a glance, and the tourists, suckers, hangers-on and rubbernecks. The girls could play the game straight—or not. Mostly, at Los Algodones there aren't many tourists.

There I saw her. The same black eyes, just like two moist ripe olives, the same full lips, the same swing to her walk, the same independent poise of her head.

A blowzy kid with staring eyes gave me a level glance of appraisal, then turned away. A cute trick came mincing up to me, talked a few words of baby talk and made a half-hearted attempt to smile winsomely. Then she went away.

The black-eyed kid came over. "Hello, pard."

"Hello."

"Looking around?"

"Looking around."

"Listen, big boy, I'm on the up and up. I'm hustling drinks. If you want to dance give me a chance. I can use the ticket. If you want to drink and want somebody to can the mush and drink alongside of you, I need the coin. If you're just rubbering don't waste my time and I won't waste yours. You look like a guy that knows the ropes and knows what he wants. I'm the kid that hands it to 'em straight."

I nodded. "We'll sit at a booth and have a couple of drinks and a talk."

She jerked her head toward the bartender and walked to a table.

"Here's mud in your eye," she said.

I looked her over. "Last time I saw you was when you were being taken to a hospital."

She straightened a bit.

"Yes?"

"Yes. How did you happen to get into this racket?"

She smiled cheerfully. "None of your damned business!" she answered.

I nodded and drank my beer. She watched me with speculative eyes. "You Bob Zane?"

"Yes; why?"

"Oh, nothing."

"Wondering about the night you lay back of a sand hill and watched a man talking to me?"

"Say, you're a wise guy, ain't you?"

"You might be surprised."

"Not me! 'Nother drink?"

"One more."

She waved a hand toward the bartender.

He started toward the booth, and the outer door opened. A sloppy man with hard eyes set in a flabby face pushed his stomach through the entrance.

"That's my call," said the girl. "Sorry, Bob Zane, but you're ditched. I wanted to talk to you, but I've got a date."

And she did what blamed few dance hall girls do to a guy who is spending—she got up and left me, cold. The bartender grinned and walked away. I turned my head so I could get a better look at the man who had entered.

Right away I saw that she had been lying. She didn't have any date with him. As far as I could see, he'd never set eyes on her before.

But she was out to make him. She tried all the wiles of the dance hall girl. And, in the end, he motioned to the cute trick with the winsome smile and the mincing walk.

The kid with the olive eyes got a chance and whispered to the cute trick. The cutie let her eyes widen, nodded her head. After a little while she pleaded some excuse, shunted the fat one to the girl with the olive eyes, and beat it.

The paunchy man and the girl who had been drinking with me talked and drank. Mostly they talked. At first it was the regular line of conversation. Then it got lower and more confidential. When I left the place the

fat man was pulling himself across the slimy surface of
the moist table by his elbows, so that his voice would
carry to the girl without his having to speak loud.

What they were talking about I couldn't tell, but
they didn't have eyes or ears for anything or any one else.

I filed that fact away, went over to the Casino, where
I tried a system at roulette. The system didn't work
but it came near enough to it so my original five dollars
lasted me pretty well through the afternoon.

The border was about to close when I got back to the
dance hall. It's a period of frantic haste. Perspiring bar-
tenders fling drinks at the crowd that's determined to
get in its last lick. Couples stop dancing, hurry to the bar
and start scurrying for the border a good ten minutes
too early—afraid of getting left.

I looked around for the girl with the olive eyes and
the fat man, and didn't get a trace of either. Then a
subtle whisper rippled the crowd; glasses clanged to the
bar, and the exodus commenced. Ten seconds, and the
bar was deserted. Another ten seconds and the doors
were closed, locked, and the street became a parade toward the border.

Tired-eyed inspectors surveyed the seething mass with
skilled eye. Occasionally their hands darted out, and some
man or woman stepped aside. They weeded the sheep
from the goats with a flicker of steely glance that penetrated the mask of indifference the smuggler tries to
wear. It's possible to smuggle a bottle across the border
—but the percentages are against it.

I got to my burro, said good night to the inspectors,
and swung toward my camp. It was dark when I got
there. I started the fire, spoke to the animals, went to the
packs to get out a fresh can of coffee; and heard a scream.

It was a thin scream, sounding as though I'd heard
it before. It was the scream of a woman locked in a strug-

gle with some adversary, losing her strength, but fighting with sheer nerve.

I kicked out the fire. No use to be outlined against flame, a perfect target. Then I went toward that scream, on the run.

I saw them when I was within forty or fifty yards; the bulk of two figures against the grayish white of the sand, the slender form of the girl swaying and swinging, the bulky figure of the man.

As I came up, he got his hands to her throat.

Then I saw it was no mere struggle between man and woman, but that he was trying to murder her. He heard my steps, and his hand relaxed from her throat as he stiffened. His hand streaked for a gun, but I was on him before his fingers touched metal.

He was like a huge bear. The strength of his arms was enormous, but he was a flabby bear. Soft living had made the tremendous muscles soft. And the desert does one thing for a man. It whipcords his strength into tireless endurance.

When those hands grasped me I knew his strength was too great for an immediate victory. But I pried loose, sank a punch into the heavy stomach and began a dancing chase, flicking blows home when I had the opportunity. Then when he was panting and puffing, I walked in, let him grasp me, and showed him that bulk never makes for a long struggle.

I was reaching for his throat, not that I actually intended to throttle him, but just to give him a taste of what he had given the girl, when he went limp in my arms. The great weight jerked me forward, broke my grip and sent me stumbling over it. The flabby man rolled to all fours, got to his feet and ran into the darkness.

I turned to the limp bundle of femininity.

An automobile roared into speed. Lights sent twin

shafts gleaming into the darkness, then swung in a half
arc; a red taillight winked mockingly, then was swallowed
in dust, and the sound of the motor became fainter.

The girl stirred in my arms.

"Get him!" she said.

It was the girl of the olive eyes.

I took her back to the camp fire. She sipped the tea
I gave her, her face bitter, her lips clamped together.

"You'll have to ride a burro to get where you want to
go," I said.

She shook her head. "I don't want to go anywhere."

I said nothing. The desert stretched about us, a great
waste of tumbled rock hills, sage and sand. Off to the east
the river lapped at the dry soil.

"I hate it!" she spat, and as she spoke the golden rim
of a moon, just past the full, swung over the red mountain rim. "God, how I hate the desert! Of all the grim,
remorseless, unjust places on earth, the desert is it."

Never have I heard a woman speak with such hatred.

"The desert," I told her, "is misunderstood. You must
know its ways, which are as the ways of a woman. When
you know it, it is a wise mother. It does justice after a
fashion of its own, but it is always justice."

I put some more sage on the fire. It flamed up into a
warm circle of ruddy light.

"Bah!" she flung at me.

I said nothing. A desert wind came up with the moon,
and the sand began its interminable whispers.

"How I hate it all! I hate the dry heat, the glittering
sand! I hate the wind that makes everything whisper.
Those whispers! They always seem to be promising something, and they lie! Sand lies, that's what they are."

"No," I said gently; "the whispers don't lie. Perhaps
your ears lie."

And then she began to talk, the words pouring from

her mouth so fast they trod on each other's heels.

"Listen. There were two men. Either of them could have given me the information that I wanted more than life itself. Either could have saved my husband from a living hell. Those two men disappeared into the desert in an old buggy. I was unconscious. By the time I came around enough to insist upon trackers following them, the damned desert had drifted sand and silt into the tracks until they couldn't be followed.

"Then I heard that you could follow a track, sometimes when it was months old, and I tried to get you. You had gone, slipped through my fingers. I saw you again this afternoon, and was going to tell you my story when the one man for whom I have been waiting came in. I tried to get the information I wanted from him. He spotted me, somehow. I came to your camp to wait for you. The border men told me where it was. He followed me. You know the rest.

"That's the justice of the desert you prate so much about! My husband was entrusted with a big shipment of gold. We had only been married three months. Three men took it from him, but under such circumstances that he was held responsible. Those three men came to the border and buried the gold. One sneaked out and changed the hiding place and rushed to Mexicali. The others followed him, found him, demanded an accounting. They went to the hiding place, but I couldn't follow because they had spotted me—I was unconscious, knocked down with a blow, nearly killed with a bullet.

"Those men disappeared. Then the third started to follow the cold trail. He traced them to Mexicali. Then he traced them in this direction. He has some information I haven't got. And he didn't want me to see you.

"Now they have all slipped through my hands. I'll never be able to establish John's innocence. I've given everything, thrown all I had into the gamble, trying to save my husband from prison. He got a jolt of fifteen years! Think of it! Fifteen years!"

I looked at her eyes, rimmed with moisture, blazing with hatred. My mind went back to that night in Mexicali when the team had gone out into the night at a gallop, carrying the two men.

"It had been raining," I muttered.

"What? When?"

"The night they took the buggy and went into the desert."

"Yes!" she snapped. "It had been raining, but it cleared up and the wind came up, and the ground dried almost immediately, and drifted over the tracks. A week later the best tracker in the border country couldn't follow the tracks."

I looked at the moon, then I thought for a moment, not daring to raise her hopes too high.

"We'll go to Yuma. We can get a car there. It'll be an hour's ride on the burro," I said.

"Why should I go to Yuma?"

"Because the desert is getting ready to show you its justice," I told her.

She rode to Yuma with me. The trip was mostly in silence. At Yuma I got a man to drive us to the place where the team had been found, northeast of Holtville. I knew a man that had a ranch near there. I got saddle stock from him. By midnight we were out on horseback, the moon blazing down with a light that turned midnight to day.

I searched for two hours before I found what I wanted. It was in a silty patch where the wind had stretched its legs and swept the ground down to bare crust.

There were two long lines of earth stretching out into the moonlight, some four or five inches high. In between

these lines of raised earth were little mushrooms of baked
dirt, flat on top, sticking up like flattened door knobs
thrust into the ground.

"What are they?" she asked.

I stopped my horse. "You've seen 'dobe houses, made
of brick that's nothing but sun-dried mud pressed into
shape?"

"Yes."

"You know how well they endure?"

"Yes. They're pretty substantial. Why?"

"Two or three months ago it rained in the desert. Two
men started out with a buggy because an automobile
couldn't travel over the slippery ground. The wheels of
the buggy, the feet of the horses, sank down into the silty
mud, pushed it into ruts."

"Well?"

"Then the sun came out. The ground dried almost
instantly and the sand and silt started to drift, and covered up the tracks so they couldn't be followed."

Her voice was impatient as she spat another question
at me.

"Well, what's the answer?"

"But the pressure of the wheels and the feet of the
horses pushed the silt into a hard mud. The sun baked it
into 'dobe. Then the winds blew for several weeks, and
in places all the light stuff was blown away. The tracks
that had become invisible became visible again, not as
ruts sunk into the ground, but as ridges, high above the
loose stuff that had blown away."

I could see her eyes glitter with black interest under
the silvery moonlight.

"These are the tracks of the buggy?"

"These are the tracks of *a* buggy driven about that
time, when the ground was wet, and with two horses."

She sighed, a peculiar, tremulous sigh.

"Let's go," she said.

We rode on, following the tracks as best we could. We could only pick them up in the silty spots where the wind had blown. But the buggy was going straight when those tracks were made, evidently piloted toward some star or natural landmark which had showed in the moonlight.

It was nearly daylight when we came to the place where the buggy had stopped. Here were crisscross ridges of earth, miscellaneous mushrooms of 'dobe.

"The rig stopped here for a long time," I told her. "Then, when it went away, it took an aimless course as though there was no driver."

She nodded.

I poked around in a sand drift. A bit of bone caught my eye. I scooped away the sand. The body, what was left of it, was that of Sam Slade. The girl wasted no time in exclamations or hysterics. She joined me in getting the sand away, and in making another search. We found Pete Lucas just as the sun went up.

There was a paper in the sand near where Slade's hand had been. It was scrawled, blotched with red stains, but it told the story:

Lucas, Carl Flint and me held up John Lorne of a big gold shipment. I sneaked the gold from the other two and buried it here. Peter Lucas found me. I offered to split fifty fifty. He agreed. Lorne's wife had us spotted and made a gun play. We beat it out here in a rig. Lucas found where the gold was and ambushed me, but I managed to get him even after he shot me in the back. I tried to get into the rig, but the horses got frightened and ran away. The desert is killing me. God, it's hot! Lorne is innocent. The gold is . . .

The scrawl became unintelligible.

I looked from the note to the sand hills, red in the

rays of the newly risen sun. It took me a few minutes to
spot the handle of a shovel. I dug it out of the drifting
sand. After that it was easy. The gold was there. I had it
uncovered and before her within half an hour.

Tears streamed down her face. The sun had turned
from a red ball to a white-hot disk. The heat rays were
shimmering over the desert.

"I'm sorry, I—"

There came the sound of something ripping through
the air, the plunk of a high-power bullet striking a sand
bank. Powdery sand scattered over us both. The bullet
had gone directly between us, a space of inches. A second later there came the sound of a thin, spiteful crack.
The sort of noise smokeless powder makes in the heat of
the desert. I flung her down against the sand. Another
bullet zipped past my arm. A third threw sand in my
face. I dug a trench, after a fashion, and got out my old
shiny forty-five from its shoulder holster. Not much good
against a rifle.

He came on then, charging, the windshield of his
automobile down, his rifle clattering a volley. Breastworks
or trenches were no good now. He was going forty miles
an hour toward our flank. I ran to one side so he'd con-
centrate his fire on me, and give the girl a chance. My
old forty-five bellowed an answer.

The automobile gave him the advantage of quick motion. But it's hard to shoot from a moving car, harder to
shoot a rifle than a revolver. And the old forty-five has
accounted for many a rabbit on the run.

I saw dust flick from the shoulder of his coat, saw the
hand drop, the arm straighten. The gun slid down, hit
the windshield support. He grabbed for it with his other
hand, and the wheels went into a skid. The rifle struck
the ground and went end over end. He slammed on the
brakes, but I was running forward.

He took in the situation with a swift glance, and did the only thing available. He stepped on the throttle. I fired twice to stop him, trying to find a rear tire, but he rounded a sand hill and got away.

The girl came to me. We picked up the rifle.

"He must have either followed us, or else had some tip we didn't know anything about."

She nodded. "But we have the gold, and Slade's confession!" Her voice showed how she felt.

I rigged a pack on my saddle and walked, leading the horse, carrying the rifle. The girl rode the other horse. The olive eyes gleamed with a deep light.

"To think that those marks would come to light after weeks!"

I couldn't resist the opportunity for a crack.

"Desert justice," I said.

And she nodded, looked out at the shimmering waste of sand, out where the horizons danced in the heat, and the mirages chased each other in a game of ripple-tag.

We got to Holtville, made a report, and organized a posse to track down Carl Flint, the flabby man with the cold eyes. It was two days before they found him. One of my bullets had punctured his gasoline tank. He'd abandoned the automobile and tried to make it for Yuma. His way lay across drifting sand hills. He hadn't made it.

The girl was to leave that night, to join her husband. The Governor had issued a pardon. The gold had been restored to its owners. There was a matter of a reward, almost five thousand dollars.

"It's yours, Bob Zane."

I shook my head. "You stayed with it, did the work. It's yours."

"No. We'll split it."

I shook my head again. "The desert keeps me supplied. You and your husband will need it."

We sat around my camp fire. Fifteen minutes and she would go toward town to take her train. The reward was all that remained, and I wouldn't change my attitude on that.

The wind came up and the sand rustled softly against the sage. She listened to it.

"The desert!" she breathed, and her voice was soft with emotion.

I thought of the three men who had robbed and cheated, and gone to the desert, of the girl who had followed, of the desert justice of the tracks that stuck in the air, the three bodies buried in the sand hills. It was the drifting sand, the whispering sand, the shifting desert that had lured them to their doom, betrayed them at the last, covered their bodies.

It was a pleasant reverie. Was the sand telling the sage about it? Had it whispered its judgment in the ears of the dying men before they had succumbed to the sentence of doom which had been pronounced?

And then, abruptly, two arms were around my neck. My startled lips felt the clinging caress of warm, moist lips.

There was moisture on my cheek where a tear-stained cheek pressed against it—and she was gone.

I listened to her feet as they crunched into the soft sand as she walked away, toward civilization, toward the train that would take her to her waiting husband—and I knew then that John Lorne was a lucky man.

The sound of the steps died away. The wind freshened, and the desert whispered soothingly to my tired ears, little sand whispers that didn't make sense, but vaguely stirred and soothed. And then the swirling sand, eddying against a dead sage, seemed to hiss the words "Desert jussssstice," and I nodded affirmation.

The desert is a wise mother when you know her ways.

Blood-Red Gold

I THE HUMAN JUGGERNAUT

NOBODY KNOWS all that happens, right at the finish, when the desert has her way with a man. It's a grim secret that only the desert herself and the buzzards can tell.

But this much is certain. Right at the last, the victim tears off his shirt and starts digging with his hands. I've found my share of bodies in the desert, and I know others who have found their share. In every case shirts torn from backs, fingers shredded by the cruel sand-gravel of the desert.

That's why we didn't take so kindly to Harry Ortley's story of what had happened—not after we found Grahame's body.

I'd first seen Harry Ortley when he drove into Randsburg. It wasn't any trouble to judge his character. He was one of those birds who played sure things. You couldn't figure him taking a chance of any kind, or giving another fellow a break.

Stringy Martin was standing with me when Ortley drove into Randsburg. He had a sedan, and he parked it in front of the Palace Restaurant, locked the ignition, locked the transmission, rolled up the windows, and locked the doors.

Stringy's lived nearly all of his life in the desert. He watched the performance, then turned to me with a grin.

"If that fellow ever raised a bet it'd be a cinch he held better than three of a kind," he said.

And, somehow or other, it was the best description of the man's character you could make. Stringy's like that— always pulling some crack that hits a bull's-eye.

Ortley walked into the restaurant.

He was fat, not paunchy fat, but the smooth, well-distributed sleek fat that comes to people who are accustomed to getting what they want. He was about forty, and his eye was as cold as the top of Telescope Peak in the winter. His cheeks were round, but his mouth was unusually small.

"Gentlemen," he said, in a thin, reedy voice, "good afternoon."

Stringy nudged me.

"He's speakin' to you," he said.

"Howdy," I said.

The cold eyes turned from Stringy to me, me to Stringy, and back to me.

"I am to meet a man named Sidney Grahame," he said.

I couldn't see how the information meant anything in my young life, but the cold eyes kept boring into mine as though I was supposed to do something about it.

"Don't know him," I said.

The eyes continued steady.

"I was to meet him here in Randsburg. He was to have a string of burros. I'd like to get started to-night."

There wasn't any apology in his tone, and there wasn't any request. He was the type that was accustomed to make his wishes known, and have men jump to do his bidding.

"Stranger," I told him, "you ain't accustomed to the desert."

The eyes never wavered.

"No. That's why I felt you might secure some information for me while I was eating. I haven't had a bite since breakfast. You should be able to find him by locating the string of burros."

And he ignored the lunch counter, sprawled his bulk in a chair at one of the tables, and picked up the bill of fare. As far as he was concerned, the incident was closed.

Stringy Martin snickered.

Mary Garland, who was running the Palace, chipped in with a bit of information. She'd heard the conversation.

"There's a gent named Sid something-or-other that's got his packs out in front of the hotel. I heard him mention he was waiting for some one."

The man looked up.

"Was the name Ortley, the one he was waiting for?"

"I d'know. I didn't hear any name."

Ortley looked at Stringy Martin.

"If you should be going by the hotel," he said, "you might tell this man that Mr. Ortley is here . . . I'll try some of the spare ribs, and you can give me a side order of roast lamb. Are your vegetables canned?"

Stringy and I walked out before we heard what Mary had to tell him about the vegetables. There he was, plunked down in the middle of the Mojave Desert, damned lucky to be getting anything, and wondering if the vegetables were canned.

Some folks get like that.

We sort of stuck around to see what happened when Ortley met his man. There were five burros tied up in front of the hotel, all packed and ready to go. Four of 'em were pack animals, and one had a riding saddle. He was a big burro, and he looked to be a good one.

The chap who was crouched down on the porch of the hotel, hugging what little shade there was, was a lunger. You couldn't miss that. But he was beating the game.

There was a luster to the brown skin, and a strong set to the jaw. His eyes had lost the feverish glitter, and were steady.

Ortley came crunching down the road after a while.

"Mr. Grahame?" he asked.

The thin chap got to his feet, his face all crinkled with a cordial smile.

"You're Harry Ortley. Mighty glad to meet you. I've got something that'll sure interest you this trip. Been waiting since morning."

"I was delayed. Did you get my message?"

"What message?"

"I sent a man to tell you I was here."

"Nobody said anything to me."

"Humph. Well, let's start."

"I ain't eaten anything. Better have a snack before we get going. We'll go pretty far to-night after it gets cool, and food will come in handy."

Ortley let his cold eyes drift over the packed burros, then turned them on Grahame.

"I doubt if we can waste time eating. You should have had your lunch. Where can I leave my car, where it will be safe?"

Sid Grahame flushed a little, then pointed to the build-ing that had a dirt floor and a galvanized iron roof.

"You can park it in there," he said.

Ortley unlocked the door, unlocked the transmission, unlocked the ignition, drove the car into the garage, and locked it all up again. He took out a hand bag, and then strapped a big forty-five about his middle.

"We'll have to take my personal belongings," he said.

"Maybe we can put 'em in a roll. A hand bag's hard to pack," said Grahame.

Ortley's cold eye held his gaze.

"I prefer my things in the bag. They are more con-venient that way."

Grahame took five minutes getting the bag tied on one of the packs. He didn't say anything while he was doing it.

"Only one saddle burro?" asked Ortley.

"Yes. We can take turns riding."

"I see," said Ortley, and climbed into the saddle.

They shuffled out into the desert and I heard Stringy Martin's chuckle in my ear as the last of the burros disappeared round the base of a sage covered hill.

"When," he asked me, "do you suppose it'll be the little guy's turn to ride the burro?"

I didn't answer the question. There wasn't any use.

II ONE MAN RETURNS

That was the first time we saw Harry Ortley.

The second was when he came back from the desert—alone.

The desert hadn't been exactly kind to him. His eyes were swollen. His skin was red and angry. His boots had been dried and cracked by the desert dust, and his flesh hung in bags under his eyes. But the eyes were as cold as ever.

He was leading the string of burros, and the packing wasn't anything to write home about. There were some sore backs in the train, but Ortley didn't mind a little thing like a burro's suffering.

He pulled up in front of the hotel and walked right to his hand bag that was tied on top of the pack. He seemed to be in a hurry because he didn't monkey with any pack rope knots. He pulled out a knife and cut the ropes. I noticed the bag seemed mighty heavy as he pulled it from the pack.

He walked right across to the garage and took a bunch of keys from his pocket. He unlocked the door of the automobile, put the hand bag in the machine, then locked the door. Then he walked across the street to us. He was walking pretty stiff, and his feet hurt him.

"I have a tragedy to report," he said.

His cold eyes were fastened on me, and I didn't like the looks of them.

"Yes?" I said.

"Yes. The gentleman who accompanied me, Sid Grahame, has perished of thirst in the desert. He became lost while prospecting for gold. I haven't seen him for three days."

"How do you know he's dead then?" I asked.

The cold eyes didn't so much as flicker. He shrugged his shoulders and waved his hand toward the desert. The gesture was as eloquent as any words would have been.

"Why in heck didn't you try to trail him and take water to him, instead of beating it back with all the water and supplies?" I said, and I could feel myself getting red in the face.

His voice was just the same steady tone I'd always heard. He didn't raise it, and he didn't apologize with it. He just spoke.

"I'm afraid I'm not adept at trailing, and it would have been dangerous for me to start out alone in the desert. I had a map showing me the way back, and I didn't take any chances."

I started to let him have it all, right then and there, but there wasn't any use, and the desert has its own code. It was a case of where minutes might be precious. A man lost in the desert is like a man overboard at sea.

We got half a dozen of the old-timers around and went to work. Ortley told us no automobile could back-track his route and he was right on that. It took us three days to find Grahame's body, and then the buzzards led us to it. It wasn't where Ortley thought it should have been—not by a long ways.

There wasn't much we could do except bury him right there. We searched the clothes for addresses, and took his watch and a cigarette case and a knife. There wasn't much else.

Stringy Martin's voice was in my ear.

"That man didn't die of thirst."

I knew it, and I knew that a couple of other men in the crowd knew it.

"Ortley's lying," I admitted.

"Let's shake him down."

"After we get the body taken care of."

We made a grave where we found him. It was the only thing to do. Then we got Ortley in the center of a ring of attentive ears and made him repeat the story.

Stringy Martin did the talking.

"Then he must have got lost thirty miles away from here."

"I guess so. I'm not accustomed to the desert. I find it all seems strange to me."

"And you didn't get anywheres near this place?"

"Not that I can remember."

"There's the remains of a camp fire a couple of miles up this cañon, and marks where blankets were unrolled in the sand. And there's a tomato tin that's been opened, and some coffee grounds spilled on the desert, and there are some burro tracks—old, but burro tracks, just the same."

Ortley's eyes held Stringy's with a disdainful sort of expression in them.

"Well?" he asked.

"And this man didn't die of thirst. He was murdered by some means or other."

"How do you make that out?"

"Because he didn't dig with his hands, and his shirt's on. A man who dies of thirst starts running, and he rips his shirt off, and he gets down and tries to dig out the sand with his hands. And he keeps on digging, until you can see the marks of the desert on what's left of his hands. This man hadn't done none of those things."

Ortley shrugged his shoulders.

"As I said, I am not accustomed to the desert. But I have given you the facts as I remember them. Of course it is possible I was near here with the pack train. We may have camped here. I don't think so, but I wouldn't swear to it. I believe there are even cases of men traveling in a big circle in the desert and thinking they are going in a straight line, aren't there?"

"How did you get back to Randsburg?"

"I trusted the burros for a while, and then I saw the outline of that peculiar peak off to the left, and got my bearings from that. I had made a map."

"Where is that map?"

"I lost it. It blew out of my hands."

Stringy Martin looked about him. What he saw in the faces of the rest of us apparently coincided with his own judgment. He started for the burros.

"Well, you'll have a chance to clean this thing up a bit before you leave Randsburg. We'll notify the sheriff when we get back to town."

Ortley said nothing. His eyes were steady, and cold.

We got in to Randsburg, and notified the sheriff over the telephone. He came out and brought the coroner with him. They put Ortley on the grill.

Ortley had money, and he fought the way people with money do. He hired a doctor from Los Angeles who specialized in testifying in court cases. That doctor came in with a suitcase filled with books, and he convinced the sheriff and the coroner that people who died with thirst didn't rip off their shirts and dig their fingers to the bone.

He laughed at the idea that any dying man would do such a thing. He quoted a lot of European doctors, and some statistics that had been compiled from Arabs in the

Sahara desert or some place, and he made the sheriff think we were a bunch of boobs.

The sheriff told us that some of the circumstances were a little suspicious, but he didn't think the district attorney would care to go any further into the matter, and then he left.

You look at a map and you'll find Randsburg's pretty well out in the middle of the Mojave Desert. As far as government goes, it's more or less of an orphan. It's in Kern County, but it's only a mile or two over the border from San Bernardino County. Both counties are bigger than some states.

Randsburg is so much like what the old mining camps were like that the wise guys will tell you there can't be such a place. It stretches along one twisting, unpaved street, a smear of sun-faded houses and rambling, false-fronted business structures.

It's a place that does pretty much what it pleases. And there's another place, not over three miles from it, that does exactly as it pleases. You understand that a mining town out in the middle of the Mojave Desert ain't governed by exactly the same rules that govern a city that's plunked down in the middle of the orange groves.

Ortley glowered at us with his cold eyes, walked to his automobile, unlocked the doors and the ignition and the transmission, and went away from there. There was nothing left behind except five burros and some desert whispers.

III COLD TRAIL

Now desert whispers are funny things. Maybe you've got to believe in the desert before you believe in desert whispers. At any rate, you've got to know what it's like to spend the long desert nights bedded down in the drifting sand before you'll know much about the desert, or the whispers, either.

The desert is peculiar. It's something that can't be described. You either feel the spell of the desert or you don't. You either hate it or you love it. In either event you'll fear it.

There it lies, miles on miles of it, dry lake beds, twisted mountains of volcanic rock, sloping sage-covered hills, clumps of Joshua trees, thickets of mesquite, bunches of giant cactus. It has the moods of a woman, and the treachery of a big cat.

And always it's vaguely restive. During the daytime the heat makes it do a devil's dance. The horizons shimmer and shake. Mirages chase one another across the dry lake beds. The winds blow like the devil from one direction, and then they turn and blow like the devil from the other direction.

Sand marches on an endless journey, coming from Lord knows where, and going across the desert in a slithering procession of whispering noise that's as dry as the sound made by a sidewinder when he crawls past your blankets.

It's at night when the desert's still and calm and the steady stars blaze down like torches that you can hear the whispers best. Then you'll lie in your blankets with your head pillowed right on the surface of the desert, and you'll hear the dry sagebrush swish in the wind. It sounds as though the leaves are whispering. Then you'll hear the sand rattling against the cactus, and it'll sound like a different kind of a whisper, a finer, more stealthy whisper.

And then, usually just before you're getting to sleep, you'll hear that finest whisper of all, the sand whispering to the sand. Of course, if you'd wake up and snap out of it, you'd know that it was just the sound made by wind-blown sand drifting across the sandy face of the desert.

But you don't wake up like that. You just drift off to
sleep, lulled by the sound of the sand whispering to the
sand.

I've never really figured it out, but I guess that's why
the desert is so full of whispers. Strange stories seep
through the desert just the way the sounds of the drifting
sand seep into your ears. Take a man who has lived a long
time in the desert, and his voice gets a dry, husking whisper in it that's like the sound of a lizard's feet scratching
along the surface of a sun-baked rock.

Everything whispers in the desert, and some of the
whispers would sound reasonable anywhere. Some of 'em
only sound reasonable when you're half asleep in the middle of the desert.

Edith Eason first came to me as a whisper.

I was camped up north of Shoshone when I heard of
her. And I swear I can't tell who it was that first told me.
It was just a whisper, a casual, seeping whisper. You'd
probably laugh if I said so, but, somehow or other, I have
an idea it was a sand whisper that first told me about her.

At any rate the name didn't sound strange to my ears
when Humpy Crane gave me the low-down on her. It's
the sort of a name that lends itself to a whisper. Sand
drifting over sand or rustling against cactus would give
forth a sound like that: "Eason—Eeeeason—Eeeasssssssson
—Edith Eassssson!"

Humpy came in to my camp fire up north of Shoshone.
I was camped on a slope of the Funeral Range, and it was
a typical desert night. Humpy saw my supper fire, and
came on over. I could hear him and his burro long before I
could see them. Their feet shuffled through the dry sand
with a sort of whispering noise that muffled the steps.

"Hello, Humpy," I said, when the fire lit on his lined
face and white hair. "Had anything to eat?"

"Nope. I'm short o' grub, an' I saw your fire. Didn't
know it was you, Bob Zane. Got any tea, or tomatoes?"

I opened the pack.

"I got a little of everything here, old-timer. Sit down while I get her ready."

We ate under the stars. The burros moved around through the dwarf sage.

"Wasn't you one of the fellows that went in after the lunger that got bumped off in the desert?"

"You mean Sid Grahame, the one that went out with Ortley?"

"Yeah."

"Uh-huh, I was; why?"

"Nothin' much. There's a red-headed girl come out from Denver. Her name's Eason. Edith Eason. She's hanging around Randsburg, lookin' for you, or for Stringy Martin, either one."

"What's she want?"

"Don't know. It's got something to do with this lunger that got croaked. She grubstaked him or something, and she thinks he found some quartz stuff and was taking Ortley in to show it to him."

I sipped a graniteware cup of tea.

"That," I told him, "is different."

Even then, I began to put two and two together, the weight of the bag when Ortley had lifted it off the burro, the eager way he'd cut the pack ropes to get it loose.

"Eason, Edith Eason—I've heard the name somewhere."

"Maybe. It's a name that's easy on the ears. You goin' in to Randsburg?"

I hadn't been headed that way, but I didn't hesitate any when Humpy asked the question.

"I'm goin' back," I told him.

Edith Eason had bright red hair and eyes that were a calm gray. She looked like a woman who could manage her own way in the world.

"Sid was working in the office with me when he devel-

oped the sickness," she told me. "The doctors said sunshine and fresh air would cure him, but he was cooped up
in a stuffy office, and he wouldn't quit because he didn't
have anything saved up and he didn't want to be a burden
on any one.

"So I pretended to get awfully interested in mining,
and then I told him I didn't want to be working for wages
all of my life, and I was going out in the desert and prospect, or else grubstake some old desert rat. He warned me
I'd get stung, and finally I worked the situation around so
it seemed logical for me to offer to grubstake him in the
desert and let him prospect.

"He was out six months in all, and he started to get
well almost from the first. He wrote to me and mailed the
letters whenever he came to a post office. Sometimes I'd
get three or four of them in one mail. The last batch of
letters said he had something that looked awfully good,
that he had a capitalist coming in to look it over and that
he'd let me know. Then the next I heard was when I read
of his death. So I wrote to the sheriff for details, and he
told me stuff that brought me out here."

She let her calm gray eyes bore right into mine, and
read my mind.

"You think I'm a fool for giving up my job and trying
to come out here, don't you?"

Out in the desert you get so you shoot straight from
the shoulder on most things, or else you get crooked all
over.

"Yes," I told her.

She nodded.

"That's the way I like men. You and I are going to get
along."

"You talk as though you were considering adopting
me," I said.

"I am," she said, and her eyes didn't even twinkle.
"You and I are going into the desert together."

"Huh?"

"Yes. I want to see where Sid's buried, and I want to try and trail where they went on their expedition."

"It's a cold trail."

"I know it. But I've heard a lot about you, Bob Zane. They say you can make the desert talk to you, that there's nothing in the Mojave you can't find out."

I told her straight from the shoulder.

"Yes, ma'am, the desert talks all right. It talks in sand whispers that are easy to believe—in the desert. They don't sound probable anywhere else. I'm afraid you've been listening to sand whispers."

She shook her head and reached her hand inside the blouse of her suit. When it came out there was a little tissue paper parcel in the palm. She unfolded the paper parcel.

"Look," she said.

I looked, and then I looked again, and then I rubbed my eyes and looked some more.

They were little nuggets of red metal. They were almost blood-red, but I knew what they were even before I scratched under the red with the point of my knife.

"Gold," I told her. "It's a gold that's alluvial, and it's been through some chemical or other that's given it a red coating. You get all sorts of gold here in the desert. They even have a black gold, that's dead black on the surface."

She nodded.

"The garage man found these. When Ortley drove off something spilled from his pockets when he took out the money to pay his bill. The garage man found these on the dirt floor."

I shook my head.

"No. This couldn't be what Sid discovered. This is a placer deposit. If he found something that needed capital, it would have been quartz. A deposit of this sort of gold could be washed out without requiring enough capital to bother about. A man all by himself could make the claim pay its way."

She stamped her foot.

"I tell you I *know*. I don't know what the explanation is. That's what I'm going in to find out. But I know that this is from Sid's mine. And Ortley insisted on taking his clothes, his shaving things, and his tooth brush and paste in a leather hand bag."

I nodded.

"Yeah. I saw that. I saw him bring the hand bag out, too, and put it in the car. That don't prove anything."

"The dickens it doesn't!" she snapped. "When they unpacked the burros, they found all of his personal things wrapped in a canvas. So what was in that bag when he brought it out?"

I did some fast thinking and remembered how he'd cut that bag loose from the pack and put it in the car before he did any talking, and I remembered how heavy the bag seemed.

"You win," I told the red-head. "Can you be ready to leave by to-morrow morning?"

The smile that twisted her lips was a funny one.

"Want to get drunk, Bob Zane?" she asked.

"No; why?"

"I wondered why you wanted to stay in town to-night."

"Lord, *I* don't want to stay. But we've got to get a couple more burros and some grub and some water cans."

"I've got them all. How long will it take for you to put the packs on?"

"About forty-five minutes, for the first packing."

"Then we can leave in an hour."

It was settled, just like that. We left in exactly fifty-seven minutes. And I did something I haven't done in the desert for a long time—I strapped my old forty-five onto my waist and got a box of fresh shells.

You get acquainted with people quick in the desert. They can't fool themselves and they can't fool you, out where there's nothing but eternity and silence. I never found out why it is, but it's so. Take a two-day trip in the desert with some one and you'll know him like a book, no matter if he doesn't say a thing.

We traveled late the first night, and we rolled our blankets under the stars. I made the girl as comfortable as I could, and then I went up the ridge a hundred yards or so, so she wouldn't feel I was intruding. I've acted as guide, off and on, for lots of women parties, and the first night they usually sleep with a gun clenched in their fist.

Funny thing about people. They'll sleep in a Pullman car with nothing between them and a lot of strangers but a little green cloth with some numbers on it; but when you get 'em out in God's outdoors they're likely to get self-conscious.

Not this girl.

She was one of the kind that was sure of herself, and of every move she made. She had the poise of a thoroughbred, and she took to the desert like a duck to water.

People are like that. They either take to the desert or they don't. They either love it or they hate it, and if they hate it, the hatred is born of fear.

That night a faint breeze sprang up out of nowhere. The stars blazed steadily. The sage leaves commenced to rustle against each other, and then the sand began to whisper. I went to sleep with the sand making little whispering noises that sounded more and more like words.

In the morning she was up, waiting for me, which I hadn't expected. It was early. The desert was cold with a dry cold that penetrated. There was just the faintest streak of dawn in the east. The stars hadn't commenced to pinpoint out before the day. They were still blazing steadily.

She threw some sage branches on the fire and the red flared up over the desert.

"Go get the burros," she said. "I can get the breakfast."

She was like a great shadow, moving between me and the fire.

"No fancy stuff," I warned. "Coffee and something we can handle quick. We've got to get started before it gets too hot."

She clattered the pans about and I could hear the gurgle of water from a canteen. I rounded up the burros, put on the saddles, and heard the beat of a spoon against a pan.

It was a good breakfast, and it came up on the dot.

"One cup of water for dishwater," I told her.

"No more than that?"

"No. You've got to get accustomed to the desert, and you might as well begin."

She didn't argue. She just measured out a cup of water and poured it in the frying pan. Fifteen minutes later we were throwing the last rope on the pack, and she knew a lot about the squaw hitch.

The east was a red gold now, the color of the gold that had fallen from Ortley's pocket, the color of bloodstained gold. She watched it as the burros shuffled their way through the sage and greasewood clumps.

"I heard whispers last night," she said.

"Sand," I told her.

She said nothing.

IV TRAIL'S END

The red faded from the east. The golden light was so strong it hurt the eyes. Purple shadows began to form and long streamers of light tinged the high points. Then the sun fairly jumped over the horizon, and it was hot.

It was a typical desert day. By eight o'clock the mountains began to shimmer. By ten, there were mirages playing tag with us. By eleven, the place was a furnace with no shade. I knew of a clump of mesquite, and I made it a little before noon.

The girl's face was red, her eyes were inflamed, and her lips were cracked, but she managed a grin. I slung off the packs and loosened the saddles. The shade was welcome, and there was a little breeze. Fierce desert flies came and nipped at us, danced in front of our eyes, buzzed in our ears, crawled on our moist skin.

I was accustomed to it, and I slept. The girl couldn't sleep. I knew she was tossing on her blanket, fighting flies, trying to shut the torture of the sun out from her eyes.

By three o'clock I slung on the saddles and we started again. The horizons were still dancing. Then the purple shadows crept stealthily out from the high ranges. The sage cast long shadows. The horizons quit jumping about, the mirages vanished, and cool fingers of soothing wind reached out over the sandy wastes.

"Here is where he's buried," I said.

She got off her burro. I showed her the grave, and then I went on for a hundred yards or so with the burros and left her there. She came up in about fifteen minutes.

"Do we camp here?"

I shook my head. "I found where they spent a night. I think it was the last night they had together. We'll camp there. We can make it by dark."

I crowded the burros, and we made it by dark. It had been a long, hard day. Most women would have had hysterics, but this red-headed campaigner wanted to cook the supper.

I parked her off to one side and made lots of hot tea and opened some of the canned delicacies I'd brought.

She drank the canned tomatoes eagerly and smiled at me with tired eyes. She ate some of the canned vegetables, nibbled at the toast, nodded her head, stiffened, took some more tea, nodded again, and fell asleep.

I took the plate from her nerveless fingers and eased her back on the blanket, put another blanket under her head for a pillow. She never stirred.

I took a flashlight and looked around.

I'd seen it all before. There was a cliff that stretched up from the desert, hollowed by wind and drifting sand into a million little caves. There was a dry wash, and then the blackened ashes of an old camp fire.

I got the camp made and went to bed.

The girl slept late in the morning, and I let her sleep. It was sunup before I called her to coffee and bacon. She grinned apologetically, and toyed with the food. The sun was commencing to do its stuff and the sand radiated the dazzling light.

Perhaps it was the angle of the sun, perhaps it was just because my eyes happened to be looking in that direction, but I saw something I'd overlooked before. It was a little scratch on the side of the cliff, a place where a nailed boot had left two parallel scratches on the surface of the soft rock.

"Do you hear whispers?" she was asking. "When you're out in the desert?"

"Yeah. Why?"

"I heard whispers again last night."

"Sand whispers."

"No, these were words. Some one kept saying something about a letter. I'm very near a letter that was left for me."

I looked at her sharply, but the calm eyes didn't falter.

"Yes," she said, "a letter."

I looked at the scratches made by the boot heel once more.

"I think," I said, "if you'll take a look in the caves up

along the face of that cliff, you might find it. I'll take the high ones, you take the low ones. Watch out for snakes."

She didn't argue. She started searching.

I was the one to find the letter. It was up in a high cave. It was addressed to Miss Edith Eason, and the address was the business address in Los Angeles.

I scaled it down to her.

It was something of a shock to her as she saw the sealed envelope, written in the hand of the dead. Coming on top of the whispers she'd been hearing, it must have seemed like a voice from the dead.

Funny thing about those whispers. They'd seemed to be trying to tell me something during the night. But I was too drowsy to hear well. Once I thought I had a message, but it had slipped my mind when I woke up.

You can't ever tell, though; maybe it was because of those whispers that I looked at those boot marks. Then again, maybe all of this whispering business was just imagination. I'm putting down the facts the way they happened. One's guess is as good as that of another.

After a while she handed me the letter.

There was a lot of personal stuff in there that I hated to read. It seemed like violating a confidence, but I knew I had to read it to get the whole sketch. The thing was just the way I'd commenced to figure.

Sidney Grahame had located a big, low-grade quartz mine. He'd interested Harry Ortley into coming in and looking it over. While they were dickering over terms, Ortley wanting to take everything in sight and have a guarantee of ten per cent more, Sid wandered off into the desert and just stumbled onto a rich placer.

He staked it out, and told Ortley he didn't need his finances, that Ortley could have the low-grade if he wanted, and welcome, and then he showed Ortley the placer.

That was where he made his mistake. He knew it before the day was done. They started back. Murder was in Ortley's eyes. Sid knew it. He wrote the letter and hid it in the cave, figuring that if anything happened, desert-wise eyes would back-track Ortley. But he didn't dare make the hiding place of the letter too obvious for fear Ortley would see it.

There was a map showing the location of the placer.

I looked up from the letter to find the girl's eyes on mine.

"Can we get there to-day?" she asked.

"No. It's two days' travel, and it's twenty miles from the nearest water. It's one of the worst bits of the desert. That's why it's never been prospected more thoroughly. I'd better go and get some witnesses before we go in there."

I looked at her eyes and saw fire in them for the first time.

"That's nonsense. You don't want witnesses. You just want to get me out of the way where I won't see what's going to happen. We'll travel hard and we'll get there to-morrow."

I tried to talk her out of it. As well argue with a gran-ite mountainside. So we started to travel. And we trav-eled plenty.

The map located the mines with reference to Pilot Butte, and I didn't have any trouble. There was the gleam of a tent in the afternoon sun as we approached the placer.

"You stay behind," I told the girl.

She just shook her head.

We rode up on the tent. Fingers of shadows were stretching across the desert.

"Hello, in there!" I yelled.

There was no answer. I got off the burro and went in. My hand was parked around my forty-five as I pulled the tent flap.

The tent was deserted, and it had been vacated in a hurry. It looked as though Ortley had seen us coming in over the desert and taken a sneak to where he could ambush us.

It was a bad break. I hadn't thought Ortley would be that wise, but he was. He'd had the breaks and played them. I went out of the tent knowing what the answer was going to be even before I heard the crack of the rifle.

Sand spurted up at my feet. The second shot gave me his line. He'd made a little fort out of rocks and sand, and had worked it over so it had all the color of the native country.

One man with a forty-five at his belt isn't going to do any good wading into a fort where a man with a high-powered rifle is holding out.

I turned loose a couple of shots just so I wouldn't be taking part in an argument where some one else was doing all the arguing, and I got the girl off her burro and down into a little swale.

By keeping down in the hollows, we managed to work off the property. At dusk I went back and rounded up the burros. I couldn't tell whether he'd intended to kill us or whether he'd merely tried to throw a scare into us. I wished I'd brought a rifle, wished I didn't have the girl along.

V   DESERT WARFARE

"What's the next move?" she asked.

"Keep him from getting out of the country," I said. "He's probably made quite a stake of gold by this time, and he'll either beat it or else try to bluff it out."

"What will we do?"

"Do you think you could find your way back to the water alone—if you had to?"

She studied my face for a moment or two to find out what the question meant.

"You mean if anything should happen to you, and I'd have to try and get back alone?"

"Yes."

"I'm afraid not. Let's see if we can't keep him where he is without taking the risk of losing your life. I know enough to know that a man with a revolver isn't any match for a man with a high-powered rifle."

"All right," I told her. "Then the only thing to do is to wait him out."

"How do you mean?"

"While he's on that claim, and has a fort to wait in, and a tent that he'll move on up to the fort under cover of darkness, we haven't got a chance. But the nearest water is at that hole twenty miles away. He hasn't got very much water left. He'll have to go for water, and he'll have to get out of the country.

"We can always follow him, keeping just out of range of his gun. We have the advantage of knowing the desert. And whenever he strikes civilization we'll have him arrested. It ain't the way I'd like to play it. I'd prefer a show-down and taking him in with his hands tied, or else letting him take me in with my feet off the ground, or plant me right here. But we are both witnesses to the finding of that letter, and if anything should happen to me and you couldn't find the water hole, it'd be playing into his hands."

She nodded.

"What do we do, camp?"

"Yes. We camp, and we keep a watch day and night. He'll be up to some treachery when he finds out what we're planning. And we go very, very sparing on the

water. We've got to make him run out of water before
we do."

We camped that night just as though the desert was
full of hostile Indians. What little fire we had was
shielded behind blankets, and we put it out as soon as
we had boiled the tea water and warmed up the *frijoles*.

I kept watch that night while the girl slept. Once or
twice I thought I heard him, trying to find our camp, but
I got down on my stomach where I could sweep my eyes
along the sky line, and couldn't see anything moving.

Morning showed he'd moved the tent, just as I'd figured he would. If the girl had been able to find her way
out alone, I'd have waited for him by the tent, but we
couldn't afford to take any chances. Dying of thirst was
too horrible a death to consider for that girl.

I'd made the camp pretty well out of rifle range of
the mining claim, and all we had to do was to keep watch
during the day. By night I'd make another camp.

He stuck in his fort all morning. After breakfast I put
my head in the shade of a big sage and tried to get caught
up on sleep.

It was hot, and the sun beat down on the sand like an
oven. The flies came and crawled and nipped, but I managed to get some sleep. I was sore, and my dreams
weren't pleasant. I'd underestimated this fellow Ortley
with his cold eyes and his efficiency of selfishness. I hadn't
figured he'd have left the empty tent to lure me into an
ambush; and I didn't figure on his having a fort, or knowing the desert well enough to play a lone hand and get by.

Evidently he was one of those mathematical thinkers
who figure out every move in the games they play. He
must have studied the desert, and had some one show
him most of the simple tricks of packing.

The girl was keeping guard, and she must be getting
a full dose of desert. I'd rigged up a little shade for her.

And I'd dug a trench we could get into at sign of any danger.

It was about four o'clock when she called me.

"He's coming," she said.

I snapped wide awake, saw the black blob of motion that was moving slowly over the glittering sand. He had both hands up in the air, and he was carrying a white rag, waving it wildly.

I didn't trust him somehow or other.

"Get down in the ditch and flatten out," I told the girl. I waited, standing in plain sight, but my hands were pretty well placed for sudden action.

It was when he was within about a hundred yards, nice rifle range, but a little uncertain revolver range, that he dropped the white flag. I saw then how damned clever he was. He'd tied his rifle between his shoulders so it hung down behind his back. And he only had to whirl around, catch the muzzle, jerk the weapon around, and there he was, ready for action.

It was a clever trick, even for an old desert fighter. For a city dweller to think it out showed the type of mind that had thought of the fort, of the ambush. If it hadn't been for the ditch I had dug, it would have been almost certain death for us.

I jerked the revolver from its holster, and showed him some speed. That was one place where I could claim the advantage. He might have a coldly efficient mind, but he didn't know how quickly a man in the desert could get his gun from its holster.

My first shot was just a trifle high and to the right. It actually nicked through the top of his shoulder. I saw the dust fly from the shirt, and I heard the little *tick* that the bullet gave.

Then the rifle cracked spitefully, and a high-velocity bullet fanned my cheek.

I dropped down into the trench I had dug, and Ortley flattened on the desert.

I tried waving my hat on a stick.

He didn't even fire. His coldly efficient mind had told him that I wouldn't wear my hat after I dropped into the ditch.

I stuffed some sand in a handkerchief, and made it look a little like the top of a man's head. I moved that slowly along the top of the little trench, and he fired.

I jumped up with the sound of the shot. He was reloading his gun, a mere jerking of a lever; but it gave me time for a snap shot.

The shot missed—for the simple reason that there wasn't enough target to shoot at at the distance. He'd carried a short-handled trowel with him, and he'd thrown up a little embankment of sand, and hollowed out a ditch.

I knew then I was up against a man who overlooked nothing. Those cold, scornful eyes, utterly emotionless, were windows for a brain that moved with ball-bearing efficiency.

I dropped back into the trench and looked for the handkerchief. It was filled with little holes. I knew that those holes had been made by spattering sand. The high-velocity bullet had hit close enough to its mark to send little gravel particles spattering up in a stinging shower.

It was good shooting. Probably Ortley, with that damned efficiency of his, had been practicing on his rifle shooting, waiting for the time which he felt might possibly come.

My respect for the man mounted as my hatred increased.

The rifle cracked again. I flattened in the trench. There sounded the unmistakable *thunk!* of a bullet plowing into solid meat. I looked at the girl anxiously. She was well down, and there was no sign of a hit.

The rifle cracked again. Once more there sounded the

impact of a high-powered bullet on something solid.

At the third crack I flung myself up from the trench, revolver ready for a snap shot. As before, I found my man was well covered. But I saw what he was doing. He was shooting our burros!

I dropped down and reloaded my revolver. There was only one thing left to do—charge and fight it out, gun against gun.

But the rifle didn't crack any more—not just then. The damned, efficient devil had figured out what I would do next, and was waiting for me, long-barreled rifle ready to claim an easy victim as I scrambled from the trench. After that, the girl would be easy.

"If anything happens to me," I warned her, "don't waste time being sentimental. Grab my gun and wait. Get him if you get a chance. If you don't get the chance —well, don't let him get you."

She nodded.

I didn't go into details. I knew the man by this time. A death of thirst in the desert is a horrible thing.

Minutes passed and there was no sound. Then there came the crack of the rifle. This time it was far to the right. I jumped up. I might as well have stayed where I was. He was out of revolver shot, anyway. And he was killing our burros with a methodical calmness, an unhurried efficiency that was like the man.

The girl didn't appreciate the situation for a minute.

"We've driven him off!" she said, and her voice was triumphant.

I started rolling up some food in a shoulder pack.

"Yes," I told her, "he's moved."

My words were punctuated by another shot. The last shot came a few minutes later. Every one of our burros was buzzard bait. And the desert seemed to reach out clutching fingers for us.

Ortley walked back toward his fort. He didn't even

look our way. That's how sure of himself and his strategy he was.

And he had good reason to be. Out there in the desert we were going to have to get the breaks if we won through. Ortley had burros and he had a high-powered rifle to protect the burros. We had nothing except provisions and water. Neither of those would last.

The desert became purple with a short twilight, and then darkness came like a cool mantle.

"How good are you at walking?" I asked the girl.

"Do we walk?"

"We do."

I rolled the shoulder pack as tight as I could get it, and took all the water I dared to carry. I made the woman travel light. We started out before it had been dark an hour.

Twenty miles is only a hop, skip, and a jump in an automobile. It's a fair ride on horseback. It's a good ride on a burro. On foot it isn't so bad if a man's accustomed to walking. But twenty miles in a burning desert with loose sand underfoot and a woman . . .

VI THE WEAPON OF DESERT KNOWLEDGE

We made the first five miles fairly easily. The girl was getting tired then. I was sweating under my shoulder pack. I gave her a little water and a ten-minute rest, and then we plugged on.

About one o'clock she asked me the question I'd been expecting to hear long before.

"Why are we running away?"

"Because Ortley holds all the trump cards. He's got a killing radius with a rifle that beats what we have with a revolver. He's got shade and shelter. He's got transportation. There's only one chance we've got. That's to beat him to water and then be able to wait him out."

"What do you mean by 'wait him out'?"

"I'll show you, when we get to water."

We plugged along for another hour. The girl stumbled once or twice. I made her take off her boots and looked at her feet. They were getting in bad shape. I had a little adhesive tape, and I bound them up as best I could. She lay flat on her back for fifteen minutes. I didn't dare to let her rest long. It was going to be a struggle.

I got her to her feet, and we plugged on. The shoulder pack was rubbing pretty badly. I'd had to take stuff that would carry and didn't have the chance to arrange it so it'd ride best. There were too many bulky objects, too little blanket.

Daylight saw us two miles from the water and the girl looked pretty white in the morning light. I began to drive her unmercifully. I taunted her with being a weakling. I told her Ortley was too smart for her, that she was too soft for the desert, that she was a drag. I told her lots of things that made me squirm as I said them, but it was the only way.

She didn't have spirit enough to reply. Her white face remained expressionless. Her calm eyes were paled with fatigue. Her feet moved as though her boots were made of lead.

And it began to get hot.

I'd gone strong on the water with her when I saw we could probably make it. We didn't really run out until the last mile.

A mile doesn't seem very far. But let me tell you that last mile was a torture, every step of it. The sun was beating down on us. The girl's feet were gone. I was carrying an awkward pack. We'd made twenty honest miles of sand and fine rock, twenty desert miles of up and down, and we'd crossed one ridge that went up two thousand feet above the rest of the desert, and it went up straight. The climb up that slope had been heartbreaking.

The girl's boots were typical department store boots of the type that are manufactured for women who want to look well in hiking clothes. They're all right for riding, but for walking they're a different thing. And a woman's feet aren't built for heavy boots.

I tried to do some more taping. But the skin had gone completely soft. It was like wet tissue paper. She was staggering and wincing, moaning, biting her lip, gasping irregular breaths.

We got to the water hole. She was all in.

I got some wet mud around the fevered feet. I soaked her wrists in cold water and I sopped her forehead. She rolled over and went to sleep. I took the things from the pack and buried the stuff that the sun would hurt. Then I sat there to fight flies and wait.

There was a little shade, some mesquite that wasn't very high or very thick. We had to keep moving around to follow that shade. The flies were bad, and it was one hot day.

She woke up around noon, so stiff she could hardly move. I fed her.

"I can never walk out of this desert," she said. "I'm not a quitter, but I just can't do it."

"I know it. I'm not asking you to—yet."

"How else could we get out?"

"Wait."

"Wait for what?"

"For about four or five days."

"Here?"

"Here."

"Why so long?"

"If it happens sooner we're licked."

"What happens?"

"Wait and see."

Five days passed, and I was afraid I'd guessed this Ortley wrong. But on the sixth day, just a little after sun-up, I saw the dots come straggling across the desert. Four burros and a man.

It was about time. The grub I'd taken hadn't been any more than enough. The flies and the heat and the continued inactivity had been awful. The girl had had plenty of water to drink and sop on her skin. I'd been afraid to get myself accustomed to too much water, so I'd kept on my regular desert ration, which was plenty short.

The burros speeded up as they neared the water.

"What now?" she asked. "He's still got the rifle."

I indicated the little trenches I'd dug.

"We can keep out of the line of his fire, no matter where he tries to shoot from."

"But he won't bother with us. He'll keep on going."

"Maybe."

"And our provisions are almost gone."

"It's a show-down now. Either we win or we lose. If we lose you've got to wait here while I walk to Randsburg and get some help. Those provisions will have to last you."

"How about you?"

"I won't bother with provisions. I'll carry water—if I have to go."

The black spots got nearer. We could see the long, dancing shadows cast by the early sun. I got up close to the little embankment I'd thrown up and got the girl placed where she'd be safe.

Ten minutes more and I could hear the crunch of their feet in the sand. When they were within about forty yards I slipped my forty-five forward and took a peek.

It was as I'd thought. Ortley had figured out what the

embankments meant. He was behind a burro, his rifle ready. At the flicker of motion I made when I raised up, he fired.

I dropped back and called to him.

"Better surrender, Ortley. You were so confident we'd left, and so damned greedy, that you waited until you'd milked the last ounce of gold from the claim, and that means you're short of water. We can hold the water hole."

His language was worse than strong. And I could hear the thick tone of his voice which told me what I'd surmised. He was out of water—had been for a few miles at least. Ortley was gold-mad, and he'd stayed on to work as much out of the claim as he could. The burros were weighted down with his plunder. He'd postponed the trip for water until the very last minute that he dared, knowing he wouldn't dare to return to the claim—not until he heard what had happened to us.

He walked around the water hole, shooting from time to time, trying to find a weak point in our defense. There wasn't any.

The burros got restive and tried to walk in. He tied them together and kept herding them out of range. I'd have shot his burros and left him in a trap, only we'd have been caught in the same trap.

Ortley had been a thinking machine, but he hadn't known the desert long enough. The desert gives its hoard to those who know her. In the desert, knowledge counts. Ortley didn't realize his position even now.

It was nearly noon before he knew what he was up against. He went almost delirious with rage. He would have charged the spring, only he knew it would be sure death. I'd have shown him no mercy, none whatever.

Finally he knew the alternative.

"Damn you! I'll win my way out. You can stay here and starve!"

I looked up after a while. He was plugging his way toward the next water, Bitter Springs. I sighed and smiled at the girl.

"Well, that's that."

"But he's gone with all the gold, and he has the burros and the grub—and everything."

I nodded.

"That's true. But he's cruel, this Ortley, and he's undoubtedly been cutting down on the water he's given his animals. You wait—and see what happens."

His first trouble came when he was less than a mile away. The thirsty burros, knowing they were being taken away from water, balked. He was cruel, this Ortley, and he got the train to moving again. It took work, and blows, and spurs, and cruelty.

I waited.

The burros became dots, finally vanished. They were making almost no time at all. The afternoon breeze sprang up. The long shadows marched across the desert.

There was the sound of hoofs, and here they came, four burros, on the trot, eager for water.

I caught them as they drank, filled up the water canteens.

"Let's go," I told the girl. "He may not be far behind."

As soon as the burros had plenty of water I took them off a couple of miles in the desert and let them feed a bit. Then I started them toward Randsburg.

We traveled until one o'clock. Then we made a short camp and were on our way again at daybreak.

"How about Ortley?"

"He'll either get back to the springs, in which event he'll be there, waiting for the sheriff—or I'll find him somewhere else, when I come back with a posse."

She didn't get it all figured out, but she didn't ask any questions, not after that.

We got to Randsburg, and I told my story. The packs of the burros were weighted down with gold. It was a blood-red gold, alluvial, in coarse chunks and colors that ran very thick and big. All the gold had the same reddish coating.

The sheriff came, and we started out.

We went to the water hole first, figuring Ortley would have found his way back there, and been trapped.

He wasn't there. So we started looking through binoculars at the horizon. We spotted the circling dots of buzzards and went to the point under which they circled.

I was glad the girl wasn't with me.

But I wished that expert doctor, who had testified that people dying of thirst didn't dig the flesh away from their fingers, had been there. The doctor's testimony had saved Ortley once. Now what was left of Ortley would have refuted the doctor.

He had been cruel. He had murdered. He had stolen the claim of a partner. But he had been punished. The desert is rather thorough in such matters, and it will be a long time before I forget the sight of those hands.

But sometimes I think the desert's cruelty is one of its best features. There's too much mercy in connection with man-made justice. After all, an immutable law that never varies is the one that gets the respect.

But that's the desert. It's a wonderful mother, and a cruel one. And the cruelty teaches self-reliance, and self-reliance is pretty nearly the object of life, after all.

But that's what makes the desert whisper to itself at night when the sand begins to blow; it's trying to pass on the stories of Ortley and his kind.

Every time I pillow my head on the sand, and listen to the little whispers that slither across the floor of the desert, I wonder how many more stories there are, stories like the story of the red gold, of Ortley, of the girl with the calm eyes, of the lunger who died of some mysterious cause.

There are lots of them, and the sand is trying to tell them, whispering the news to the cactus as it drifts by, telling the stories to the other sands. And then, finally, as the breeze freshens, the other sands stir to life and repeat the stories they have heard, until the desert becomes just a great bowl of whispers.

That's what the sand has to tell the sand as it drifts by. That's why the sand whispers seem more than sand whispers—just before you drop off to sleep of nights. The stars blaze steadily down, telling of faith, and of fair dealing, and of upright manhood. And the desert, by way of warning, whispers the stories of Ortley and his kind.

Carved in Sand

I TENDERFOOT CONTRAPTION

WHEN A MAN lives a great deal in the open, little things sometimes stick in his mind. That was the way with the remark the college professor made to me.

"Everything in nature," he said, "has two points of manifestation."

"Meaning positive and negative?" I asked him, just to let him know that he wasn't going to spring any theory on me that I couldn't, at least, talk about.

"Not exactly that," he said. "It's something a little more subtle."

I swept my hand in a half-circle, including in the gesture the sweep of sun-glittering sand and cacti-studded desert. "What would be the double manifestation of that?" I asked him.

"I don't know," he said. "I'm not enough of a desert man to know its manifestations. But you know it. If you'll only watch it, you'll find that it does have a dual manifestation."

It was only a little thing perhaps, but somehow it stuck in my mind; and it seemed that I'd found the answer in Pete Ayers. Pete was desert born and desert bred, and the shifting sands had got into his blood. He was as restless as a swirl of loose sand in the embrace of a desert wind.

Of course the desert leaves its mark on everybody who lives in it. Most of the men who have lived in the desert have gray eyes, firm lips, a slow, deliberate way of moving about that is deceptive to a man who doesn't know the breed. When occasion requires they are as fast as greased lightning, and as deadly as a cornered lion. Ayers was different. He was just a happy-go-lucky kid who was forever rolling into mischief and stumbling out. He was always in trouble, always getting out of it by some fluke.

Now he lay stretched out beside me on the edge of the rim rock, the hot desert sun beating down on our backs. He handed me the binoculars.

"Brother," he said, "watch where the bullet strikes. I'm betting even money that I don't miss him by more than two inches, and I'll bet on a direct hit for reasonable odds."

That was the way with Pete; always making a bet, always willing to wager his shirt on the outcome of whatever he happened to be doing.

"Wait a minute, Pete," I said as he cocked the rifle. "Let's make certain that it's a coyote. He's acting sort of funny for a coyote."

"He's going to act a lot funnier," said Pete as he nestled his cheek against the stock of the rifle, "in just about one minute."

I focused the binoculars on the slope across the long dry cañon. Ordinarily I don't go in much for binoculars in the desert, because a desert man cannot afford to be cluttered up with a lot of weight. The tenderfoot always carries a camera, binoculars, hunting knife, and compass. They're things that are all right in their way, but the real desert man starts out with a six-gun, a canteen, a pocket knife, a box of matches and a sack of tobacco. That's about all he needs.

The binoculars were good ones that Pete had won from a tenderfoot in a poker game the night before. They

brought up the opposite slope of the cañon with a clear-
ness that made the black shadows transparent.

"Hold everything, Pete!" I said. "It's a police dog!"

I heard Pete's grunt of incredulity, but he lowered the
rifle and turned startled blue eyes to me.

"Hell," he said, "you're crazy! There aren't any police
dogs out here. Them's tenderfoot binoculars and there's
mebbe a sort of tenderfoot influence about 'em."

"Take a look yourself," I said.

Pete put down the rifle and reached for the binoculars.
He focused them to his eyes, and then gave a low whistle.

"Hell!" he said. "And I'll bet I'd have hit him!"

I said nothing. We watched the animal for several
seconds.

"What the hell's he doing here?" asked Pete.

I didn't know any more than he did—not as much, in
fact, so I couldn't say anything. We lay there in silence,
with the desert sun beating down on the glittering expanse of waste, making the black rim rock on the other
side of the cañon twist and writhe in the heat waves.

After a while Pete passed the binoculars across to me.
I found the dog again, steadied my elbows on the hot
rock, and watched closely.

"He's running around in little circles, looking for a
scent of some kind," I said. "Now it looks as though he's
found it. He runs along straight for ten or fifteen yards,
then stops and circles, and then starts going straight. Now,
he's found what he wants. He's running close to the
ground—and making time."

"Hell," said Pete drily, "you don't need to tell me
everything he's doin', I got eyes, even if they don't mag-
nify eight diameters."

The police dog fascinated me. I couldn't understand
what he was doing out here in the desert. I kept the
binoculars on him and watched him as he angled down

the slope. He was running rapidly now, wagging his tail as he ran, and apparently following the scent without difficulty. He ran down around the edge of the slope, rounded an outcropping of rock, crossed the cañon, and vanished behind a ledge of the rim rock on our side of the cañon.

"Well," said Pete, "the show's over."

"No," I told him, "I'm going to find out what that dog's doing out here."

"That's just the way with you," he said. "Filled full of curiosity."

But I could see from the light in his blue eyes that he was curious, and that he also favored giving the dog a break. A police dog can't live long in the desert. A coyote can get by nicely, but not a dog, no matter how big or how strong he is. It's a question of generations of training, and the coyote has something that no dog has: a certain toughness that enables him to get by.

We moved along the rim rock. I was holding the binoculars by the strap when we reached the next little peak from which we could look down in the cañon.

Pete's exclamation at my elbow showed me that he had seen the camp. I raised the binoculars, and through them saw an automobile, rather battered and dilapidated; a white tent; a canteen; a cot; a box of provisions. Then I saw a woman's bare arm reach out around the edge of the tent and pick something from the box.

"Looks like a woman down there," I said.

"What the devil would anybody want to camp in that cañon for?" asked Pete.

"Prospector maybe," I told him.

"A woman prospector?" he asked.

"Maybe. She had a white arm. Looked like she was city-bred."

"Just the arm showed?" asked Pete.

"That was all," I said.

"All right," he said. "Keep the binoculars then."

Suddenly the woman came out from around the edge of the tent. I could see at once that she was city-bred. The cut of her clothes, the delicacy of her complexion, the angry red sunburn on the backs of her forearms, all told the story. But the thing that interested me and held me breathlessly watching was the expression on her face. It was an expression of sheer terror.

The police dog had evidently been out with her and had lost her. He had been smelling along the dry sand of the desert, trying to pick up her trail; and now he was trotting along at her side, wagging his tail. Yet the woman's face was twisted and distorted with terror.

She was carrying something in her hand, and she ran twenty or thirty yards back up the slope to the roots of a sage brush and started digging with her left hand. Her right hand pushed something into the little hole, and then she patted the sand over it, got to her feet, and walked back toward the camp.

I handed the binoculars to Pete, and as my eyes focused on the camp I saw two dots moving from around the slope of the cañon. I saw the police dog grow rigid, and after a few seconds I could hear the sound of his bark.

"Hell," said Pete, "she looks scared."

"She is," I said. "Look at the two dots coming around the slope there, about half a mile down the cañon, Pete."

He raised the glasses and grunted as his eyes took in the two dots. "Two men," he said, "with rifles and six-guns. They've got cartridges in the belts of the six-guns, and they look as though they were getting ready to shoot."

"Are they coming toward the camp?" I asked.

"Toward the camp," he said. "Hell, Bob, after this I think I'm going to carry these tenderfoot contraptions all the time. In the meantime, I'm going down and cut in on that deal."

"Count me in," I told him.

He snapped the binoculars back into the case.

"Going back to get the burros?" I asked him.

"They'll wait," he told me. "Let's go."

The rim rock was a good ten feet in a straight drop. Then there was some loose sand, and the sheer slope of the side of the cañon.

Pete went over the rim rock without hesitation, lit in the sand, threw up a flurry of dust, made two jumps, and started sliding down the ridge. I didn't make quite so clean a leap, and I felt the impact as I struck the sand. My feet went out from under me, I rolled over a couple of times, got to my feet, and started sprinting down the slope, digging my heels into the soil, grabbing at the little clumps of sagebrush and taking long jumps to avoid the patches of rock.

Pete kept gaining on me. I don't know why he didn't go down head over heels, but he managed to bound down as lightly as a mountain goat.

II MANNERS IN THE DESERT

Apparently the girl didn't see or hear us. She was looking at two men who were approaching.

The police dog heard us, however, and whirled, starting to bark. With that the woman turned and saw us, of course. She called the dog back and stood staring at us, and once more I caught the expression of terror on her face.

Pete's bronze hand went to his sombrero, swept it off in a bow, and he said, "Pardon me, ma'am, we just dropped in."

There was a ghost of a smile on her face, but it still held that expression of terror.

"It was almost a drop," she said, looking back up the slope where the dust clouds were still drifting about in the hot sun. "Who are you and what do you want?"

Pete jerked his head toward the direction of the approaching figures. "Just thought," he said, "that we'd see if you needed any assistance."

I saw her mouth tighten. "No," she said, "you can't be of any assistance to me."

I didn't beat about the bush at all. "Do you know the men who are coming?" I asked.

"I think so," she said.

"What do they want?" I asked.

"Me," she said.

I waited for an explanation, but there wasn't any. The dog was growling in his throat, but he was lying on the ground where she had ordered him to stay, his yellow eyes glinting from us to the men who were coming up the dry wash.

The two men came up with the tense, watchful attitude of men who are expecting to engage in gun play at almost any minute. They looked us over and they looked the girl over. One of them stepped off to one side and said to the girl, "You're Margaret Blake?"

She nodded her head.

"You know who we are and why we are here?" he said.

She said nothing.

He looked from her over to us. "Who are these men?" he asked.

"I don't know," she said.

The man shifted his attention to Pete. "What's your connection with this?" he asked.

Pete grinned at him, a cold, frosty grin. "Don't you know who I am?" he asked.

"No," said the other man, his eyes narrowing, "who are you?"

"I'm the guy," said Pete, "who is going to see that the young woman here gets a square deal."

"This woman," said the man, "is under arrest."

"Arrest for what?" asked Pete.

"As an accessory," said the man.

"To what?"

"Murder."

Pete laughed. "She don't look like she'd be good at murder," he said.

"You can't always tell by looks," said one of the men. "Now, you two fellows get started out of here. I don't like the way you horned in on this party."

"Don't you, now?" said Pete.

The other man said in a low voice, "Make them give up their guns, Charlie. We can't let them go out in the desert with their guns. They might ambush us."

"Yes," said Charlie. "You fellows will have to leave your guns here."

"Now *I'll* tell one," I told him.

I saw grinning devils appear at the corners of Pete's mouth, caught the glint of his blue eyes as he reached slowly to his gun, pulled it out of the holster and looked at it almost meditatively.

"You don't want me to give *this* gun up?" he asked.

"That's what we want," said Charlie.

"This gun," said Pete, "is a funny gun. It goes off accidentally, every once in a while."

"Pete!" I cautioned him.

The warning came too late. There was a spurt of flame from Pete's gun. I heard the impact of the heavy bullet as it struck the stock of the rifle in the hands of the man nearest Pete.

There was nothing to do but back his play, and so I

made what speed I could snaking my six-gun from its holster.

The two men were taken completely by surprise. They had thought that their rifles were sufficient to command the situation. As a matter of fact, at close quarters a rifle is very likely to prove a cumbersome weapon, particularly when a man tries to take in too much territory with it.

"Drop it!" I told the man.

His eyes looked into the barrel of my Colt, and there was a minute when I didn't know exactly what was going to happen. Then the gun thudded to the sand. The bullet had jerked the other's gun from his grasp.

"All right, Bob," said Pete, "they'll get their hands in the air, and you can unbuckle the belts and let their six-guns slip off."

"First, let's make sure they've got their hands in the air," I told him.

Two pairs of hands came up slowly.

"You boys are making the mistake of your lives," said Charlie. "You're going to find yourselves in the pen for this."

"Please don't," the girl pled with us. "I'll go with them. It's inevitable."

"No," said Pete, "I don't like their manners—and I always play my hunches."

I unbuckled the guns, let them drop to the ground.

"We're officers," Charlie started to explain, "and you—"

"Sure," said Pete. "I knew you were officers as soon as I saw you. You've got that look about you—and your manners are so rotten. Now turn around and start walking back the way you came. I suppose you've got an automobile staked out around the edge of the slope, haven't you?"

They didn't say anything.

Pete shook his head. "Rotten manners," he said. "You don't answer courteous questions."

"Please!" said the girl. "Don't do this for me. He's right in what he says. You're going to get into serious trouble."

"Miss," said Pete, "getting into serious trouble is something that I'm accustomed to. I get into a new kind of trouble every day. Come on you two, let's march."

We turned them around, but it took a prod with the muzzle of my six-gun to get Charlie started. After they had started they moved along doggedly and steadily.

We rounded the slope and found their car parked in a little draw. Pete's gun pointed the road to town.

"I'm going to be standing here," he said, "until that car is just a little black spot in the middle of a dust cloud, 'way over on the desert there. And if you should hesitate or turn around and start back, something tells me that you'll have tire trouble right away."

The men didn't say a word. They climbed into the automobile. The starting motor whirred, the engine responded, and the car crept along the sandy wash, struck the harder road, and rattled into speed. Pete and I stood there until the machine had vanished in the distance, leaving behind it nothing but a wisp of dust.

Pete looked at me and grinned. "Sore, Bob?" he asked.

"No," I told him. "I had to back your play, but I wish you'd use a little discretion sometimes."

"Discretion, hell!" he said. "There's no fun in discretion. Let's go back and talk with the woman. You can figure it out for yourself, Bob. She's okay. Those men were on the wrong track, that's all."

I wasn't so certain, but I holstered my weapon. We started trudging back through the sand. When we rounded the edge of the slope and could look up the cañon, I could see dust settling in the afternoon sunlight.

"Two dust clouds," I told him grimly.

Sure enough, the camp was still there; but the automobile, the young woman, and the police dog had gone.

Pete looked at me, and his face was ludicrous in its crestfallen surprise. "Hell!" he said.

"It's going to take them about two hours to get to town," I said. "Then they'll get some more guns, a couple of others to help them, and start back. The next question is, where can we be in two hours?"

Pete's eyes started to twinkle once more. "I know a swell bunch of country where there's an old cabin," he said, "and I don't think the burros would leave much of a trail getting up there."

"How far can we be on that trail in two hours?" I wanted to know.

"We can be pretty near there."

"Okay," I told him. "Let's go."

We climbed back up to the burros, got the string lined up, and started plodding up the slope toward the old cabin that Pete knew about.

After about an hour the country changed, and we began to run into stunted cedar, glimpsing pines up on the high slopes of the mountain country beyond. Another half-hour, and we were well up in the mountains, from where we could look back over the desert.

I paused and pointed back toward the place where I knew the little desert town was situated. "Pete," I said, "you've got those binoculars. Take a look and see if you can see anything that looks like pursuit."

He was focusing the binoculars on the road when I heard a peculiar throbbing sound which grew in volume. I raised my eyes and picked out a little speck against the blue sky—a speck that might have been a buzzard, except that it was moving forward across the sky with steady purpose.

I tapped Pete on the shoulder and pointed with my finger. He raised the binoculars, looked for a minute, and then twisted his face into a grimace.

"They'll pick her up with that," I said, "before she's gone thirty miles."

"There's lots of places she could go inside of thirty miles," Pete said.

"Not with that automobile," I told him, "and not in this country."

Pete shrugged his shoulders. "How the hell did we know they were going to get an airplane to chase her with?"

"How the hell did I know that you were going to start gun play?" I told him, with some irritation in my voice.

"You should have been able to tell that," said Pete, "by looking at the woman. She was too pretty."

I sighed. "Well," I told him, "I always wanted to know what it felt like to be a fugitive from justice."

"Hell!" said Pete from the depths of his experience. "There ain't no novelty to it—not after the first time or two. It feels just like anything else."

I didn't say anything more. I merely watched the airplane as it diminished in the distance. I was still looking at it when I saw two other planes coming from the west. The plane I had seen first tilted from side to side, making signaling motions, and the other two planes swung in behind it. I focused the binoculars on them and saw them fly in formation, until suddenly they started down toward the desert.

The sun was just setting. The valley was filled with deep purple shadows. In the high places was the hush of coming twilight.

"What did you see?" asked Pete.

"Two more planes," I told him, snapping the binoculars into the leather case.

Pete grinned at me. "That," he said, "isn't going to keep us from eating, is it?"

"Not this meal," I told him, "but I don't know about the next."

III ACCESSORIES TO THE CRIME

Pete had his blankets spread out on the other side of a little ridge. I was careful not to disturb him as I got up and sat there in the moonlight, looking down on the dark mystery of the shadow-filled valleys below. It was cold up here, but I had a blanket wrapped around me, Indian fashion.

Down below, as far as the eye could reach, stretched the desert; a great waste of level spaces, broken by jagged mountain spurs—mountains that were still a part of the desert, dry, arid, covered with juniper, stunted cedar, and an occasional pine. There were no tumbling streams, no dense underbrush—just barren rock and dry trees that rustled in the wind which was blowing from the desert.

Looking down into the black splotches of darkness in the valleys, I knew what was going on in the desert. The wind was stirring the sand into soft whispers, typifying the restlessness of the desert. For the desert is ever restless, ever changing. Its moods change as frequently as the appearance of the desert mountains is changed by sunlight and shadow.

Even up here in this cold, high place the desert seemed to be whispering its mysterious messages; the noise made by drifting sand as it scours against the soft desert rocks, carving them into weird structures, polishing, cutting, drifting, changing, ever changing.

I sat there for three or four hours, watching the moon climb over the eastern rim of the mountains, watching the black pools of mysterious shadow in the cañons gradually recede until the golden surface of the desert glinted up at me from below. Several times I listened to hear Pete's snores, but no sound came from his direction.

After a while I felt somewhat relaxed, and rolled back into my blankets, where it was warmer. In fifteen or twenty minutes I began to feel drowsy, and drifted off to sleep. After all, as Pete had remarked, being a fugitive from justice didn't feel particularly unique, once one had become accustomed to it.

I woke early in the morning and watched the east taking on a brassy hue. It was still and cold. There was not a sound, not a breath. The stars, which had blazed steadily during the night, had now receded to mere needle points of light; and soon they became invisible.

I kicked back the blankets, put on my boots and leather jacket, stamped my feet to get the circulation in them, and walked around the little ledge, to the place where Pete had spread his blankets. The blankets were there, but Pete wasn't.

I looked over the ground, and felt of the blankets. There was frost on the inside of them, where they had been turned back when Pete slipped out. I studied the tracks as well as I could, and then I knew that Pete had slipped one over on me. He had pulled out long before I had got up to watch the moonlight.

Fifty yards from camp I found a piece of paper stuck on a bush. When he had to be, Pete was glib with his tongue, and glib with a pencil if he couldn't talk. He was one of those fellows who expressed himself well.

I unfolded the note and read:

Dear Bob:

I got you into this, and there's no reason why I shouldn't take the blame. You didn't do anything except follow my lead. I don't know how serious it is, but I'm going to find out. You sit tight until I come back.

(Signed)   *Pete*

I should have known that Pete would have done something like that, and I felt irritated that I hadn't guessed it in advance and guarded against it.

It was all right for Pete to claim that I had been blameless and that he was going to take the responsibility. I probably wouldn't have started things if Pete hadn't been there—and then again I might have. But I didn't need a nurse or a guardian, and when I pulled a gun on an officer it was my own free and voluntary act. I didn't like the way Pete was trying to shield me, as though I were a child, instead of a man ten years his senior.

I got some firewood together, got the coffee to boiling, and sat crouched by the fire, warming my hands and waiting for a while before I drank the coffee, hoping that Pete would show up. When he didn't show up, I drank a couple of cups of coffee, but kept the pot hot so that he could have some when he came in.

The sun climbed slowly up the blue-black of the desert sky, and there was still no sign of Pete. I went out on a projecting rock where I could look down into the valley, and kept watch on what was going on. Toward ten o'clock I heard the sound of automobiles, and I could make them out through the glasses, two carloads of men jolting their way along the floor of the valley.

An hour later, I heard them coming back; and the glasses showed me that which I had dreaded to see, yet expected. In the rear seat of the first automobile was a man and a woman. At that distance I couldn't make out their features, but I didn't have much doubt who they were.

I waited until the machines had gone the length of the valley and turned through the pass into the level desert, then I threw packs on the burros and started back down the mountain. Pete knew exactly where I had been camped, and he also knew that I had the binoculars. I figured that he probably would have a chance to use his pencil once more.

I hit the trail of the automobiles and started following along, keeping my eyes pretty much on the ground. Within half a mile I found what I was looking for, a folded piece of paper lying by the side of the road, catching the glint of the hot desert sun. I unfolded the paper. It was a note from Pete, all right. He hadn't put any heading on it at all, so that if the officers discovered it, it wouldn't give them any clew which would lead to me. The note read simply:

> *They caught me. I put up a fight, but they got me, and I guess they got me dead to rights. The woman is the daughter of Sam Blake. Blake killed a prospector named Skinner who had a cabin over in Sidewinder Cañon. They jailed him, and the woman helped him escape. They caught him again and are holding her as an accessory. I don't know what they're going to put against me. I told them you didn't know anything about it and had backed my play with an empty gun. I don't think they're going to look for you.*

I knew Bob Skinner, and I also knew the place over in Sidewinder Cañon. It was fifteen or twenty miles over the mountains.

There was nothing much to be done except trail along behind the automobiles, so I plugged along doggedly through the desert sunshine. All the time, I kept thinking about the stuff the woman had buried at the foot of the sagebrush when she saw the two men coming from the direction of the road. When I got near that first camp of hers, I made a detour and went into it. The officers had been all through it, probably looking for evidence.

I climbed back into the shade cast by a spur of rock,

and got out the tenderfoot's binoculars again. When I was sure that I had the desert all to myself, I went over to the clump of sagebrush and dug in the sand.

I found a package done up in a newspaper. The package had hacksaw blades and a gun. The hacksaw blades had been used, and I figured that was how Sam Blake had managed to slip out of jail. As far as I could tell, the gun hadn't been fired.

It was a .45 single-action Colt, and it had been carried around quite a bit in a holster.

I looked at the newspaper. It was an extra edition, hurriedly thrown together; one of those little hand-printed efforts put out in small desert towns, usually once a week or once every two weeks.

Ordinarily they contained nothing more exciting than a chronicle of the comings and goings of people who live in a small community.

But this paper was different. Across the top, in big blotchy headlines, black type announced:

BLAKE BREAKS JAIL

Down below:

OFFICERS SUSPECT WOMAN ACCOMPLICE

I sat down on my heels in the sand, and read everything that the paper contained. It was an account of the jail break, which didn't interest me particularly, and an account of the crime, which interested me more.

Sam Blake charged that Bob Skinner had jumped a claim which Blake had staked, stripping the claim of the valuable gold that was in a pocket and then skipping out.

I knew Skinner. He was the sort of customer who would be likely to do that very thing. Blake asserted that Skinner had picked up more than five thousand dollars in gold from the pocket, and so Blake had taken his gun and gone down into Sidewinder Cañon.

A lunger by the name of Ernest Peterman had seen him going down toward Skinner's cabin. Peterman had a little cabin up on the summit of a ridge on the east side of Sidewinder Cañon. He'd seen Blake coming along the trail which led to the cañon, and had recognized him. He'd watched him go down to Skinner's cabin. It had been about two-thirty in the afternoon, and Peterman said he knew that Skinner was alive at the time because there was a lot of smoke coming out of the chimney of Skinner's shack. He hadn't paid any particular attention to it, however; he'd just given the scene a casual glance and then gone out to take his afternoon sun bath.

It happened that a ranger had dropped in to see Skinner sometime the next day. He'd found Skinner dead, with a bullet hole in his forehead and a knife wound in his heart. He'd found horse tracks in the trail, and had been able to mark them because of a broken shoe on the right hind foot. He'd trailed the horse into the little settlement, had found it, identified it as belonging to Blake, and had finally forced Blake to admit that he'd been to the cabin.

At first Blake denied it. Later on, he admitted that he'd gone down to have a settlement with Skinner, but he claimed that Skinner was dead when he got there. Things looked black for him because he hadn't reported the murder, and because at first he'd denied that he'd gone down to see Skinner at all. But the thing that clinched the case against him was the testimony of the lunger. If smoke had been coming out of the chimney at the time Blake hit the shack, it was a cinch Skinner had been alive then. Nobody doubted the good faith of the lunger.

I read the paper and frowned. I could see that Pete Ayers had acted on impulse, and the impulse had led him into trouble. We were going to be hooked as accessories, along with the girl. The authorities didn't like the idea

of Blake sawing the bars of the jail window and slipping
out into the night.

I led the burros over to a nearby spring, saw that they
had water, and then started on the long journey over the
mountains to Sidewinder Cañon. I didn't dare to strike
the main trails. On the other hand, with burros I could
keep moving over the desert mountains, particularly after
the moon came up.

IV THE DESERT WHISPERS

It was well past daylight when I came out of the jagged
mountain formation on the west and into Sidewinder
Cañon. I could look down the twisting cañon and see the
roof of the prospector's shack. I staked out the burros,
and went down on foot.

I could see where the officers and the curious ones
had been tramping around the shack. It sat out on a little
sandy plateau, and there had been a desert wind in the
night which had wiped out most of the tracks; yet they
showed as confused indentations in the sand.

It looked as though at least ten or a dozen people had
milled around the shack, tracking down the ground.

I went into the cabin. The door was open, of course,
as is customary in mountain or desert cabins. There was
the damp, musty smell of places which are shaded from
the purifying effect of direct sunlight. There was also
another musty smell which was more ominous and unforgettable; the smell of death.

I found the bed where Skinner had been sleeping. I
found red stains, dry and crusted, on the blankets; stains
also on the floor. Lazy flies buzzed in circles over the red
stains. It was not a pleasant place to be.

I made but a casual inspection. I knew that others had been there before, and that every inch of the cabin had been searched. Doubtless some of the searchers had been desert men.

I walked out into the sunlight and took a great breath of fresh air, looking up into the clear blue of the cloudless sky, then over at the glittering expanse of jagged, barren ranges which hemmed in the cañon. Everything was still and silent.

Far up in the heavens a black dot marked a circling buzzard.

I started to look around.

It was ten minutes later that I saw something I couldn't explain. That was a fresh break in the little corral back of the house. It was a crazy structure of weatherbeaten lumber, held together by rusted nails and supported by posts set into the soft sand at various angles. It was the place where Bob Skinner had kept his prospecting burros; and I could see that a horse had been in the corral recently, and it looked to me as though the break in the corral had been done recently. In one place a board had been splintered, and the splinters hadn't as yet become dulled by the desert sunlight. The clean board showed out from beneath its weatherbeaten veneer.

I looked over the stretch of sand around the corral. Useless to look for tracks there. The wind had leveled the sand out and made it into miniature drifts. It was right in line with the opening of a little cañon, down which the night wind would sweep with concentrated force.

I rolled a cigarette and sat looking at that break in the corral fence. After a while I started up the cañon. By the time I had gone a hundred yards I came to a little sheltered place, where there was some soft sand that hadn't been blown by the wind. I saw the tracks of a horse, and to one side the print of a booted foot.

The sun was climbing higher now, and the walls of the little cañon began to radiate heat. I plugged my way along over the rocks, searching for the faintest sign of tracks. A little later on I found more tracks. Then I struck a little trail that ran along the side of the cañon, and in this trail it was easy to follow the tracks. They were the tracks of a horse, and behind the horse, the tracks of a man.

I worked along the little dry cañon, and struck a level place. The horse was running here, and the tracks of the man were heavy on the toes and lighter on the heels.

After a while I got into country that didn't have much sand, but I could follow the tracks better because there hadn't been anything to drift with the desert night wind. I saw the tracks of the horse climb up a ridge, and I followed them.

Near the top of the ridge I struck horse tracks again, and farther on I struck horse tracks and no man tracks. I followed the horse tracks off and on for three or four hundred yards, looking for man tracks. There weren't any.

I went back and tried to pick up the man tracks. I couldn't find them again. They had gone to the top of the ridge and then vanished.

I sat down on my heels, rolled another cigarette, and thought for a while.

There was a spring down the ridge, and three or four miles over toward the head of Sidewinder Cañon. It wasn't a particularly good spring—just a trickle of brackish water, thick with alkali—but it was a spring just the same. I started working down toward that spring.

I didn't see any man tracks until I was within fifty yards of the spring; then I picked up the tracks of booted feet again. As nearly as I could tell, they were the same tracks that I had seen following along behind the horse tracks.

I searched around the spring, and found horse tracks. These didn't look like the same horse tracks that I had seen earlier in the day. They were the tracks of a bigger horse, and they seemed to be fresher. I went over to the trail which led into the spring, and I could see where the horse had come in along this trail and gone out along it.

I kept poking along, looking in the sagebrush, and finally I found a hole dug in the side of the mountain. It was about a foot deep by two feet long. I poked around in the hole. It wasn't a hole that had been dug with a shovel, but something that had been scooped in the side of the mountain, and half filled in with slag from the side of the bank above. There wasn't anything in the hole.

I went down and followed the tracks of the horse. They went down the trail, evenly spaced and at regular intervals.

I turned back from that trail and went back up the ridges the way I had come into the spring. It was hot now, and the sun was beating down with steady, eye-dazzling fury.

I managed to get back up to the last place where I had found the horse tracks, and started tracking the horse. That was comparatively easy. The horse had worked over toward the west and north, following down a ridge which wasn't quite so rocky, and on which there was a more dusty soil to hold the tracks.

I knew that my burros were trained in the ways of the desert and could shift for themselves until I got back; but I was in need of food, and the inside of my mouth felt raw from drinking the alkali water at the little spring. Nevertheless I kept pushing on, working against time, and at length I found where the horse had started wandering back and forth from a direct line, as though looking for something to graze on.

I followed the tracks until it got dark, and then I

built a little fire and huddled over it, keeping warm until
the moon came up. Then I began my tracking once more.
It was slow work, but I took no chances of getting off the
trail. I just worked slowly along the trail, following it
along the sides of the ridges; and finally I came to something black lying on the ground.

I saw that it was a saddle, and feeling the tie in the
latigo, I could tell that the saddle had been bucked off.
The horn was smashed, and there were places where the
iron hoofs had cut the leather of the saddle. The horse
had evidently bucked and twisted, and had walked out
from under the saddle. The blankets were off to one side.
Rocks were pushed loose from the indentations in the
earth which had held them, as though the horse had been
standing on his head and striking out with all four feet.

I marked the place where the saddle was, and kept on
working down the slope.

It was still dark when I heard a horse whinny.

I called to him. Then I heard his shod feet ringing on
the rocks as he came up to me. He was glad to see me.
Right then, a man represented food and water to him,
and he was eager for human companionship. There wasn't
any rope around his neck, but I didn't need any. I twisted
my fingers in his mane, and he followed along with me
like a dog. When I came back to the place where the
saddle lay, I got it back on him, and climbed into it.

He had lost his bridle, but I cut off the strings from
the saddle, roped them together and made a rough hack-
amore.

The horse was weak, thirsty and tired; but he was
glad to yield to human direction once more, and he carried me back over the ridges.

It was two hours past daylight when I came to the
spring, where the horse drank greedily. I let him rest for
half or three quarters of an hour, and gave him a chance
to browse on some of the greenery which grew around

the edges of the water. Then I sent him down the trail and found my burros, standing with full stomachs and closed eyes, their long ears drooping forward.

I got a rope from my pack, slipped it around the neck of the horse, and started along the trail which led up the east slope of the mountains on the side of the cañon. When I got to the top I poked around, looking for a camp, and after a while I saw the glint of the sun on something white. A man rolled over in the sunlight, pulled a blanket around his nude figure, and got to his feet. He stood grinning at me sheepishly.

I rode over to him. "You're Ernest Peterman?" I asked.

He nodded. He was getting back his health there in the high places of the desert, I knew. That much could be seen in the bronzed skin, the clear eye, and the poise of his head.

Man has devised many different methods for combating various ills, but he has never yet devised anything which is superior to the healing hand of nature in the desert. Let a man get into the high places of the dry desert atmosphere, where the sun beats down from a cloudless sky; let him live a simple life, bathing in sunshine, and resting with the cold night air fresh in his nostrils, and there is nothing which is incurable.

"I wanted you to take a little ride with me," I told him.

"How far?" he asked.

"Just up to the top of the ridge."

"All right. In an hour or so?"

"No," I told him. "Now. I want to get there about a certain time in the afternoon."

"What time?" he asked.

"The same time that you saw Sam Blake go down into Sidewinder Cañon," I told him.

He shrugged his shoulders and shook his head, as

though trying to shake loose some disagreeable memory.

"I didn't want to do it," he said.

"Do what?" I asked.

"Testify," he told me.

"I didn't say you did."

"I know," he said. "It isn't that. It's just the thoughts that have been worrying me lately. Have you seen his daughter?"

I nodded.

"A wonderful girl," he said. "I don't think her father could be a murderer."

"He went down there with a gun, didn't he?" I asked.

"Yes."

"You don't suppose he just went down there to pay a social call, do you?"

"I don't know. He'd been robbed. Everybody seems to think that Skinner really robbed him."

"Did you know Skinner at all well?" I asked.

He shook his head.

"Ever get up to the top of the ridge much?"

"I've been up there once or twice in the morning."

"How did you happen to be up there on that particular afternoon?"

"I don't know. I was restless, and I just started walking up there. It was a hot day. I took it easy."

"And the shadows were just beginning to form on the western rim of the mountains?" I asked.

He nodded.

"And you could look down on Skinner's little shack?"

He nodded again.

"All right," I said, "I'd like to have you take a ride up there with me."

I let him ride the horse, and he seemed to feel a lot easier when I had a rope around the horse's neck, leading him. I took it that Peterman was pretty much of a tenderfoot in the desert.

"How did you happen to come to the desert country?" I asked him.

"I've tried everything else."

"Are you afraid of it?"

"Yes," he said, "I was dreadfully afraid at first. And then I got so I wasn't afraid."

"How did that happen?" I wanted to know. "Usually when a man sees the desert he either loves it or he hates it. If he hates it his hatred is founded on fear."

"I know," he said. "I hated it at first, and I hated it because I was afraid of it. I'm willing to admit it."

"What changed you?"

"You'd laugh if I told you," he said.

I looked at him, at the bronzed skin, the clear eye, the steady poise of the head, and I smiled. "Perhaps," I said, "I wouldn't laugh."

"It was the whispers," he said. "The whispers at night."

"You mean the sand whispers?" I asked.

He nodded. "There was something reassuring about them," he said. "At first they frightened me. It seemed as though voices were whispering at me; and then, gradually, I began to see that this was the desert, trying to talk; that it was whispering words of reassurance."

I nodded, and we didn't say anything more until we got to the summit of the ridge. I looked over the ridge, and checked Peterman as he started to look over.

"Not yet," I said. "Wait about fifteen minutes."

He sat and looked at me as though he thought I might be a little bit off in my upper story. But already the desert had begun to put its mark upon him; and so he didn't say anything, merely watched me as I smoked a cigarette.

When I had finished two cigarettes, I nodded my head.

"All right," I said. "Now look over."

He got up and looked over the top of the ridge. He

looked around for a moment and said, "I don't see anything."

"Look down at Skinner's cabin."

He looked down, and all of a sudden I heard him give
an exclamation, his eyes widening in surprise.

I unstrapped the binoculars and handed them to him.
"All right," I said, "take another look."

V MAKE WAY FOR A WITNESS

Sun beat down upon the little desert town with its dusty
main street and its unpainted board structures squatting
in the gray desert which lined either side of the road. A
big pile of tin cans marked the two ends of the main
street, and these piled-up tin cans were bordered by a
nondescript collection of junk which spread out over the
desert, interspersed with clumps of sagebrush.

There were occasional automobiles on the street;
automobiles, for the most part, of an ancient vintage,
innocent of finish and as weatherbeaten and dust-covered
as the board structures themselves. There were also horses
tied to the hitching rack in front of the general merchandise store, and a couple of sleepy burros rested on three
legs at a time, casting black shadows on a dusty street.

We rode toward the building where the preliminary
hearing was being held. A crowd of people were jammed
into the little structure, despite the intense sunlight which
beat down upon the roof. Other people crowded around
the outside of the building, blocking the windows, cran-
ing their necks to listen. Out in the street little groups,
recognizing the futility of trying to hear what was going
on inside, formed gabbing centers of gossip to discuss the
case.

I climbed from the saddle burro and dropped the rope

reins over his head. "Make way for a witness," I said.

Men looked around at men. "Hell! It's Bob Zane," someone said. "Make way, you fellows, here comes Bob Zane."

I pushed my way into the courtroom. The tenderfoot clung to my blue shirt. He was sort of frightened and subdued. The atmosphere of the place reeked with the odor of packed bodies and many breaths. People stared at us with cold, curious eyes.

Abruptly, the little space around the judge's desk opened ahead of us, and the two officers stared with startled eyes into my face. One of them went for his gun.

"There he is now!" shouted Charlie, the deputy.

"Order in the courtroom!" yelled a wizened justice of the peace, whose white goatee quavered with indignation.

The officer pulled out the gun and swung it in my direction. "The man who was the accomplice of Pete Ayers, one of the defendants in this case," he shouted.

The judge banged on the desk. "Order in the court! Order in the court! Order in the court!" he screamed in a high piping voice.

I squared myself and planted my feet, conscious of the business end of the gun that was trained at my middle.

"Just a minute," I said. "I came to surrender myself and demand an immediate hearing. I'm charged with being an accessory in a murder case. I can't be an accessory unless there's been a murder, and unless the person I aided is guilty. I've got a witness with me who wants to change his testimony."

I half turned, and pushed forward the tenderfoot.

Peterman looked about him, gulped and nodded.

"You can't interrupt proceedings this way!" piped the judge.

"Don't you want to hear the evidence?" I asked.

"Of course," he said, "but you aren't a witness."

I held up my right hand and moved a step forward, holding him with my eyes. "All right," I said, "swear me in."

He hesitated a moment, then his head nodded approvingly as his shrill, falsetto voice intoned the formal oath of a witness.

I moved abruptly toward the witness chair. One of the officers started toward me with handcuffs, but I turned to face the judge. I began to speak rapidly, without waiting to be questioned by anybody.

"The man who killed Bob Skinner," I said, "put a horse in Skinner's corral. When he had finished killing Skinner, there was blood on his hands, and when he tried to catch the horse, the horse smelled the blood, and lunged away from him. The man chased after the horse in a frenzy of haste, and the horse broke through the corral fence and started up the cañon, back of the house. The man followed along behind him, trying to catch the horse.

"A wind storm obliterated the tracks in the sand in front of the corral and around the house, so that the tracks couldn't have been seen unless the officers had appreciated the significance of that break in the corral fence and had gone on up the cañon looking for tracks. I took the course that a horse would naturally have taken, and I picked up the tracks again, up the cañon. And also, the tracks of the man who was following."

Having gone that far, I could see that I wasn't going to be interrupted. I looked out over the courtroom and saw eyes that were trained upon me, sparkling with curiosity. I saw that the judge was leaning forward on the edge of his chair. The two officers had ceased their advance and were standing rooted to the spot.

Pete Ayers, who had stared at me with consternation

when I pushed my way into the courtroom, was now grinning happily. Damn him! I don't suppose he ever knows what it is to worry over anything. He is as happy-go-lucky as a cloud of drifting sand in the desert. The girl was staring at me with a white face and bloodless lips. She didn't yet appreciate what my coming meant; but Pete knew me, and his face was twisted into that gleeful grin which characterizes him when he is getting out of a tight place.

"All right," snapped the judge in that high, piping voice of his, "go on. What did you find?"

"I followed the horse tracks to the top of the ridge," I said, "and I found where the man had quit chasing the horse. Then I followed the man tracks a way, and lost them. But I figured what a man would do who was out in the desert and hot from chasing a horse he couldn't catch. So I worked on down the ridge to a spring, and once more found the tracks, this time at the spring. I looked around and found where the man had dug a hole and had buried something near the spring. Then I found where he had walked out, secured another horse, ridden back to the spring, pulled whatever had been in the hole out of its place of concealment, and ridden away. He hadn't bothered to look after the horse that had been left in the mountains, figuring that it would die in the desert from lack of water and food.

"I then went back to the place where I had left the horse tracks, and started following the horse. Eventually I found the saddle, and then I found the horse."

There was a commotion in the courtroom. The officers conferred together in whispers, and one of them started toward the door. I quit talking for a little while and watched the officer who was pushing his way through the swirling group of men.

Outside the building a horse whinnied, and the whinny sounded remarkably significant, upon the hot, still air and the sudden silence of that room—a silence broken only by the irregular breathing of men who are packed into the narrow quarters, and who must breathe through their mouths.

"Well?" rasped the judge. "Go on. What happened?"

"I found the saddle," I said, "and I found the horse. I brought the horse back and I brought the saddle back."

"What does all that prove?" asked the judge, curiously.

"It proves," I said, "that the murderer of Bob Skinner wasn't Sam Blake. It proves that Sam Blake came down to call for a showdown with Bob Skinner, but Skinner was dead when he got there. Somebody had murdered Skinner in order to take the gold from his cabin, and the horse had balked at the odor of blood. The murderer had chased the horse for a while, but he couldn't continue to chase him, because he was carrying enough gold to make it difficult for him to keep going after the horse. So he went down to the spring and cached the gold; then he went out to get another horse, and later came back after the gold."

The judge's glittering eyes swung as unerringly as those of a vulture spotting a dead rabbit to the bronzed face of Ernest Peterman, the tenderfoot.

"That man," he said, "swears that he saw smoke coming out of Bob Skinner's cabin just before Sam Blake went in there."

"He *thought* he saw smoke, your honor," I said. "He's a tenderfoot, and new to the desert. He didn't go up on the ridge very often, and he wasn't familiar with Bob Skinner's cabin. Particularly when the afternoon sunlight throws a black shadow from the western ridge."

"What's the shadow got to do with it?" asked the judge.

"It furnishes a black background for the tree that's growing just back of the house, right in line with the chimney on Skinner's cabin."

"A tree?" piped the judge. "What's a tree got to do with it?"

"The tree," I said slowly, "is a blue Palo Verde tree."

"What's a blue Palo Verde tree?" the judge inquired petulantly.

"One that you've seen many times, your honor," I said, "in certain sections of the desert. It only grows in a very few places in the desert. It requires a certain type of soil and a certain type of climate. It isn't referred to as a Palo Verde tree in these parts. Your honor has probably heard it called a smoke tree."

I sat back and let that shot crash home.

The blue Palo Verde grows in the desert. The Indians called it the smoke tree because it sends up long, lacy branches that are of a bluish-green; and when the sun is just right, seen against a black shadow, the smoke tree looks for all the world like a cloud of smoke rising up out of the desert.

Peterman was a tenderfoot, and he'd climbed up on the ridge just when the western shadows had furnished a black background for the smoke tree behind Skinner's cabin. He had taken a look at the scene and decided that smoke was coming out of the chimney. No one had ever thought to have him go back and take a look at the cabin under similar circumstances. They had been so certain that Sam Blake was guilty of the murder that they hadn't bothered to check the evidence closely.

The judge was staring at me as though I had destroyed some pet hobby of his. "Do you mean to say that a man mistook a smoke tree for smoke coming from a chimney?" he asked.

I nodded. "Keener eyes than his have made the same mistake, your honor," I said, "which is the reason the Indians called the tree the smoke tree."

"Then who owned the horse?" asked the judge. "Who

was it that went in there before Sam Blake called at the cabin?"

I pointed my finger dramatically at the place where the officers had been standing.

"I had hoped," I said, "that the guilty man would betray himself by his actions. I notice that one of the men has left the courtroom hurriedly."

As I spoke, there was the sound of a terrific commotion from outside. A shot was fired, a man screamed, a horse gave a shrill squeal of agony; then there was the sound of a heavy, thudding impact, and the stamping of many feet.

Men turned and started pushing toward the narrow exit which led from the place where the hearing was being conducted. They were men who were accustomed to the freedom of the outdoors. When they started to go through a door, they all started at once.

It was a struggling rush of bodies that pulled and jostled. Some men made for the windows, some climbed on the shoulders and heads of others and fought their way over the struggling mass of humanity. Futilely, the judge pounded his gavel again and again. Margaret Blake screamed, and I saw Pete Ayers slip a circling arm around her shoulder and draw her close to him.

I thought it was a good time to explain to the judge.

"That horse I found, your honor," I said, pushing close to him so that I could make my voice heard above the bedlam of sound, "was a nervous bronco. He made up to me all right because he was thirsty and hungry, but he was a high-strung, high-spirited horse. I left him tied to the rack out in front. I thought perhaps the owner of the horse might try to climb on his back and escape, hoping to take that bit of four-legged evidence with him. But horses have long memories. The last time the horse had seen that man, he had smelled the odor of human blood and had gone crazy with fright."

The crowd thinned out of the courtroom. Here and

there a man who had been pushed against a wall or tram-
pled underfoot, cursed and ran, doubled over with pain,
or limping upon a bad leg; but the courtroom had emptied
with startling speed.

I crossed to the window as the judge laid down his
gavel. Impelled by curiosity, he crowded to my side. Outside, we saw, the men were circling about a huddled figure
on the sidewalk. The horse, his ears laid back, his nostrils
showing red, his eyes rolled in his head until the whites
were visible, was tugging and pulling against the rope
that held him to the hitching rack. I noticed that there
were red stains on one forehoof, and a bullet wound in his
side.

Lying on the sidewalk, a rude affair of worn boards,
was the crumpled body of the deputy who had helped to
make the arrest of Margaret Blake that first time we had
seen her. The whole top of his head seemed to have been
beaten in by an iron hoof.

The judge looked and gasped. He started for the door,
then caught himself with an appreciation of the dignity
which he, as a magistrate, owed to himself. He walked
gravely back to the raised desk which sat on the wooden
platform, raised the gavel and banged it down hard on the
desk.

"Court," he said, "is adjourned!"

It wasn't until after Pete Ayers and Margaret Blake
had started out in the desert on their honeymoon that I
got to thinking of the words of the college professor.

The desert is a funny place. It's hard to know it long
without thinking that there's something alive about it.
You get to thinking those sand whispers are not just a
hissing of dry sand particles against rock or sagebrush, but
real whispers from the heart of the desert.

The desert shows itself in two ways. There's the grim
cruelty which is really a kindness, because it trains men to

rely upon themselves and never to make mistakes. Then there's the other side of the desert, the care-free dust clouds that drift here and there. They're as free as the air itself.

Pete Ayers was a part of the desert. The desert had branded him with the brand of care-free sunlight and the scurrying dust cloud.

The desert had recorded the tell-tale tracks that had led to the discovery of the real murderer. Every man is entitled to his own thoughts. Mine are that it's all just two sides of the desert, the grim side that holds justice for murderers, and the happy side that leaves its stamp on men like Pete Ayers.

Pete Ayers clapped me on the back. His bride stared at me with starry eyes.

"We owe it all to you, Bob Zane!" she said, her lips quivering.

But I looked out at the desert. The white heat of an afternoon sun had started the horizons to dancing in the heat waves. Mirages glinted in the distance. A gust of wind whipped up a little desert dust-spout, and it scurried along, the sagebrush bending its head as the dust-spout danced over it.

"No," I told her, "you owe it to the desert. The desert is kind to those who love it. She held the evidence, carved in sand, for the righting of a wrong and the betrayal of a real culprit to justice."

Pete Ayers grinned at me and said, "You're getting so you talk just like that swivel-eyed college professor you guided around last month."

But his smiling eyes shifted over my shoulder and caught sight of the swirling dust cloud scampering merrily over the desert. I watched his expression soften as his eyes followed the swirling sand. And then I knew that college professor was right.

Fall Guy

YES, SIR, taken any way you've a mind to look at it, the desert's a queer place. And the desert along the Mexican border is in a class by itself. Almost anything can happen down here. Not only can happen, but does. Most of it ain't believed, though.

Why, just the other day I was mentioning about the wheel ruts sticking up in the air, and some dude pitched in and says, "You mean the ruts are indented in the soil, my good man." Of course, I told him I wasn't his good man an' that I meant the ruts stuck *up* in the air, like I said.

Finally I'm hanged if I didn't have to take him out and show him.

There they were, wheel tracks sticking up eight inches above the surface of the desert, and where the horse had walked in between the wheels, there was mushrooms of earth sticking almost a foot up in the air.

The dude rubbed his eyes, and then sat right down on the desert and swore he'd never come west of the Rockies again. He said it was bad enough to have all the people crazy without having the country go crazy, too.

He was so flabbergasted I didn't tell him how it happened. Simple enough. You know the desert, you've probably seen 'em yourself. It happens in the Colorado Basin where the desert soil is mostly a fine silt. They make good 'dobe bricks out of that soil.

A light rain comes along once or twice a year. If somebody drives a wagon over the ground then, the wheels sink down into the soil and so do the horse's hoofs. But it packs that light silt into a regular 'dobe. Then when the sun does its stuff and the wind blows the powdery silt around this way and that, the 'dobe stays put. After a year or so the tracks'll be sticking right up in the air. I've seen 'em eighteen inches high with regular hills where the horse stepped.

That's the way with the desert. Strange things happen down there. If you know how they happen they don't seem so strange. If you just see 'em, and don't know how they happened, you naturally think the country's gone crazy.

Take the Desert Queen, for instance. Ever hear of her? No, I don't mean a mine of that name, I mean a regular woman, the Desert Queen—and she's a sure enough queen if there ever was one.

I'd heard whispers of her for a couple of years, but I'd never seen her. You know how the desert is, full of whispers. Why, even the sand whispers. You'll hear it of nights when you're laid out in your blankets, sand rustling against the cactus stalks and sounding like whispers. Then you'll hear the sand rustling against the sand, making regular sand whispers. Sometimes it seems as though you can hear what the sand's saying . . . just before you drop off to sleep, sort of.

But this here Desert Queen ain't got nothing to do with sand whispers. She's a real flesh and blood queen. But I thought for a long while she wasn't anything but a Sand Whisper.

I heard of her first down in Los Algodones. The roulette table was out four thousand. The proprietor said it was an olive-skinned girl with smoky eyes and a cowboy hat who played a system. I listened to him and grinned. Those gamblers are always inventing stories of people who made big killings. It acts as a come-on for the suckers —their customers.

But six months later I heard of her in Tia Juana. Four thousand again. She seemed to play a system and quit when she got four thousand.

Well, I was sitting right here in this very *cantina* one night, a year or so later, when I noticed a commotion over at the roulette table. See how this big horseshoe bar winds around? And there's the house-girls, asking you to dance and buy a drink, over on one side, and the roulette wheel on the other!

I was sitting right about here, and I saw something was happening over at the roulette table. So I got up and strolled over.

She was a slender kid with black hair and smoky eyes, and the eyes were the big part of her face. She was an American, all right, and a beauty. Her skin was a smooth olive, the lips were a dark red, and they weren't colored up any, either. She was a regular daughter of the desert, the kind that can stay out in the blistering sun and still have a smooth skin and velvet complexion.

She had a cowboy hat and riding boots, a buckskin skirt and a big belt around the waist. There wasn't any gun in the belt, but you could see where a holster was usually worn. The sun had tanned the rest of the belt a different color. The place where the holster was usually kept was darker.

She was playing a system all right. I don't know much about roulette systems. Most of 'em are the bunk. But they tell me that if you'll wait until a certain sequence of colors comes an' then slide out your bets, you've got a better than two-to-one chance.

This girl sure knew her system, and she could control her play. There's lots of good mathematical systems at roulette. The trouble is most people ain't got the self-control necessary to stand up an' play a system. They get to gambling on the side, and then they're finished.

Personally, I got my own system with roulette. I leave it alone. That keeps me from losing, and that's more than you can say about most systems.

But this girl was playing as cool and calm as though everybody in the room wasn't watching her. She'd watch the numbers fall for a few minutes, then make a bet. If she lost she'd double it the next time, and keep doubling. But she didn't lose. She seemed to know just about where that little ball was goin' to hop.

I watched her for a while, and then went back and sat down.

Phil Ryan came over and sat down next to me.

" 'Lo, Sid."

" 'Lo, Phil. How's tricks?"

"So-so."

"Anything new?"

"I got a job for you, Sid."

That sounded good to me. Phil and I were buddies for quite a while, and I wanted a chance to get goin' with him again.

Phil's another one of those things you wouldn't believe. He's a Western gunman. Thought there weren't any more, didn't you? Just like those wheel tracks in the desert. You don't believe 'em until you have 'em explained.

Well, Phil's like that. He's what they call a guard. He learned to handle a gun in the Big Scrap. Me, I'm an old-timer, and I've packed a Colt over more desert than most people ever see. But Phil was a youngster, one of the new school.

Oh, the gunmen ain't killers any more. They're just fellows who can do some fancy shootin' when the occasion calls for it. There's lots of capital in the desert country now, and that capital has to keep moving in the form of cash. There's the out-of-the-way mines with the big payroll, and there's the tourist resorts on the border with their big stocks of cash, always coming and going.

The border's still a tough place, for all the tinsel and all the tourist traps. And they employ us fellows to sort of chaperon the coin shipments. We don't have nothing much to do except to ride along. Mostly just being on hand is all the protection we need to give to a shipment.

No highwayman is likely to tackle a job where he knows there's a couple of men standing guard who can shoot with either hand and shoot fast.

I ain't so fast as I used to be. In the old days when Tombstone was still running I could go for iron with the best of them, even if I do say it. But I'm no spring chicken any more. But this here Phil Ryan's fast, awful fast. I've seen lots of fast fellows in the old days, and Phil's as fast as any of 'em. You could have put him back with the Earps and the Clantons, and he'd have made history—maybe would have made it a lot different from what it was.

Anyhow, I was glad to get a job that Phil had dug up. I knew it'd be ridin' with him, and I always liked Phil.

"What's this here job?" I asked.

"Chaperonin' a bunch of gold bars up to the border from the Dry Canteen Mine."

"Why the reinforcements? You been holdin' down that job by yourself for quite some time."

"They got a tip. Pedro Gallivan's got an eye on the shipment."

I whistled a little bit.

Pedro was a border character just like all the rest that had gone before. He wasn't Mex and he wasn't American. Sort of a mixture, was Pedro, and he was too slick ever to get caught.

The border has done lots of things to civilization, and civilization has done lots of things to the border. Dope, booze, and Chinks get run across, and that business is all cash. Pedro specialized in finding out where the cash was. He was a hijacker of cash. He didn't monkey with petty running of hooch or dope or Chinks, but he sure did swoop down on the money.

He lived in a big *hacienda* with palm trees and servants, and he had a shell of respectability about the place that made him seem like a retired banker. But there were plenty of whispers around about Pedro Gallivan. He didn't ever pull much in person. He always had a "fall guy" to take the blame if anything went wrong, and he had plenty of people working for him.

It was whispered that he furnished some of the big imports for shipment. He had people with him who were polished, educated, and crooked. Pedro was the head of the system. God help a man, or woman, for that matter, that Pedro got into his clutches. He made 'em work for him and work hard until he needed a fall guy, and then— well, dead people don't tell tales in the border country any more than they do anywheres else.

"What makes you think Pedro's going after the mine gold?" I wanted to know.

Phil glanced around him. His lips got tight. "A tip."

"He never has monkeyed with any of that sort of stuff. Always worked on the border runners."

"This is a straight tip."

We sat and looked at each other for a while.

"Count me in," I said.

He nodded, happened to glance toward the roulette,

and sat down his beer glass so hard the bottom bumped the table.

"What's doing?" he asked.

"A smoky-eyed jane with a system."

He was on his feet before I knew what he was going to do, and halfway over to the roulette table before I had a chance to say anything.

She looked up and saw him coming.

Her face changed color for an instant, then the smoky eyes bored straight into his and the lips came back from pearly teeth.

Phil swept off his sweat-stained sombrero, and the girl cashed in her chips. They went out together and the crowd gawked.

I stuck around until midnight. That was when we were scheduled to start out. Phil showed on the dot. The border was closed and all the tourists had gone home. The place was quiet.

"The broncs are out front," he said.

I followed him without saying anything.

My stirrups had to be lengthened, and I wanted to take a good look at the rifle that was in the saddle scabbard. I had my own guns, and I got 'em from the room where I was hanging out. We started about quarter past twelve.

The desert was silent, just crammed full of stars. The horses didn't make much noise, plumping their feet down into the soft sand. We rode in silence for over an hour.

"What are the plans?" I asked.

"We intercept the shipment about ten miles farther south, and we escort it to the road. There they've got armed automobiles waiting. If there's any trouble it'll be on the trail."

I rode along for another half hour.

We'd left the desert floor and were following a trail

along the steep sides of the barren desert mountains that
show soft and purple from the floor of the desert, but are
very devils to ride over, being mostly straight up and down
with all sorts of volcanic rock and what-not sticking out
and playing thunder with a horse.

"Who was the girl?"

"Miss Dixie Carson."

"She the one they call the Desert Queen?"

"Yes. Ever met her?"

"No. Never saw her before. Heard of her. Sort of whispers, nothing much definite."

He didn't say anything for a quarter of a mile. Then
he half turned in his saddle.

"I love her," he said.

"You should," I told him. "I'm for you."

He grunted and swung back into the saddle.

That was all there was to it. But he knew and I knew.
Out there in the star-filled silence of a desert night a fellow
doesn't need to talk much to get an idea across. Phil knew
I wasn't going to babble anything, and that if he ever
needed me to back his play I'd be there.

We finished our short cut and came to the main trail
from the mine half an hour before the burro train got
there. It showed up about daylight with a clatter of little
bells and the sound of shuffling feet and soft, Mexican
voices.

Phil hailed the leader, and then we rode on ahead. A
couple of *rurales* were in the rear.

The east got brassy and the stars became little needle
points. I could look back and see the burro train, twisting
like some big serpent as it wound its way around the side
of the hills, following a pass through the mountains.

I loosened up my rifle, looked up at the ridges of the
mountains.

"Good place for an ambush, Phil."

"Yeah. Let's ride on ahead a ways."

We touched the broncs with the spurs and went on ahead. After a while we couldn't hear the little bells any more.

The sun touched the purple peaks of the high mountains.

"Phil," I said, "my eyes ain't as good as they used to be any more, but take a look at that bush up on the slope about two hundred yards, just below that outcropping of red rock."

Phil swung his head up.

"Hm—" he began, and then it happened.

There was the cough of a high-powered rifle, and the bullet plunked into solid meat. I didn't have time to see whether it was Phil or the bronc. I had the spurs into my own cayuse, and we were off the trail and going hell-for-leather down the side of the mountain.

There was a dry wash at the bottom, and some boulders in the bottom. I grabbed the gun as the horse scrambled into the boulders, and kicked my feet free from the stirrups when I felt air between me and the saddle.

Bullets were chipping bits of rock off of the boulders all around me. It was like a hailstorm on a lake. I could hear the pop of guns and the spatter of bullets. One of the horses was screaming with pain or terror or both.

I was glad we'd come on ahead of the pack train. It would have been plain hell to have the burros trapped in that cañon, each with a load of gold bars. As it was, there wasn't anybody except Phil and myself, and Phil was able to take care of himself—or else it was all over with him.

I dropped back of a rock where there was plenty of shelter and cut loose at the bush up on the ridge. I couldn't see anybody, but I wanted to let Phil know I was all right and, besides, to warn the *rurales* back with the pack train.

Then I heard Phil's gun roar up above me, and knew

we were sittin' pretty. Phil would be almost sure to try for the ridge, and he'd count on me to cover him from down in the cañon. My legs ain't much for runnin' uphill any more, but I can still see between the sights.

I knew Phil was out and running from the way the bullets quit spatterin' against my rock. I flung up over it. A man's head and shoulders were outlined against the sky above the ridge. He was sighting a gun up on the slope where Phil was jumping for a bush.

I cut loose and beat that guy to it.

He settled, slumped, rolled, and lay still.

Somebody clipped a hole through my sombrero. But then, it was gettin' old, anyway. I slammed home a shell and took a snap shot at a bit of motion on top of the ridge. I didn't hit him, but I threw enough dust in his eyes to put him out of the fight for a while—and the fight wasn't goin' to last long.

Phil was out in the open now, walkin' toward the ridge, trustin' to me to see that nobody got up to take a shot. One fellow tried it. I think I hit him in the leg, from the way he went down.

Then there wasn't any more firing. I heard the drum of a horse's hoofs, and then the whinny of another horse. Phil broke into a run, and I saw him bring his gun to his shoulder as he took a couple of long distance shots.

That was all there was to it.

We got the *rurales*, and the man who was dead was properly checked off. He was a guy we had seen a couple of times with Pedro Gallivan. But he didn't have anything that showed he'd ever belonged to Pedro, except a bullet hole in the back of his head. My bullet had gone through his shoulder and down into his innards. It'd probably have been fatal. But he might have talked a little bit if it hadn't been for that bullet hole in the back of his head.

That was one of Pedro's little tricks. Dead men didn't talk, any.

The fellow I'd wounded in the leg had evidently made his bronc all right. There was only one horse left behind. It had been stolen from north of the border the night before.

Pedro was a clever cuss when it came to covering his tracks, and if somebody had to take a tumble, he always left a fall guy.

After that Phil and I got a new job. The mine owners hadn't paid much attention to Pedro as long as he only went after money paid for booze and Chinks. But when he started going after bars of gold, he was getting too close to home for the big lads to take any comfort, so they told Phil and me to take a couple of months, ride trail on Pedro, and wipe him out when we got a good excuse.

But Pedro knew when he'd bit off more than he could chew. He kept pretty close to first base, and Phil and I just sort of stuck around where we could keep tabs on what was going on at his *hacienda*.

I think Pedro had us spotted. It wasn't that he said anything; but the Mex who tried to knife Phil one night, and the gent of undetermined nationality who took a shot at me from ambush one full moon, made it look as though somebody knew what we were there for.

But Pedro was respectably at home in the *hacienda* both times.

We rode up there to make sure. He welcomed us with oily eyes and suave comments. We answered him with polite remarks that didn't fool anybody. And that was the way things stood.

Then Walter Hedley showed up.

Hedley was just a bit of human wreckage, nothing

more. He was the sort of backwater flotsam that collects at the border. They're always more or less the same. Drink is the big thing in their lives.

Hedley must have had some pretty good stock in him. He was a gentleman after he got drunk, and that's about the best indication of breeding you can get—along the border, anyway.

Pedro looked Hedley over and invited him up to the *hacienda*.

Phil and I knew what that meant. Pedro was in need of some more fall guys. He liked the fellows who had breeding and education. He shifted 'em from booze to dope, got them so they could put up a good front when they were hopped up, and sent 'em out on border business that wouldn't bear too much of a searchlight.

We didn't want fall guys. We wanted Pedro. So we discussed how maybe we could get this guy Hedley to talkin' with us before Pedro got him branded.

But it was the Desert Queen who dealt herself in on the hand. I don't know how she found out what it was all about, but she called herself in on the play, and from then on things moved fast.

Through Phil, I'd found out more about this girl they called the Desert Queen, the one whose real name was Dixie Carson. She made a specialty of getting the human wreckage of the border, patching it up so it could sail once more, and starting it off on another voyage.

Mostly she dealt in the sort of women who are thrown into the border and left there. She had a secluded ranch way south and she built up the people she took in down there, gave 'em lots of fresh air, staked 'em with money, and gave 'em self-respect.

That was why she raided the roulette every once in a while. She was a genius on mathematics, had a college degree in it, and she'd figured out things about a roulette

wheel. Phil said she called it the Calculus of Chance, or
something like that.

Anyhow, the Queen got track of Walter Hedley, and
he fell for her like a ton of brick. The Queen wanted Hedley to straighten him up. Pedro wanted Hedley to drag
him down. It was a battle.

Pedro got Hedley to visit him at his *hacienda*. Dixie
got Hedley one night, invited him to her place, and drove
off with him the next morning. A week later Phil came
to me.

"I'm quittin'," he said.

"Quittin' the job, Phil?"

"Yeah."

"What's the matter, son?"

"Goin' to work for the Queen."

I looked him over. He didn't ring true somehow.

"What's the big idea, she won a lot of gold she wants
guarded?"

"Nope. She wants me to take Walt Hedley out into the
desert an' make a man of him. Pedro got him started using
dope while he was at the *hacienda*. She can cure him of
booze, but he keeps getting out and smuggling in dope.
She says he wants to kill himself when he realizes what
he's done, but when the craving gets on him he can't
resist."

I didn't say anything. I ain't never craved dope myself,
and a man who hasn't had any particular craving ain't in
any position to pass judgment on a guy that has it.

"When do you start?"

"To-night."

"The mine people sending in anybody to work with
me?"

"No. They figure Pedro's lying low as long as somebody's watchin' him, and they figure one man can watch
him just as well and twice as cheap as two men."

I grunted. Mine people get that way. Some smart bookkeeper out in New York was auditing the books and telling the superintendent in Mexico how to handle a slick bandit like Pedro Gallivan. But I let it go. It was bread and butter for me, and that's one thing I won't fight with.

"Where you goin'?" I asked.

"Out to the Phillips prospect. If you get out that way, drop in."

"You don't seem cheerful, son."

He looked down his nose.

"She loves him," he said.

There wasn't anything I could say, so I put one of my hands on his shoulder.

"Things have a way of workin' out all right, Phil, old-timer. Stay with it."

He grunted and walked away.

I saw them start that night. The dude was sittin' erect and straight, his jaw fairly oozin' resolution an' determination. That's the way with people who know they ain't goin' to last. They put on twice as much determination as the situation calls for, just to fool themselves.

Phil sat slumped in the saddle takin' it easy, the way a man does when he's in for a long fight and knows he's goin' to come through somewheres near the top or know why.

Out where they were goin' it was too hot to ride in the daytime. They had to make it at night. They had a packhorse, and there was a trickle of water at the place. It was an old abandoned prospect, baked by the sun, swept by the drifting sands. There was just sky, sun, cactus, and sand, nothing else, and it didn't vary from day to day.

I figured I'd ride out that way after a week or so. I didn't like the idea of those two men being cooped up in that loneliness, both of 'em in love with the same girl, one of 'em the successful one, and havin' a streak of yellow, the other all man, and tryin' to make a man outa the yellow one.

The desert does things to men. It's the utter silence, the emptiness, the loneliness of the place. A man either hates it or loves it the first time he gets into it. But even if he loves it, he can't stand too much of it.

Things began to happen out at the *hacienda*, however, that kept me busy. Pedro had riders comin' in at nights, and there were times when the house was all dark as though people had gone to bed, but there'd be the tinkle of glasses and the hum of voices far into the night.

I cached a roll of blankets within hearing distance of the corral and got to sleeping out there under the stars.

Twice riders saddled up and left the place, and I couldn't follow them on account of the darkness. The third time there was a moon, and the fellow who rode away into the desert was a wiry little Mexican. I knew him. He'd been a gambler in Mexicali until Pedro enlisted him. He was a resourceful little cuss.

I followed for a couple of hours before I realized he was takin' a trail toward the Phillips prospect. Then I closed up the gap.

I was close to him when it happened.

A shadow rose up out of the ground.

"Is it you, *amigo*?" asked the rider.

"It is not the one you expect, but the one who expects you," said the voice of Phil Ryan, speaking in Spanish. "You will leave what you bring here with me, and you will tell the one who sent you that there will be nothing more sent."

The rider sat very still and straight for a few seconds.

I got the picture then. Pedro had been sending in dope to Walter Hedley, and Phil was breaking up his little game.

"*Señor*," said the rider, speaking too softly, too smoothly, "you ask for that which I have. Take it then!"

He was fast, that bird.

I ain't so speedy as I used to be in the old days, and my hand was still coming up from the holster, tugging at the hammer on my gun, when I saw the moonlight glisten on his leveled weapon.

But Phil Ryan's gun crashed and I saw the Mexican's right wrist wilt.

"Go back, and tell your master I want no more fall guys. Tell him to come in person the next time he has business with me," said Phil's voice.

Phil was fast on the draw, awfully fast.

I got back out of the way and let the rider pass. Then I rode in for a chat with Phil.

"She loves him," said Phil. "She's been out here twice. I can see how it is. She wants him to get well."

"And him?"

Phil shrugged his shoulders.

"Is he a yellow one at heart, underneath all that smooth bearing?" I asked.

"I can't tell," said Phil.

Which was a lie. When a man's spent that long in the desert with another chap, he can tell everything about him. But if Phil wanted to be generous about it, I wasn't going to interfere. I have a hunch that things come out right in the desert if you just give 'em time enough.

I rode away and left Phil with his dude.

I saw Dixie Carson after that, and I took the risk of talking to her.

"If you want him, you're going about it the wrong way. He's from a good family. If he gets cured there'll be some society bud coming to claim him," I said.

It was none of my business, but I had to say it to hear with my own ears whether she really loved him. And I'd got to know her better since I'd been ridin' with Phil.

The olive skin didn't change color. The eyes still remained smoky, impassive.

"That," she said slowly, "is my own business."

I let it go at that because she was right.

Pedro was still lying low. Such riders as went from his place were going on border hijacking business. They never once went toward the trails that came in from the mines.

I rather guessed Pedro's one experience with mine guards had sort of convinced him he'd better leave the outfits alone. But I just kept right on the job.

Then Phil showed up with the news his dude was cured.

He was, too. I saw Hedley when he rode in. The shoulders were back and the eyes were steady. He'd lost that look of too much determination that had gripped him when he went into the desert.

He had a long talk with Dixie Carson; and after that, he sent a telegram.

Then Phil told me a funny thing. It seemed there was a girl who came from a good family and who was engaged to this here dude. Now that Hedley had got full control of himself, he'd wired her, telling her the whole situation, offering to release her or to go through with it any way she wanted.

It was a couple of days before he got an answer.

He was around the border resorts, looking at the people swigging booze over the bar, looking at the gambling, sneering, and keeping straight.

Personally I didn't like that sneer.

If he'd been a real thoroughbred and had been cured, he wouldn't have been so sneery at the poor unfortunates who were hitting it up. That self-righteousness in a man who has been down in the gutter don't impress me. But I didn't say anything. I'd said too much already.

The second day the girl came, in person. She wanted to see Hedley before she answered one way or another.

To my eye she was a washout. She was one of those

society blondes with a funny way of pronouncing her "a's."

Walter Hedley made quite a fuss over her. She held the reins and she showed it. With the Desert Queen she rubbed it in. Walter made the presentation with something of a flourish. A man always does take delight in presenting two women who love him, one to the other. He thinks they'd oughta get along well together! Seems like men would never learn.

"Miss Westing, may I present Miss Dixie Carson, the girl who helped me find myself."

The Desert Queen held out her hand cordially enough.

The blonde looked her over from head to foot.

"I thought, Walter, you'd abandoned all your old associates," she said. Then she walked away.

The Desert Queen's face got a darkish color, but her eyes remained steady.

"Good-by, Walter," she said, and turned.

The dude hesitated for ten or fifteen seconds, then went over to the blonde. I was glad Phil wasn't there to see that.

After that things moved fast at the border. First came the stock crash. You wouldn't think it'd affect the border, but it did, lots of ways. Mines shut down, for one thing. And the blonde did some telegraphing, for another. What her dad wired back evidently wasn't so reassuring. She slit the telegram open, read it, then stamped her foot.

"I do wish fawther wouldn't be so downright stupid," she said.

Half a dozen people heard her, and the news traveled.

That night she bucked the roulette wheel and won about three hundred. The next day she met Pedro Gallivan. The next evening she and Walter were "visiting" at the Gallivan *hacienda*.

By that time I'd developed a fat Mexican cook to give

me the lowdown on Pedro. She was working daytimes at the *hacienda*. She spent the nights with her family. It took lots of *dinero* to bribe her to cough up such information as she picked up, but she had a good memory.

She told me about the blonde and Walter.

The Westing girl, it seemed, was playing Pedro and Walter, one against the other. Walter didn't want to stay out there, and he was sore. The girl had a talk with him about lots of things, and they stayed.

I pumped the Mex to find out if Pedro was riding.

She didn't know. She only knew that Pedro was looking at the gringo girl with melting eyes and making protestations of affection.

I asked her where Walter had been.

She said Walter had been sent on an errand.

I thought over that being sent on an errand business. It didn't sound so good. I looked around for Phil. He wasn't in town. I lost ten dollars making fool bets on roulette and went to bed.

About two o'clock I heard shots and tumbled to the floor, reaching for my boots with one hand and my cartridge belt with the other.

There was the clatter of horses coming at a breakneck pace, and there was the tattoo of pistol shots, the rattle of rifle fire, and something dropped to the ground with a thud that jarred the pictures on my wall.

The *rurales* were there about the time I was.

The dead man was Walter Hedley.

The *rurales* told of a boldly planned holdup to clean out the cash that was held over in the casino. It was one of those wildly foolish affairs that seemed to be foredoomed to failure, but it had almost worked. A chance alarm had brought the *rurales*. Maybe that alarm hadn't been so much of a chance after all.

Walter Hedley was pretty well riddled with lead. There was a look of puzzled bewilderment on his face.

The *rurales* must have been shooting exceptionally well that night. Or maybe they'd had a little help.

The posse swept on after the rest of the gang. They came back inside of half an hour. The Mexes had one dead bandit, and a fall guy is all they look for. The robbery hadn't been a success, the "ringleader" was dead, what more could one ask for?

They consumed much *tequila*, and assumed a great deal of credit for straight shooting.

Pedro had a perfect alibi. I investigated it.

The little Mex gambler that had been taking the dope into the Phillips prospect, the one Phil Ryan had shot in the wrist, didn't have any alibi. But you can't hang anything on a man just because he hasn't an alibi.

The blond girl wept vigorously over her "fallen hero." The Desert Queen took the news in silence. After that she sat for a long while, looking at the horizon with unmoist eyes.

Two nights later my spy tipped me off that Pedro was riding, and she had heard some mention of bars of gold.

Another shipment was due from the Dry Canteen Mine, and I got in touch with Phil and asked him if he wanted to ride, just for old times' sake.

I didn't like the expression on his face when he said he did.

"Don't try to ride into no bullets, son, and get killed on the field of duty," I ventured to suggest.

He snorted. "Nobody'd care if I did."

"That's a coward's game," I said shortly.

"I ain't a coward."

"Don't think coward thoughts, then, and you won't get to be one."

I had to let it go at that.

We lay in wait where we could see the corral back of Pedro's *hacienda*. We moved in after dark, and there was a wind blowing, a wind that whipped the fine silt in little whirlwinds, sent them dancing off over the face of the desert.

About midnight we saw shadowy figures about the corral. Horses got saddled. Then we could hear riders.

"No fall guys this time," muttered Phil.

I grunted assent. We were between the riders and the *hacienda*, and we intended to keep between them.

It was tough work, trailing the party ahead, yet keeping out of sight and hearing. There was a moon, and the little band rode fast.

They took a short-cut trail. I hadn't known of it before. Once I thought we had lost sight of them. The wind was bad up along the ridges, and there was a cloud scud forming over the moon.

But we caught up to them in a box cañon below, almost ran onto them before we knew it. They'd evidently stopped for a palaver. We trailed them easy from there until they staked out their broncs in a clump of trees just below a spring.

The men climbed up a ridge and settled themselves. It was getting gray dawn now, and Phil and I had to work pretty carefully to keep from being discovered.

There were six horses in the party. Two of 'em were packhorses with empty *alforjas*—empty saddle bags. The other four were prime saddle stock.

Below the ridge ran the automobile road.

"S'pose they're going to tackle the armed cars?"

Phil shrugged his shoulders.

We waited. It was all there was to do.

An automobile showed up. Behind it came another. The tops were down, men sat in the cars, and the men had rifles. The top of the ridge spouted fire.

One of the cars swerved drunkenly.

The driver of the other car ran it to a stop, turned, and spoke to the men with him.

The crackle of rifles still sounded on the ridge.

We could see it all, then. Pedro had bought over some of the guards. They were throwing in with him. I glanced at Phil.

He nodded.

I took a fine sight at a huddled figure and cut loose. Phil's gun roared in my ear. That cross fire smoked 'em out. They tried to get us, but we were well covered, and we had lots of time. They were fighting against time.

The guards below came to life and began to do some shooting. Pedro's gang started for their broncs. So we made for ours.

I could hear the sweep of hoofs ahead of me and the sound of shooting. Phil was riding stirrup to stirrup with me and we were holding our fire until we could see something to shoot at.

The sun was just making thin purple lines of reddish color along the tops of the ridges. The wind was blowing and it was cold. We were between the riders and the *hacienda.*

"You double back and keep 'em from getting to the *hacienda.* I can haze 'em along the trail," yelled Phil.

I didn't like the idea, but he pointed out, "It's our best chance. We can't catch 'em, and they'll double around on a secret trail somewhere. They know the mountains."

Phil sounded right, so I swung back.

They did just what he'd predicted, took a cut-off trail, and swung back into the *hacienda* trail. I was there waiting for 'em. Phil was behind 'em.

They dropped behind boulders and got real deadly.

They were fighting for their lives and knew it, this time. And the time element didn't bother 'em so much now. They were four against two.

We had 'em pocketed, and they had us boxed. It was a question of making every shot count and waiting for developments. I built a little fire behind a rock and sent up a smoke signal. The fight got warmer after that.

But the bandits couldn't get out. The wind did things to my smoke signal, but I figured there'd be keen eyes searching the trails.

The *rurales* rode up in an hour.

They called on the little group to surrender. The bandits just laughed and started to sell their lives as dearly as possible. The Mexican government ain't gentle with bandits. When they get trapped, they might as well see it through.

These did.

I surveyed the wreckage afterward. The little gambler was there, and a couple of others, but there wasn't any sign of Pedro.

I looked at Phil and he looked at me.

"Suppose he could have laid low on that ridge and started the others with the horses?" I asked.

Phil thought things over, then he nodded.

We rode back, and the trail told us what we wanted to know. One of the horsemen hadn't started with the others. He'd kept up on the ridge, probably playing dead. Then, after the galloping horses had decoyed us into pursuit he'd come to life, gone down, got his own bronc, and rode away by himself.

But he hadn't ridden toward the *hacienda.*

Pedro must have known the game was up at last. He was headed into the hills, straight for the border desert country. A man could live a long time in that country.

Phil and I looked at the ridges. The trail followed the cañon. There was no use following it, while there was one chance in ten on the ridges.

"You take the left, me the right," I said.

Phil nodded, filled up his cartridge belt from his saddle bags and took the ridge. I took the other.

I didn't see anything. Once I thought I heard shooting.

When it got dark I gave it up and made a camp. The next day I backtracked into the *hacienda*. The *rurales* were in charge.

"Got clean away," I reported.

Phil was there. He didn't say anything.

I noticed a bullet had splintered the horn of his saddle and there were two shells missing from his belt.

"Any action, Phil?"

He shook his head.

"No. And I'm glad, too."

"Why glad?"

"Oh, under the circumstances, I wouldn't want to go through a lot of red tape. I wasn't a regular officer, you know, just a special guard, and I was off duty."

His words sounded sort of casual. I took a good look at the splintered saddle horn again. Then I climbed a peak and got out my binoculars.

Far off toward the east I could see a little bunch of circling dots, swinging, twisting, spiraling, settling. It was along the ridge Phil had taken, and they were turkey buzzards.

I put up my glasses, rode back to the *hacienda*, took another look at Phil's saddle, scratched my head. He saw me, and came out.

"Close call," I said.

He nodded.

"Guess the New York office will want a report on what's happened," I said. "Would you like to write it?"

He shook his head.

"Saw some buzzards over the east ridge," I hinted.

"Yeah?"

"Yeah"

"Ever see the president of this company?" asked Phil.

"No. Why?"

"He's a pot-bellied cuss that's awful cold-blooded. Know what'd happen if you'd bumped off Pedro and reported it?"

"Reward?" I asked.

"Naw. He'd fire you to cut down the overhead. He'd figure that with the bandit dead there was no need of a guard."

"How about you?" I asked.

"I'm quittin' the guardin' business. Dixie and I are gettin' married."

I got to thinking about those buzzards some more. Then I got to thinking about what Phil had said. He'd met the president, and he knew. After all, there was that time they'd deliberately cut the force in two and left me without any reinforcements. I decided I wouldn't ride over toward the east ridge.

That's why I'm still chaperonin' the gold shipments for the Dry Canteen Mine. It's been a year since the Big Scrap, but they're afraid Pedro may show up again, and they keep me on the payroll.

There's strange things happen down here in the border country.

The girl? You mean the blonde? Her father went through bankruptcy, lost everything in the crash.

Where is she now?

Oh. See the third one from the end there, the house girl that's solicitin' dances for a cut on the drinks, the washy-eyed blonde? That's her. She and Pedro decoyed Walter Hedley into the holdup, then tipped off the *rurales*. That got rid of Walter. Pedro was to marry the girl—or said he was.

She was Pedro's last fall guy. That's why I started to tell you about this border country. It's a queer place.

Priestess of the Sun

THE TOWN OF Mojave squats in the sunlight like a gigantic spider sitting in the center of a web of railroad lines, a main automobile highway, and little, single-tracked dirt roads that stretch out and out until they are lost in the heat waves which shimmer on the horizon.

Mojave is an outpost of civilization. Back of it lies the land of whispers.

My shadow was short and black as I walked across the main street of Mojave, headed toward the railroad tracks. That meant the sun was almost directly overhead, and that, in turn, meant that it was hot.

To the west, the Tehachapi Mountains rippled in a heat-tortured dance. To the east stretched the great barren waste that man has called the Mojave Desert—the land of whispers.

To the south, a long string of black dots emitted a spurt of white steam. Seconds later the hot silence of the desert parted long enough to let the sound of the train's whistle seep through.

The string of black dots presently showed as dust-stained Pullmans. The glittering black monster that pulled the train up the grade from Lancaster hissed puffingly along steel rails that were so sun-heated they would blister an ungloved hand.

The train lurched to a creaking stop.

Passengers stared listlessly with tired eyes. The steel Pullmans were ovens. Perspiring skins caught and held the flour-fine desert dust that seeped through doors and windows.

I saw my package come from the express car, provisions shipped direct from Los Angeles, ready to be transferred to the back of my pack burros. I moved forward, and almost ran into her as she got off the train.

First I saw a pair of snakeskin shoes, a trim ankle, and the neat expanse of feminine leg which fashion then decreed as proper. Then I saw the hem of a blue suit, a flutter of feminine finery as she jumped, and she was on the ground, standing right in front of me, vivacious, slender, attractive—and tired.

Her eyes were tired. Her mouth drooped. But she was full of pep, the pep of civilization, the pep that comes from forcing oneself to appear full of life and spontaneity.

"You're Pedro Madrone!" she said to me and I saw the flash of her teeth and the outstretched hand.

I took the hand, apologetically.

"I'm sorry—" I began.

Her voice interrupted me. It wasn't a sweet voice. It was too rapid-fire to be sweet, and, like her eyes, it showed more than a trace of nerve strain.

"I'm Jean Stiles, the one that Ramsay wrote you about. Surely you got that letter?"

"But I'm not Pedro Madrone."

Her face lost its smile. The eyes flashed a how-dare-you expression, and she jerked her hand from mine.

"Damn!" she said, and turned away.

Just that, no more, no less. Perhaps it was her nerves. Perhaps it was just her way. I walked on up to the express truck and didn't bother about it one way or the other.

❋   ❋   ❋

The next time I saw those snakeskin shoes was six months later and a hundred miles away. I saw them by moonlight and there were circumstances attending the seeing which robbed me of sleep.

It was full moon.

I lay rolled in my blankets far out in the Mojave Desert, in a place where few men have penetrated. There was no water, there were no roads. My water was almost gone. One more day and I would have to turn back to Randsburg, and even then I'd have to use all of my desert knowledge to make it.

The moon seemed so close I could have chipped a piece from it with a rifle shot. The cool, breathless silence was utterly void of any sound. My ears rang from the stillness. The silvery basin of desolate desert was flooded with moonlight.

I closed my eyes, lay back and relaxed.

Something stirred—a bit of sage rustling in one of the sudden desert winds which spring up from nowhere, blow fiercely for a while and then die down just as suddenly.

I listened for the whispers.

Soon they came, desert whispers which are only for the ears of those who know and love the desert. Sand rustled against sage. Then, as the wind grew stronger, the sand rustled against sand, and the rustlings were as whispers, hissing, sibilant moonlit whispers of mystery.

I lay and listened to the whispers, and they lulled me to the threshold of sleep. Just as I was dropping off, the whispers suddenly ceased to be mere sibilants of drifting sand, but became a definite message.

I snapped wide awake, and the memory of that message slipped from my mind like a vanishing mirage. But it was somehow disquieting. The desert was whispering something that made my hair tingle, made little chills race along my spine. I settled back, shivered, pulled my blankets tighter about my chin and tried to sleep. Sleep was not for me. The moon beat down upon my face. The wind grew stronger, and the sand reached a hissing crescendo.

I kicked back the blankets and dressed—and the desert wind stopped blowing as though it had been scooped from the face of the earth. The desert was white and silent once more.

But I pulled on my boots and started walking, toward the northwest, toward the first slopes of the red and purple mountains.

I walked for a hundred yards, straight toward a clump of cacti. Then I saw something white in the middle of that clump, a rounded something that glittered in the moonlight as only one thing can glitter—a sun-bleached bone.

I hesitated, looked again.

There were more rounded streaks of white. These would be ribs, buzzard-picked ribs which loomed in the moonlight as gruesome reminders of the grim power of the desert.

I took a doubtful step, shook off the strange feeling which gripped me, took a deep breath and forged ahead. Ten steps and I knew the bones were not those of a human. Then I walked faster.

Moonlight in the desert is composed of glittering glare and inky shadows. There seems to be no halfway line. Where the sand reflects the brilliance of the moon it almost seems that there is a dazzling brilliance. Where the shadows of the desert fall there is jet-black darkness.

The skeleton was half in moonlight, half in shadow, and it took me a few moments to make it out. It was the skeleton of a burro, and he had died in harness. There was a packsaddle, and a rotted leather strap, baked stiff, and still offensive to the nostrils. Leather holds the odor of carrion for a long time, even in the hot, dry air of the desert.

I peered down into the blackness of the bone litter and caught a glimpse of cloth. It was too dark to try poking around. Out in the desert we get to read the sand like a printed page, and to mess around in the darkness would be to destroy clews.

I was back at the skeleton by the time daylight was gilding the tops of the red and purple mountains to the north. I had held myself back to make sure the light would be strong enough.

There wasn't enough animal life in this section of the desert for a coyote to live on; but there were buzzards, and the buzzards had pulled the bones around some. Even so, I was able to tell that the burro had been headed to the westward, along the rolling base of the jagged mountains. And he had died almost in his tracks.

I found the long leg bones and checked each in turn, but the legs were all sound. I had rather expected to find a broken leg. Even so, his owner would have taken off the saddle.

I walked to the skull. There were three holes. Two where the eyes had been, one that was small and round.

The burro had been walking along the rounded slope. Some one had shot him with a high-powered rifle.

I delved into the bones and rescued the *alforjas*, twin bags of rawhide made to swing from either side of the packsaddle. Decay, sunlight and time had done things to the contents of those bags, but I spread them out carefully, an article at a time.

There were silken undergarments that came to bits in my hands, and had no recognizable laundry marks. There were feminine toilet articles. And there was a pair of snakeskin, high-heeled shoes. I thought of the woman who had stepped from the train at Mojave.

The sun leaped over the rise of ground to the east and burned into my back. Flies droned about the dark hide and stinking remnants. Tracks had been obliterated. Everything but hide, saddle, and bones had gone the way of all things perishable.

A shot, dead in the center of the skull, squarely between the eyes, meant accurate shooting. This, on a walking burro, probably meant a close range. There was a clump of cacti some sixty yards ahead when I faced in the direction the burro had been traveling.

I went to that clump. Any tracks that might have been there had long been blotted out, but I was searching for something that would remain, and I got to my hands and knees and searched the ground bit by bit.

The sun glittered on it and I raked it out of a lodgement in between the spines of a giant cactus. It was a thirty-thirty shell. I looked it over.

The firing pin had not hit exactly in the center. That frequently happens. But in the bottle neck, just where the shell tapered down to seat the bullet, there were two little cracks, forced by the explosion of the shell. The relation of those split marks to the firing pin impression might tell something.

I dropped the shell in my pocket.

Looking back toward the skeleton, I reconstructed the scene. The burro was walking slowly around the mountain slope, had just emerged over a little crest. Perhaps there was a woman walking beside him; perhaps a man was with her.

The single shot. The burro had collapsed.

What of the woman?

I went back to the skeleton and pretended that I had

been walking up the little incline, that a rifle had barked from the cacti clump and the burro had thudded to the ground.

What would I do?

Two things. First and foremost, the water canteen. I would stoop for it. Then shelter.

I stooped to the skeleton and reached for the horn of the packsaddle. Then, while I was in that position, I looked around over my shoulder for a place of shelter.

There was a rock halfway down the little slope.

I went to it on the run, trying to do just what the woman, or the man and the woman, would have done. But I began to doubt the presence of a man. There were no empty shells near the burro bones.

I skidded around the rock.

There was a canteen, and in the bottom of the canteen was a double hole. I looked at it carefully. The double hole marked the course of a steel-jacketed bullet.

I figured just how I would stand to conceal myself from the clump of cacti where the first shot had been fired. Then I put the canteen over my shoulder and flattened myself against the rock. That gave me a direction at right angles as being the first place from which the canteen would be visible.

There was no cover in that direction.

I marked a line and walked along it very slowly. Fifty yards along that line I found another empty shell, a thirty-thirty with double split checks in the bottle neck and a firing pin that was just slightly off center.

I dropped it into my pocket, along with the other.

Then I looked around some more. I found nothing else. The sun-swept surface of the desert glinted mockingly in the sun's light.

I returned to the rock and figured what I would do if

I had been crouched there and some one had shot at me and bored a hole in my canteen. There was a rocky wash twenty yards down the slope. I ran toward it.

There I found a bit of white cloth, bleached and rotted by the sun. I had been a sack, and it had been dropped at the base of a stunted bush. I stooped to pick up the ragged fragment, and paused, arrested in mid-motion by the yellow glitter which my eyes beheld.

There was gold, a regular pile of it, virgin gold, alluvial. There were nuggets and there were grains of dust the size of wheat grains. It had evidently been in the cloth bag, which had rotted and spilled the gold.

So much the desert had to tell me, and no more.

I spent the morning in a search and found nothing else. Those were the elements of tragedy which the whispers had hissed in the moonlight. The story, I knew, was unfinished. But I could not find the closing chapter, the sun-bleached bones of a woman—or perhaps those of a man and a woman.

Somewhere out in that glittering expanse of hot sand those bones must be lying, but I couldn't find them.

I rounded up my burros and started the march back to water. It would be an all-day trip. That was the nearest water. Impossible that a woman should have reached it on foot even now when there was a hint of a cool breath in the desert. Doubly impossible that a woman could have walked there six months ago when the desert was an inferno of heat.

A mile of the march slipped behind me. I was in the middle of the second mile when I found the ashes of a camp fire. I paused to look it over.

There was nothing, absolutely nothing save the blackened circle of camp fire embers. That meant that the one who had made that fire was an outdoor man, accustomed

to woodcraft and the open. Otherwise there would have
been a litter of empty tin cans, old papers, discarded odds
and ends of various sorts.

I resumed my march. An hour's travel and I caught
the glint of sunlight on tin. I went to the place. It was an
empty tomato can, cut open with a heavy steel hunting
knife. And there was the blackened circle of embers from
an old camp fire.

Tomatoes in cans are indispensable in the desert. They
are one of the few canned things a man who knows the
desert will carry. Taken once in a while they neutralize
the burning acidity of a body that must continually give
off perspiration. Even so, they are carried only on long
trips by the men who have accustomed themselves to the
desert.

The two camp fires were less than three miles apart.

I checked that fact for future reference and went on.
Within the next mile I found three more camp fires. Each
was made as the others had been made. They were the
overnight camp fires of one who knew the desert.

Why had so many overnight camps been made on the
one ridge?

There could only be one answer. That answer was in
the gold which had been imprisoned in that cloth bag.
Some one had hunted, not for that particular gold, but for
the deposit from which it had been taken.

I got to water, filled my canteens, rested a day and
went on to Randsburg.

At Randsburg I made discreet inquiries. The name of
Pedro Madrone still stuck in my mind. But I found that
Pedro Madrone was unknown in Randsburg. I asked men
who came from Mojave, and from other sections of the
desert; and always the name was the preface to a shake of
the head.

I told of finding the skeleton of the pack burro in the

desert. Then I waited around Randsburg for the news to travel.

Nothing happened.

As an experiment, I told of finding the sun-bleached bones of a woman far out in the trackless waste of the Mojave Desert. I waited a few days for that story to seep through the camp.

Still nothing happened. I must try another tack.

I was moved by an inspiration. I mentioned that near the bones of this woman I had found a folded paper, bleached and yellowed by the sun, but still bearing lines that could be traced.

After that, plenty happened—yet, hardly what I had expected.

The moon was half full again. I had made my camp half a mile outside of the town in a little valley where one could sleep under the stars. The wind blew and the desert whispered, and once more it seemed that the whispers were trying to convey a message. I became vaguely uneasy, with a desert man's intuition of trouble. Sleep would not come. I dressed, and walked into the desert.

Behind me, my camp showed peaceful and serene in the moonlight. The desert was a white silence of mystery. Somewhere, I thought I heard the sound of a foot crunching over a wind-blown stretch of desert gravel. I listened.

A dry bit of sage snapped beneath the weight of a skulking object.

I turned and started toward the place.

A rifle roared and I heard the unmistakable *thunk!* of a striking bullet. My bed roll gave a peculiar twitch, then was still again.

I could hear running steps, but I was unarmed and the would-be murderer had a rifle and he knew how to use it too.

That was the reason I didn't do any following, but

squatted down in the shelter of a clump of greasewood and waited for the moon to set. After that I rescued my blankets and rolled in back of some rocks.

Daylight found me scouting around where the noise of the feet on gravel had first come to my ears. The cartridge was in plain sight, a thirty-thirty with two little checks on the bottle neck.

I was sure of my ground now. I packed my stuff on my burro back, took my rifle from its holster, and headed out into the desert, back toward the place where I had found the skeleton of the burro.

It wasn't a case for the sheriff—not yet. But I had thrown out the bait that had brought to me the man I wanted. What was to follow could better happen out in the waste spaces where the arm of the law reaches but gropingly.

In one way it was not up to me, but I remembered the vital magnetism of the young woman who had stepped off the train. And then again, there is such a thing as justice. I didn't lose sight of that.

We who live in the desert get pretty close to nature. We don't ask for much. But we want a square deal, and we like to have other people get a square deal.

It was on the morning of the second day that I found a man camped by the side of the trail I was following. He was stooped a trifle, and the sun had been unkind to his skin. His face was an angry red and the nose was commencing to peel. The eyes were flecked with red streaks and his lips were cracked. He had city and tenderfoot written all over him.

That last crack of mine about finding a paper had brought results. Some one was very, very anxious to find the paper that had been beside the skeleton of the woman I was supposed to have found. But he was even more anxious to keep me from using it than to find the paper himself. That was the explanation of the rifle shot.

So the paper I should have had wasn't simply a writing accusing him of murder. It was more. How much more I couldn't tell.

My plan was to go directly into the desert. Then any man who insisted upon making camp with me would be the man who was following.

But this tenderfoot seemed hardly the man to have shot a burro squarely between the eyes at sixty yards with a single shot.

Still one can never tell—in the desert.

"Headed west?" I asked.

He gently patted the sunburned tip of his nose. "You're going east, aren't you?"

"Yes."

"I'm going east."

"I see. Camped rather early, didn't you?"

"I guess so. I'm not accustomed to travel. It's rather done me up. You see, I don't know the desert very well."

That much was self-evident. From the heavy, hot boots to the whipcord sport clothes he shrieked of newness to the desert.

He looked at me longingly, wistfully.

"Well, I'll be headed on," I said.

He gulped.

"Could I—er—join up with you?"

There it was, right like that. I had set a trap for the man who wanted to kill me, and this tenderfoot with his sunburned nose and heavy boots was walking into it.

Was he the man I must guard against? Was he a tool? Or had he merely happened along?

"You couldn't keep up," I told him. "I'm traveling fast and far."

"I'll keep up," he promised.

"All right," I said. "I'll camp here to-night with you,

and we'll start early in the morning. Guess I'd better shoot a jackrabbit. Got a rifle handy? Mine's got some trouble in the lock."

"Thirty-thirty in my saddle scabbard," he told me, pointing with his long arm.

I went to the scabbard and took out the rifle, sighted it.

It was a gun that had seen use, lots of it, and desert use at that.

"I'll throw the packs and then take a turn out through the sage," I told him.

"I ain't seen a rabbit," he said.

I just nodded. I knew what I was looking for and where to find it. He was watching me, so I wanted to have a mark when I fired.

Jackrabbits work their way into the middle of a sage clump and get down into a ball. Along in the afternoon, by making a noise and keeping on the east side of the bush you're looking at you can generally make them raise their ears. The sun shines through the thin cartilage of a rabbit's ears with a reddish color. There's no red naturally in the sage, so all you have to do is to make plenty of noise and watch for a pinkish glow from the sage.

I spotted one inside of the first hundred yards.

I walked up toward the sagebrush, looking just below the pink bit of color for something solid. He broke cover before I found the mark I wanted. I flung down on him and he bowled over at the crack of the rifle.

He was a young one and all right for eating.

I picked up the rabbit and moved back along my back trail. When I came to the place where I'd been standing when I shot, I dropped the rabbit, stooped and picked him up, and picked up the empty cartridge as well.

It was half an hour later that I had a chance to study that cartridge. It had an impression of the firing pin that was just a bit off center, and had two little split marks in the bottle neck.

I slept that night, but not in my blankets and not until late. But the city chap seemed to hit it off regular all night. He'd given his name as Jack Melford. I was puzzled in the morning.

"How long have you had that rifle?" I asked him.

"Just about half a day," he said. "A dark fellow named Madrone was through here, and he sold it to me."

I nodded. Maybe—and again maybe not. I couldn't be sure.

The third night I knew there was some one ahead of us. There were tracks, and the burros wiggled their ears at each other. We caught up to him just before making camp. We traveled in the evening moonlight. It was easier on the stock and easier on us. He had a camp fire going and he was standing back out of the circle of light.

"Hello," he called, and his voice was the voice of a man who doesn't welcome company.

He came in out of the darkness, a soft shadow of gliding caution, and tried to urge us onward by some excuse about the spring being muddied.

"We're stopping," I told the man.

"I'll put on some tea," was all he said, and flung some fresh wood on the fire, sage roots that flare up in crackling flames and make solid coals for cooking.

I got a look at him then. Part Mexican he was, and his eyes had that smoky tinge of dark mystery which comes from the Indian side of the Mexican blood.

"Pablo Sandoval," he said and flashed his teeth in a smile as he thrust out a brown hand.

We unpacked, had tea and *tortillas*. I managed to get a look at the rifle in Sandoval's scabbard. It was a thirty-thirty, and it was old, but it hadn't been carried much in a saddle scabbard. The stock showed it.

I managed to work Melford off to one side.

"Melford, did you ever see this man before?"

"No, why?"

"Sure he wasn't the man that sold you your rifle?"

"Heavens, no! It was Madrone who sold me the rifle, a black Mexican with a big stomach, fat, greasy."

I nodded and let it go at that, but there was something in the wind, and this tenderfoot was mixed in it, either as a tool or not. City gangsters have been known to come to the desert.

I didn't sleep until after the moon went down. That was late. Then I slept, but not in my blanket roll. Dawn found me tired, but ready to go.

I could strike the ridge where I'd found the bones of the dead burro by cutting across with a long march.

"I'm leaving you two," I said. "You'll be company for each other."

"But," said Sandoval, "I am traveling alone."

"And I'm going east," said Melford. "Why can't I stay on with you?"

"Because," I said, "I am not going east from here. I am going to the northeast."

"Oh," said Melford.

Sandoval said nothing.

We got on the packs. I noticed Melford studying a folded paper he surreptitiously took from his pocket. "Perhaps," he said dubiously, "I could get where I'm going by heading northeast from here—but I'm supposed to go east for one more day, and then north. There's a water hole east of here?"

"Yes," I said curtly, and swung my burros to the northeast.

From back of a rock outcropping on the top of a rise I watched them go. They went east. I pushed the burros fast and far. It was ten o'clock at night when I got to the ridge of the skeleton.

In the morning I started a systematic search.

Fifty yards from camp I found a track. It was made with a moccasined foot, but not the foot of an Indian. It was a small foot, and it didn't come down exactly in the line of travel. A line drawn through the heel and toe missed the next footprint by an inch and a half.

Some one had been over that ridge in the moonlight, after I'd made camp. It was impossible that that person hadn't seen my camp. It was also impossible for any one to exist in that stretch of the desert without a base of supplies, a burro loaded with provisions and water.

I lost the tracks in a rocky wash. I spent the day in fruitless search, and I was worried. The desert has a code of its own, and I had deliberately flung down a challenge to a murderer. It was up to me to notice trifles.

That afternoon I watched to the south. If Jack Melford found some excuse to join me again it would be almost a declaration of guilt. Paths do not cross in the desert without some reason.

Just before dusk I saw a cloud of dust. Then I made out burros and packs. I got out my rifle and saw that it was loaded with fresh shells, thoroughly oiled, and that the sights hadn't been jiggled any.

It got as dark as it could get with the big moon hanging in the eastern heavens. I made a small camp fire, and then waited in the shadow of a cactus.

It took the burros an hour and a half to reach my camp. Melford's voice boomed out across the desert.

"Good evening," he said.

"Howdy," I remarked, and slipped the rifle forward.

Then I saw there was another with him.

"Howdy," said the voice of Pablo Sandoval, and this time the voice was placating.

"Thought you fellows were going east," I said.

"And north," remarked Melford.

"And north," echoed Pablo Sandoval.

"I'll make you tea," I said, and walked in toward the camp fire. My rifle I left concealed back of the cactus. My six-shooter was on my hip, in plain sight, and my right hand was never far from the holster.

I made them tea, as is the code of the desert when a weary traveler comes to the camp of one who has already eaten.

Pablo Sandoval caught my eye and flickered a glance toward the desert. There was just the slightest inclination of the head, a gesture of beckoning.

"We've got to get some more wood," he said, and was on his feet like a cat, melting into the shadows.

"I'll help him. Sit still, Melford," I said, after a second or two, and went in the opposite direction.

I circled warily. Sandoval stood, outlined in the moonlight, motionless, his hands clasped back of his head. The gesture showed that he knew of my suspicions.

I approached him, and my right hand was on the butt of my six-shooter.

"Well?"

He came toward me so that I could hear his lowered voice.

"You're wondering why I came."

I remained silent.

"It is to save your life," he blurted.

"My life," I told him, "has always been able to save itself before. Perhaps, if you had *not* come, you might have saved a life."

I didn't tell him whose. I left that to soak in.

"*Señor*," he hissed, and leaned toward me, "he plans to murder you. I found that out, and I came to warn you."

"The tenderfoot?"

"Yes, the tenderfoot! He is a killer of the city, but dangerous even in the desert. He was here six months ago, and he killed then. I have heard admissions from his own lips!"

He was speaking in the Spanish language, this off-spring of three races, and he was talking rapidly.

"You're sure?"

"*Señor*, I am Pablo Sandoval, and I come of an old and honored family. I have warned. That is enough!" And he turned on his heel and strode away.

They are proud, these Mexicans, even when their blood has been well thinned with racial mixtures. I saw him stooping to gather wood, and I made no attempt to follow, but swung well to the left, gathering wood and waiting by my rifle until I saw him return to the camp fire.

I brought in my load of wood. We piled up the fire, then I dragged my blankets back of a clump of grease-wood. Melford yawned, nodded, smiled sheepishly.

"Last two days have used me up," he said.

He dragged his own blankets from the place where he had spread them to a place from which he could command a view of my own bed. That action might have been accidental, but it drew me a meaning glance from Pablo Sandoval.

Sandoval took his blankets far out into the desert.

"The light of the camp fire keeps me awake, and sometimes sparks blow," he said, by way of apology.

I kicked off my shoes and crawled under the blankets.

The moon was a ball of white fire, blazing steadily. The desert showed dazzlingly brilliant under the flooding moonlight, the sagebrush and greasewood casting black shadows, motionless sentinels guarding the silent sand.

I squirmed my blankets deeper into the clump of brush, and slipped from them on the dark side when Melford had his back turned to me. I wadded the clothes up so the blankets seemed to outline the form of a sleeper. I was tired of this stalling about. It was time for a showdown.

My hand was on my six-gun as I waited, watching Melford, waiting for a glint of moonlight on metal.

It did not come. Melford was sleeping. The regular breathing, the rhythmic snores all told their own story. And I was tired. The prospect of another sleepless night did not appeal to me.

I slipped forward over the sand, cautiously, noiselessly. Melford stirred when I was within a few feet of him. His eyes snapped open and saw the business end of my six-shooter boring into his chest.

"What—huh?"

"I'm taking no chances to-night," I whispered. "Get your hands up, out of the covers, over your head!"

"But—"

I jabbed him with the gun.

He took a deep breath. I knew what he intended to do, to shout to Sandoval. I punched him in the solar plexus with the butt of the gun, and the air whooshed from him. His jaw sagged and he gasped.

I knotted a pack rope around his wrists. Then I thrust a gag into his mouth and tied his wrists.

"Move and you'll stop lead," I warned, and glided into the shadows. My rifle was where I had left it. I holstered the six-gun and squatted, hugging the rifle.

Half an hour passed. The shadows shifted. There was a faint stirring of breeze. Soon the sand would commence to drift, and, as it drifted, would utter those desert whispers which mean nothing, yet which mean everything.

I wondered if I owed Pablo Sandoval an apology.

And then, even as I wondered, he came, a soft furtive shadow, stalking as skillfully as a cat, wary, ominous, deadly. And he was stalking my blankets. In his hand was a rifle.

I determined that I had been sufficiently long-suffering. When Pablo Sandoval raised his rifle I would call to him and step from behind the bush. Then we would shoot it out.

He inched his way around the concealment of a mesquite and raised the rifle. I raised my own rifle, got to one knee, prepared to call. And a moving shadow stopped me.

It was a shadow that came around the side of a clump of cacti, paused for a moment, then came forward. It was the shadow of a human being who walked on noiseless feet.

The moonlight flooded the desert as she emerged from behind the cacti, and I caught my breath.

She was almost naked, yet the nude body gave no hint of impropriety. It was the type of nudity which fits in with its surroundings, just as one would expect a rare marble to be nude, or a painting of a nymph at a pool.

She wore a little fragment of animal skin about her hips and there were moccasins on her feet. Her hair was around her shoulders, and there was a short bow with a pointed arrow in her hand.

She walked with that perfect muscular coördination which makes for grace in a deer, for noiseless power in a stalking mountain lion.

She was almost on Sandoval when she stopped and raised the bow.

Sandoval squinted down the barrel of the gun and pulled the trigger.

A spurt of flame, the roar of a rifle shattering the unechoing silence of the desert, and the *thunk* of the bullet. I knew there would be another bullet hole in my blanket roll, and I intended it to be the last. I cocked my rifle.

Then I realized there would be no need. The girl was drawing back the powerful bow, and her body was a song of grace.

Something warned him.

He glanced over his shoulder. He yelled, gave one startled leap. The bowstring twanged a deeply resonant hum. The arrow flashed like a streak of death-dealing shadow, but his leap saved him.

He flung around the rifle, and I pressed my own weapon to my shoulder.

Then he saw her face.

The rifle wavered in his grasp, dropped from nerveless fingers. He made the sign of the cross, mechanically, dazedly. The girl flicked a hand to the little quiver which was at her waist, tied to the fragment of skin which covered the contour of her hips. Another arrow was on the string.

But Pablo Sandoval seemed not to heed the menace of that arrow. It was the face that held his attention. One staring look he gave it, and then screamed. He whirled and took to his heels.

I heard him scream for the second time as he tore past me. I heard his third scream as he dashed blindly through a clump of spiny cactus. Then there were no more screams for an interval, while he rattled the gravel of the dry wash with panic-driven feet.

He came out on the other side, running blindly, and he screamed again. This time his scream contained a new note. It was a note of desert madness, that peculiar knife-like something that is always present in the hysterical yapping of a coyote, that fiendish undertone of malice which is in the voice of a mountain lion.

I knew then that he would never come back. I have heard men give screams before, screams that held that same note, and run madly into the desert. None ever came back.

A woman's voice was in my ear.

"You may put away the rifle."

Was it a threat or merely a statement? I turned to her. She was closer now and the moonlight was on her face. But I had no need of the moonlight. I had known who she would be as soon as I had seen the look of mad terror on the features of Pablo Sandoval.

She was the woman of the snakeskin shoes, the woman who had descended from the train at Mojave.

But she had changed.

Her face held none of the eye-puffs, none of the sagging lines, none of the tired droop. Her features were bronzed and they were as firm as the features of a fifteen-year-old child. Her eyes were clear and steady, and the magnificently beautiful lines of her rounded body were hardened to graceful strength.

I lowered the rifle.

"Did you bring Jack?" she asked; and then I saw a great light.

"I tied and gagged him," I said.

She followed the direction of my pointing finger. I saw her stoop over the form in the blankets. There was the sound of a knife cutting rope, and then two arms came around her.

I walked away, sat down and waited.

It was some time before they came to me, arm in arm. He had given her some of his extra clothes, and she looked uncomfortable. She did the talking.

"I am Jean Stiles," she said. "It all started with a map an Indian drew for my father years ago. We all took it for a joke, but when I got fed up with civilization and parties and all that, I decided to hunt up the place. I wrote to an acquaintance, and I guess I told him too much. He referred me to 'Pedro Madrone.'

"There never was any such person. But Sandoval posed as Madrone to me. It was an accomplice who met

Jack, sent him out into the desert, and even sold him Sandoval's rifle, either as a passport to Sandoval or to get rid of a piece of evidence."

That was a fine bit of Mexican irony!

"Sandoval told me you were the guide," Melford said to me, "who led Jean into the desert. We were to spy on you, force you to confess."

The girl went on:

"Sandoval guided me into the desert and kept trying to get the map. I'd only given him a copy of a part of it. I knew he was a dangerous man, and when I got near the gold I left him one night, packed the burro and went on by myself.

"He let me get the gold, then demanded the map and the gold. I'd hidden the map. He shot the burro and left me on foot without provisions, then he shot a hole in the water canteen. He figured thirst would force me into submission.

"He tried to trail me, carrying a canteen of water, figuring to trade me water for gold when my thirst became desperate. But I had four bags of gold. I ran and dropped the gold, and he spent so much time looking for the sacks I'd dropped that it got dark.

"Then a windstorm came up. I guess it blotted out my trail. He never followed me. He had the rest of the burros hidden somewhere. I tried to find them, couldn't and went back to the place of the gold. There was a spring there, and some food, and the place can't be found without a map. It's in a hidden cañon.

"It took all of my strength to get back. And I couldn't leave the place. There was a store of corn there, and an Indian, an old, old man who taught me to shoot the bow. There was game, there was corn. There were no burros, no means of reaching civilization. I think the Indian could have made it on foot, but he wouldn't go. He said I had been sent as a Priestess of the Sun.

"I grew to like it. I've never felt so well in my life. And I knew, sooner or later, Jack would come . . . Ugh, these clothes are scratchy. I feel as though my skin were suffocating!"

"You'll have to get accustomed to them again, Jean," Melford warned.

She met his eyes.

"Why?" she asked.

"Why—er—why, because! You can't go back to the city as you were!"

She nodded slowly, raised her face to the moon, and then looked out over the desert, over past the red and purple mountains.

"Listen," she said dreamily, "and I'll sing you the Song of the Sun. It's a whispered song, and it's to be sung only at sunrise."

And she laughed nervously. Then, when no one said anything, she started chanting the Song of the Sun. It was pure Indian all right.

When she had finished, the silence of the desert settled on us. Then she began to whisper, after a while.

"There's life there, health, sunshine, fresh air; gold, lots of gold, all the gold one would want. Back in the city I'd go mad again; and your lungs, Jack . . ."

Her voice trailed off in a whisper.

I went to my blankets.

"You youngsters sit up and talk all night if you want to. I've been dodging sleep for the last three weeks, and having holes shot in my bed roll. I'm going to sleep. In the morning we'll try and trail Sandoval."

And I kicked off my boots.

"He thought he was seeing my ghost," said the girl.

Then she added dreamily: "If he hadn't jumped, I'd have killed him with the arrow."

"Jean!" exclaimed the tenderfoot in a shocked voice.

She looked at him speculatively. Then she touched his face with the tips of her fingers, and laughed, a low, crooning laugh. It was the laugh I've heard an Indian girl give to her lover; I never heard a white woman laugh that way before.

I doubled my coat under my head and dropped off to sleep. When I awoke the east was a long streamer of vermilion with banners of gold. The tops of the red and purple hills were catching enough light to show in color instead of a black outline.

I looked for Melford. His blankets were empty. He had gone. And the girl had gone.

Then I found a pile of clothes. The extra clothes he had given to the girl. They lay in a pile where she had dropped them. They had been too "scratchy."

Over near my blankets was a sack of skin, filled with gold. There was enough gold in that sack to make a neat little nest egg.

There wasn't any note. And they hadn't taken anything with them. I knew that the Priestess of the Sun had gone back to the desert she had learned to love and had taken her mate with her.

I tried to trail Sandoval. He was running the last I saw of his tracks. He hit the slope of the red and purple mountains, and the rocks didn't show any more tracks.

I waited two nights, waiting for them to come back, the Priestess of the Sun and her man. They didn't come back. I wanted to give them a chance to change their minds, but they didn't change 'em.

Daytimes it all seemed like a dream. It seemed that I should go and bring them back. It seemed that a girl had no right to throw herself away from civilization.

Then would come the moonlight, the velvety night, and the sand whispers, and it would seem the most natural thing in the world that the girl should want to stay with the desert. I thought of her as I had seen her get off the train, soft, flabby, tired of mouth, puffs under her eyes.

Then I remembered her as she had drifted into camp, bronzed, graceful, moving with the easy stride of perfect health. And Melford's lungs needed the desert sunshine.

Often I've wondered how they're making out, the Priestess of the Sun and her mate. Sometimes, just before I drop off to sleep, I think the sand has a message to me, a message directly from them; and there's always a smile on my lips at what the sand seems to whisper.

Out in the desert we get closer to fundamental truths than you do in the cities.

Golden Bullets

I NIGHT SUMMONS

Go THROUGH THE desert in a Pullman car and you'll be bored. Travel through it in an automobile and you'll be mildly interested, but disappointed.

"So this is the desert," you'll think. "This is the place about which I've heard so much! Shucks, it's nothing much, just sand and mountains, cacti and sunshine; gasoline stations, not quite so handy."

But get away from the beaten trail in the desert. Get out with your camp equipment loaded on the backs of burros. Or even take a flivver and get off the main roads. See what happens.

The spell of the desert will grip you before you've left the main road five miles behind. That night you'll sleep beneath steady stars and listen to the whispers that are the night noises of the desert.

By morning you'll either hate and fear it, or you'll love it. I never knew any middle point, not with any one. The desert engenders either fear or fascination, either love or hate.

And if you're one of those who love it, you'll get to the point where the whispers mean much.

You won't hear 'em until you get in your blankets and the camp fire has died down to a mere blotch of dull red against the gray sand of the desert. Then a wind will stir up from some place. The embers will fan into a golden glow, and you'll hear the whispers. Of course you'll know it's just the sand rattling against the cacti. Maybe, if the wind gets stronger, it'll be sand rustling against sand.

But those are the desert whispers, and you'll get so you listen for them. You'll finally get so you can almost interpret 'em. Sounds funny, but it isn't. It'll come just as you're dropping off to sleep. You'll hear the sand whisper to the sand, and the sand answer, and you'll be just drowsy enough so you'll nod your head in confirmation. But the next morning you can't tell what it was you were agreeing to.

I've made my stake out of the desert, and I feel kindly toward it. I've got enough now to wear fine clothes and have a chauffeur to drive me the places I want to go. I've struck it rich, and people nudge each other when I go to the theater and point me out—Bob Zane, the man that opened the virgin lode.

At first I thought I'd never go back to the desert. I was tired of living on rationed water. I wanted to be where I could take a bath every day, twice a day if I wanted. I craved fresh linen, vegetables, cream in my coffee, beautiful women, theaters, newspapers.

I thought I was satisfied.

I'd stand on Hollywood Boulevard at the corner of Cahuenga and watch 'em pass, the well-fleshed, firm-skinned beauties with their peach-and-cream throats, their red lips, and their exploring eyes.

But I got sick of it without even knowing I was.

It happened one afternoon. She was a Spanish girl, and she wasn't of the boulevards. Her skin didn't have the smooth gloss of city life. It had been baked by sun, caressed by wind, moistened by infrequent rain. She was slender, almost stringy. But she moved with a lithe grace that her city sisters couldn't ape; she was vital as a panther.

I thought of her often that evening. I couldn't get her out of my mind.

I drifted into a palatial picture theater. The sound picture wailed through its action. There was a desert scene. I slipped forward to the edge of my chair. And then something happened to the lights. The house was dark. When the picture machine went on the blink you could hardly see your hand in front of your face.

Some one called for patience, that the break was temporary and would be repaired in less than thirty seconds.

The audience sat there in the gloom, and started to whisper. Funny about men, that way. In the dark they seem to lack confidence. They whispered as surreptitiously as though they were afraid of the gloom, afraid a loud noise might bring some night animal pouncing down upon them—instinct, I guess, carry-over memories of past lives when men were food for animals, instead of animals being food for men.

That whisper started in the back of the house. It grew in volume, like a desert wind sweeping down a cañon, sending rustling sand against the cacti. Soon the whisper swept around me, hissing in my very ears, a vast composite of sound—and the lights went on, showing the desert scene on the screen.

I got to my feet as one in a daze.

I tramped on somebody's feet, and he growled. A woman tittered. I didn't even notice them. I stumbled to the aisle, walked rapidly toward the door. My chauffeur was coming at ten thirty. I didn't have time to wait for him, couldn't even stop to telephone him.

I caught a taxi and went to the Arcade Depot. There

was a train for Yuma in twenty minutes. I got a lower. Daylight found me at Yuma. I got a flivver and some blankets, a canteen, some grub. I didn't get much. I was too impatient, like a man who has been too long separated from a loving mistress.

By ten o'clock I was well out in the desert.

That night I sat by a little camp fire. The stars blazed steadily. The little winds were dancing about, making the embers flare up to gold, then dull to russet red. I stretched in my blankets and listened.

Pretty soon I began to hear them, the whispers of the desert.

All about me was that heavy, oppressive silence that stretches down from the very stars. It was broken only by the whispers. Those whispers were so faint I couldn't hear 'em at first. Then the wind freshened, and I could hear the sand whispering to the sand.

I thought it was the desert giving me a welcome back to it, and I smiled a sleepy smile. Then I thought I heard the word "Tucson," and I straightened and snapped my eyes open. The word had sounded awful plain.

But it was just a funny sound the sand had made against the cacti, and I closed my eyes and drowsed again, half listening, half sleeping. I dozed, awoke, sighed and settled to sleep.

And the whispers became plainer. I could hear words, soft, hissing, whispered words.

"The *señor* will come?" asked a hissing voice. There seemed to be something more to it than a sand whisper.

"But the *señor* must come! The man dies."

And there was a warm breath on my cheek. I fancied a soft hand caressed my hair, drew itself along my forehead.

"Softly; to awaken suddenly is bad. The *señor* must open his eyes—"

I snapped my eyes open to see her.

She was dark-skinned, and her oval face was bent over my own, her lips half parted. The eyes were catching the starlight, sending it back. They seemed limpid pools of dark romance, swimming in reflected starlight.

I straightened, and she drew back.

"It is all right, *señor*," she said in the language of Mexico. "I feared to awaken you suddenly. It is bad for you, and you might have reached for your gun and gone '*boom!*' and it would have been all over for poor little me."

She laughed, and the stars caught the glint of her pearly teeth and showed them against the warm mystery of her pink mouth.

"You must come," she said.

I struggled to a sitting posture.

"Why must I come, and where?"

"You must come with me to save one of your race who is dying. We have no automobile, nothing but a burro cart, and the heat of the sun would kill him before he reached the main road. But you have your automobile. We saw the lights of your car, saw your camp fire, and it was decided that I should come. I have walked for more than two hours, *señor*, and the camp was hard to find. You made a very small fire, and you let it go out early."

I nodded.

"I wanted to listen to the sand," I said, before I thought.

She lost her smile as she regarded me.

"The *señor*, then, knows the desert," she said. "It is well, otherwise he would not believe."

"What wouldn't I believe?"

"That which you are to hear. But come."

I kicked the blankets off. She sat silent while I dressed. None of the false modesty of city maidens, none of the curiosity of the morbid, none of the brazenness of the hard-faced women of the camps. She was what she was, a child of the desert; and because I also was of the desert, we were in perfect accord.

I knew that I was to go on some errand of mercy, that this young woman had walked miles through soft sand that clung to her ankles, that she was worried about the one I must try to save. I knew that speed counted for something, and I pulled into my clothes, flung the canteen in the car, tossed in the blankets without waiting to roll them, and motioned her to the seat beside me.

"Which way?" I asked.

She pointed to a star.

"That way, *señor*."

"There is a road?"

"There is desert. The *señor* will have to watch and drive with care."

I put the car in low and swung away from my camp, out toward the star.

Twice we had to make detours of direction to get level ground, swinging around the heads of dry washes. Once we got into such deep sand that I had to let some air out of the tires. Finally we saw a hill blotting out the lower stars, showing as a dim silhouette.

"Señor," she said, placing her soft hand upon the back of mine, "it is here."

I saw the rudiments of a road, and floor-boarded the throttle. We crept up the hill, making a terrific noise of snarling motor, grinding transmission, spinning tires.

There was a house at the top. A door flung open into a lighted oblong, and a fat woman stood as a black blotch, framed in gold. She screamed a comment in Spanish. I shut off the motor, and the girl vaulted over the door and ran with flashing ankles. I followed, more slowly. The fat woman showered blessings upon my head, hailed me as one sent from the gods.

The house had that indefinable odor of a place where sickness reigns.

An oil lamp furnished a reddish illumination. There were beds in the single room, a table, a stove, a rude fireplace. A couple of boxes did for chairs. It was a desert home, no better and perhaps a little worse than the average.

On the bed next to the far wall something tossed and turned. Over this bed the girl was stooped, her cool hands soothing in fluttered caresses.

I walked to her.

He was a white man, and he was far gone. His red-rimmed eyes told of wasting fever. The gaunt face seemed but pale skin stretched over white bones. His beard had grown in rough stubble. The hair was matted, the lips tinged with blue.

About the bed was a foul odor, the odor of decomposition.

I knew then that the man was wounded, that it was an old wound, and that he could not be moved. I had seen death before, and I knew the shadow of its fluttering wings.

I wondered how I might break the news to the man on the bed and to the girl. It was hard to say. There was, perhaps, a chance in a million if the man lay there, if he had plenty of water, if his wound were cauterized and treated with proper antiseptics.

To move him over the jolting surface of the desert would mean certain death. Yet the girl had set her heart on his being moved. She recognized the slow march of death in the man's present surroundings. Had I come there a day sooner it might not have been too late. But his face was already graying.

It was the man who broke the silence. He turned his feverish eyes upon me and smiled. As his lips parted I could smell the fever on his breath.

II YAQUI BULLETS

"Tina says she got you, to move me," he said. "It is too late; but I am glad you have come. Draw up a box and listen—listen carefully, for I cannot repeat. I will tell you everything, and then the tax on my strength will bring about the end. So you must listen, and not interrupt, not argue, not question."

I grinned reassuringly.

"Oh, it's not that bad. You can tell me a little, then get some sleep. To-morrow you'll be better. Maybe you can be moved by to-morrow night."

He shook his head, rolling it from side to side upon the flour-sacked bundle that served as a pillow.

"Don't argue! Don't try to salve me over. I know what I know. I'm a surgeon. I know the symptoms. I'll be good for twenty-four hours if I conserve my strength. If I talk I'll go any minute. But I've got to talk. The end is the same in any event. Come closer, don't waste time."

I knew he spoke the truth. The girl felt it. She gave a choking sob, grabbed his hand in hers, pressed it to her lips. He smiled at her, and the fever-reddened eyes grew tender; then he turned to me.

"Take my wrist in your hand. Hold your middle finger there, on the pulse. As long as it beats firm don't interrupt me. When you feel it skip a few beats and then race rapidly in little, stringy pulses, that means I am going. Then tell me to be fast. Until then, let me tell it my own way, don't interrupt."

I nodded a promise. He was half delirious, fighting for sanity, and his pulse was rapid, bounding, but regular.

I held the fever-parched flesh, felt the throbbing pulse as it pounded away the life stream beneath my fingers, and listened.

"I am a Los Angeles surgeon. I had an office in one of the new buildings on Wilshire. My name doesn't matter. Civilization had gripped me. I was money mad. I wanted power, and I wanted money.

"I had some measure of success in my profession. I thought I was progressing. I invested and made money. Then came the crash of the stock market. I was wiped out. And I was fighting mad, desperate. I'd have robbed a bank if I could have been certain of getting away with it. You know the frame of mind."

I nodded, because he was half delirious and because I wanted him to get over the preliminaries and get down to business. He went on:

"Then a girl came into my office. She was just a young thing, society stamped all over her, class in every line of her bearing. But she was in some sort of trouble. There were dark circles under her eyes. Her glance was nervous.

"I thought I knew the symptoms, but I didn't. There was an old man with her, a fellow who was all dried out by desert winds. He must have been about sixty. There was some strange bond between him and the girl, yet she didn't trust him.

"The girl did the talking: 'This man wants an X-ray of his shoulder,' she said.

"I said nothing, but took the X-ray. It would be a cash case and a good fee. I'd see to that, and I knew these cases where they don't give names and talk as though they've carefully rehearsed what they're going to say—which is the case.

"The X-ray showed a bullet under the right scapula. It was an old wound. The scar was nearly faded to normal color. I showed them the plate.

" 'Remove that bullet,' said the girl.

"I shook my head. 'It's not advisable,' I told her; 'the wound is an old one, and the bullet has been isolated by the tissues. It's not interfering with the bone or muscle motion, and there's always danger of infection from an operation.'

"She scowled at me. 'We want it removed. If you won't do it, some one else will. There's a good fee in it for you if you do it, nothing if you don't.'

" 'Can you go to the hospital this afternoon?' I asked the man.

" 'Hospital—hell!' blazed the girl. 'It's a case for an operation right here and now. You've got the equipment.'

" 'I'd have to get a nurse.'

" 'I'll be your nurse.'

" 'You! You'd get sick at the sight of blood!'

" 'Try me.'

"I tried her. I got her to help with the anaesthetic, and I performed the operation there on my office operating table. I dug out the bullet, sewed up the cut, put on bandages, and turned to her. She was white-faced, and her lips were tight, but she was standing it one hundred per cent.

" 'It's all over,' I told her. 'It'll be a couple of hours before he comes out from under. Then he can be taken home in a cab or an ambulance. He'll be feeling pretty groggy.'

"She nodded, and began fishing among the packings I'd used and dumped into the bowl at the foot of the table. I asked what she wanted.

" 'The bullet, of course.'

" 'I have it here,' I said, and handed it over.

"And at that time the door opened and Miss Marlan, my regular office nurse, came strolling into the room.

" 'I've missed you,' I said, and my tone wasn't too cordial. I'd almost lost the operation fee over her absence. She'd been due an hour earlier. She looked like the fag end of a big party. She made some carefully thought up excuse, a lie that I didn't even bother to listen to.

" 'I want this bullet tested,' said the girl.

" 'Tested?' I wanted to know. 'What for?'

" 'Gold,' she said.

" 'Bullets,' I explained, speaking as one would speak to a child, 'are made of lead alloy. This one is discolored from having been embedded in the living tissues.'

" '*Will* you please test it?' she stormed.

"To please her I got out some acid, a little graduate, cleaned the bullet under a water faucet, and dropped it into the graduate with the tips of my forceps.

"Then I got the surprise of my life. The bullet was almost pure gold!

"My nurse crowded close, watching the test. I'd as soon Miss Marlan hadn't been there. The girl seemed not the least surprised at what the bullet was. She called for an ambulance, paid my fee for the operation, and had the unconscious man removed.

"When she had gone, Miss Marlan, the nurse, looked after her with eyes that were smoky with thought.

" 'Know who she was?' she asked.

" 'No,' I said; 'do you?'

"The nurse shook her head, but I knew she was lying, and that aroused my curiosity."

The surgeon quit speaking as a fit of coughing seized him. The Mexican girl flung herself upon him, wiping his forehead with a wet rag. She pressed a little bottle of whisky to his lips. He drank, then resumed his story.

"My nurse, Miss Marlan, took occasion to become impertinent a couple of days later, and I discharged her. At the time I thought there was a smirk on her face when I let her go. It seemed to be just what she wanted me to do.

"Then chance gave a clew as to the identity of the girl who had ordered the mysterious operation. She was Stella McRae, daughter of a man who had lost everything in the market. She was engaged to marry a chap named Craleigh, and it was more than rumored that Craleigh was a big creditor of the old man. He had agreed to take the daughter in payment of the debt.

"The girl, Stella, was reported to be visiting friends in the Imperial Valley. I read of that in the society column. But it wasn't until I learned that my nurse, Miss Marlan, and the chap she was going with, a fellow named Lugger, had gone into the desert on a prospecting trip, that I suddenly took a tumble. I got busy and traced them, then.

"The society girl, Stella McRae, had run onto this old prospector, and he'd told her of a secret mine somewhere in Mexico, probably in the Yaqui country. The Indians there are outlaws, and they use gold and silver for bullets. That's the old story. I've heard it since, a dozen times.

"Stella McRae wanted to buy her freedom, so she could marry for love instead of for money. My nurse had doped it out and she'd gone down to hijack the mine when it was located. And I had been partially responsible.

"I went after them. I don't know why. Perhaps it was the lure of the money. Perhaps it was because I wanted to do the square thing by the girl. Perhaps it was greed, perhaps it was sympathy. Anyway, I went.

"I traced Miss Marlan and Carl Lugger into the desert. They went through here. Tina knows the way. She acted as guide until I sent her back. That was when the country got dangerous. I was a fool not to have some one who knew the desert with me. I was just a tenderfoot. But I found them; and I was the one who blundered. It was too much smoke from a camp fire, I guess. At any rate, I got the Indians into the country, and then the trouble started."

The dying doctor got that far and then there was another spell of coughing. I felt the form writhing and twisting beneath my hand, felt the pulse grow weak and stringy. I bent forward.

"Be calm," I told him.

He knew it was the end. His eyes grew glassy with effort, but the coughing twisted his system, and then, when he got over the coughing, he was so weak he could hardly speak.

I figured he'd opened up bleeding in the wounds again, and told the girl to bring me some hot water and rags.

The doctor rolled his head in a half circle on the dirty pillow, gasped, and whispered to me in a husky voice.

"You'll go . . . This is important—bend closer—got to tell you this or they'll trap you . . . When you see a painted face on the rock, watch out for—"

And that was as far as he got.

The threadlike pulse stopped. The eyes snapped into some peculiar expression, the iris expanding, then contracting. The head ceased to roll. The whisper died into a rattle and then was silent.

It was a wail from the fat woman that conveyed the news to the girl.

"He is dead," she wailed.

The girl fell forward, her shoulders heaving in sobs, and I comforted them as best I could.

I stayed the night there, and we buried him the next day. He'd been badly shot up, and there had been infection. Why a city physician should have been possessed of the wild urge to go after a secret mine in the Yaqui country was more than I knew.

As for the golden bullets—well, I'd heard whispers of golden bullets, but, then, one hears all sorts of whispers in the desert. It doesn't do to take 'em too seriously.

But I got to wondering if what he said was true, and before we buried him I explored around a bit in the infected wounds, and I finally carved out a bullet.

The girl came in the room just then, and I dropped the bullet into my pocket. I didn't want her to know. She seemed to be taking it awfully hard as it was.

We buried him in a sandy grave with a little ceremony that wasn't orthodox, but it sounded solemn, and the Mexicans cried and covered their heads with their skirts as I filled in the dirt.

Then we erected a cross, and put a monument of stones on the grave.

After that I got a chance to examine the bullet. I whistled when I'd made a few tests. The bullet was almost pure gold.

That night the girl came to me as I sat by the fire, and slipped her hand in mine.

"He wanted you to go," she said.

I nodded.

"I will go with you part of the way, to show you where the trail is."

The old Mexican wailed a protest, but the girl turned flashing eyes upon her and spat forth sentences that sounded as the rattle of gunfire. The old woman dried up.

It was a strange thing: golden bullets, Yaqui country, a girl for a guide. Would the Indians be expecting some one to come in, following the wounded man's outbound trail?

The Yaquis are queer chaps. They respect a white man as long as a white man respects them. They're fiendishly cruel when the occasion warrants. The Mexicans persecute them, and they torture the Mexicans when they get a chance. They're proud, and they're independent, and they live in one of the richest mineral countries in the world.

They tell stories of the Yaquis following up the main ridge of the Sierra Madre range, and coming in to trade

for rifles with certain tight-lipped traders who slink down
from Arizona. It's a grim business, and the story goes that
a rifle brings its weight in gold.

I'd heard whispers of the rifle traffic, as has every one
who has lived in the desert. And I'd heard of the reloading tools the Yaquis buy; and I'd heard of golden bullets.

The story goes that they won't bother to pack lead
back to their homes because gold and silver make good
bullets, and they have all they want of them and more.
But I'd never seen any golden bullets, nothing but whispers which had been through the desert, just like the
whispers of the lost mines.

But now a tenderfoot had gone into the country and
had found a golden bullet. He'd found too many of 'em;
but then, he was a tenderfoot. If his story was true, there
was a society girl in there somewhere, and a nurse who
had taken her lover and gone in on a hijacking expedition,
and the country would be swarming with Yaquis—perhaps.

There was always the chance the Indians had only
stumbled onto the surgeon, shot him up, and figured he
was the only miner in the country.

"You will go, *señor*?" crooned the girl.

I nodded and squeezed her hand.

"If you will show me the way, Tina."

And then she put her head on my shoulder and cried.

"He wished it so," she muttered between her sobs.

III   SECRET CAMPS

We started before dawn, trying to get as many miles as
possible behind us before it got hot. We had burros, and
we were traveling light. The fat Mexican—an aunt or

something, I never did get her relationship to Tina straightened out—stood in the doorway of the shack, her head bowed and covered with her skirt, and the sound of her wailing followed us out over the dark grayness that enfolds the desert before dawn.

I'd crossed the Mexican line that night when I came with the girl to see the dying doctor, so I didn't bother too much about border patrols. We were seven or eight miles south of the border at the start.

The country was rolling, sandy, covered with cactus and some mesquite. The mountains were to the left, blotting out the light that began to ooze through the higher passes as the eastern sky got rosy. We were following a rough trail, and it was hard going.

The girl walked mechanically. Her eyes were filled with grief, but she never complained of fatigue or the cruel rocks that sprinkled the trail as we climbed higher into the mountains.

We stopped about eleven in the shadow of a mesquite and had some cold tortillas and beans. Then I spread the blankets for a pillow, and we got some sleep. It was hot, and the flies were bothersome, but we were tired enough to sleep anywhere.

By two o'clock in the afternoon we were up, and we had a little water from the canteens. Then I tightened the cinches on the pack burros, and we started on again.

We went on until well after dark. It was the sort of travel that took it out of a man, hard, steady, hot, tedious. The girl seemed as fresh as when we had started that morning. Her eyes were a little darker, perhaps. Her lips remained unsmiling, and she seemed in something of a daze, but she traveled at a pace that ate up the miles.

We camped that night. I don't think she slept much. Once, when the whispers began to drift over the face of the desert, I heard her sobbing to herself. But I didn't keep awake to listen to her. I was dog tired, and I knew talk would do no good. It was one of those things time alone can heal. She had loved him, and she had loved him with a wealth of passion that only the Latin blood can know.

Perhaps the night wind was stirring the whispering sand until she thought she could hear the sound of his voice. I don't know. I only know that the wind sent the whispering sand skidding and whirling through the draw where we had camped, and that the girl sobbed, and that the burros were restless and the stars blazed down steadily.

Early in the morning she was up, and she had the fire going and a little coffee water bubbling by the time I woke up. It was the smell of the coffee that awakened me.

I caught up the burros and saddled the packs. We started as the east was just getting a faint brassy hue that made the stars retire to needle points. It was cold with the dry cold of the desert places. Soon it would be hot. We were rationing ourselves on the water.

Near ten o'clock the girl stopped.

"Can we camp here?" she asked.

I looked at the sun.

"We could make another hour before the siesta," I said. "Of course, if you are tired—"

She shook her head impatiently.

"*We* camped here, the second night," she said, and then I saw the blackened ashes of a little camp fire off to one side.

I nodded and flung the packs off the burros. She crouched down beside the blackened embers and lived with her memories.

The sun was beating down on that little circle of charcoal, but she didn't seem to mind.

After a while I dozed off.

When the flies woke me up she was still sitting there.

That afternoon we crossed the railroad on an angle and then struck up into the Sierra Madre range. The going got rough, and we ran into some timber. There was more water here, and it was cooler.

After a week we were in a well-watered country, and we began to go pretty careful. I made small fires out of bone-dry wood, and I didn't make any fire at all at night.

On the tenth day the girl pointed to a little rock-bound depression. From the looks of the trees I figured there was a spring there and some green grass.

"That is where he left me. I camped there and was unmolested. He came back three days later, and—he was as you saw him, shot."

I nodded.

He'd have stood more chance if she had kept him there and put herbs on the wounds, but there was no use making her feel sorry; and they'd both been pretty well scared. The Yaqui is none too gentle.

"I shall wait there for you," she said.

I shook my head. "You'll go back! Now, which way did the *señor* go from here?"

She shrugged her pretty shoulders.

"I know not the way he went, and I will not go back. I wait. My place is here. You are doing that which *he* asked. Every night he whispers to me of what I am to do."

"No, you'll have to go back. It'll take me a long time to accomplish what I have in mind. I'll leave you a burro with plenty of grub."

She pouted.

"I could be of more use here."

"No."

"But we can camp there to-night, in our old camp?"

"To-night only, and there will be no fire."

She accepted my word as law. We camped there in

the dark. There was no sand to whisper now. But the trees rustled in the wind that came up before dawn, and they gave soft whispers, vague promises. It was spooky.

I got her burro packed in the morning. She kissed me good-by. I watched her out of sight and then began to explore the country. I felt certain I could find anything that a tenderfoot had found.

There were jagged mountains, covered with pine, dry air that blew over the ridges, vaulted blue black sky, great cañons that were filled with purple tinged shadows. Everywhere was grim silence, save for the rustle of wind in the tops of the trees.

Somewhere ahead was the place where Indians found gold more plentiful than lead. It was up to me to find that place, and to see that my burros were in condition to bring out much of that treasure.

I found a box cañon with a spring, and I worked all day making a rock enclosure that would keep the burros in the cañon. There was plenty of feed and water.

I camped without a fire.

In the morning I started out, a little parched corn meal tied in a sack at my belt, a little bacon rolled up in a blanket on my back, my rifle and plenty of shells, a six-gun at my hip for work at close quarters.

I went slowly, looking for tracks and hugging the shadows. I saw several deer, and the fresh meat looked tempting, but I wouldn't risk a shot.

That night I camped high on a ridge by a trickling spring. I made no fire. The single blanket I carried barely served to turn the wind that sprang up about midnight. I lay and shivered, catching a little sleep.

I listened to the wind in the pines, thought of the apartment I had fixed up in Hollywood, my car, the chauffeur—and I was satisfied it was all a mistake, trying to live in civilization. I had gotten soft. The elevation and the wind kept me from being comfortable in a single blanket. That was what beds and mattresses, hot baths, and servants had done for me.

Toward morning I got more sleep.

As I rolled up my blanket and chewed on a little parched corn meal, I got the idea some one was watching me. I got back in the shadow of the pines and waited for more than an hour. But nothing moved that I could see, except some deer that came in to the water hole.

I oozed out of the shadow and slipped down the ridge. Here and there I could see tracks, Indian tracks. Then I came to some softer soil and saw shod tracks, those of a woman and those of a man.

I studied those tracks. They'd been made right after a light rain, and then the sun had baked them in the soil. They were running tracks. The woman went first. Back of her, covering her retreat, the man plodded along.

I could see where he'd fired a gun from time to time, a thirty-thirty. The brass shells were along the side of the trail he'd made. It hadn't been an Indian firing those shots or he'd have picked up the cartridges.

Then I came to where Indian tracks had intercepted the man tracks. The girl seemed to have gotten away. The Indians and the man milled around in something of a mess, and then there were no more tracks of a man's shoes.

I crept along cautiously, watching, waiting. It looked like a poor time to be trying to sneak a mine out of the Yaqui country. It has been done, but only when a man could slip into the country, work fast and silently, and slip out again.

Apparently the society girl and the prospector had run into trouble. He'd probably told her the story of the mine, one he'd discovered earlier, only to be shot up and driven out. She'd had the bullet removed for proof, then financed the expedition. And it looked as if the prospector were out of the game.

Twice that afternoon I had the idea I was being followed. So that night I built a little fire, well screened by brush, let it die down to coals. Then I took some brush tips and filled out my blanket so it looked like a sleeper. I placed the dummy right close to the circle of coals and climbed a tree to wait.

Half an hour passed without anything happening. I was getting ready to come down, figuring my ideas of being followed had all been the bunk. Then I saw a shadow cautiously gliding toward the camp. I crouched in the tree, saw that my six-gun was loose in the holster, and waited.

I was unprepared for that which followed.

They shot in a crashing volley without warning. I could see the flashes of their guns, hear the whine of the bullets, see the dummy figure jump and twitch as the bullets crashed into it.

Then everything was silent.

I waited for them to come up to plunder. Then, if there weren't too many, I'd show them the difference between shooting down a tenderfoot doctor and tackling a fellow that had spent most of his life in the desert.

But they didn't come in. They were satisfied.

I saw them moving off, a compact little group.

I waited an hour, got down the tree, went to my blanket. There were half a dozen holes in it. I dug into the ground back of the blanket, probing after bullets. I got a couple. They were golden, and they looked as though they'd been but freshly molded.

Usually the Yaquis will give one warning to a white man in their country. That warning takes the shape of an Indian standing with upraised palm, motioning the traveler to go back. When one has that warning, if he's

wise, he goes back. I'd been trying to keep under cover
and not get that warning. But they weren't giving any.

IV BY THE PAINTED ROCK

The way this play stacked up, there was just one thing
to do, and it was up to me to do that quickly.

Sometimes a fellow can get away with a stake from
the Yaqui country. It has been done. Sneak into it along
the backbone of the Sierra Madres, keep quiet, find a
mine, take what can be taken, and leave. It's a big country, and if a man keeps well under cover he can stay in it
for weeks without any one being the wiser.

Now I was up against it right. Something had riled
the boys more than usual. I didn't know just what, but
I wasn't staying to find out; not after they had me spotted.

I shouldered my pack and started out.

Traveling a rough country in the dead of night isn't
what it's cracked up to be. In the first place, very few
people realize how utterly dead dark the country can get.
They're accustomed to some sort of street light.

But I had the stars, and there'd be a lemon peel of
moon sometime before dawn. I did the best I could,
watching to see I didn't sprain an ankle.

After a while I struck easier going. Then the moon
came up. Then it got gray dawn, and I slipped along at
a half run. By the time the east was turning rosy I'd
picked my hiding place, a little patch of scrub brush, way
up on a naked shoulder of mountain. The black shadows
would contrast with the glitter of sunlight on that bare
slope when the day got well started, and I'd be pretty
safe from detection. If anybody did start coming my way

I'd have lots of open country to scatter lead over.

I dozed off because I was tired. The flies woke me up. I was cramped. My hip was on a rock. I moved, batted at the flies, shifted my weight to the other hip, and dozed off.

I thought I smelled smoke. Then I thought I heard the high notes of a woman's laugh. I frowned. It was a poor place to get goofy ideas.

Then I heard the bass rumble of a man's voice.

I sat up, looked around carefully, and then began to bore my eyes into the shadows below me.

There was a little cañon opening up below the bare shoulder of mountain. It ran down in a steep gash of boulder and gravel until it hit a patch of pines. Then there was some brush, and, lower down, dense shade. I thought I could hear the trickle of water. And on the ledge a face had been painted.

Then my eyes caught a flicker of motion, and a girl walked out of the shade.

She must have been four hundred yards away. I couldn't see too many details, but she was slender, grace-ful-limbed, and she was white.

A man called to her, and she stepped back.

It was a bad situation, but my duty was clear. They were whites, and I'd probably drawn the Indians to them. There was an even chance the Yaquis would pick up my trail sometime during the day and follow it up. I'd have to warn those people, get 'em to take cover with me, make a stand during the day, travel at night.

I broke cover and came down the side of the slope, intent only on getting across that patch of sunlit space in the shortest possible time.

I hit the boulders, jumped from rock to rock, clatter-ing my way down to the bottom. Yet they didn't spot me. They must have been the worst sort of tenderfeet.

I slipped through the shadow and came on them.

It was a pretty scene. She was in his arms, his head bent down over her lips, one arm around her waist, pulling her toward him.

"I hate to interrupt, folks," I said.

They gave one swift jump. The girl darted to one side. The man swung a hand toward a new, shiny gun that dangled from a leather holster that showed a hardware-store yellow.

"Forget it!" I snapped. "You're in Yaqui country. The Indians are on the warpath over something or other, and I'm afraid they're trailing me. I stumbled onto your camp and so had to warn you."

The man's hand slowly left his hip, but his eyes were hard and watchful.

"Who are you?" he asked.

I let him have it in bunches. There wasn't much time to waste.

"Zane's the name, Bob Zane. Came into this country at the request of a dying doctor, looking for a lost patient, Stella McRae . . . and, maybe, hoping to dig up a little metal for my pains."

Their eyes flickered from face to face.

"I'm Stella McRae," said the girl.

"Figured you'd have to be her, or else the nurse, Miss Marlan. Who's the man?"

She sighed.

"That's Ned Craleigh." Then, as if feeling more explanation was due me, added: "He was the man whom I hated. Now I love him."

The man nodded. "Her father interceded to get her to marry me. She thought I'd bought him. She wanted to get money to square the account. She did it. I followed her. She wanted to buy me off, but she came to realize my affection was on the level."

I let his words seep through my mind, trying to figure everything they meant.

"In other words, you've found the mine?"

It was the girl who answered.

"And how!" she said.

I looked her over. She was a dark kid with smoky eyes and red lips. There was a brazen way she had of looking at one. Her clothes were outing stuff, but class from top to bottom. She smiled into my eyes.

"Like my looks?" she asked.

I caught a glimpse of the man's face. It was twisted into black hatred. Only for an instant did the expression flicker on his features, and then he was smiling again.

"Come on and I'll show you what we've found," he said.

I followed him. The girl came behind me.

There was a little spring, a stream, some piles of dirt that had evidently been washed, a gold pan. The man tugged at a flour sack, which was doubled back and sewed to reënforce it.

I caught a glimpse of yellow metal.

"Gold?" I asked.

"Gold," he said, and his lips mouthed the word as though the very thought had started a flow of saliva.

I gave a swift look at the way the place had been worked—amateurish.

"There's lots more here," I said.

The man nodded. "It goes down from the grass roots."

"You haven't any burros. I've got some pack stock cached a few miles from here. Maybe we can make a dicker. But we've got to get out now. We can't stay here."

He looked at the girl. She nodded.

I rubbered around some more. Somehow or other, things didn't seem just right. Then I caught a glimpse of some clothes, woman's clothes they were: silk undies, hiking stuff, boots, a jacket.

The girl followed the direction of my glance.

"Sloppy housekeeping," she said, and moved over to the pile.

She tucked the silk out of sight, threw the other clothes over her arm. Something rolled from the pocket of the trousers, something that glittered. I picked it up. It was a compact.

"How about making a deal on the burro transportation?" I asked.

The man laughed.

"Don't be foolish. We've got burros cached out ourselves. How'd you think we got in here?"

There was a rasping something in his tone I didn't like. The girl's hand was stretched out for the compact.

The cover was loose. I had a peep inside, and I saw it was an outfit for a blonde. This girl was a brunette. And I saw the print of a woman's bare foot in the mud by the stream.

I jumped back.

The man's hand streaked for his gun. It was the girl that got me, though. She went through the air in a flying tackle. By the time my rifle was halfway around she was clinging to my arm.

"Shoot him, Carl!" she screamed.

And I found the end of Carl's gun boring into my eyes.

"Drop the rifle," he ordered.

V DESERT TORTURE

I hesitated until I saw something in Carl's eyes that glittered, and the girl's teeth sank into my arm. Then I dropped the gun. The girl unbuckled my belt, and the six-gun and cartridges dropped to the ground.

"You're a damn fool," said the man.

I said nothing. I could only agree with him. The girl laughed, just the sort of a laugh I'd expect from her.

"We've got to beat it, Carl. Kill him."

He shook his head.

"We'll treat him the same way we did the girl. It's a Yaqui trick. I've read of it. If any one finds him they'll never believe but what the Indians did it."

I knew then what he meant, and what they'd done with the girl who had found the mine.

The Yaquis have done it. They've done lots of things.

It's simple. Simply strip the victim stark naked and turn him loose. There is lots of cactus in the country. There's lots of blistering sunlight, and there are lots of sharp rocks. The ground gets so hot under that light that you can cook an egg by simply leaving it out in the sun for fifteen minutes. And civilized feet don't go well over sharp rocks, not with a few hundred miles of travel over an arid country staring one in the face.

As a matter of fact, about all one would have to do in that country would be to take a man's canteen away from him.

He'd have a hard time getting out. It's sixty miles between water holes in places.

The girl prodded me in the ribs.

"Strip," she said.

The man nodded and backed up his nod with a gesture of the weapon he held.

I had one chance of outwitting them. It was a poor chance, but I took it rather than jump at sure death from the gun. I stripped off my clothes. They left me nothing, not even a scrap of covering.

"March," said the man, "and march up the cañon. I want to see you well over the top of the hill."

I marched.

My feet struck the sharp rocks, and I lurched forward to lessen the pain. The girl laughed, a cruel, cutting laugh.

"Faster," said the man. "We can't wait here all day. We've got work to do."

I made some progress. The sharp rocks cut my feet. Then I staggered out of the shadow into the blinding sunlight. It fastened on my skin at once, a blistering blanket. The rocks under my feet became burning coals. I tried standing on one foot for a while, then the other. It was no good. The torture on the one foot more than made up for the temporary relief the other got.

I knew that by standing in one place until I had drawn the heat out of the stones I could get some relief. But the man was yelling at me to get started, and there was a tone in his voice I didn't like.

I went on as best I could. The tortured skin, hot and puffed, offered no resistance to the sharp edges of the rocks. The soles were cut in half a dozen places by the time I'd gained the top of the ridge.

I went over and looked for shelter, but I didn't dare to stay too close—not with what I had in mind.

Finally, when I was satisfied they'd lost me, I ducked into some shade.

The punishment a mile of travel had inflicted on my feet had made them a mass of sores. The sun had burned into my skin, and the flies followed me in droves. It was simply plain hell.

Civilized man is pretty much a creature of environment.

But the man Carl had mentioned his burros. There was one place where he'd be almost certain to leave them. After half an hour's rest I set about cutting branches with sharp rocks, stripping off the bark, and trying to tie the sticks onto my feet with it.

It was only a partial success. My feet were already

swollen, bleeding, and hot dirt was ground into the cuts. There were blisters forming under the skin. Every step was like ten thousand hot knives working up into my agonized feet.

The bark wasn't strong enough to hold the "sandals" together, and it wore through after a few steps, but I made progress, and I kept to the shadows. All the time I had the feeling that Yaqui eyes were watching me. It was not a comfortable feeling.

I thought of the girl who had preceded me—a blonde, with the skin of a blonde. I thought of what the sun would do to that skin.

And we were miles and miles from the nearest succor.

It was mid-afternoon before I gained the place where I wanted to go, and I was burned red, my feet were masses of raw flesh, swollen, tortured. I left bloody prints on the hot ground.

But Carl's burros were there.

I managed to catch one after an agony that seemed an eternity of suffering, and got on his back. I steered him by pulling his ears, turning his head this way and that, and I prodded him along with the point of a sharp rock.

The couple were still up the cañon above. Once I heard the girl laugh.

It was a care-free, voluptuous laugh. The sound churned up anger in my soul, but I was a sick man. Ten thousand times more foolish to try to sneak up on them and get a weapon by surprise than to do what I had in mind. It was a slim chance, and an only chance.

I prodded the burro along at a snail's pace. I was afraid I might be discovered at any time. It was ten miles to where I'd cached my own stock, and I was naked, sun-burned, wounded by stone bruises, weaponless in the midst of the Yaqui country.

The burro plodded on.

The coolness of dusk was like a benediction to my parched skin, but the fever was commencing, and soon I burned just as though ten thousand suns were beating down upon my skin. The burro wanted to quit for the night, and I had trouble with him.

Then, just as I was figuring it was hopeless, after all, there was a flicker of motion in the dark shadows, and something jumped toward me.

The burro started, shied, and I spilled to the ground.

Tina was on me, muttering soothing words, crooning, patting my hot skin, her fingers at my feet. Then she caught the burro, put me back on, slipped a rope around his neck, and started to lead him.

The next three hours were like a nightmare, but we came to her camp. Tina had herbs—where she'd gotten them, I don't know. She put them on my skin, making sort of a paste by bruising the leaves between smooth rocks and spreading them over me. There were other herbs she put on my sore feet. I slept.

In the morning Tina was there again, and with her was another girl, a blonde, who was swathed in a light blanket and who limped as she walked.

"You?" I asked.

She nodded.

"I'm Stella McRae."

"You found the mine?"

"Yes, I kept on after the Indians got the old prospector, and found it. I knew a little something about placer work. I had dabbled around in geology in college, and I washed out quite a bit of gold. Then the girl and the man came. . . . You know what they did."

"How did you get here?"

"Tina was scouting around. She was worried about you. She found me, put leaves on my skin, and hid me in the shade. She walked here, got a burro, came back to me, carried me in, then started to look for you. You tried to send Tina home, but she doubled back."

I held out my hand to Tina. There were tears in her dark eyes.

"*He* whispered to me," she said.

I didn't know about that. But I'd left an extra revolver with Tina, and somebody or something was doing a lot more than whisper to me about what I was going to do with it.

I didn't say anything, though; I let the girls think we were starting back.

Stella McRae never said a word about the lost gold, yet I knew what that gold meant to her.

It was well after midnight of the third day that I felt well enough to try it. I'd manufactured some sandals out of a pack saddle. My clothes were mostly flour sacks.

The girls were sleeping. I took a burro and the gun, left a note scribbled with charcoal, and started.

It was dark, pitch-dark, but I could get the direction from the stars, and the burro could feel out the road to travel. By gray dawn I was near where I wanted to be.

I slipped off the burro and started a stalk, and I'd never stalked a deer with more caution.

I came to the cañon just as the first rays of dawn were making things light, and I hugged the cold shadows, my gun held at ready. Carl Lugger wasn't going to get any breaks, not if I knew it. My sore feet made walking an agony, but there was that in my soul which transcended any bodily pain.

The sun came up over the top of the ridge, but the rays wouldn't penetrate into the cañon for a couple of hours yet. A faint wind stirred through the trees. The water rippled and purled over the rocks.

I saw the cold ashes of a dead fire, and then I saw

something white, bulky. I bent forward. It looked like a flour sack. I reached for it.

It was the sack of gold, so much of it that it would have torn the double cloth unless handled carefully. That was strange. Why would they leave the gold out in the open in this manner? As a trap?

I looked swiftly about me, and then my eye caught a pile of cloth.

I looked, rubbed my eyes, and looked again.

There were silk undies, well-tailored outing clothes, khaki hiking jacket. And there were a man's clothes, even down to the underwear.

I looked more closely, saw the barefoot tracks leading up the cañon.

And then I saw the tracks made by Yaqui Indians. The cañon was full of them. I'd been so intent upon detecting the sleepers I hadn't bothered to peer into the dim light for tracks.

There was no sign of weapons. The Indians had cleaned them out. But they'd not bothered with the gold. That was typical Yaqui psychology. There was plenty of gold in the country. They didn't do much bartering, and, when they did, they used the gold as sparingly as possible. They knew that gold attracted unwelcome visitors.

I judged the tracks were about two days old.

The girl was a brunette. Her skin would withstand the sunlight better than the man's. But that blazing sunlight at a high elevation with the actinic rays working overtime . . . and two days!

I shrugged my shoulders.

Doubtless the Yaquis had been watching the camp for some time. They'd seen the couple send their two victims out into the sunlight, stripped naked, barefooted. And the Yaquis had doubtless chuckled at the performance.

They are cruel, those Yaquis, when the occasion de-

mands, and they are fighting to keep their remaining country free from invaders. But they are also just, with a justice
that is not tempered by mercy.

I loaded the gold on the burro and started back,
reaching the camp well toward noon. I handed the gold
to Stella McRae.

"Yours," I said.

She asked me questions. I did not answer them then,
and I haven't answered them later. Neither did I try
to return to the cañon for more gold, nor to follow the
barefoot tracks of the two who had been driven from
that shade.

I knew what I would find. First the prints of bare
feet. Then a little spot of blood. After that, more blood,
until finally the whole imprint of the foot would be found
outlined in blood, blood that was baked black beneath
the rays of the fierce sun. And if I followed those bloody
tracks . . .

We were unmolested on the return journey.

Stella McRae gave some gold to the fat Mexican, a
good deal to Tina. She wanted me to take half. I refused.
She would probably need it all. Perhaps, some day when
things had blown over, I'd slip back into that Yaqui country, traveling alone and light, and bring out some more
gold. I hoped it would not be in the form of a bullet.

We parted at the shack. Stella McRae and I left the
others. Tina and the fat Mexican kissed me good-by.
Stella and I flivvered off across the desert. We were silent
during most of the trip.

She kissed me good-by at Yuma. There were tears in
her eyes, and she made me promise to call on her. Me,
a sun-browned desert adventurer, calling upon a society
girl! And yet—

I didn't return to Hollywood immediately. I waited
a couple of nights on the desert. I wanted to hear the

sand whisper again. Finally I loaded up and drove back.

My chauffeur looked as though he was seeing a ghost.

"We thought you'd been kidnaped, sir—taken for a ride."

"Nothing as exciting as that."

He looked at me with something of wistfulness in his tired eyes.

"Gosh, it must be great to be able to duck out whenever you feel like an adventure. But they tell me there ain't any real adventures left in the desert any more. . . . Say, what's that new stickpin you've got?"

He came closer.

"Looks like it was a gold bullet mounted on a pin!"

I shrugged my shoulders and turned to the papers.

I was reading of the breaking off of the engagement between Stella McRae, the leader of the younger set, and the wealthy broker, Ned Craleigh, when the chauffeur interrupted me again.

"By gosh, I'll bet you've been places in the last three or four weeks."

"And done things," I echoed.